Plain
Brown
Wrapper

To Karen —
who has excellent
taste in names)
Thanks so much
supporting. Alex Burse!

All bom zatzr
"Grisom zatz
for 2005

Plain Brown Wrapper

An Alex Powell Novel

Karen Grigsby Bates

AVON BOOKS
An Imprint of HarperCollins Publishers

Plain Brown Wrapper is a work of fiction. Any resemblance between the central characters and persons living, dead, or semicomatose are entirely the product of the author's admittedly overworked imagination.

FIRST EDITION

Designed by Nancy B. Field

Library of Congress Cataloging-in-Publication Data

Bates, Karen Grigsby.
    Plain brown wrapper : an Alex Powell novel / by Karen Grigsby Bates.
        p.   cm.
    ISBN 0-380-80890-0
    1. African American women journalists—Fiction.   2. Martha's
Vineyard (Mass.)—Fiction.   3. Los Angeles, Calif.—Fiction.
    I. Title.

    PS3602.A86 P58   2001
    813'.54—dc21   2001018925

01   02   03   04   05   RRD   10   9   8   7   6   5   4   3   2   1

For Bruce and Jordan

We should never be afraid to tell the truth, my dear—
but sometimes it's kinder to do it in fiction.

—ELEANOR ROOSEVELT

Acknowledgments

I'd like to thank:

Faith Hampton Childs, good friend and agent *extraordinaire* who "got" Alex Powell early on, and saw that she was delivered into the right hands.

My editor, Carrie Feron, whose hands were indeed the right ones, and her assistant, Aviva Meyerowitz, and the marketing team at Morrow/Avon, especially Dee Dee DeBartlo and Leesa Belt.

My writer and journalist friends for their generosity and support: Tina McElroy Ansa, A'lelia Bundles, Eric V. Copage, Carolina Garcia-Aguilera, Shirlee Taylor Haizlip, Gar Anthony Haywood, Karen E. Hudson, Sujata Massey, Courtland Milloy, Sylvester Monroe, Barbara Neeley, Jill Nelson, Gary Phillips, Catherine Seipp, Gayle Pollard Terry, Valerie Wilson Wesley, Paula Woods, and two who are no longer with us: Donald Rawley and Kate Ross.

Friends and colleagues, past and present, at *People* magazine's West Coast bureau.

Babes on Books—after six full years, I don't care anymore whether we're a book club or a group therapy session: I just care that we keep doing it.

The Norton Thanksgiving Group: May our glasses always be half-full.

The many kind people at the L.A. County Sheriff's Department, the Los Angeles Police Department, the County Coroner's Office, and several newspapers around the country. Any mistakes are mine, not theirs.

Patient readers Callie Crossley, Lauren Adams de Leon, Marcy DeVeaux, Jovon Gilhom, and Jamie Marshall, and dear friends Anita Addison and Maria Miller.

And finally, my deepest appreciation to my family, especially my sister, Pat, mother, Miriam, husband, Bruce, and son, Jordan.

KGB

Winter 2001

Plain Brown Wrapper

1

A sixty-eight-year-old woman being shot on her own front lawn in broad daylight is not normally a laughing matter, but every time I tried to describe the particulars of this specific incidence of urban violence, I ended up laughing so hard I feared I'd never finish my column in time for deadline.

My name is Alex Powell; I'm a journalist. My column runs in the Metro section of the *Los Angeles Standard* twice a week, Sundays and Thursdays. Basically I can write whatever I want, as long as it reflects life in the fractious jumble of communities that make up greater Los Angeles. Sometimes the stories actually do make a positive difference in people's lives. Occasionally, they're even life-changing.

Like the one I wrote about Adrienne Pierce, a seventeen-year-old South Central girl who, after her parents' deaths from AIDS, was struggling to care for her younger siblings so they wouldn't be broken up and distributed in the wasteland of foster care. An honors student at a local public school, she'd given up hope of going to college (no money, and who would look after the kids?) and had resigned herself to working in fast-food joints and slipping in a class or two at a local junior college whenever she could manage it. After the column ran, she was offered a full scholarship to the University of Southern California, and an anonymous benefactor prepaid the freight for the little Pierces for four years in a university-affiliated day-care center, so they'd be cared for after school while Adrienne was finishing her own classes. That was three years ago and they still send me notes from time to time, letting me know how they're doing.

My column about the Fernandez family won a local reporting award and, more importantly, helped a family of hardworking immigrants in a moment of severe crisis. Aurelio Fernandez and his family had been firebombed out of their small home near Watts when some Latino gang members mistakenly thought Aurelio was a police informant in a drug sting that had nabbed some of their colleagues. In retaliation, they torched the house—in the middle of the night, with the six Fernandezes inside. The family made it out with their lives but very little else. Little Sylvia Fernandez, a bubbly five-year-old, was badly burned over 30 percent of her body, and the family was homeless and totally without medical insurance. When the *Standard* ran the news story and my column (an interview with Aurelio and his wife, Alta Gracia, which I managed to get the day after the fire), help poured in. A local real estate developer who normally deals in the luxury end of the market gave them a small home, rent-free, for two years, and the possibility of buying it after that. Three of the country's best reconstructive surgeons teamed together to give Sylvia the operations she'd need to look like herself again. Catholic Charities provided counseling for the traumatized family. And a black sorority at UCLA took turns baby-sitting the younger Fernandez kids for six months, so Aurelio and Alta Gracia could remain by Sylvia's bedside while she was in ICU and rehab.

Those kinds of stories make me realize why I wanted to be a reporter. Those kinds of stories are life-enhancing, maybe even transforming.

The shooting story, however, wasn't one of them. Which was why I was having such a hard time finishing it without . . . well, I may as well just show you what I handed in, and you can decide for yourself:

The Grass Is Always Greener—for a Reason

By Alex Powell
Standard columnist

Up here in View Park, the neighbors take their property seriously. The streets wind randomly upward from the noise and hustle of Crenshaw Boulevard. On still summer days, if you leave the windows open, you can hear the congas from the drummers assembled in Leimert Park, a half mile away. The lawns are uniformly green and wide, the homes large and well-kept. It is a house-proud section of South L.A., full of people who don't joke about the responsibilities of domestic upkeep.

Emmaline Andrews is no slacker in that department. Her lawn is the pride of Mount Vernon Drive—"velvet green," her neighbors like to call it. A widowed retired high school principal, Mrs. Andrews lovingly tends her lawn and garden daily; joggers huffing up the hill in the early morning wave to her as she pinches back the deadheads on her rosebushes. In the evening, she chats with the neighbors as their automatic sprinklers pop up and hiss moisture where it's needed. The errant piece of trash doesn't stay too long on Mrs. Andrews's sidewalk: "Anything out there, once she notices it, that's it; it's gone," says Roscoe Washington, a neighbor for almost 25 years. "Emma takes no mess."

Apparently, she doesn't like any left on her lawn, either. Which is why the normally easygoing community volunteer would get after Robert Mawbry, a new resident, who liked to walk his twin rottweilers off their leashes, letting them do their business where they might. Most neighbors resented it but weren't around to catch Mawbry in the act. The few who did and protested say Mawbry just shrugged. "That's what dogs do, man. When they gotta go, they go."

Maybe it was the timing. Maybe the moon was squared in something assertive, like Aries, which makes even mild-mannered people grow fangs and growl. Whatever the reason, Emmaline Andrews had arisen for the third time that week to find twin steaming piles on the strip of grass between the sidewalk and the street. "You know, I don't think I even thought twice about it," she told me later. "I just saw those piles of—well, you know—and I guess I just snapped."

You could say that. What else would possess a 5-foot-3-inch, 110-pound grandmother of four to run, in her pink slippers, down the front steps to the lawn, pick up a warm pile of dog feces in her bare well-manicured hands, yell "Hey, you forgot something!" and then heave that pile of poop at the retreating back of the offender—who, by the way, outweighed her by more than 100 pounds? Temporary insanity, more likely than not.

Robert Mawbry, outraged, scraped the poop from the back of his neck (in addition to being a vigilant gardener, Mrs. Andrews pitches during the season with the senior baseball league at Christ the Good Shepherd Episcopal Church), screamed something about her mental instability, and left.

He returned about a half hour later, having showered, tethered the dogs, and picked up a gun. The neighbors were still rehashing Mrs. Andrews's perfect pitch and taking guesses as to whether this would reform Mr. Mawbry once and for all, when Mr. Mawbry himself appeared, with his firearm. Mr. Washington, a retired pharmacist, described it: "Emma was just telling me how she threw the stuff at that boy, when here he comes—with a gun! I tried to tell her to hit the deck, but he was quick. Before I got the words out of my mouth good, he just aimed and shot her."

In the buttocks. The gun was actually a toy. It belonged to Mr. Mawbry's nephew, who had left it behind on a recent visit. It was loaded not with BBs but with leftover gravel from an aquarium project. The doctors at Cedars Sinai, where Mrs. Andrews was rushed, facedown, to the emergency room, say her prognosis is excellent. She and Mr. Mawbry were all set to sue each other (he for assault with a firearm . . . she for grievous bodily harm) when Presiding Judge, Haskell Lange, addressed them both in court.

"Look," Hizzoner intoned, staring at both parties over his steel half-rims, "I have a full docket and this is the least of my problems. Let's resolve this quickly. *You.*" He pointed to Bob Mawbry. "Under California law, I'm entitled to sentence you as if that weapon were the real thing: If she'd had a heart attack and died when you were coming after her with what appeared to be a shotgun, you'd have gone up for life." He paused. "I can't say this occurred entirely without provocation, so I'm going to give you a break. Go home and thank God I'm in a benign mood this morning. But hear this, Mr. Mawbry: Walk your dogs whenever you like, but clean up after them—*always*. If I have any complaints that you aren't, it's an automatic $1,000 fine—every time. $2,500 and a year's probation." *Crack!* went the gavel.

"And *you!*"—peering at Emmaline Andrews—"kindly refrain from assaulting your neighbors with dog doo. I hear of you pitching any ca-ca curveballs again, and neighbor or no neighbor (the judge lives up the street from Mrs. Andrews) it's a week for you at Sibyl Brand, understand?" *Crack!*

Everybody understood. Everybody was satisfied. Mrs. Andrews had no interest in spending time in the city's infamous women's prison. And $1,000 a pop—excuse me, a poop—would seriously eat into Mr. Mawbry's disposable income; he might have to trade his black Boxter in for a Geo, a fate worse than jail for the circles in which he moved.

So the judge went on to more serious cases. And last I heard, the only manure on anyone's lawn on Mount Vernon Drive these days is the kind that's bought and paid for at the hardware store. There's a lesson in here somewhere—but I can't stop laughing long enough to figure out what it is.

It wasn't as if the piece was hard to write. I'd done the research and interviewed the pertinent parties. I'd be moving along at a good clip; then I'd get to the part about the turd-throwing grandma and just lose it. Which meant I'd have to start all over again. Which is why it took almost three times as long to write the damn column than it usually does. Which explains why I was just now easing into my seat at the National Association of Black Journalists' annual convention. Luckily for me, they were meeting in Los Angeles, so I was able to slip away for the afternoon, finish the column, and return, albeit late, in time for the NABJ awards dinner.

"Colored and late," observed my friend Signe Tucker, as she pulled out my chair. "*Such* an attractive combination." Signe is a stickler for time, among other things.

"Sorry, but I had to change. I couldn't go to the newsroom in cocktail clothes, and you'd have died if I'd worn wrinkled linen after six." I gestured to myself: black silk sleeveless dress, coral cashmere shawl, black evening bag shaped like a 3-D trapezoid, with a silk tassel swinging from the bottom. Signe, also a stickler for the right dress at the right time, nodded approval.

As if on cue, my little satin bag began to buzz like a hive of hornets being used for piñata practice.

"Girl, you better pick up that phone." Signe grinned. "Somebody calling you at seven o'clock on Saturday night can only mean two things."

"Oh, really?"

"Uh-huh, and since you ain't got no man, it can only mean one thing."

"That being?" I hoped I was sounding arch.

"That's the Paddyroller page, girlfriend. Your WPs have run you down!"

While my purse continued its angry buzzing, I pondered my options. I could pretend I'd left the phone someplace, like on the dresser in my hotel room. I could maybe talk a passerby into barking *wrong number*! and hanging up for me. Or I could do what Miss Smug knew I was going to do, which was, reluctantly, answer it.

Damn. What was the point of taking a few days away from the office if the office had to receive a bulletin every time you sneezed? I'd come to NABJ to get *away* from my editors—or one in particular, truth be told—and here they were, tracking me down anyway. I was in a ballroom in a nice black dress, not racing through the woods in hopsack rags, but no matter: same shit, different century. Signe was probably right. More than likely, my white people (WPs in Signe-speak) had indeed tracked me down. Not that Signe was psychic or anything. My particular master, A.S. Fine, had buzzed me twice in the past two days; nobody else had, so it was a good guess this was him again. It was equally likely he wanted nothing in particular—just checking up. ("Nosy." Signe giggled. "They're dyin' to know what we say about them when they're not in the room!")

The buzzing started up again and I gave up. Pulling the drawstring mouth of the purse wide, I fished out the tiny cell phone, flipped it open, and sighed. "Okay, A.S., what is it this time?"

"You ain't trained your white folks no better than that, they think they can interrupt your vacation?"

It wasn't A.S. Fine at all. That staccato 'Bama voice belonged to Everett Carson, whose chocolate self was supposed to be sitting up on the ballroom dais with all the other Big Black Publishers. Especially since he was receiving, as he well knew, the Journalist of the Year award. Very big stuff.

"Number one," I explained for the umpteenth time, "they are not *my* white folks; I bear no personal ownership of or responsibility for them. Number two, aren't you supposed to be here already?"

I looked around the ballroom. *Le tout* black journalism was here, from the crème de la crème, basking in the admiration of younger, less-experienced journalists, to subsidized journalism students and everybody in between. It was *the* annual national professional development activity for black reporters, writers, editors, anchors, and producers. And as a fringe benefit, it included some amazing social activities. Which explained why some women arrived at the convention hotel with as much luggage as the Duchess of Windsor once used. The telebabes, as Signe called them, were the worst: On-air women in the major markets changed their outfits twice, sometimes three times a day. The women from lesser markets wore bright colors and big jewelry, with perfectly done hair and makeup. The Major Market mamas were less uptight about hair and makeup; their clothes were sleek, usually neutral in color, and expensive. Regardless of status or income, almost all the women sported some sort of brooch made of precious metal and semiprecious stones, à la Barbara, Jane, and Diane. (Minor Markets, of course, wore expensive "fashion" jewelry; the sophisticates among them opted for simple shapes in sterling silver.)

The men were dressed in their gender equivalent: Minor Markets wore stuff from the Men's Warehouse and fifty-dollar ties; Major Markets wore sleek Italian or high-end American off-the-rack (and, in one self-important case, the real thing from Savile Row) and ties that could run upward of two hundred dollars. Of course, their stations paid for all this with liberal clothing allowances.

Ev interrupted my visual assessment of the room. "I'ma be there in about a half hour. I just wanted someone to know I might be a few minutes late."

"Everett, you wear a watch that costs more than my car. Why can't you look at it every now and again and get your sorry butt where it's supposed to be on time?"

"Powell, if I wore a *Timex* it would cost more than your car! Bet you ain't you traded that raggedy-ass tin can yet."

"I know you're not talking about my automobile and expecting me to do you any *favors*—"

He wasn't listening. It sounded as if he was giving instructions to someone who'd just arrived. I could hear the squeak of a room service cart and the muffled clink of glassware.

"Yeah, thank ya, you can put it down right on the coffee table. Here you go." A door slammed in the distance. "Powell? You there?"

"I shouldn't be, but I am."

"Okay, listen. Just tell Sandra Mebane I'll be down in about forty-five minutes. That's plenty of time."

Like I didn't know what for. "Look, Stud Muffin, I am your girl, and I've had your back so many times that if I hadn't, you'd look like colored Swiss cheese. But I'm warning you, boy, don't fuck up. Not tonight."

The earpiece was filled with a burst of laughter and then a string of tsk-tsks. "Powell, your language! You eat with that mouth?"

"I kiss my mother with this mouth too, smart guy. Or do you want to see if Signe here will do your dirty work instead of me? She's rubbing her hands together now, just anticipating the fun."

"Tell Sig-nee I'll deal with her when I get there." And he hung up. I folded the phone and stuck it back in the bag. Signe looked at me expectantly.

"Well? What up?" She only speaks in the vernacular when she's among us folks. Otherwise it's the Queen's English all the way. While she's very proud of her Memphis accent and background, Signe has a horror of people—especially Yankees and WPs—thinking black Southerners only speak in dialect.

"He sends regards to Sig-nee." I grinned.

"Oh, no, he didn't. I know that Negro did *not* call me out my name!" That was the one thing guaranteed to set Signe off—that and rudeness. If she told you how to pronounce her name ("Signe— like I'll be *see'n ya*, get it? It's French"), you were, by God, supposed to remember.

"If you had a name like Ruth or Emily or Beulah or Shaniqua— something *regular*," I teased, "he wouldn't be *able* to call you out your name."

"Humph! Won't have a mouth left to mangle anybody's name *with*, he don't watch it," Signe pouted. She wouldn't hurt a fly, but she did like her name, and it irked her when people questioned her mother's choice in giving it to her. Many's the time I'd heard her meet the innocent query—"Signe? What kind of name is that? Never heard of a black girl named Signe"—with a very crisp "It's *French*, okay? And do I look anything but black to you?" After that, the questioner always left hurriedly, as if unsure exactly how volatile Signe might be.

I looked around the ballroom. "Lot of people here," I said.

Signe was kind enough to refrain from punctuating my observation with her usual "Duh!" Instead she said, "Girl, you know they haven't seen this many Negroes in one white folks' room since we marched on Rich's in the sixties!"

You could just hear the magnolia petals drop with each syllable. Signe was one of my very best friends, an unreconstructed Memphis belle. She sneakily disguised her laser-beam intelligence with a pair of world-class dimples and that Scarlett O'Hara drawl. To some folks, "southern accent" and "stupid" are synonymous, so when people who underestimate Signe discover the error of their ways, it is usually too late.

Magnolia Mouth had, for instance, lulled the senior senator from Kentucky into relaxing enough during a routine lion-in-winter profile to confide that, even though he'd voted for it ("demograph- ics, you know, more of them vote now than when I was fu'st run- nin'"), affirmative action did have its downside. "You know, my daughter had to search for months before she could find a nice col- ored lady to stay with her children. When I was coming along, there were always plenty. Now they all want to work for the telephone company or the post office or somesuch place!"

Signe had clucked sympathetically while the old boy rattled on. "Then"—she chuckled wickedly—"I raced back to my laptop and modemed that sucker straight to New York!" Her story ran front-page, above the fold, two days later (KENTUCKY'S LYNWOOD: *Good Help Is So Hard to Find*). When the fertilizer hit the fan, she was interviewed by most major networks, and shortly after her scoop she got a promotion to national correspondent for the *New York Times*.

Senator Lynwood, completely dazed by the hoo-rah, was convinced to retire by his mortified Republican backers, and the following year, a much younger, marginally more progressive senator was elected in his place. Stealth Signe had struck again. But I digress—a very bad habit I have no intention of giving up.

"Think they're gonna count the silverware before they let us leave?" I teased. The hotel we were meeting in, the Millennium, was new, on the critically Caucasian Westside, and owned by the Saudis, who were not known to be particularly Negro-friendly. Signe shrugged one of those it-wouldn't-surprise-me-a-bit shrugs and gestured to a table a few feet away.

"If anybody was of a mind to take some, wouldn't be those honeys. There's not even room enough to stash a demitasse spoon in any of those dresses." She sniffed with obvious disapproval.

The table in question held a bouquet of women in what my mother would dryly describe as "varying degrees of undress." They were eight in all, ranging from deepest chocolate to pale pecan. Each had carefully dressed in her party-girl best: décolletage here, plunging back there, impeccably applied makeup and stiletto heels all around.

"The girls are out to catch," Signe said.

As if I needed to be told. For women attending NABJ, there is a tacit dress code almost as complicated as the way West African women wear their headdresses to indicate marital status. Or how, in the last century, calling cards were turned.

Anthropologically speaking, you knew a girl was single here if she was dressed like the table o' gals: short snug skirt, high heels, advantageous display of her best asset—and that keen room-sweeping glance like an old-fashioned lighthouse beam. No new male face went unnoticed. The sighting was usually followed by a request for information. "What's the 411 on . . ." would be whispered all evening.

Signe and I, on the other hand, while single, were of another caste. In our simple cocktail sheaths, mid-heel sandals, and spare ("but real," as Signe likes to point out) jewelry, we advertised that we were *not* out to catch.

Our reasons, however, were totally different. I truly was not interested in any man I might meet at NABJ. Company inkwell and all that. After an intense months-long relationship with a fellow reporter ended disastrously, I'd decided that relationships with civilian men would be best for everyone involved. So I dated lawyers, bankers, and starving artists—mostly, to my mother's dismay, the last.

Signe was single but attached. In junior year at the women's college we'd both attended, she'd started going out with Otha Collins, a literature major at the men's school down the road. Fifteen years later, they were in many respects an old married couple, even though they'd not bothered actually to jump the broom. Every few years, they thought about it, came close, dismissed it, and went right back to going steady—to the consternation of most of their friends and both sets of parents.

Signe laughs that her mother "thinks she'll have to put SHE WAS ALMOST THE BELOVED WIFE OF on my headstone."

I've often thought that they haven't married till now because Signe keeps getting cold feet, but if that's true, Otha doesn't mind. "I'm a patient man" is all he'll say.

If I had to bet, I'd bet on him. Anybody who can sit perfectly still for hours on a lake waiting for fish to bite has a pretty good chance of reeling Signe in eventually.

I must have been frowning without realizing it, because Signe laughed at my expression and stuck a (dry) stirrer in my pursed lips.

"Ooooh." She grinned. "If your face freezes like that, you're gonna have some ug-lee nasolabial folds, honey." I just glared. But I could feel myself trying to relax those pesky muscles. Signe was probably right, damn her.

"Let me guess: He's going to be late but there's a good reason, right?"

I sighed. " 'Something came up.' "

Signe snorted. "The same part of him that's always coming up."

Like most everybody, she knew Ev had a hard time keeping his zipper closed. It was a marvel to all of us. Here was a man who was a workaholic, who cared very little for the niceties of courtship, who was constitutionally incapable of being faithful for longer than five minutes—and he was beating women off with a stick. "I mean, it's not like he looks like Billy Dee or anything," Signe once pointed out.

Indeed, Ev was entirely ordinary-looking in every way. Exactly six feet. Deep brown skin. Small even teeth, sporting a trademark gap. A build that now took a 42-regular suit. (He'd lost some weight recently and was quite proud of himself.) He even took his coffee regular. But whatever he had, it was in heavy demand. I'd spent countless confer-ences assuring pouting women that Ev and I were merely friends and colleagues, and by all means they should feel free to go for it. It got so I was grabbing stray male friends and batting my lashes at them just so it would look like I was occupied—and therefore not a threat to any babe with Ev on her agenda—because Ev tended to attract women who were jealous and possessive. And, occasionally, violent.

One of his past girlfriends had actually gotten him barred forever from The Refuge, a great bar on New York's Upper West Side, because she'd cold-cocked a waitress who'd had the temerity to flirt with him—maybe in the attempt to boost her tip—while serving them drinks. There were other places he was no longer welcome for much the same reason.

"I suppose I should tell somebody official the guest of honor is going to be late, huh?"

Signe looked around. We both caught sight of Sandra Mebane, NABJ's president, at the same time. She was dressed like she could have sat at the table o' gals, and she was not looking very happy.

"There she is, girlfriend. In her usual pleasant mood. Good luck."

I sighed and reluctantly made my way toward Sandra. En route, I nodded at the Four Cocksmen of the Apocalypse—middle-aged senior editors of competing newsweeklies—who were basking in the admiration of four journalism students young enough to be their daughters. (Actually, two of them *did* have daughters about that age.) The young lovelies' crystalline giggles floated over the stemware and blended into the general ballroom noise.

One of the guys motioned for me to come over, but I waved and kept on going. I'd once asked Ev why, given his reputed prowess, he wasn't one of the group, and he'd laughed. "Girl, them boys is amateurs. I'm in a class by myself."

"King of the Cocksmen?" I'd hooted. He'd lowered his eyes just like a girl being congratulated on getting pinned and, I swear to God, he actually giggled.

"Well, it ain't for *me* to say, Powell." He didn't need to; enough women said it for him—regularly, gratefully!

Finally I reached Sandra. "Alex." The president nodded. In the year since she'd been elected, Sandra had tried very hard to make the NABJ trains run on time and had, by and large, succeeded. Now here was Ev screwing up her one big chance to show, in a highly visible way, how well she'd whipped us all into shape. This was not going to be pretty. I took a deep breath.

"Sandra, Ev just called, and he says he's going to be about twenty-five minutes late. He apologizes, but apparently it couldn't be avoided."

Sandra's impeccably shaped brows drew together in a fierce frown. "Uh-huh. What's her name?" She'd actually gone out with Ev for about two months, and she knew about his excuses.

"Uh, I don't think it's anything like that, really. But he swears he'll be here in time to receive the award." As if on cue, my purse began to buzz again. I opened it eagerly.

"Well, hey, Ev. I'm standing here talking to Sandra Mebane right this minute."

"Oh, shit! Powell, whatever you do, don't—"

"Let me speak with him," Sandra snapped, and before I could protest she snatched the little phone right out of my hands.

"Everett, this is Sandra. . . . Don't 'hey, baby' me, don't even *start*. Now you listen here. Everybody, and I do mean *everybody* who counts in publishing, is here tonight. And they've come *on time* to see you receive the Journalist of the Year award. So if you know what's good for you, you will hop off whatever skank you're on, jam your black ass into your pants, and get over here this minute. Because if you don't, I will personally be responsible for breaking the as-told-to story for NABJ's conference newspaper as to how you decided to come out. *Of the closet, asshole*. You have exactly twenty minutes."

She snapped the phone shut, took what Yoga adherents like to refer to as a *cleansing breath*, and handed it back to me.

"Thank you, Alex. I believe we'll be seeing Ev before his award is announced." And she turned her cranky back to me and left.

Sandra was probably right. The combination of a southern Baptist upbringing and natural black-man macho had made Ev predictably homophobic in many ways. Some of his best friends weren't, for instance, homosexual.

And he'd die to be mistaken for one. On the other hand, this was the same guy who'd gone to the mat when his art director, who was brilliant and openly gay, was denied insurance because he was HIV-positive. Ev himself had gone to the insurance company and screamed at the president.

"I don't give a shit *how* he got it, he does good work and he's one of my people and you gonna treat him right, you hear?"

Given the decibel level, everybody heard, and the art director got his insurance. Thanks to Ev—and protease cocktails—he's alive and asymptomatic today. And he's still doing good work for Ev.

But there was a vast difference to Ev between fighting for gay rights and having people assume *he* was gay and campaigning on *his* behalf.

Signe agreed. "He'll be here in twenty minutes if he's gotta pay

Scotty to beam him up." She giggled. "Bless his little provincial self!"

As usual, Magnolia Mouth was right on target. Almost twenty minutes on the stroke, the hornets began buzzing again.

"Yes?" I asked sweetly.

"Okay, Powell, now listen," Ev began. I could hear a vaguely familiar sound, maybe water running, in the background.

"Uh, Ev, you seem not to be here," I pointed out helpfully.

"Dammit, I know I ain't there yet, that's what I called to tell you. I'm *almost* there."

"Isn't that the same thing as not being here? I just want to make sure."

I could hear Ev sigh with exasperation. He sounded like people do when they call from the health club on their cellulars while they're on the treadmill or the stair-stepper.

"Powell"—puff puff!—"just keep that harpy Sandra in line a little . . . longer . . . ?" His voice trailed off oddly.

"Ev, are you okay? You sound funny."

"I'm fine . . . just having a little trouble catching my breath. Allergy season. I'ma hit the inhaler in just a minute. . . ."

I could hear him fumbling with something—then a soft *whoosh!*—then nothing.

"Ev? Everett?"

Sandra Mebane was bearing down on me, eyes glittering with rage. Why me, Lord? The phone continued to relay a blank silence. Then nothing. The little digital readout said DISCONNECT.

"Where *is* that sonofabitch? I swear to God, if he embarrasses me—"

"Sandra, something's wrong. I was talking with him from somewhere here in the hotel, and he stopped and the line went dead. Why would he not be here if he could, especially considering your threat?"

"I don't know, Alex. But you'd better go and see about your boy. You've got fifteen minutes, outside."

Signe waved her hand at me, making a *shoo!* motion. "Maybe

something *is* wrong. Go see; I'll save your place and let you know what you missed."

Mighty white of her to offer, since we were the only ones at our table, and we both knew damn well I would miss exactly zilch by going upstairs to find out what was keeping Ev from his public.

2

I hadn't even gotten partway around our embarrassingly empty table when a set of half-frozen fingers grabbed my elbow. They belonged to Paul Butler, a syndicated columnist in the *New York Times* Washington bureau.

"Hey, where you off to? I was just coming to sit with you guys." He held two frosted glasses in his free hand, the probable explanation for why my elbow was now turning blue.

"Upstairs, Chilly Willy. I've got to go find out what's keeping Ev. Sandra is just about beside herself that he isn't here yet, and—lucky me—I've been given the assignment. Ol' Signe, yonder, has graciously conceded to wait down here and save our places." Signe stuck out her tongue merrily and crossed her eyes. "It's going to be tough, but I know the sister is up to it."

Before he could concur in his usual affable manner, Paul found himself dragooned into service. Signe did this regularly, with men she knew and men she didn't. They always obeyed. Probably some Memphis voodoo.

"Oh, no. Ladies do *not* go up to gentlemen's hotel rooms without an escort. Paul," Signe instructed, in her magnificently bossy way, "go on and take Alex up there."

"Me? I'm not even in the middle of this. Why don't *you* go, Signe?"

Signe gave him one of her *Yankees—what can you expect?*

glances and said, with exquisite patience, "Because, darling, every *civilized* person knows that *two* ladies in this kind of situation aren't much more use than *one* lady. And," she added shrewdly, "Everett ain't the liberated type. What do you think he's going to say if he opens the door from doing the nasty and only Alex is standing there?"

I looked at Paul expectantly. "She has a point. For once."

Magnolia Mouth just arched her eyebrows in response as she returned to her milky drink. I've seen cats before cream bowls with the same expression.

Paul sighed. "Okay, okay. Let's go and see what kind of trouble Everett's gotten himself into *this* year. We'll be back in a minute."

"Yes," I assured Signe, "we will. And while we're gone, your mission—and you have no choice but to accept it—will be to get Sandra to change the order of this way-too-long program so Ev can get down here in time."

"It is done." Signe stood, saluted us both, and drained her glass with a flourish. Delicately blotting her mouth, she straightened her shoulders, made a precise military quarter turn, and marched smartly off in the direction of the increasingly fidgety Sandra Mebane, who, if she knew what was good for her, would obligingly rearrange the order of the early part of the evening. I'm not much of a betting woman, but I'd bet Signe's evil against Sandra's evil any day.

On the way up to the eighteenth floor, Paul and I chatted about inconsequential things. I met him when I went to work at the *Washington Trib*. He'd been the best friend of Tim Carter, the guy who eventually inspired me to make the date-civilians-only rule.

Actually, I met both men at the same time. Paul was working Metro and Tim was doing the Maryland state legislature, which meant he lived in Annapolis half the year, listening to them drone on about stuff like sewage bonds and intercounty emergency programs. Exciting stuff. I was reporting to one of the suburban desks, covering northern Virginia, a region that was right outside the District line—and a world away. While Tim was watching the legislators stab themselves in the back—using the requisite flowery language, of course—Paul was doing homicides, urban development, and the D.C. City Council. And I was writing about, among other things, how previously all-white suburban schools were adjusting to the large influx of Southeast Asians who were swiftly remaking the face of these bedroom communities.

I expected to be bored, but I wasn't. There was a gold mine of human-interest stories to report, and the fringe benefit of some of the best Asian food around for lunch. I had pho, the national soup of Vietnam (North and South) in Arlington, and pad thai in Alexandria. I attended Presbyterian churches that offered services almost entirely in Korean and interviewed one of South Vietnam's most famous—and most reviled—generals in a Franco-Vietnamese diner he and his wife ran just off Highway 66. It was a great job; I loved it.

In the beginning I also liked it because—I'll admit it—of Tim. Tim had come to the *Trib* from the *Chicago Sun-Times* and was already making a name for himself. We shared a table in the cafeteria one day, and things just seemed to progress from that point. For a year or so, we dated each other exclusively; toward the end, we were half living in each other's apartments. Many people, me included, thought we were on our way to being a Serious Couple.

Except somewhere along the way, Tim's natural proclivity to be a man (and hence walk on all four legs) overtook him at a critical point. Some background: After a relatively chaste period in college—I'd given it up but pretty much stayed with the brother who'd grabbed the golden ring, until graduation—I went through an experimental period when I lived in New York. No numbers you had to tally with a calculator or anything; truth be told, you could have used both hands and still had a couple of fingers left over. Still, I retired to my real, more sedate self after my experimental, uh, spurt was done, and I promised myself I would not go to bed with any man unless he had Serious Potential.

Tim Carter had Serious Potential. He was smart (a necessity), funny (what good, after all, is smart if it doesn't come spiced with a sense of humor?), good-looking in a self-conscious kind of way (that I'm-cute-you-know-you-want-me way), and he loved to argue. Frankly, that probably clinched it for me. We spent many happy hours debating everything. We contested each other's points of view through museums, at the theater, in restaurants, and at parties. I was pleasantly surprised to realize, after several months of having a bathroom cabinet with some just-in-case contraceptive goo stored in it, that I was actually squeezing the tube on a regular basis.

Tim also came with Paul Butler, a best friend who would appear at the most inconvenient times. Like when you were planning a romantic dinner à deux. Or when you wanted to go see a foreign film—and he just happened to have floor tickets (two, of course) for the Bullets–Knicks game. Or when you wanted the two of you to go out alone, and there Paul was with the Snotty Professional Babe of the Week—and never the same one, not that any of them were women you'd enjoy seeing more than once. But Paul's scathingly sarcastic presence was a small price to pay. When he was there, I managed. When he wasn't, I had a man with Serious Potential all to myself.

And then the boy, to employ a Signe-ism, started barking.

I was, to be sure, fun, engaging, and attractive, but Mr. Carter was apparently feeling constricted and having second thoughts about being part of a couple. Instead of pulling my coat to that and making like Sammy Davis ("I gotta be free . . . I gotta be me"), he made like Patti LaBelle and got his ya-yas here—and there—and mostly everywhere he was welcomed. Being male, single, attractive, and affluent in D.C., as Paul liked to point out, to my intense irritation, "is like being a Visa card—*everybody*'ll take you!"

Well, I thought of myself more like a Platinum American Express card: Not everybody can have me, but for those who qualify the benefits are worth the hassle. When I discovered Tim's late evenings weren't being spent in the newsroom or hanging out with Paul, I threw the goo away (no huge waste; there wasn't much left in the tube). Then I invited Tim to dinner, hinting it would be romantic and al fresco.

He arrived that evening to find on my front stoop a silverplated dog bowl with TIMMY engraved on the front (at lunchtime, I'd taken it to one of those places downtown that does engraving-while-you-wait). The bowl had an unopened can of Alpo nestled inside with a delicate paper doily underneath and, next to it, a bud vase with one perfect just-opened pink rose. This feast was carefully placed on an embroidered linen place mat. Next to it, on a pale-blue correspondence card, I'd written *Bone appétit. And bone voyage.*

What I didn't know then was this: Tim wasn't alone. Paul had walked from the paper up Connecticut Avenue to Columbia Road with him. Paul had left the *Trib* for the *Washington Post* a couple of years earlier, but he and Tim still spent a fair amount of time together. He'd actually been planning to stop off long enough to say hey and have the drink Tim had so rashly promised I'd offer. I heard later (because of course this story was too good for Paul to keep to himself) that when he saw the table setting I'd left for Tim, he'd burst out laughing.

"Boy, you'd better come on down the street with me to get some dinner. 'Cause from the looks of it you are getting *nothing* here. Ever again." Give that man a job at the Psychic Network!

The next day, I gave the dog bowl to a pet shelter and the food to my neighbor's schnauzer. Tim sent a huge bouquet of flowers (why do men find you so much more interesting when you treat them badly?), which I promptly carried over to the Washington Hospice. Shortly after that, he went to NBC as an on-air reporter. Good riddance. I'm a CNN girl myself.

As the old folks like to say, all things happen for a reason. Very shortly after Tim Carter went electronic, the *Trib* folded, victim of the public's increasing reliance on televised news, and Washington became a one-paper town. Paul went to the *Post* for a couple of years, as did about a third of the *Trib* staff, and after a year in London came back to accept an offer covering Metro Washington for the *New York Times*, where he's been happily ensconced ever since.

I'd freelanced for Everett Carson for practically nothing when he was starting *Diaspora* on a shoestring, so he returned the favor by offering me a temporary full-time job at *Diaspora* writing features and editing freelance writers. It—and he—saved my professional life: *Diaspora* paid the rent and got me some gorgeous clips. And the clips got me two big features in *Vanity Fair*, back when being in *Vanity Fair* still meant something.

Ev couldn't afford to keep me forever, but he kept me long enough for a senior editor at the *Los Angeles Standard* to call and casually inquire whether I'd be interested in coming out and talking with them. I did and, over the protests of some reporters who'd been there longer than I and thought, based on seniority, they deserved the job, was offered a column in the Metro section. I was supposed to see Los Angeles through fresh eyes, the editors explained to me.

I'd never lived west of the Mississippi in my life, but it was time for a change. The *Standard* was one of the country's half-dozen best papers—senior management likes to think of it as third, after the *New York Times* and the *Washington Post* and before the *Wall Street Journal*—and no one who works there has the heart (or the *cojones*) to correct senior management. It would be a good place to spend a few years.

So here I am, five years later, and it's been a good move. I see Signe as often as possible. I've made good female friends here. And I see colleagues from my former life back east once a year at this conference. I mostly ignore Tim, after the initial greeting. (I see him on TV every now and again, and that's enough.) And Paul and I usually get together and have a drink and catch up during the week. Post-Tim, we've actually become pretty good friends—as good as you can get with someone you see and talk to once a year. He'll teasingly point out eligible prospects here and there, and I always tell him firmly to mind his own business and remind him about the civilians-only rule. It has gotten to be a kind of in-joke.

On the eighteenth floor, we got out and walked toward 1802. The heavy runners and fabric-covered walls absorbed sound completely. It was quiet enough that we could hear the pearls in my drop earrings rattling against each other.

The door to 1802 was cracked slightly. Paul rang the bell, then pushed the door open.

"Ev?" he asked.

No answer.

"Everett?" A little louder. Silence.

We were in the living room of a suite. A glossy shopping bag from a high-end store in the Millennium Plaza across the street from the hotel was in one corner. A pair of black suede men's evening pumps lay untidily on the rug in front of the sofa. Hastily stuffed into them were a pair of black silk dress socks.

In the dining area, a double-breasted dinner jacket with notched lapels was draped across a chair. I peeked at the black label: GIORGIO ARMANI it announced, in stylized block letters.

"Looks like *Diaspora* pays pretty well," I murmured, half to myself.

"Well enough that there might be pants to go with the jacket?" Paul asked, looking around.

We stepped closer to the dressing area that connected the two rooms. Crumpled before the bedroom door were the trousers to the jacket; their peau de soie stripe gleamed softly in the half-dark. A slice of yellow light from the bedroom made an elongated wedge into the gloom of the dressing room.

"Paul, if he's in there screwing somebody, I'm going to *kill* him," I hissed. "You go see."

"Me? Why me? *I* don't want to see him naked any more than *you* do!" Paul whispered. I had heard that tone before; it was his "I'm not letting you sweet-talk me into doing what you want so just forget it" voice.

"Yes, but you're a man, so it's okay for you to see him naked. *If* he's naked. It's like what happens in a locker room." I had never been in a men's locker room, but how wrong could I be?

Paul sighed. "Okay, okay." He took a deep breath and pushed the door a bit.

"Ev?"

I waited outside.

"You can come in, he's just sleeping." Paul sounded relieved. He stood facing Ev's back. "Wild sleeper, though."

So he was. Turned on his side, away from us, the evening's guest of honor was snoozing silently, a sheet drawn up to his waist, his nude brown back exposed. The bedclothes looked like they'd been through a Waring blender. Next to the bed, a bottle of Veuve Clicquot was upended in a pedestal bucket full of ice that was beginning to melt. Two glass flutes were on the night table; one was smudged with a brilliant poppy-colored lipstick.

Whoever the lipstick belonged to had left—but not so long ago. The air was still scented with her presence. It was a rich combination of white flowers, with a touch of vanilla and something else . . . sandalwood, maybe. I, who pride myself on being a Sherlock Holmes of perfume, couldn't place the scent. All I knew was it smelled foreign—and rare. You wouldn't see the girls on the first floor at Bloomingdale's offering to spritz you with it as you passed by.

Paul walked over to Sleeping Beauty and shook him. "Yo, brother, while you're up here sleeping the sleep of the dead everybody's downstairs waiting for—*Oh, shit!*"

"Oh, shit *what?*" I asked, retrieving Ev's pants from the doorway.

Paul was quiet for a moment; then he walked around to Ev's other side. "Look at this."

I sucked in my breath and came nearer. Ev was smiling slightly, but there was no exhalation of breath fogging the surface of the compact mirror I'd fished out of my evening bag and theatrically held beneath his nose. Actually it was more of a grimace than a true smile. There was a some creamy froth around his lips—the kind of bubbles that people who snore heavily sometimes produce. He was still warm to the touch, but it was clear he was assuming room temperature. Quickly.

"God, Paul—he *is* dead!"

We looked at each other.

"We'd better tell somebody," I said.

He nodded. "I'll call hotel security and stay here. You'd better go downstairs to the dinner and let them know what's happened. Just say he's really sick. The police will probably want to sort out the rest."

"All right," I agreed. "Will you be okay here by yourself?"

"Alex, the man is *dead*," Paul said, a trifle impatiently. "What's he going to do to me now? Anyway," he added as an afterthought, "when I covered Jonestown for the *Trib*, it was a hundred times worse than this—*several* hundred times worse. I can handle it."

Against my will, I fleetingly envisioned hundreds of bloated bodies rotting in Guyana's bright sun, the South American fields dotted with big tubs of poisoned grape drink. He was right.

"Okay, then. I'll come back up as soon as I can get things straightened out downstairs."

"We'll be waiting," he said, with a tight little smile. "Everett, let's make a phone call." I left while he was asking the operator to connect him to security.

Downstairs, the room was in full roar. Some wise soul had decided to start the program while dinner was being served, and the ravenous guests had fallen to with gusto. I slipped to the dais and signaled Sandra Mebane.

"So? What did you find out? Am I going to have to light him up or what?" Sandra looked like she was going to lose it any moment. She was speaking through clenched jaws.

"Um, Sandra, there's going to have to be a change in the program."

"Oh?" she asked, lifting one carefully waxed brow.

"Everett won't be able to join us for the ceremony after all," I said. "He seems to be very—ill."

"*How* ill?" Sandra asked, searching my face closely for signs of complicity.

"Seriously ill. Perhaps even deathly ill."

"Oh, that's horrible!" Sandra said, all sympathy now that Ev was legitimately sick. "Well, we'll read the citation and give the plaque to his managing editor. Is she here?"

"He," I corrected. "Henry Adams. Yes, he's over there, at table twenty-one."

An earnest, conservative-looking Henry was in deep conversation with two editors from the *Atlanta Journal-Constitution*.

"I'll tell him, Sandra; then I've got to get back upstairs to Ev and see if the doctor's come. Paul Butler was calling him as I left to come down here."

I walked over and told Henry, who assumed an expression of appropriate solemnity befitting Ev's sudden illness and agreed to make some gracious impromptu remarks on Ev's behalf.

"God, I hope it wasn't lunch," he muttered, rubbing his stomach anxiously. "We were at the same table." It was typical of what little I knew of Henry: obsessed with how things were going to affect *him*, above all else.

"Henry, I don't think it was, or everyone else at that banquet would be sick by now too," I said, in what I hoped was a professionally reassuring tone. Myself, I had skipped the luncheon and had had a sandwich when Signe and I slipped away for some therapeutic shopping, before I raced back to work to finish that damn ca-ca column.

When I left to return upstairs, dessert was be-ing passed. Henry was scribbling furiously in a small leather-covered note pad, and up on the dais, the editors of *Onyx*, *Aspire*, and *Radiance* were deep in friendly, animated conversation. Everett's empty chair was a yawning space between them.

3

About half an hour after I'd left Ev's room, I was back again. I figured, given what had happened, there'd have been much more commotion, but the hallway was as quiet as before. Hotels, apparently, are very discreet when it comes to removing dead people. It was only after I'd rung the bell and the door to 1802 swung open that I could tell something important—or at least unusual—had happened.

The living-room area was awash in light. Ev's briefcase had been tagged with some official-looking label; it waited by the door, along with his laptop and his burgundy agenda. They were tagged too. From the partly open bedroom door, I could hear the soft *pop!* of a flash, followed by a *whir*; the dressing-room walls reflected the flashes, treating us to mini lightning explosions. The murmur of men's voices floated softly back to the living room, where a lone man sat at the dining room table, scribbling notes into a small flip-top binder.

He had longish hair—for a cop, anyway. But he had a standard-issue cop mustache, medium-sized and clipped neatly to within an inch of its life. He was prematurely gray with a wiry runner's build. His steel-rimmed glasses kept falling down on his skinny nose.

"Nobody's supposed to be in here; who are *you?*" he asked abruptly, shoving the recalcitrant frames up his slender bridge.

"What, give you that information with no identification? On the television shows they flip a badge at you and *then* ask you to identify yourself."

"Jesus Christ!" Mr. Policeman snapped in annoyance. He reached into the pocket of his linen jacket, dug out a battered leather wallet, flipped it open, and flashed it. It contained the gold shield of a detective first class of the Los Angeles Police Department and identified him as James V. Marron.

"I assume this is real," I said, returning the wallet to him. "Do you have a driver's license, so I can double-check?"

He looked at me, utterly unamused. "Do you have a name?" he asked, with exaggerated patience.

"Yup." I handed him my business card; he took it and gave it a quick perusal.

"Well, Miss Alexa Powell—or is it Mrs.?"

"It's Ms., actually."

He rolled his eyes. "Of course. Why should I not have guessed you'd be one of *them*? Well, *Ms.* Powell, as you can see, there's been a death here."

"One of *them* whom? And duh, I know Ev's dead; that's why we *called* you. Immediately, I might add."

"Feminists, that's whom. And you also *left* before the police arrived. That's a no-no."

Now *I* was annoyed. "Yes, I did. Since Mr. Carson was the evening's keynote speaker, I thought the people waiting for him to appear might appreciate some word indicating that he wouldn't be joining us. Mr. Butler, as you can see, waited for the authorities—that, I suppose, would be you. As soon as I notified the award-givers, I returned. Is there a problem with that? Do you want the names of the people I talked to who saw me down there, so you can establish my whereabouts?"

The detective started to speak but was interrupted by Paul's arrival from the other room.

Paul stopped and stared for a moment at both of us, glaring at each other, then spoke to the cop.

"Let me guess. She's pissed you off already, hasn't she?"

Marron sighed. "Oh, yeah."

They exchanged smug glances. Which of course immediately pissed *me* off.

"It's fabulous you guys have bonded, but could a mere fallopian ask one teensy question? What, exactly, happened to Ev?"

"We won't know *exactly* what happened to him until we do an autopsy," Marron said. "Let's just say this cannot automatically be assumed to be death from natural causes."

"Why would you think somebody killed him? Looked like he had some sort of heart attack or stroke or something."

"I'm saying it's *possible* somebody may have killed him. We can't say definitively until the autopsy's done. Do you know anybody who'd want him dead?"

Paul and I exchanged glances.

"A lot of people weren't terribly fond of Ev," he said slowly. "If he accidentally stepped in front of a truck, some people might even want to open a bottle of champagne. But I don't think anyone would *shove* him."

Marron looked at me. "What about you? You think the same thing?"

I frowned. "I guess. Ev could be very abrasive, very arrogant. On the one hand, it made him really good at what he did for a living. On the other, it didn't make most folks want to spend a whole lot of time with him socially. Paul's right. A lot of people are going to sigh with satisfaction when they read Ev's obituary, but I can't imagine anyone who hated him enough to kill him or have him killed."

Marron sighed. "Too bad. If the coroner's report indicates foul play, we have nowhere to start. And it doesn't help that everybody here will be going home in a few hours. It's not like I can padlock the ballroom and make them stay till we interview each of them."

"Why not?"

"Because, as I understand it, there are some very important people down there."

"Who should be glad to cooperate with the authorities, just as we are, right?"

He looked at me over his glasses, which had again slipped down to the end of his nose, and grinned ruefully.

"You are so-o-o young. Think the mayor wants to get complaints from the likes of the publishers of the country's biggest papers? Are *you* going to ask Rupert Murdoch to make himself comfortable, thanks, this will all be finished in about forty-eight hours?"

He was right, dammit. The keynote dinner was the highlight of the week; most people left early the next morning, to give themselves a chance to recuperate a little before the work week began on Monday. If somebody at the conference had had anything to do with Ev's death, it would be infinitely harder to find out who—and why—once everyone scattered back to their respective parts of the country. And everyone else who didn't kill him would start screaming about how the LAPD was doing its racist thing again, detaining black people in their standard double-tiered administration of justice, blah, blah, blah.

"You think somebody *here* did it?" I asked.

"Odds are pretty good that's the case," Marron said dryly.

Wow. One of my peers. Somebody we *knew*. Of course, how Marron and his people would find whoever it was would be difficult, since unfortunately all black folks still look alike to much of the LAPD's rank and file.

"If you're going to find who did this, you'll need some help, I think."

"I beg your pardon?" Marron was genuinely startled.

"Well," I said, "between the two of us, Paul and I know almost all the major players. Let us ask around a little. Some people are more likely than others to benefit from Ev's death. Maybe we can help to narrow your possibilities. 'Cause if we don't, it's not like anybody is going to expend a whole lot of energy over one more dead black man in this city."

"We happen to expend a considerable amount of energy on *every* dead citizen in this city, regardless of race or gender. There are scores of dead bodies that claim our attention every single day. And for your information, Ms. Powell, real homicide doesn't work like it does on cop shows." Marron sneered. "You want to get your jollies playing Jessica Fletcher, you'll have to do it somewhere else."

"Would you excuse us for a moment, Jim?" Paul asked. Grasping me very firmly by the arm, he propelled me into the guest bathroom in the foyer. He shut the door, slammed the lid to the toilet seat down, and shoved me onto it. "Have a seat," he said abruptly.

"*Jim?*" I mocked. "Are we on a first-name basis with the authorities now?"

Paul's normally unperturbed face was totally devoid of its usual cynical cool. "Let me tell you something, Nancy Drew. This is *not* funny. Everett has probably been killed, probably by somebody we know. You know what cops tend to do in instances like this?"

"No, but I'm sure you're going to tell me."

"Damn right I'm going to tell you. Cops, Little Bo Peep, tend to look close to home when homicides occur. They often consider the obvious first. In this case, *we* found him—which automatically makes us suspects, if not to Jim Marron then to someone else on his team. The *last* thing he wants is some smart-ass offer from *you* to play detective. And if you don't start speaking to him a little more respectfully, you might find yourself spending a lot of time in one of those designer rooms all police stations have. Let me tell you something, little girl: They do *not* come with nice white rugs; room service brings you lukewarm coffee from a machine, and unlike here at the Millennium, you cannot just check out when you want to."

It was a long speech for Paul. I knew him well enough to know that when he's angry, he clams up. Which must make it maddening to have a good fight with him. But that didn't seem to be my problem right this minute. He might have been jawed up in the figurative sense, but he certainly was flapping his mandibles in the real.

I sat on the oversized toilet seat and considered things. In his days as a beat reporter, he had covered many, many more homicides than I (okay, I'd covered exactly two and hated every minute of both), and having done that, he probably knew the inner workings of the police mind, such as it was, better than I did. And he was a man, which means men would automatically give him more consideration than they would me. Maybe he was right; maybe I should just finish packing, go home tomorrow morning, and let the LAPD figure it out.

"Powell, have you heard *anything* I've said to you?"

I looked up; that little vein in his temple was pounding away under his glossy pecan skin; his hands were on his slender hips. They were beautiful hands—long thin fingers that should have belonged to a surgeon or a concert pianist. Funny I'd never noticed that before.

"I heard everything you said," I told him, preparing to rise from my throne.

"And?"

"And you're right. Any place that serves lukewarm coffee—from a machine, for God's sake—isn't a place in which I'd want to spend a lot of time. So I guess I'll go out and withdraw the offer and go home and mind my own business."

I tried to look properly contrite.

Paul inspected me minutely for any sign that what I said might be at variance with what I intended, squeezed past me, and opened the door. A welcome *whoosh* of cool air wafted in. Apparently satisfied, he turned back to me.

"Good. Let's get out of here."

Back in the living-dining room, the paramedics were packing up. Some people from the coroner's office had arrived; they were dressed in bright blue jumpsuits with their department emblazoned in gold across the back. Actually the jumpsuits were very cool, in a ghoulish kind of way. They were placing a body bag that I assumed contained Ev on a collapsible gurney.

"You'd be surprised how many of those get stolen every year."

The police photographer, a young guy in baggy khakis and a big ID running through his belt loop, shrugged toward the jumpsuits. He was zipping a big Polaroid camera—that would explain the *whir* that followed the pop of the flash—into his shoulder bag. He placed a stack of instant photos in a Ziploc bag and slipped them in an outside pocket.

The assistant medical examiner was putting away what looked like a big meat thermometer. He looked up, saw my puzzled expression, and said one word: "Liver." Eeeww! I'd read enough murder mysteries to know that the temperature of a body's liver can help to pinpoint time of death. I didn't want to know *how* they took the liver's temperature while it was still in the body, but I would guess that punching through a few layers of skin and muscle might be involved. Yuck.

The hotel manager was helping the medical examiner's assistant carefully drape a white damask tablecloth over the white plastic bag. He saw me looking and answered my unasked question.

"At this hour, miss, it's unlikely we'll run into anyone in the corridor, but in case we do, we've found it's less distressing for guests to see a cart draped with a sheet than . . ."

"Than the corpse du jour being wheeled about like room service?"

The manager made a moue of distaste. "Close enough."

"You leaving later on this morning?" Jim Marron asked. I looked at my watch: 1:03 A.M. Tomorrow was here already.

"Yes, I'd planned to, unless you need us to stick around." Big of me to offer, since I live here anyway. But I could see Paul was looking pained at the possibility of having to change his plans.

Marron looked at Paul and me speculatively, then sighed. "Nah. Not much point. Just leave your numbers and let me know if you're planning to leave your respective hometowns for any reason."

We each wrote down our addresses and numbers on the backs of our cards and silently handed them to him. Marron placed them in his wallet.

"Take a couple of days to think about it, but if you have any thoughts on why someone would do this, I'd be interested in hearing them."

"By the way," he said, looking at me as he shook Paul's hand, "you look different from the picture they run with your column in the paper."

"Interesting. I wouldn't have thought you'd *read* my column. Too far left for you."

"Can't say as I do—not regularly, anyway. But it shows up from time to time in the station house—usually strategically placed somewhere in the men's room." His eyes were actually twinkling.

I was surprised that he read it, but I knew where my photo was hung: I'd already heard from a couple of friendly cops I take to lunch from time to time that when they're annoyed with my ideology down at Parker Center and in the station houses, they tape the column above the urinal and address their complaints to my picture while they take a whiz. *So* mature.

"Well, if it helps you guys achieve a steady stream, I guess I'm doing my job."

He gave us a mock salute and stepped into the waiting elevator. The Millennium's manager and the people from the coroner's office had already—silently—disappeared.

Paul and I waved at Marron and walked in the opposite direction, toward the guest elevators. It was very, very quiet.

"Drink?" he asked.

"Not possible. The bar closed at one, and it's too late for any decent room service," I pointed out, wishing fervently that it was a half hour earlier. I could use something to drink. And eat, since we'd missed dinner. Whatever it had been.

"I've got some odds and ends in my room. Let's see what we can find."

So we took the elevator down two floors and walked the silent halls to 1609. Paul's room looked as if no one had stayed there, it was that neat. (I don't trust neat people; chronic neatness indicates an ungenerosity of spirit. Or creativity. *Something.*) A small stack of magazines and newspapers were on the glass-top coffee table, and his briefcase was placed next to a chair in the dining area.

I walked to the balcony, opened the sliding glass doors, and stepped out. The city air was uncharacteristically warm and slightly humid. A lot of visitors to L.A. are taken aback that the evenings can be so cool. But we are on the edge of the desert, and, in true desert fashion, when the sun goes down it gets chilly. Even in summer— except for a few nights.

Tonight was apparently one of them, because it was comfortable even though I was wearing a sleeveless dress. A slight breeze wafted through the open doors, making the sheer curtain liners flutter gently. Below me, palms rustled near the pool, and headlights made bright streamer patterns down busy Santa Monica Boulevard. Everything looked so normal—but the last few hours had been anything but.

Paul's voice startled me. "The Ethics Committee had its meeting up here during lunch. Some of the leftovers look pretty good."

I turned. Paul had moved the magazines aside and set an over-sized glass plate on the table. It contained a few generous wedges of Brie and Gouda, a pile of red grapes, some apples and pears—and a huge slab of *pâté de volaille*. The pâté looked fabulous. I tried to squelch the picture of the assistant coroner packing up his liver thermometer. I was hungry, dammit.

A basket of assorted crackers was next to the plate, and two open half bottles of wine, one red, one white, stood next to two empty glasses.

"No Twinkies? A girl's gotta have dessert."

"Black women—never satisfied. And then you-all wonder why Quincy and Sidney and all those other brothers are dating Miss Daisy."

"I don't wonder, I *know*. But that's another conversation entirely, one I'm much too hungry to have right now."

"Thank the Lord!" Paul laughed. "Red or white?"

"Red," I said, tucking my feet up beneath me. "Paul, do you think somebody we know killed Ev?"

His forehead crinkled in concentration. "I don't know. But if you were to be absolutely cold-blooded about it, there *are* some people who might have wanted to whack him if they thought they could get away with it."

"I know; I've been thinking about it all night. Who's on your list?"

Paul sighed heavily. "I don't even want to say it out loud. There are, for my money, a couple of folks."

I shoved a hotel note pad toward him. "Write them down. And I'll write mine on this one."

Paul uncapped his fountain pen and started to write, stopped, then continued. I wrote down all my names quickly, with the plastic ballpoint that was next to the guest stationery.

"Now let's exchange pads," I urged.

We did—and were intrigued to see the same three names, in different order:

Jake Jackson, Frankie Harper, Chip Wiley

We'd each targeted the black publishers of Ev's closest competition—the people who'd gallantly helped him start *Diaspora*, only to have him go after big chunks of their readership soon afterward.

I looked at Paul. "They had the most to gain if Ev's magazine shut down," I said slowly.

"Different reasons, of course," Paul agreed.

"Of course."

"But we aren't police, and the police will make their own evaluations as to who the suspects are or should be, right?"

"Absolutely," I agreed. "In fact, pleasant as it's been, I'd better leave and go pack so I can check out and not have to pay extra when all those Negroes make the predictable last-minute rush to do the same thing."

Paul didn't try to persuade me to stay; he walked me to the door and hugged me tightly. "It's been a strange night, but I kind of like the fact that I spent it with you."

"Thanks—I think." I laughed and kissed him lightly on the cheek.

"I'll walk you down to your room," he offered. His good manners—the fact that he actually had them, unlike many men his age—were something I'd always liked about him, even when I was finding him annoying.

"Not necessary; I'm only a floor below you. And despite what happened to Ev tonight, I feel perfectly safe."

"I don't care, I'm walking you down anyway."

"What if I say I won't let you?"

He shook his head and handed me my shoes. Then, to my surprise, he swept me up in his arms and let the door slam behind him.

"*Let* ain't got nothin' to do with it."

I was stupefied. He strode easily down the hall.

"Hit the button, will you?" He dipped so I could.

The doors opened and we rode down in silence. If you'd asked me before, I couldn't have imagined that I'd have liked being manhandled that way, but after the shock wore off it was actually rather pleasant. He was wearing a light citrus-scented aftershave with a hint of, if I wasn't mistaken, violets.

"What's that scent you're wearing?"

"Something from the thirties. Acqua di Parma. I've worn it for years, since before it was rediscovered." Paul prided himself on not being a follower.

"Nice." I sniffed appreciatively. "I never noticed it before."

"Never picked you up before." He laughed. "This is you."

Paul gently deposited me in front of my door, and waited till I opened it. The pleasant smell of Acqua di Parma was still in my nostrils.

"See you next year, Powell. Try to stay out of trouble till then. And stop staring at me! It was worth the potential hernia just to see you speechless."

I waved silently and watched in wonder as he walked down the hall, still chuckling to himself.

Five minutes later I was fast asleep—teeth brushed but makeup still firmly in place. My skin would probably look like hell in the morning, but at least my teeth weren't going to fall out. The last thing I remember thinking before I conked out was "Hernia? I am *not* that heavy!"

4

For a number of conference-goers, it's become something of a tradition for groups of friends to get together for brunch. Sometimes registrants choose to attend the gospel brunch that usually has corporate sponsorship boosting the hallelujahs and amens. Wherever they went, Sunday morning was the last chance for folks to meet up before scattering in their different directions. But I was in no mood for the questions about Ev's death I knew would dog me if I tried to have breakfast downstairs in the grill. So around seven-thirty I had room service deliver strong coffee, a bowl of fresh fruit, and some yogurt—penance for having consumed almost that entire block of pâté by myself last night.

It's not like I could have gotten out of the room anyway; at about 6:45, the phone had started ringing. I'd spent part of the morning talking with Henry Adams, who was understandably distressed that his boss had expired overnight.

"I'm sure you'll handle whatever comes up, Henry," I said, trying to sound as if I cared. "You always come through in a pinch."

After more meaningless reassurances from me, Henry, at my suggestion, finally hung up to call Jim Marron and make the necessary inquiries as to when Ev's body might be released for shipping. He'd already talked to Ev's family, and they wanted him sent home. Paul called a half hour later to say good-bye, just before he left for the airport. And various NABJ members had begun ringing as the news of Ev's death—and its hazy circumstances—began to leak out. Whoever said good news travels fast hadn't clocked bad news' speedometer.

By 10 A.M. I was dressed, packed, and standing in an ever-lengthening line waiting to check out. The buzz was incessant, as worried NABJ members canvassed each other about Ev's untimely end. To pass time more quickly, I amused myself by eavesdropping. It is a bad habit I'd had since childhood, but one that proved eminently useful—then and now. Woodward and Bernstein probably eavesdropped too, and look what it got them.

"God, they thought he was asleep when they found him."

"Hear he died with a smile on his face; wouldn't have hurt my feelings none."

"You are *so* crude! Sex didn't have anything to do with it—the man was *poisoned!*"

Uh-oh. Word had spread faster than I'd imagined it would. The woman in front of me heaved a heavy sigh. I didn't know her, but she was dressed in expensive sportswear and reeked of senior editor authority. The tag on her briefcase carried the logo of one of the nation's premier newsweeklies in big red letters.

"I'll say this: If it *was* murder, thank God the killer didn't do it with a knife or a gun. Nothing drives me crazier than to have to edit reports of black people who die niggers' deaths. You'd think the only way we had to kill ourselves was with Saturday night specials and butcher knives!"

"So déclassé," I murmured, grateful that it was my turn to check out and I didn't have to continue in this vein. Ms. Authority was expanding on her point with the woman behind her, a sister dressed in vivid tropical colors and an intricate set of tiny braids. Braids was nodding in emphatic agreement, as her fashionable gold matte earrings swung vigorously with each movement of her head.

"Thank you for staying at the Millennium," the pretty Asian desk clerk cooed. "I hope your visit with us was a pleasant one."

It was—until last night, I thought grimly. The surface me merely nodded pleasantly, picked up my garment bag and briefcase, and left to find Signe. I'd promised to drive her to the airport.

"Can't miss this baby." Signe laughed as we stuffed her oversized garment bag into my old BMW 2002's trunk. "You know," she huffed, as she tried slamming down her side of the trunk, "this thing would fit in there if you didn't use your trunk like a rolling file cabinet. You *have* a file cabinet at work!"

"You sound like Paul," I muttered, juggling my ancient key in the ancient lock.

I'd bought the car fifteen years ago; it was five years old then and had been driven by a little old lady who truly used it to tootle through the hands-down whitest part of Washington: from home in Spring Valley to the National Cathedral for church and, once a month, over to Embassy Row for meetings of the Cincinnatus Club. It barely had gone 10,000 miles when she sold it. I don't know what had possessed her to buy an orange car—with a stick shift, yet—I think I remember her saying something about finding the neon-tangerine hue "cheery." Whatever her decision to order one in what the BMW people called Inka, the little car's pulsing color looked much more at home in my Adams-Morgan neighborhood, with its bodegas, Ethiopian restaurants, and Third World art galleries, than I imagined it had back in Richard Nixon's old stomping grounds. The only thing Inka over there were some of the live-in nannies.

"You know," Signe suggested, picking the slowly disintegrating raffia that was the passenger seat's stuffing off her linen pant leg, "you *could* give in and buy a car with seats that aren't crumbling. And some air-conditioning would be nice." She fanned herself vigorously with a program from the awards banquet as I drove from the cool depths of self-park into the midday heat.

"Hey—it's a twenty-year-old car, it runs, and it's paid for. Does air-conditioning mean so much to you that you'd rather spend thirty-five dollars on a taxi, cause that *is* an option."

"Girl, please! Don't be getting all huffy 'cause I pointed out your little ol' car has a few problems. I'm sure you'll get a grown-up car one day—maybe before you're too old drive it!" She pantomined the universal little old lady, going slowly and peering warily over the steering wheel.

We both cracked up. Signe and I have been fussing with each other like this since college; it was a cherished ritual. And when we spend time together, we always fuss more just before we separate. So the ante on the fussing was being upped because we both knew we were going to miss each other when she got on that plane to go back to New York.

Despite its age and now-faded tangerine color, my little car worked like a charm. And it would until the next time it needed to have something fixed, which, according to schedule, should be about four weeks from now. Even with regular visits to Dave, my miracle-worker mechanic, eight weeks was about what you could expect for a twenty-year-old car that was maintained with loving indifference.

"Girl, what a mess! Do you suppose they'll have the funeral in Washington?" Signe asked, as I eased off Santa Monica onto Sepulveda. She looked out the window as we whizzed down the almost-empty ramp to the 405 South.

"I guess. But I remember him telling me once about how everybody in his family is buried in the same place, someplace really tiny in the South Carolina countryside. They all go back there every third summer for a family reunion. Didn't you include him in your black family reunion piece that ran a few years ago?"

Signe's head swiveled around and she snapped her fingers. "You're right! For somebody who's getting old quick, you've got a good memory. They meet in, if you can believe it, Ninety-Nine Miles. It's about forty minutes outside of Columbia. I had to rent a car at the Columbia airport and drive there. Talk about getting *lost!*" Signe's huge brown eyes dance in remembered amusement. "But that's another story." She waved a mahogany hand in airy dismissal. "Poor Ev," she said softly.

"Yeah, poor Ev," I echoed.

Ten seconds later, Signe's mourning period had apparently ended. Her next question came immediately after, and it startled me. That and the eighteen-wheeler that was drifting into our lane. I beeped to let him know we wouldn't take being demolished kindly. A hairy white arm popped out the window in a half wave of acknowledgment.

"So, Alex, who do you think did it? I hear those wheels turning."

"Me? I don't know . . . it could have been a lot of people, I guess."

"Uh-huh, and all of them bleed once a month."

"Signe!" I was almost really shocked. And intrigued. "Why do you think a woman did it?"

"Girl, *please*—because Ev was such a dog, God bless him." Signe's eyebrows arched towards her hairline, and tiny wrinkles disappeared into her short wavy natural.

A thought occurred. "Signe, did you—"

Signe snorted. "Not hardly. For one thing, I'd never do that to Otha. For another, I like my men monogamous, and monogamous and Everett Carson did not live in the same house. He always had one woman ringing the front bell while he was hurrying another out the back."

I thought back to several NABJ conferences where those precise scenarios had been enacted many times (and not only by Ev either), and I nodded. "I guess."

"There are two sisters I can think of who could have real sound motive for killing him. One didn't come this year, but the other one was there."

"Who didn't come, and how do we know she didn't sneak in, do it, and leave without anybody seeing her?" I wondered aloud.

"Because that girl wasn't going nowhere, honey," Signe said, with rock-ribbed certainty. "On Saturday night she was fully dilated and pushing and screaming at Lenox Hill Hospital; baby Michael *Preston* Robertson was born when we were at Happy Hour. Sandra told me."

"Pam Preston—and Ev?" Really, the things we don't know.

"For a hot minute, about three years ago, he was *totally* into this girl: flowers every other day, lots of public exposure as a couple. Then—poof!"

"Why?"

"The usual. Commitment anxiety. *And* he'd found someone else to charm, so he dropped Pam. Never had the balls to tell her why. Of course she was mortified. She and her girlfriends at WNXT were already deciding on where she'd register and who'd design her dress. *Major* face crunch."

I considered. That kind of embarrassment could make someone, in the heat of passion, expunge the source of the mortification. But Pam had gotten over it, gotten married, gone on to another life. Even if she had some hard feelings, it would have taken something much more motivating than anger at being dumped to hop on a plane in your ninth month, especially when you're about to drop a baby any moment. Pam, for my money, was not a likely subject.

"Who's the other possibility?"

Signe grinned. "Fasten your seat belt."

"Signe, my seat belt's *already* fastened! Now *who*?"

"Nobody knows this—*nobody*, hear?"

"Yeah, yeah: Cross my heart, hope to die, poke a nail into my eye, yadda yadda yadda."

"I'll take that as a promise you won't blab it around. Remember last month when you came to see me for the Fourth, and we invited Ev over for dinner, and he begged off?"

"Yes—which I consider a blessing, since I wasn't frying chicken in ninety-two-degree weather in a Manhattan apartment with no good vent—"

"Like *you're* the one who was gonna be cookin' that bird! Well, he didn't come because he was too busy."

"Which I thought was odd at the time. I mean, how often are we all in the same city at the same time? He must have been busy."

"He was. With Nellie Pointer."

I looked at Signe. Clearly the heat had gotten to her. Nellie was Henry Adams's predecessor and had done an admirable job of bringing *Diaspora* into the twenty-first century. She'd overseen the installation of a computer network, so editing, billing, and circulation were all plugged into the same system. She'd overhauled the contracts for writers, photographers, artists, and vendors and made them comprehensible to normal people while remaining acceptable to the lawyers who had inserted the indecipherable language in the first place. And she'd worked her buns off in the interest of making *Diaspora* a first-class magazine.

She did have her drawbacks, though. She was extremely emotional, shrill and prone to tears at the drop of the hat—especially when stressed or angry. And Ev, with his constant needling, his unwillingness to let his editors edit without his interference, had Nellie in tears almost every other day. She'd been fired eight months after he'd hired her. "No offense, but we ain't each other's kinda people. I got to have a right hand I can work with." Which meant, basically, a right hand that could reach down and scratch its testicles every now and again.

Nellie's feelings were hurt. And despite a generous severance package, and the fact that she picked up another job at a bigger magazine almost immediately, she was not interested in letting water run under this particular bridge. No, Nellie was damming the river farther downstream and would sometime in the near future plan to flood Ev's fields however she could. Whoever claimed revenge was a dish best eaten cold didn't know Nellie: she'd sit in front of the oven with a knife and fork and a napkin tied around her neck, just waiting for it to be done, and scald her tongue while scarfing it down. So Signe's news made no sense.

"Uh, when you say he was *busy* with Nellie, you mean they were laying out a story or something?"

"Nope." Signe grinned, enjoying my amazement. "They were just laying out. With each other."

"You liar!"—beat—"How do you know?"

"I actually ran into them one evening a few weeks after you left. Otha and I had gone up to One hundred and Seventh and Broadway for some Eritrean food—you know that little place—and there they were, walking up toward Columbia. I think she lives on One Hundred Twelfth and Riverside. She was all hugged up on him, and he was trying to pretend they weren't a couple. But they were for that night."

I applied the brakes. Traffic had come to a complete halt, for no apparent reason. Typical L.A. And the airport was still twenty minutes or so away. Signe never even glanced at her watch; she was so used to me playing Hoke to her Miss Daisy whenever she came to L.A., she just assumed I'd get her there on time.

"Damn. She's not even his *type*." Ev didn't date assertive women, and Nellie's assertiveness was her trademark. "What did they see in each other, do you think?"

"She'd just broken up with someone, and he—well, hell, Alex, he's *Ev*. She offered and he took; then he split. You can say a lot about him, but you can't say he's inconsistent. Remember the personalized plates on the boy's Jeep?"

We both mentally envisioned Ev's navy Jeep Grand Cherokee. Its plates were notorious around D.C. because they read HITNRUN.

Traffic was picking up again, and soon we were back to speed. The scraggly palms swabbed West L.A.'s smoggy skies like ineffectual bottle brushes.

"Nothing, I guess, in terms of MO. But he barely spoke to her civilly in the office; how could they have . . . you know?"

Signe laughed heartily. "Ev will 'you know' with just about anybody, and that's what Nellie was: any body. He told me later he'd just succumbed in a weak moment, and he shouldn't have. But that's Ev."

The American terminal finally came into sight.

"So you think Nellie might have killed him, because he fired her or because he stopped seeing her in his trademark abrupt fashion?"

"Either of those—or the fact that she thought she might be pregnant with you-know-who's little darlin'."

I was so astonished I almost rear-ended a shiny black Lexus that had smoothly swooped in front of me to the curb. The driver, a blow-dried guy with multi-pleated silk trousers, tassel loafers, and no socks, lifted a thin lip to sneer at my battered little coupe. Your mama, I mouthed silently. He blinked, uncomprehending.

I turned back to Signe. "How on earth do you know these things?"

"Gotta be in the right place at the right time, girlfriend. In my case, the right place was in the ladies while you were upstairs with

Paul and the Po-leece, 'cause Nellie was in the stall next to me, crying her eyes out. And you know Nellie: She can't keep a secret."

"But if she was in the stall, how'd you know it *was* Nellie?"

"Please. You can smell her Calyx coming and going. It's like being around a big ol' grapefruit. Anyway, when I knocked and asked her if she was all right, she came blubbering out the stall and told me her period hadn't come and—"

"Oh, God, no!"

"Yeah. She was hysterical. Said her mother would *die*, and you know how close she is to her mother."

I'd met Nellie's mother. She was one of the first black women in the country to receive an MBA in the early fifties and had been a serious career woman ever since. She was very elegant, very icy. Nellie was constantly trying to please her and constantly not quite getting there. She was right to be worried: Arthurine Pointer probably wouldn't have been happy to show baby pictures of her unwed daughter's child at the next convention.

"Anyway," Signe said cheerfully, gathering her purse and tote bag, "it all ended well, because when I saw her in checkout this morning, she was all bright and chirpy. And in that typical Nellie way, stage-whispered across two lines of people, "Everything's okay! I'm going home with my Friend!"

Well, subtlety was never Nellie's strong suit—and who knows? Most people don't even remember that "my friend is visiting" was the fifties euphemism for Big Red's presence. But if she got her period on Sunday, that meant Nellie still thought she might be pregnant on Saturday night. Could she have been angry enough with Ev—and herself—to kill him?

It wasn't an answer we were going to get right away, because Jerk Boy had finally hoisted himself into his Lexus and zoomed off. I jockeyed into his space with room to spare, and we both hopped out.

"You'll have to hustle if you're going to make the noon plane. Call me if you find out anything else. I'll keep my ears open at this end." We placed Signe's monster bag on the ground and hugged good-bye.

"Ladies, may I be of assistance?"

A distinguished-looking older man in a skycap's uniform smoothly took the unwieldy bag and held his hand out for tickets. "Where to, young ladies?"

"New York," I said, "and only *that* lady is going. Although if she doesn't move she won't get herself *or* her bags on the plane."

"Oh, yes, she will; haven't let a pretty woman miss a plane yet," the golden-skinned gentleman assured me. Signe was dimpling like cellulite on a middle-aged thigh.

When I pulled away—seconds before the evil sister whose sole joy in life is derived from handing out $50 tickets and reminding people, none too nicely, that "the *white* zone is for loading and unloading *only*"—I could see Signe and the baggage brother flirting outrageously. He had to be all of sixty. And there was no doubt both her bags and her booty would be on that plane.

About thirty minutes later, I'd driven through the hilltop ranch homes of Baldwin Hills, down into the bungalowed flats again, through the Fairfax District's stucco duplexes and into Hancock Park. As I pulled into the drive, weekend runners were gliding under the great green canopy of trees that lined my street. Underground sprinklers were sending rainbow-hued spray over lush green lawns.

Somewhere inside my house, there were unpaid bills and laundry to be done. It was time to get back to real life without room service and dulcet-toned wake-up calls. I pulled through the open gates and set the emergency brake and hoped I didn't drip oil in the motor court.

Home again, home again, jiggedy-jig.

5

I should explain about where I live, because a person could get the wrong impression if he only knew my address. Marvin Gaye was right about people needing to believe only half of what they see.

When I first moved to Los Angeles, the *Standard* put me up in a downtown hotel for a month while I read the want ads and spent several lunch hours and way too many weekend afternoons inspecting potential living spaces. I looked at high-rise condos in Westwood (too sterile), garden apartments in West Hollywood (cute, but the parking is horrible and it's not quiet enough), duplexes in the mid-Wilshire Corridor (even worse parking than West Hollywood), and a one-bedroom penthouse in Los Feliz (lovely, but too expensive).

Certain parts of the city were out, period: Beverly Hills had an attitude problem—mine about it as much as its about everyone who didn't reside within its glided confines. The Hollywood Hills were too scary for East Coast me; standing on the front porch of one of the sweetest, most affordable, bougainvillea-hung bungalows, my overactive imagination could just see a Charlie Manson-type threading his way up the narrow winding roads, hiding in wait in the inky shadows between old-fashioned, glass-globe streetlights (not the ugly but more efficient mercury-vapor types that discourage crime), waiting to do me in one winter evening when I returned home after working late. No, thanks. And Brentwood and Culver City were too far away from work; I worried I'd spend an hour each way commuting. Back East, you drive for an hour you're in another state, for God's sake. (That was before I became used to the idea of spending as much time in my car as I do now.)

Just as my month of subsidized living was coming to an end and I was considering whose sofa I was going to beg to crash on for a week or so, and wondering if I could afford to lease one of those totally furnished executive-suite numbers, fate intervened courtesy of homesickness and an uncharacteristic need for physical fitness. One of my Metro colleagues, another East Coast immigrant, had told me a week or so earlier that he'd found two places in L.A. that reminded him of home: Pasadena and Hancock Park. "Maybe you should drive around a bit, get a feel for them, and see what's available."

I'd visited Pasadena several times, and my co-worker was right; it was very East Coast in many ways. It had, for instance, trees with deciduous leaves, an important bit of ambiance for those of us who like watching leaves succumb to the forces of gravity come autumn. It had gorgeous homes, quiet streets, and, in some places, beautiful views of the San Gabriel Mountains. But it had problems too. Pasadena was one of the *whitest* cities I'd ever seen, and working where I did and having integrated enough other things in my life, I had no interest in ever integrating anything again. Call me after the Spookometer goes over 15 percent, and we can talk.

Pasadena also has some of the worst pollution in the L.A. basin— which is saying something. In the last century, the city's air was so clean that wealthy Easterners chose to winter there. These days, its air is often so bad you can't even see the mountains the city is built directly beneath. People with severe respiratory problems are urged to leave in the summer, it's *that* bad. Call me naive, but I figured if I worked for the *Los Angeles Standard*, it would be nice if I lived in Los Angeles, if for no other reason than to ensure I was exposed to some ethnic diversity. The *Standard* did a brave job of writing and talking about multiculturalism at every turn, but its newsroom—and certainly its management—still looked very Pasadena. (Not coincidental, I guess, since many of them lived there.)

That September Saturday, I left the hotel in my rent-a-car and drove maybe fifteen minutes south and a little east to the edge of Hancock Park. I parked around Second and Irving and started walking, confident I could find my way back again easily enough. I realized, once I started walking, how much I missed the regular exercise. Back home, I usually walked to work. In the few weeks I'd been in L.A., most of my walking was done to and from the car. So I was really enjoying this little ambulatory expedition.

There was no logic to my trajectory; I simply went where my fancy took me. I saw large houses deeply set back from the streets with lush, neatly tended lawns. In style, they ranged from Mediterranean Hacienda, from Craftsman to good old East Coast Colonial. Several people seemed to favor Tudors (a little too dark and brooding for me; reminded me too much of the dorms at boarding school). And there were a few of what real estate people insisted on repetitiously labeling "French Normandy." (Where, please, is Normandy located if not in northern France?) On the whole, a beautiful neighborhood, but, considering my *Standard* salary, clearly out of my league.

I kept walking west and north and, several blocks later, found myself on a small commercial strip. It looked like Main Street probably did thirty years ago; there was a butcher, a baker, several antiques dealers, a newsstand, a few restaurants, and a general store. I followed the intoxicating scent of freshly brewed coffee and turned into Cafe El Lay for a fix. And there, over a currant scone and a big *caffe* latte, fate intervened. Turned out I was in Larchmont Village, the commercial strip in Hancock Park. And the Village had its own newspaper, the *Larchmont Chronicle*. And the newspaper had a page of folksy classifieds.

Just to leave no stone unturned, I turned to the real estate listings. I skimmed past the ridiculous ones ("Trad. elegance: 4 bdr plus md's, mstr w/sauna & Jacuzzi, lib w/wbf, fml dr, Smallbone kitchen, $10,000 per mo") to something that caught my eye: "Guest Hse, Hnck Park. Available immed."

It listed a number but no information on price or size.

What the hell, I'd thought, and plunked my 35 cents in the phone slot. A brisk voice answered on the third ring.

"Yes?"

"Hello, I'm calling about your ad in the *Larchmont Chronicle*. I've just moved here from the East Coast, and I wondered whether I might see the space—that is, if you've not already leased it. And," I added, as the thought occurred to me, "if I can afford it. You didn't list a price."

"We'll talk price *after* you've seen it and *if* you decide to take it," the voice snapped. "Can you come now? It won't be convenient to show it after this afternoon."

"Sure. I'm in the Village. What's the address?"

She told me and gave me instructions how to get there on foot. "It should take about fifteen minutes, unless you're as old as I am."

I laughed and started to hang up.

"Just a minute!" the voice snapped. "What's your name?"

"Alexa Powell. You won't have any trouble recognizing me," I assured her sweetly. "I'm black." I hung up. Let her chew *that* over. Might as well get it out of the way right off and find out who I'm dealing with here.

She was standing by the gate when I turned up the driveway, a tiny lady immaculately dressed in charcoal-gray sweats and spotless white leather sneakers. Her silver hair was twisted up in a French knot, and gray South Sea pearls glowed in her ears.

"You must be Alexa; I'm Sally Fergueson." We shook hands; her grasp was dry, cool, and surprisingly firm. "Good thing you told me you were black," she cackled. "I might not have caught on for days."

I raised my eyebrows. I find it extremely irritating when white folks presume anything when it comes to my blackness. If Sally Fergueson noticed my annoyance, she didn't let on. In fact, she *kept* on.

"Well, face it, honey, I'm darker than you after a weekend in Palm Springs! I'll bet some people say things they wish they hadn't when they find out what you are." She chuckled, and she was right. Sometimes strangers did express intemperate opinions about mah peeples and then blanch when I calmly informed them I was one, too. She was still laughing when she swung wide the wrought-iron gate and gestured me in.

I had entered paradise. On the other side of the high stucco wall, a huge green backyard dozed in the midafternoon sun. A flagstone patio outside the main house was dotted with wrought-iron tables and chairs, and a good-sized pool threw iridescent sparkles as the sun hit the waves made by the automatic sweeper. At the opposite end of the pool was another, smaller patio with a shallow wall about it, maybe two feet high. A similar table—wrought iron, but a bit more modern—had four chairs around it, and a furled patio umbrella stood guard over the whole arrangement.

I held my breath. This was too good to be true.

"That, as you can see, is the guest house. Come on, I'll show you the inside." We walked about seventy-five feet, stepped onto the small patio, and Mrs. Fergueson opened the honey-oak door. It probably wasn't the smartest thing to do, since I had no idea what she'd charge—*if* she decided to rent to me—but I couldn't help it: I gasped when I walked over the threshold.

The front of the house was one room, a large living-dining area. The sun streamed through large casement windows onto the hard-wood floor. To the left, a large fireplace stood stacked with split logs. Hand-hewn beams spanned the ceiling.

At the rear of the big room, a set of folding French doors had been pushed back to reveal a small but adequate kitchen. The stucco walls were stark white; blue and white Portuguese tiles lined the backsplash and counter. The sink clinched the deal for me: I'd never seen anything like it in a kitchen. It was totally impractical. I wanted it—bad. Oval shaped, it was white porcelain with a hand-painted scene of a little boy chasing dolphins around its rim. A steel chemist's faucet—the kind that loops up and over—stood like a sentry over the boy and his fish. It would have to be wiped off after every use, especially after dumping coffee grounds or leftover spaghetti sauce. I didn't give a damn.

There would be adequate cabinet space in the glass-fronted bleached-wood cabinets for my dish collection, I thought. There was an expensive refrigerator, a gas range top, and a double oven (one convection, one microwave) in a cabinet next to the stove. The floors were terra-cotta Mexican pavers.

To the left of the kitchen, behind the living room, was a master bedroom. It wasn't huge, but my queen-sized bed would fit in with no problems. Opposite the space where the bed would go was a smaller fireplace than the one in the living room, and a dressing room with built-in bureaus and closet rods. This room connected to a small bath with old-fashioned porcelain fixtures (plain ivory, no dolphins). Just off the kitchen was a second bedroom that was empty. It would make a fine library/office/crash pad for visitors.

"So? What do you think? Can you stand it?"

"I can stand it," I said dryly, knowing Murphy's Law was about to kick in: Now that I'd found it and wanted it so badly, it would be unaffordable.

"It only has one bathroom, and you're going to have to walk up front to get your mail since, technically, we're not allowed to rent these places out," Mrs. Ferguson was saying. "And you'll have to park your car on the other side of the house; there's a garage space for you, and you can use the walkway over there that connects the yard with the motor court."

I sighed. "Now tell me the bad news. How much?"

Sally Ferguson looked at me speculatively. "I was planning to ask eight hundred dollars. Can you handle that?"

I couldn't believe my ears. "Eight hundred dollars?" I repeated, just to make sure.

"Well, utilities *are* included, and it's pretty nice space, if I do say so myself. It was okay before, but I spent some money five years ago and redecorated it for my daughter. Louise was going to leave her tiresome husband and move in. I was looking forward to having her here, if you want to know the truth. Unfortunately, they reconciled, so it's just been sitting empty since then." She shook her head. "Too bad. . . . On the other hand"—she grinned—"I got another grand-child after they made up. Taylor's almost two."

Then she went back to business.

"So—what do you think?" She was going around, firmly shutting all the cupboards and drawers we'd opened during the kitchen inspection.

"I love the house—it's a *great* house. But are you sure you only want eight hundred for it?"

"I'd rather charge what I want and get who I want in here"—*slam*—"some other people called, but you got here first. If you do take it, I should tell you now: I don't care what you do in here"—*slam*—"as long as it's legal and respects the neighbors' need for quiet. I'm old enough to be your mother—but I'm not going to mother-hen you. Agreed?"

"Yes, *ma'am!*"

"And call me Sally."

"Yes, ma'am—uh, *Sally*."

So we shook on it. I came inside, she made coffee, and we chatted for a minute. Seems Sally was related, on her mother's side, to several pioneer Los Angeles families, including the ones who had engineered the basin's irrigation and, by extension, its growth. Through them she was cousins to the *Standard*'s owners, the Oatley Hansomes, although she was considered somewhat of a black sheep. Her politics were too liberal and she voted the wrong way. She loathed, for instance, the current governor, a sawed-off little opportunist the *Standard* had endorsed, despite—or maybe because of—his initiative to round up all illegal (or illegal-*looking*) immigrants for deportation.

"That stupid proposition to send all the Latinos back!" She sniffed indignantly. "Who do they think will watch their precious babies, serve at their parties, and trim their shrubbery? And who do they think is going to be running the state in just a few years? Oatley must have had rocks in his head to let the editorial page endorse that gremlin!" My sentiments exactly. I'd said so in a column, much to my editor's discomfort. They don't like making Oatley mad at the *Standard*.

The big house was exactly that: big. The furniture was stately; the beams across its living room ceiling were tremendous. The fireplace was so large I could stand up in it without crouching; it looked as if it had been shipped from some sixteenth-century Lake Como estate. Despite its size, it felt warm and homey, and the lines were beautifully proportionate.

"Oh, you'll be interested in this," Sally said casually, as I filled out the requisite information about income and employer, "a black man built this house. The guest house too."

She went on to tell me that Paul Revere Williams, architect of such landmarks as the Polo Lounge and Chasen's, had designed the house for her husband's parents in 1928. Twenty years later, both died within months of each other, and Neville and Sally Fergueson, with their small children, Louise and Harris, had moved in. She'd been there ever since. Williams had apparently designed many of the nicest homes in Hancock Park, "even though he couldn't live here at the time. Restrictions, you know. We didn't even have Jews back then. And, to the pro-covenant folks, even worse than Jews were movie stars. Now, of course, we have some of everybody in here, gay, straight, black, white, you name it—including movie people. Nobody cares—or if they do, they're not rude enough to say so. Money. The great equalizer."

I picked up my purse and prepared to clear out. There was a handsome leather satchel in the foyer's corner that looked as if its owner was ready to pick it up and scram. I didn't want to overstay my welcome—especially if that might taint Sally's decision as to whether or not she was going to lease to me.

"So you'll call me after you check references and let me know?"

"Oh, shoot!" Sally flipped a hand tipped in coral polish. "I do it the old-fashioned way. If my instinct says you're okay, you're okay. So just tell me when you want to move. If you'll come by next week after work, I'll give you keys and the code to the alarm. That about cover it?"

And it had been that stress-free ever since. Despite the differences in our races, ages, and incomes, we'd become quite good friends. I didn't see much of Sally; on weekends, she spent a lot of time in local WASPy watering holes like Coronado, La Jolla, and Santa Barbara, and she was forever lunching with this or that enameled remnant of old Los Angeles society. She minded her own business—not that I had any for her to mind very often—and occasionally had me over to the big house, where her house-keeper, Josefina (who was almost as old as she was), made tea and little sandwiches for us on weekend afternoons or wine and cheese and pâté in the evenings. I would tease Sally about her crowded social calendar, and she would lecture me about my lack of one.

"Really, Alex, you need to get out more. Hell, you need to get out, *period*! It's a shame when an old lady like me spends more time having fun than you do."

I laughed. "Talk to your cousin, Sally. He runs a tight ship with long hours."

"I would, if I thought you wouldn't kill me if I did." She winked.

We both knew better. Sally barely saw the Hansomes except at the requisite premieres at the Music Center and the annual cotillions that drew out the equivalent of Los Angeles's cliff-dwelling society. They were pleasant but distant, recognizing that, as the last shreds of old Los Angeles (which was quickly being eclipsed by what I called Nueva Los Angeles), the tiny tribe was obligated to make a united showing occasionally. In general, Sally's relatives were people who would eventually fade into heavily moneyed oblivion. They would disappear behind the high gates of neighborhoods that would, somehow, always remain restricted, if only on a street-by-street basis, where the owners of the huge homes would always be white, the help would always be some shade of brown, the grass would grow eternally green, and their fellow tribesmen would wax nostalgic, over cocktails and canapés, about the Old Los Angeles.

"Remember tea at Bullock's Wilshire?"

"Remember when you knew what everybody was saying, because we all spoke the same language?"

"Remember when there was no traffic? It only took twenty minutes to get to Santa Monica!"

"Remember when everybody knew everybody else?"

Sally, however, was making the transition. She spoke Spanish fluently ("Had to; what good was my French going to do me here? And Latin—forget it!") and could argue with her gardener in his own language about whether he was cutting back the hydrangea too much. She was the Story Lady at Pio Pico Elementary School on Wednesday afternoons and regaled the mostly Latino children with tales of Old L.A. between requests for *The Cat in the Hat* and *Curious George—en español*. The endlessly analyzed browning of Los Angeles didn't much seem to freak her out.

"Oh, honestly! The fuss they're making, you'd think this hadn't happened before. How do you think the *Californios* felt when they saw waves of white pioneers like my family pouring into the territory?"

"There goes the neighborhood?"

"Exactly!"

We hooted, confident that we were survivors, that Nueva Los Angeles was not a frightening prospect to us and our open-minded kind.

All in all, I couldn't have asked for a better landlady.

I pushed open the door I'd been walking through for five years now, and appreciated anew how lucky I had been to find this space. I turned off the alarm and was walking forward to dump my bags in the center of the room when I nearly fell on my face; I'd slipped on something I hadn't noticed beneath my sandals.

Looking down, I saw I was standing on a heavy ecru envelope—had to be Sally. She ordered them once a year from the same stationer she'd used since she was a bride. His wares were discreet, tasteful, and one of the last reliable physical remnants of Old Los Angeles.

The monogrammed card, once I wrestled it out of its celadon-lined envelope, welcomed me back and told me my mail was waiting for me in the front hall:

*In the usual place. Though you might be tired after your week
away. Josefina made her marvelous enchiladas and wanted me to
let you know there is a pan in the refrigerator with your name on
it. Am off to Santa Barbara until Tuesday. Number is on kitchen
bulletin board if something comes up.
Ciao!
S*

The mere mention of Josefina's fabulous enchiladas made my
mouth water. And as my mouth watered, I also realized that breakfast was hours and hours ago. Enchiladas would hit the spot. I
opened the broom closet, grabbed the extra keys to Sally's house,
and crossed the rear lawn.

Inside, the big house was dark, cool, and quiet. Josefina was usually gone until late Sunday night, but I called out, just to make sure.

No answer.

I walked back to the kitchen and opened Sally's big commercial
refrigerator. As promised, a good-sized pan wrapped in tinfoil had
Miss Alex in Josefina's convent-school cursive. Next to it was a small
head of romaine that also was intended for me, as it, too, had my
name on it. I fetched the mail—bills and junk—returned to my little house, and blasted two enchiladas in the microwave while I
washed, dried, and tore the romaine and drizzled it with low-fat
Caesar. Low-fat salad dressing is one of my tradeoffs; I'd rather waste
those calories on chocolate, any day.

I feasted on Josefina's generosity while I read the Sunday paper.
When I finished, it being siesta time, I decided to take a little nap.

The "little nap" lasted almost six hours, until
eight-thirty. If I stripped off my clothes and went to bed for real, I'd
be awake and crazy by 4 A.M. Instead, I willed myself to stay awake
by unpacking my week's worth of NABJ clothes, laundering the
washables, and placing the stuff to be dropped off at the cleaner's by
the door, so I wouldn't forget.

Then I sorted all the mail that had accumulated in my absence (nothing important), threw away the junk, and placed bills to be paid on my desk. I skimmed the back papers to see what had happened while I was gone. (Same stuff, different day: more city council infighting, more Westside residents fighting the latest incursion into their sacred "lifestyle"—in this case, a hospice for pediatric AIDS patients, most of whom were low-income and, ipso facto, minority. And the usual high-temp smog-choked weather.)

Finally, I inspected my closet for something appropriate to wear to work tomorrow, took a shower, and washed and dried my hair.

All that atypical domestic industriousness exhausted me. By that time, it was ten-fifty. I sat up and watched the news, then went to bed and slept until six-thirty the next morning, when the telephone woke me up.

6

I was dreaming: In a long hall at the Millen-
nium Hotel, the door to 1802 was open but people in blue Coroner's
Department jumpsuits were hurrying everyone away from the door.
There was a loudspeaker announcement in the halls, like the kind on
the PA system in high school, and an alarm kept ringing and ring-
ing. . . .

I awoke in a panic. The phone was on its fourth ring because I
heard the answering machine pick up.

Hi, this is Alex Powell. . . .

I hate that message: too damn perky. I plan to replace it with
something more sober-sounding whenever I think about it, but I
always forget. This morning, my cheery phone persona wasn't welcome noise to the real me, which was still having a hard time struggling to sleep's surface.

"Hello," I gasped, in what I hoped approximated the crisp voice
of an awake human being. In the background I heard the voice-
activated machine snap off.

"Mrs. Fletcher!" The voice was vaguely familiar and as disgust-
ingly cheerful as the canned one on my answering machine. And it
had the wrong number. Shit.

"Sorry," I mumbled. "You have the wrong number."

"No, I don't." The irritatingly up voice plowed on. "Isn't this the
famous girl detective who offered me her services a scant few hours

ago? How quickly they forget." I heard the sound of coffee being slurped. Loudly. A light went on.

"Detective Marron."

"Anybody ever tell you you'd clean up on *Jeopardy*?"

"Didn't the new police chief say he was going to give demerits to cops with bad manners? Waking innocent civilians at an ungodly hour and slurping your coffee in their ear sounds pretty unmannerly to me. What time *is* it, anyway?" Without my contact lenses, I squinted to decipher the digital readout on my bedside clock. The numbers swam before me, but they had to be wrong. "Six-thirty! Are you *crazy*?"

"Not at all," the cheerful voice continued between slurps. "I figured you'd be one of those early-rising granola-heads. Guess I figured wrong."

Something told me to not hold my breath for an apology. "Excuse me, but your last words to me were, in effect, 'Little girl, stay out of it; I'll call you if I need you.' I took your advice and stayed out of it. Now you're calling me. Why?"

Marron sighed audibly. "Jessica, I have some bad news. The preliminary pharm report came back on your Mr. Carson, and it looks like he may have had some help dying. Pathology says there are trace elements of a couple drugs that he probably didn't take for medical reasons. The logical guess is somebody whacked him."

I could feel my eyebrows involuntarily floating up, up, up, the skeptic's natural reflex. "I thought it took weeks to get this kind of information back."

"To be absolutely certain, it does. But the preliminary information is pretty reliable in most cases, and this looks like the other lab reports will bear it out."

"So what was the substance?"

"Or substances. Can't tell you till the report's been officially released."

"So you're just calling to be neighborly, or did you want to know something specific? I can't help you with any information on Ev's health. We never discussed it, and I've never known him to be sick."

"He wasn't. He was unnaturally healthy. His doctor told us he saw him once every couple years for a physical and that's it. Only 'scrip was for an antihistamine to deal with seasonal allergies. Plus an inhaler for mild asthma."

"Couldn't that have been it?"

"Antihistamines usually don't kill you, unless you've got extremely high blood pressure or a few other medical complications Everett Carson didn't have. So we're back to square one. Which is where you come in."

"I can't *wait* to hear how."

I could hear Marron taking a deep breath. "Okay, look. I'll beg if you make me, but I'd rather not. I have a proposition for you."

Silence.

"Hardball, huh? Okay, listen: I want you to forget you offered to play detective for a moment, then forget you rescinded the offer."

Oh, yeah. That made *plenty* of sense. Why hadn't I remembered to turn on the coffeemaker's timer before I went to bed? I could have been sniffing the tantalizing vapors of Sumatra or Viennese right now. Instead, I was listening to Marron slurp what was probably deli coffee in one of those paper cups with the Greek key frieze running along the top . . .

Paper cup! I just realized I'd given the coffeemaker away to a nonprofit organization and started buying coffee on my way to work. It had seemed like a smart decision at the time, but right now I'd kill for a cup of coffee. Even a cup of bad coffee.

"Done. I've forgotten my offer and your instructions. That was easy." I could just slip on my shoes and run the few blocks to the village and be wired in about five minutes flat.

"Okay, now forget what I asked you to forget: I don't want you to play detective, but I do want you to discreetly gather some information for a few days."

"Huh? Sounds like somebody's been using the extra crank the Narc boys keep in the Evidence Room."

"No, listen, it makes sense, for all the reasons you said on Saturday. You and Paul know the players—"

"If you think Paul would even *consider* this—"

"He did. He will if you will. I asked him already. Remember, they're three hours ahead of us back east."

"Why are you up so early?"

"Double shift."

"And why, please, would I be interested in using up my hard-won vacation time, not to mention money, to do your job for you? Aren't my taxes enough? Were the last round of budget cuts that devastating?"

"In a word, yes. About the budget cuts, I mean. But to answer your first question: Think of the exclusive you'd have for your news-paper. This could make you famous."

"Right. I've always wanted to be on *Oprah*. You have another, better reason?"

"Well, don't take this the wrong way, but you and Paul blend in—better than I would, anyway. You know that your people some-times have uneasy relationships with my people."

"That's because your people keep shooting my people. Often indiscriminately and without provocation, I might add."

"Now that is *total* bullshit! You get one or two assholes who act like cowboys and all of us end up paying for it, partly because you media types—"

"Cry me a river at a decent hour, Marron, and cut to the chase. What you really want is someone who can go incognegro among the natives to do your dirty work for you. And if that's what you want, you'd better start acting a whole lot nicer to me."

I heard a deep breath and silence. Maybe he was doing that cleansing-breath thing too.

"I hear there's going to be some kind of memorial service planned for Carson at the end of the week. Are you planning to go?"

"I'd been considering it, if I can get the time off. Why?"

" 'Cause if you do go, I'd like to know who was there and how they were acting—the usual."

"Uh-huh. And after I tattle to you, what are you going to do with the information?"

"Cogitate on it. I'm working up a profile. Want to see who might fit it."

"So let me get this straight: I go to my friend's funeral, sniff around, tell you any good stuff I see and hear, and then you randomly assign blame to someone based on information I've passed along? I . . . don't . . . think . . . so."

I had gotten up by this time and was rooting around for my running shoes. Having found them, I was hopping into my underwear as I spoke.

"Gee, that's too bad," Marron purred. "I ran this down to your editor last night, and he and the *Standard*'s management were quite amenable. Especially since I pointed out how we'd been screwed on the Lambert case."

The Lambert case had caused a significant furor last year when one of our Metro reporters got ahead of himself and wrote a story the police had given him access to on condition that he embargo it for twenty-four hours. He'd filed it before the deadline but forgot, while making his umpteenth revision, to place that caveat on top of the story in boldface, so the night editor just ran it for the next edition. And Leonard Lambert, an alleged rapist whose priors and sighting by an eyewitness made him a lead-pipe cinch for conviction this time in the rape of a fifteen-year-old deaf girl, almost walked. According to his slimeball high-priced lawyer, we'd nearly screwed up Lambert's constitutional right to a fair trial. The LAPD was still steamed about that, and so were the victim's parents. Can't blame them one bit.

"Well, no offense, Marron, but that was somebody else's screwup. I don't owe you squat."

"But your *paper* does, Powell, and they're okay with using you to ante up. Anyway, they've agreed to give you a few days off so you can do us this favor. Strictly off the record, of course. And with the explicit understanding that you'll be in no physical danger whatsoever."

"Or what? If something happens and I'm offed, you give them a chit that they take to the nearest auction block and simply buy another one?"

I heard an exasperated sigh at the other end. "C'mon, relax! *Everything* is not about race." Now he *really* sounded like my editors.

"This from somebody so white he's transparent. And please, spare me the 'I marched for Martin Luther King' speech."

"*I* didn't. I was too young. My mother did, though. I have pictures."

Probably explains his distinctively conservative attitude; don't theorists say we strive to be exactly like our parents—or, if the relationship isn't a happy one, their opposite? The clock said six-forty-five. If I hung up, I could still take the speed walk I'd considered skipping and get to work relatively on time.

"I'll think about it. Let me get back to you."

"I'll pretend to believe you actually have a choice in this and just say 'Sure, Powell.' "

I hung up without saying good-bye.

Lacing on my running shoes, I decided to speed-walk and think about Marron's proposition and see what burbled to the surface. Hopping on the treadmill at the gym or into the shower always manages to help me sort things out. When I'm really worried, I'm the best-toned, cleanest person in L.A. When life is normal (as it had been for a few months now), walking or showering provides story ideas or suggestions for leads. The latter were promptly obliterated by editors, who usually consider it their prerogative—no, their mission in life—to tamper with the clever heads we writers place on our own copy. I have a plaque in my office, prominently placed on one of my cubicle's walls. It says:

EDITOR : WRITER = DOG : FIRE HYDRANT

I think that's a fair analogy.

Walking quickly through the neighborhood, I put my body on automatic pilot and let my mind wander. Usually, that's when the ideas start to come, but today's walk merely worked off the enchi-

ladas I'd scarfed down last night. When I got home, I surveyed my
bath gels and made a choice. The shower's built-in seat is lined with
many different scented soaps for my various moods and purposes:
vanilla, almond, marine algae, hydrangea, grapefruit, and so on.
Spending money on bath stuff is one of my few material vices. I
reached for a bottle of eucalyptus gel. "Invigorating!" the label
promised.

I thought I'd get some sort of answer then, too, but all I got was
clean.

Back on the plantation, it was if I'd been away
for a whole month. There was a little cleared space on my desk, but
my towering in-basket more than compensated for the clean horizontal space. A quick glance showed it was mostly bureaucratic
effluvia and mass mailings from publicists hoping for a nibble on
their clients' behalf. And as soon as I logged onto my computer, I
could see that my electronic mailbox was totally stuffed. I hadn't had
that much E-mail since the *Standard* had initiated a huge buyout
two years before, and the electronic couriers were busy zinging sen-
tences on who was and who wasn't taking which offer. Of course, it
worked exactly 180 degrees from what management had planned.
Most of the good people went to our competitors with prematurely
lined pockets and prominent vertical moves, and the deadwood continued to collect a weekly paycheck.

Scanning the message list, I saw indeed that 80 percent of my
mail was gossip: the people who hadn't gone to NABJ wanting to
know the scoop and the people who had wanting updates. I'd get to
them later. As I was clearing the last E-mail from my screen, my
phone rang.

"Powell," I barked.

"Hey, Shorty. Heard you were back. When you coming down
this way to fill a sister in?"

It was Georgie Marks. Most people call her by her nickname,
because her real first name, Georgina, is, as she likes to say, "a little
too." Georgie was one of four Marks sisters—"the counterpart to the

Marx brothers," people told her again and again, like it was an original observation. She bore it with good patience.

"Yep," she'd say, "there's the Marx boys—Groucho, Harpo, Zeppo, and Chico. And there's the Marks girls."

Besides being female and spelling their name differently, there were some other things that set the Marks sisters apart from the famous comedians. The boys were white and Jewish. And short. The girls are black and Anglican. And the shortest one is nearly six feet tall. They got taller as they got younger, and Georgie, the next to youngest, is six-one in her size-11-triple-A stocking feet.

"I be down tereckly." I laughed. "Gotta report to the overseer first."

"Ooooh," Georgie breathed. "Have a fab time. I hear the little one is *not* pleased this morning."

"Couldn't be nothing *I* did," I assured her. "Haven't been here for almost a week."

"Maybe he's missed you." I could hear her grin over the phone.

"Oh, yeah. Like he'd miss herpes if he had it."

"I don't even want to speculate on that one's sex life."

"You liar. You speculate on *everyone's* sex life!"

"Only if I like them—or if they're a prospect. The little one doesn't fit into either category."

"Thank God for small favors. I'll call you when I'm freed."

"Okay, babe—I'll fire up the teapot when you're on the way down."

I wove my way through the newsroom, waving halfheartedly at people who were gesturing for me to come over and gossip about Ev. Later. The Man could not wait.

When I first got to the paper one of my more irreverent colleagues told me that the initials in A.S. Fine's name stood for Ape Shit, "because that's how he goes when he's really pissed off." There was some truth to that. Allan Spencer Fine was small—maybe five feet six inches—boyishly trim, and literally the fair-haired guy in Metro. Word was he might be the big enchilada at the paper one day. He wore old-fashioned hippie-style wire-rimmed glasses (a retro version by a Parisian occulist favored by young movie stars) and Paul Stuart clothes, top to bottom. Rumor had it he grew up as the only Jew in his class in a ferociously WASP New Hampshire boarding school.

Like me, A.S. was integrating joints before multicultural became cool. Newsroom folklore says he carefully neglected to mention his ethnic background to his mostly Protestant classmates, who assumed that anyone blond from Philadelphia could not possibly be different from them in any meaningful way. The few openly Jewish boys at St. Filbert's Academy were hazed and harassed in hundreds of covertly mean ways by spoiled rich kids who smiled whitely as they tortured their ethnic charges. The ones who were passing gritted their teeth and hoped they wouldn't be outed by their braver brothers. The Jewish boys (and, later, the first black ones) endured that eternal hazing in the interests of the superior education St. Filbert's offered. And those who weren't irreparably damaged by the experience—which, happily, was most of them—turned out to be more successful than their calculatedly inbred classmates.

A.S. kept his mouth shut and kept to himself and as a result of attending St. Filbert's had submerged any ethnicity he might otherwise have possessed. He snorted when I wished him happy new year on Rosh Hashanah and refused to celebrate Hanukkah because he claimed, "It's a minor holiday; I don't even do the major ones." (Mr. Grinchstein!)

A.S. played squash at the downtown Y twice a week; once in passing by the bulletin board on my way to aerobics, I noticed he was at the top of the squash ladder. And he'd married Arianna Hayes Whitley, whose people had helped to found the Massachusetts Bay Colony at approximately the same time *his* people were being burned out of their shtetls by Cossacks. Fine was so repressed about being a Jew and in such consequent denial about anti-Semitism, he couldn't countenance any corollary observation that race was a slight problem for the rest of the country—and, on a micro level, for the *Standard*. "All that stuff" was supposed to have been fixed by the civil rights movement. After, say, 1969, anyone who noticed any trouble in the American family was, for A.S.'s money, a malcontent, an anti-American, or, worst of all, a crybaby.

Subsequently, he and I clashed regularly over my proclivity to trouble the waters on things where a racial element was apparent. We'd often have discussions about our differences of opinion at maximum decibel level, with people around us pretending they couldn't hear what they obviously could, because the door to his glass-box office was wide open.

Our most recent set-to was over gun control—my argument being, What's good for the homies is also good for the suburban Harrys.

Ultimately, we'd agreed to disagree about that particular issue. My column ran, despite A.S.'s misgivings, and I got a bunch of angry mail, including one wounded one from the president himself, whose clipping service probably passed it along. That made A.S.'s day: West Coast editors are pathetically grateful when they're noticed by the East Coast establishment. A week or so later, I'd left for the conference with my boss's blessing.

Entering his office, I smiled to myself. Now that I'd cooled down (comparatively speaking), I'd actually missed the little bugger.

"So." He looked up from his designer frames. No *Hello, nice to see you*. Typical A.S. "Looks like you're going to be doing a little research for a week or so, hmm?"

"Do *I* have any say in this, or did you already make arrangements with the overseer?"

A.S. sighed. "Oh, please. Do we *have* to do the race thing this morning?"

"If not now, when? If not us, who?"

A.S. laughed, despite himself. "You're a pain in the ass, Powell, but I can't ever fault your grammar or your diction."

"Why, thank ya, Massa Abe. Is ahm gwine ta work fer Mars' Jim soon?"

A.S. threw up his hands in resignation. "Okay, *okay*! Do you *want* to do this? Of course you aren't *obligated*—"

"But you want something from them, don't you?"

"Well, truth be told—"

"And it always must; this *is* a newspaper, after all."

A.S. gave me a glance that was supposed to make me quake. But it's hard to quake before a skinny white guy who's five-six and not carrying a weapon, even if he *is* your boss.

"As I was saying. . . ."

He paused and waited for me to interrupt. I didn't.

"Right now, we could stand to make a few friends down at Parker Center. Between the Rodneys"—that's what everyone called the trials of the L.A. cops who'd pulverized Rodney King—"and O. J. One and Two, we could stand to deposit some capital in their goodwill bank. Some days, I'm surprised they speak to us at all. So if they're asking for *you* of all people—"

"Look, just because the former chief of police called to express his displeasure with my opinion every now and then—"

"Powell, I must have gotten a fax a week from that man! You practically gave him heart failure."

"Well, he should've been in better shape. He was a *cop*, for chrissake!"

The previous chief's girth had been grist for hundreds of editorial cartoonists and local stand-up comedians and a source of resentment from many in the rank and file. They, after all, were routinely subjected to a series of physical fitness tests. If they didn't pass, they'd be suspended until they shaped up and lost the extra pounds. I thought it was fitting to comment on that irony, something the top cop allegedly expressed his displeasure about all the way up to Oatley Hansome. Eventually, the "do as I say, not as I do" ethos earned him a one-way ticket to another job. The current police chief was reed-thin and so good looking he'd been featured as one of the Fifty Most Beautiful in *People* magazine's annual issue. He stayed in shape, kept his credentials up on the firing range, and had actually made a couple of arrests on the street, single-handed. Best of all, I'd never had a bit of trouble from him.

A.S. pulled off his specs and gave me the Look. It was the visual equivalent of a two-minute warning.

"*Okay!* I'll be happy to cooperate. For the good of the paper, of course. Which will, of course, *not* count this as vacation time. And which *will*, of course, cover any incidental expenses associated with this little adventure."

My editor sighed. It really hurt him to envision all those lovely per diems piling up. "Yeah yeah yeah. Blah blah blah." Not even yadda yadda yadda. See what I mean about being repressed? "Just remember the ground rules."

"And they are?"

"You are *not* doing this on behalf of the *Standard* in any official capacity. You *will* refrain from putting yourself in any physical danger whatsoever. And whether or not you find out anything useful, you *will* have your butt back here in seven—count 'em, seven—days."

"Boy, you sure know how to suck all the fun out of a homicide investigation," I complained. "Okay, I agree. Even if it's the story of the year, my highly desirable, well-aerobicized butt will be back here on time."

"I have no idea what your butt looks like." A.S. snorted. "Or anybody else's, either. You women have screwed things up so badly with this sexual harassment business—which is usually *totally* specious, I might add—that I don't look anywhere *ever*."

He almost wasn't kidding. One of his former writers, José Johnson, a bright Stanford educated Buppie, had been nailed by two interns and an *editor*, for God's sake, for his salacious language and tawdry suggestions. All of NABJ was asnicker because José was the anointed one as far as the *Standard*'s management went. "You never hear *him* whining about race," editors would chide. "I don't understand why you people dislike him so."

Yes, José's white folks had been berry, berry good to him. So to see their star colored boy end up as a dart on the *Columbia Journalism Review*'s "Darts and Laurels" page was highly embarrassing.

Lowering their Standard: A Dart to the editors in Los Angeles for dithering while José Johnson fondles the female news staff. It's not the fifties anymore, guys!

After a profuse and nauseatingly public apology to the offended women in question, José kept his job but adopted a much lower profile. And his old-boy colleagues in the newsroom took note and altered their own behavior.

"Listen, I'd love to wax nostalgic with you about the good old days of newspapering, when men were men and women fetched the coffee," I said sweetly, "but I've some work to do before I go. See you in exactly seven days, boss."

A.S. had returned to his terminal and was busily turning some poor reporter's copy into editorial hamburger. His keyboard was *click-click*ing like crazy. He waved absentmindedly as I opened the door to leave. His eyes never left the screen.

I wasn't fooled; he'd be counting the days till I returned to make him miserable again.

I shut the door and picked up the phone on the nearest empty desk.

"Polly, put the kettle on."

7

I successfully navigated around the Nosy Rosies
in the newsroom once more and wound my way through the paper-
strewn desks in State and Metro over to the "soft" section of the
paper, where Style and Arts and Leisure are located. Although she
worked for one of the "lesser" parts of the paper (the hard-section
types like to point out it's called a *news*paper for a reason), Georgie
was an editor, which meant that like A.S. she had an office. She was
the fashion editor, so it was an interior office—no panoramas of
downtown L.A. (Not that you'd see anything from the third floor
anyway, that was a perk reserved for the editor in chief, the publisher, and similarly lofty types, whose spacious aeries were on the
top floor.)

But what Georgie didn't have in space, she made up for in style.
The harsh overhead lighting had been ignored in favor of plenty of
indirect lighting that could be turned up or down via dimmers.
There was a Tabriz in muted cream-of-tomato colors on top of the
blah corporate wall-to-wall. Pastel orchids in porcelain cachepots
topped one antique bookcase, nurtured at night by a special grow
light. A mini–stereo system was hidden away behind the battered
doors of an old pine safe. Georgie's mother, who writes catalogs for
auction houses, had found this treasure while traveling through
Indiana. ("No museums or restaurants to speak of," her mother had
remarked flatly, "but the furniture was *fabulous*.") The heady scent

of Lapsang souchong complemented Georgie's Green Tea aromatherapy candle. Two antique cups, paper-thin and strewn with roses (another one of Mama Marks's finds) stood waiting on a tole tray.

"What *are* you wearing?"

Georgie and her elegant room were in distinct contrast to each other. Amid the English this and the American-nineteenth-century that Georgie, all six-feet-one of her, was wearing navy sateen warm-up pants. The broad white stripe running down each side of the dark pull-ons made her long legs look even longer. On top, she had a silk-and-cashmere twin set in pale, pale blue—perfect for her cocoa complexion—and around her long neck she'd twisted several silver chains of varying thicknesses and heft. Big silver hoops glinted in her ears, and a huge steel Rolex with a diamond bezel glittered on her right wrist (she's left-handed), while a two-carat emerald-cut aquamarine flashed on her opposite hand. She stuck out her foot. The unzipped edges of the athletic pants flapped around to-die-for platinum patent sandals; a diamond toe ring sparkled on her middle toe. Her toes were painted to match her lips—azalea.

"What do you think?" she asked, staring at me through her cat's-eye tortoise shells. (Georgie is as blind as a bat. If you run into her and she isn't wearing glasses, ask her to pop out a contact lens, so you can be sure her vision really is being corrected. If she can't produce a lens, run for safety. And under *no* circumstances should you accept a ride with her if she's in that condition.)

"You look like a gang-banger with a trust fund. Is this a look?"

Georgie burst out laughing. "Yes, darling, it's a look. It's called GhettoFabulous, and it's filtering up from the streets. Karl showed it for Chanel a couple of years ago, and it didn't do well—"

"Surprise, surprise!"

"—but the Italians are reinterpreting it this year, and *I* think it's happening."

Well, the people Karl Lagerfeld dresses have money to burn, but I still can't see it. The Italians are, in general, more laid back than the French. But even *they* have to draw the line somewhere.

"When Marella Angelli shows up in it, call me."

I felt safe, knowing the wife of Fiat's chairman wouldn't be caught dead looking like that. I may not know much, but I do know this: Part of style is knowing what you can't get away with, as well as what you can.

Georgie handed me a translucent cup full of amber liquid that gave off a deliciously smoky scent.

"Milk?"

"A little, thanks." She didn't offer sugar—she thinks sweetening tea is for children only.

"Now, tell me what happened. And what you're going to do about it."

So we sipped tea and talked through what would have been our lunch hour. The door was closed. The scented candles were unraveling my knotted-up thoughts. Georgie's common-sense approach was better than therapy. Before we'd left, I'd made up my mind.

The police were going to do very little to find Ev's killer. The situation was almost impossible: a crowded room with three thousand suspects who all leave the next day? Forget it. Add the fact that there were bodies on slabs in the L.A. morgue right this minute that *did* have leads that might bear fruit, plus a backload of cold cases to handle, and it looked even less likely that they would find anything without help.

And, as Georgie pointed out, "You owe him, babe. You wouldn't *have* this fabulous job if *Vanity Fair* hadn't seen your *Diaspora* clips. You could have been working in Hole-inna-wall, Nebraska, or OhLawdy, Louisiana, trying to get back to a real newspaper when the *Herald* folded. You and I both know we have *Herald* friends who are still trying to get somewhere where they've got a decent deli and a Crate and Barrel—which isn't asking for much, but you see what I mean about how dire your circumstances could have been, don't you?"

I did, and Georgie, bless her snotty little self, was absolutely correct. I owed Ev, so I would do what I could to make sure whoever killed him didn't get away with it. Yes, it was a large world out there. And yes, smarter folks had deemed this a hard nut to crack—and then backed me into doing their work for them. But I had an advantage they didn't: I'm black, and I knew people the Smart Folks didn't. Besides, I wasn't ready to go back to work yet.

"So what will you wear while you're back east? Given it any thought yet?"

"Since we've only just decided, I'd say I haven't. Rest assured, though, I will not be GhettoFabulous."

"Like you could if you wanted to be!"

Georgie threw back her head and laughed. Her shoulder-length hair fell straight back, like a heavy black curtain.

"Well, excuse me. I may not be the fashion editor for the *Standard*, and I may not have lived in Paris and Rome and London, subsidized by Mummy and Daddy while freelancing for *Le Monde* and *Tattler* and *Italian Vogue*, but I *do* think I can throw a few outfits together."

Georgie grinned. She was absolutely comfortable being who she is, which is the daughter of a Bajan chutney magnate, now retired and living on Hilton Head Island, and his antiques-acquiring wife. "It's the 'throwing things together' part I worry about, hon. I mean, we *are* talking about someone who thinks Target is a major department store."

"Chew the root, Jemima."

"See? 'Chew the root.' You know your problem, Alex?"

"I'm waiting to be enlightened."

"Inside your little yellow self is a white girl just screaming to get out."

"Yeah, well, this white girl's been insulted enough. She's picking up her skirts and leaving—this minute."

We both laughed. Georgie is fond of calling me her "very own Afro-Saxon." I always reply that this is the pot calling the kettle names.

"*My* mama ain't got a signed photograph from Queen Elizabeth displayed in the library. And *I* ain't one of four girls with names straight out of Jane Austen: Eugenia, Charlotte, Georgina, and Edwina. And pardon me, but we don't eat Christmas cake or celebrate Boxing Day like *some* people I could name."

"True—but you do come close, in your own uptight New England way."

We have this discussion at least twice a year. If Georgie can arrange it, we do it at a corporate cocktail party; white people, inevitably eavesdropping, are utterly fascinated and mystified. Queen Elizabeth in the library never fails to pique their already considerable curiosity.

"Gotta go, diva. Stay black."

"I will, babe. And you give it a try too."

That Georgie. You've always gotta stay awake, or you'll fall behind.

8

Being a procrastinator from way back, it took
me a couple of days to reschedule appointments for interviews I'd
made, pull up a couple of "Evergreen" columns to run in my
absences, and clear off my desk. Having done that, I finally arrived
in Washington at noon on Thursday, just in time to dump my bags
at Paul's place, change in the guest bathroom, and catch a cab with
him to the edge of downtown. We walked up the stairs of St. Philip's
just as Ev's memorial service was beginning.

St. Philip's-on-the-Square was a small nondenominational church
with a mostly youngish population: journalists and other godless
types who had recently found their way back to organized religion.
The services were short, the sermons were always topical, and, given
her checkered flock, it was not unusual for the Reverend Winifred
Forsythe to entertain questions from the pulpit. Nor was Dr. Forsythe,
a product of Episcopal Theological Seminary in Cambridge, above
telling her sometimes-overzealous congregants when they'd crossed
the line.

She was famous for having sternly admonished Greg Hunter, a
national correspondent for CBS during one of these hootenannyish
Q-and-As. Greg, in his trademark bullying interview manner, had
aggressively pressed the priest to provide "hard evidence" of God's
benevolence "in the face of so much earthly misery." Shaking her
head in fond exasperation, Rev. Winnie had instructed Hunter,

"Check that tone, my darling. The *president* may allow you to badger him, but he's not a black woman, now, is he? . . . Although he probably *knows* black women better than anyone since Thomas Jefferson," she added, as laughter ricocheted around the room. The current president's eye for good-looking sisters was the talk of Washington. "The fact that you are here, living and breathing, is testimony to God's infinite benevolence. His *taste*, however," she'd added dryly, "is another matter entirely."

The entire church had howled as Greg resumed his seat, red-faced. Nobody with any intelligence messed with Rev. Winnie. She was nearly six feet tall, with beautiful mocha skin, piercing eyes, and thick soaring brows that seemed permanently poised to question someone or something. Although her manner and bearing were usually described as regal, Rev. Winnie did not put on airs; she'd been seen dusting the pews, serving coffee during fellowship hour, and sweating buckets as she ran in the church's annual 10K fundraiser.

Today she stood at the pulpit, majestic and austere in her plain black robes, and spoke quietly and fondly of Ev. Her voice, alto and touched with just a hint of her parents' Jamaican homeland washed soothingly over us in the quiet little chapel. The only noise was the muffled sound of midweek afternoon traffic filtering through the old-fashioned stained-glass windows and the steady hum from the sanctuary's old air conditioner. Ev's great-aunt, a large dignified woman whom everyone seemed to refer to as M'Dear, cried soundlessly as she listened to Rev. Winnie's words, nodding every now and then at a particularly appropriate passage.

I looked around. A number of Ev's colleagues from his past service at several of the country's leading dailies were there, as were about two dozen young reporters whom he'd mentored and who had gone on to do him proud in newspapers and magazines around the country. He proudly referred to them as "my kids." ("If I get absent-minded and step in front of a bus one day," Ev had once told me, "I ain't worried about having made my mark. My kids will give the white folks hell long after I'm gone.") And Frankie, Chip, and Jake were there, sitting next to *Diaspora*'s staff. I caught Signe's eye; she nodded slightly in response. She'd taken the train from New York with another *Times* staffer, whose face was familiar but whose name I couldn't recall.

Looking around the chapel, I realized there was a disproportionate number of women in the congregation. "So what?" Paul whispered out of the side of his mouth when I hissed my observation. "This is Washington, remember?"

Well, yes, it was, and the rumor that there were seventy bajillion women to every man just wouldn't die—despite the fact that the numbers had never seemed that staggering to me—but these didn't all look like Washington women, either. From the aggressively fashionable outfits, some definitely had NEW YORK, CHICAGO, or ATLANTA stamped on them. Most were sniffing audibly and carefully dabbing their eyes so their mascara wouldn't run.

One mourner caught my eye in particular. She was bronze all over—that's the only way to describe her. Bronze hair, done up in large graceful West African braids. Deep copper-colored skin. Hazel eyes. She sat in a middle pew, not too far from us, with her arms around two little boys who looked exactly alike and who snuggled next to her. They were striking, these kids: dark velvety brown with hazel eyes and deep dimples. They wore matching navy suits with little red bow ties and brown-and-black saddle shoes. They were so perfect-looking, they could have been plucked from the back of one of those fans the funeral parlors use to advertise, the ones with little brown children, their hands steepled, eyes cast prayerfully heavenward, their knees just grazing the popsicle-stick handle.

"So we all wish Everett well on his journey"—I snapped to; Rev. Winnie was winding up her eulogy while my mind had been wandering—"and plan to reunite with him when our own turn comes, as come it must. In the meantime, may God welcome him into everlasting joy. May He shelter and keep him, and also watch over his friends and loved ones, whose lives made his own so rich. May He bring special comfort to Everett's auntie, Mrs. Harrietta Carson Weeks; his sons, Micah and Ezekiel, and their mother, Eileen"—Rev. Winnie ignored the rustle of two hundred heads whipping around in unison and continued smoothly—"and his coworkers at the magazine for which he lived. He is at peace, and with God, and would wish for us to move along with the business of life. Let us bow our heads."

So saying, Rev. Winnie returned our heads to their proper positions and intoned the traditional blessing before departure.

"May the Lord bless you and keep you. May He make his countenance to shine upon you while we are absent from one another. May He give you shelter beneath the shadow of His great wings and grant you peace. Amen."

Paul, Signe, her colleague Ellen Campbell, and I shared a cab from St. Philip's to the Mall. "I'll let you ladies share the back seat." Paul grinned as he held the door for us. "I'm sure you have *lots* to discuss." We stuck out our tongues at him, but as soon as he and the driver began an animated discussion of D.C. politics (and the plexiglass partition was slammed shut), we turned to each other.

"*Girl!*" Signe breathed. "Did you have any *idea?*" (Signe's Memphis drawl stressed the first syllable: "*eye*-deah.")

"Nope." I shook my head and turned to Ellen. "You?"

"Nope," Ellen said. "You can bet if the Daily Word over there didn't know, I didn't."

I chuckled. Signe had been called the Daily Word, or sometimes just the Word, for as long as I'd known her, which was at least fifteen years. Obviously, she and Ellen were good friends.

"You and Ev were ace boons all that time, Signe, and you never knew he had children?"

Signe shook her head slowly. "I knew he spent a couple of weekends a month in Stamford or somewhere, but it never occurred to me that *kids* were involved. The only child I've ever seen him with is his godchild, Nathan, and he's much older."

That was true. Nathan was the son of Ev's best friend, Nate Brooks. Nate had been an extremely promising editor at *U.S. News & World Report* who'd died, three years ago, of leukemia. Ev spent lots of time with young Nathan, even after Nate's wife remarried last year. It was not unusual to see the two of them hanging out on weekends in *Diaspora*'s offices. Fourteen-year-old Nate Junior would play video games on the computer while Ev edited copy. The boy was going to Choate in the fall, thanks to his own good grades and Ev's early alert to the headmaster, whom he'd once interviewed and for whom he occasionally acted as a referral service.

So we knew about Nathan. But Mike and Zeke had been a well-kept secret.

"So he must have been spending time with his kids on those weekends," Signe mused.

"Thank God for that! At least he was taking an active part in their lives." Ellen sighed.

We didn't have time to compare notes beyond that, because the taxi had stopped. Paul had paid the driver and was opening the door. "Figure out where Ev'd been stashing the kids and why?" His eyes snapped with mirth.

"Don't be ridiculous," I replied, as we swept past him indignantly. "We were discussing newsroom politics. You really have a *very* low opinion of women."

"Uh-huh," Paul said blandly.

I didn't have to turn around to see he was laughing silently as he followed us. Some things you just know.

The reception was held in the Museum of African Art's sculpture court, a broad, sunny expanse of atrium studded with African sculptures. The crowd moved easily among the Baoulé animals and Bambara *chi'waras*. Elegant bronze masks from Benin stared impassively down at the people milling about below. In the corner, a formally dressed string quartet from Howard University played classical music. Several waitpersons circulated discreetly among the guests, bearing silver trays with flutes of champagne and glasses of white and red wines. Others passed salvers of small expensive hors d'oeuvres: grilled skewers of shrimp and chicken, crab-stuffed baby artichoke hearts, small red potatoes with little clouds of sour cream, glistening with caviar and lots of thinly sliced gravlax on buttered rye.

"Too bad Ev couldn't be at his own party," I said to Signe, as we each took a flute. "He would have loved this."

"He would've, wouldn't he? All these Nicely Dressed Negroes with not a stitch of polyester in sight!"

We both laughed. Ev was a notorious clothes snob. When he'd first come to *Diaspora*, he'd made the rounds, introduced himself to the staff, and gave a couple of pointed suggestions re wardrobe.

"I can't send you out to interview the labor secretary in a tie that looks like it came from Wal-Mart," he'd snapped to one of his assistant editors. Whereupon he took off his own tie, gave it to the guy, and sent him on his way with two admonitions: "Make sure your tape recorder works, because you know how these motherfuckers are; they'll swear something was taken out of context, and they all lie"; and "Bring that tie back when you're finished with it, boy— *with no spots*. And don't ever let me see you looking like you from Mayberry again, hear? Lord knows I pay y'all enough to dress decently."

The story might have been apocryphal, but it was vintage Ev.

"Well"—Signe sighed, lifting her glass to me—"here's to Ev." We touched rims and drank. Signe's eyes widened. "This is *very* good champagne. Who's throwing this party, anyway?"

That was an interesting question. I'd have to find out. I glanced around the room for someone who might know, but my eye stopped before I'd made a complete circle.

Ev's great-aunt sat in an armchair near a beautiful Benin mask. With her high cheekbones, smooth brown skin, and heavy-lidded eyes, Mrs. Weeks looked as if she could have been its direct descendant. Since most of us can't trace our ancestors back to a specific place or tribe in Africa, who knew? Perhaps she was.

A steady stream of people came over to say a few words to her about Ev, and she received each one graciously, nodding and sometimes smiling at something the visitor was saying. She wore a black linen suit, a high-crowned black polished-straw hat with a small veil that had been pushed back off her face—"Coretta couture," Signe whispered—and was only one of two women there to wear gloves. Except she wasn't really *wearing* gloves: right now they were off, held next to her patent-leather purse, which gently nudged a matching low-heeled pump. She was dressed exactly as my two grandmothers, both long dead, would have been in similar circumstances. Maybe they were all given a Proper Colored Lady's Handbook, back in the day.

I turned to Signe. "We should say something to her." She nodded.

So we waited to walk over until the crowd thinned a little. We shook her hand—her skin was soft, but the grasp was steely—and introduced ourselves, telling her a bit about how we'd come to know Ev. A waiter miraculously appeared with two garden chairs, so we sat.

"I'm so glad to know you both," Harrietta Weeks said softly. "And you came from so far away to say good-bye to my Everett. I do appreciate it."

"We were happy to come," I assured her.

"And you look so nice, too." Mrs. Weeks nodded approvingly, taking in our plain suits, my black silk and Signe's creamy linen. High necklines, long sleeves. No fussy jewelry.

("Proper," Signe had said earlier, "unlike a *few* people here I could mention"; "Be nice," I'd chided; "Well, really. I don't think spandex is appropriate for mourning." It *was* Washington, and *some* women are not above using any large gathering to catch, even a funeral.)

"Well, you know Ev, Mrs. Weeks." Signe smiled now, still holding the older woman's hand. "If we hadn't come dressed properly he would have haunted us."

Mrs. Weeks exploded in hearty laughter. "Yes, child, I guess he would have! You know my baby. He's been like that since he was old enough to talk."

And she regaled us with stories of Ev's persnickety clothing habits, from toddlerhood up to the time he demanded two sets of clothes if he was going to subject himself to full-immersion baptism. " 'Auntie,' he told me"—she pronounced it ontee—" 'I'm sposta let that preacher try to drown me *and* sit around in wet clothes afterward? Uh-uh! And you *know* that river is full of mud!' So we got him a second set of clothes, and when Reverend Lewis had finished baptizing him, that boy disappeared and changed. Ten minutes later, he walked in wearing a snow-white suit—you'd never know he'd been touched by water!" We all wiped our eyes.

"Lord, it feels good to laugh a little." She sighed. "Hasn't been much of that lately."

She patted both our hands.

"Did you see my grandbabies? I call them that, even though they're my great-nephews, because Ev always felt more like a grandchild to me. His parents died when he was real small, you know. Drunk white man in a truck hit 'em head on when Ev was about the age those kids are now. Cracker hasn't apologized to this day. So I took their only child, and he's been my baby every since." She sighed deeply and nodded across the courtyard, where the two little boys were sitting on a bench eating fruit from a single plate. "And now M'Dear will look after those little ones, too."

"They're moving to South Carolina with you?" I asked, surprised.

"Oh, no! Their mama'd miss 'em something awful. She's a good girl, Eileen. I thought she and Everett were going to marry once, but . . . well, you can't tell young people anything, can you? Everett was crazy about her, but she said he was too . . . what did she say? Oh—*overwhelming*. Something about needing to be on her own. No, they'll stay with their mama, that's the best thing. But they'll come to see me for the whole summer now, instead of three weeks, so their mama can finish her degree. She's getting her Ph.D. And maybe I'll go see them some too, though to tell the truth I never did much like the North."

Signe nodded emphatically. "I know exactly what you mean! I'm from Memphis." Mrs. Weeks smiled and looked at me expectantly. I knew what was coming. "Poor old Alex here"—Signe grinned slyly—"is a Yankee."

Mrs. Weeks looked at me in mute sympathy.

"But her mother's from North Carolina," Signe went on helpfully. "That's why she has such nice manners."

I smiled weakly. I was going to *kill* Signe as soon as I got the chance.

"Well, that's good, honey. Your mama did a good job. *Good*

home trainin'. I'd never have known you're from up here, 'cept for your accent." Which sounded exactly like *cep' fo' yo' ack-scent. My* accent?

"Well, I try to keep it under control. I'm glad we got to meet you, Mrs. Weeks."

"Me too. Ev used to talk about M'Dear all the time. We used to threaten to call you if he wasn't acting right." Signe gave her a hug, and Mrs. Weeks hugged her back, patting her gently as she did.

"Come on over here, Yankee, and give me some sugar too." She winked. I laughed and got my very own hug-pat.

"Now you girls, you keep in touch with me, hear? I know what they're saying about what happened to my baby"—Signe and I exchanged quick glances; it was the first time Mrs. Weeks had alluded to the fact that she was aware of Ev's possible poisoning— "and I want to find out the truth, no matter what the truth is." She looked at us sternly. "Promise me you'll let me know if you hear something."

We nodded meekly. "Yes, ma'am."

"Well, I'm going to send you along, then, so you can get some-thing to eat."

She waved us away when we asked if we could bring her a plate.

"No, children. We're all staying at Everett's place. We had us a big lunch before we came, and we're going to have a decent dinner when we leave here. I'm not interested in this little bitty food they're sending around. But you-all better eat, neither one of you is bigger than a minute. And I suppose I need to spend some time talking with the white folks."

We looked across the room. Several antsy-looking white folks did, indeed, seem to be hanging around and looking anxiously in our direction. Signe and I had probably delayed their departure for at least fifteen minutes. Tough.

We waved good-bye, and Mrs. Weeks settled herself to accept more condolences. But we noticed she had the waiters take the extra chairs away, just in case the white folks (two of Ev's former publish-ers, some fellow reporters, and the CEO of some urban venture-type company) decided they wanted to stay awhile.

"She sure is sweet." Signe sighed. "I can see why Ev loved her to death."

"Um-hm. But I'll bet, when it's necessary, M'Dear has a steel spine."

"You know that's true. But speaking of people who *don't*, let's step over and visit with *those* folks for a minute. They definitely look like they could use a little cheering up."

I followed the direction of Signe's nod and saw Frankie Harper, Jake Jackson, and Chip Wiley chatting near the doors to the garden. Jake and Chip looked suitably sober—Jake looked like a mortician, actually, all five feet four inches of him stuffed into an old-fashioned black gabardine suit. Chip wore a tropical-weight charcoal-gray suit, double-breasted as usual. Frankie wore gray too, a silvery silk duiponi suit, and a simple string of pearls; like Mrs. Weeks, she carried a pair of over-the-wrist white gloves, which she now slapped back and forth from hand to hand. All three of them looked as if they were waiting to be ushered in for a little gum surgery.

Their seemingly intense conversation ended abruptly when Signe and I came over to say hello.

"Ladies." Chip nodded curtly. Frankie and Jake dipped their heads too.

"Such a lovely service, don't you think?" Signe asked, using her best Magnolia Blossom dimples. "Ev would have been delighted that so many of his friends showed up."

Was it my imagination, or did Frankie wince when Signe emphasized *friends*?

"Yes, well, he wasn't only a friend, he was a peer," Frankie said gently. "There are so few black magazine editor-publishers in the country. And now"—she sighed, her eyes beginning to tear—"there's one less."

Chip and Jake looked at her with undisguised condescension and exchanged a glance. Women, the glance seemed to say, can't control themselves worth a damn!

"Well," I ventured cautiously, "it's definitely a reception worthy of a CEO. Except I wouldn't have thought Mrs. Weeks would have had the wherewithal to do all this. Or know whom to invite."

Chip snorted. "Please! Those country spooks had all they could do to get up here for the funeral. You know she told me she actually *brought lunch* on the train?" He shuddered. "I can just imagine what they ate."

"Same thing you ate on the way down to see you own granny, nigger, don't be puttin' on airs with us. We *know* you came from Dipshit, Virginia!" Jake snapped.

I grinned—internally, of course.

"Danville," Chip said, through tight lips. *"Danville."*

"Whatever. You had to lug a box lunch, just like the rest of us. You ain't *that* much younger than me that you don't remember having to do it. Don't even try."

Chip scowled but remained silent. We took that as a nolo contendere. ("How do you plead?" "Country, Your Honor—with extenuating circumstances.")

"Anyway," I offered brightly, "train food certainly isn't what it used to be, so Mrs. Weeks was smart to bring something that wasn't plastic. I once saw Vernon Jordan on the Metroliner take an apple from his briefcase and eat it."

"An apple is one thing, fried chicken is another," Chip pointed out. Before Jake could challenge him with 'What's-wrong-with-fried-chicken?' Paul's voice chimed in. He had just joined us.

"Well, it's moot, isn't it? Not a wing to be seen anywhere in this room," he offered smoothly.

"Plenty of legs and thighs, though." Jake chuckled, shaking Paul's hand.

And breasts, the men were thinking, but managed to restrain themselves.

Signe sighed and excused herself to greet friends nearby. "Your Cro-Magnons, girlfriend," her silent look seemed to say, "and welcome to them."

"So who *did* foot the bill for all this?" I asked.

Chip, Frankie, and Jake looked at one another. "We did," Frankie said quietly. "The three of us. We didn't know whether his family could afford it, and we thought it would be a nice thing to do."

"One publisher to another," Jake added.

"And besides, it's deductible." Ah, Chip! The powdered skim milk of human kindness flows freely in his veins!

"First-class job," Paul said. Chip nodded, satisfied that someone recognized his superior taste and generosity.

"So who did you hire to take care of all the details?" I asked.

"Esmé Marshall. We always use her. She's the best," Chip asserted.

Esmé Marshall. They really *had* spent some money, because the Marshall Plan doesn't come cheap. Esmé was *the* black publicist and event coordinator of note; she did personal PR for movie stars, orchestrated celebrity weddings—and now, I guess, funerals.

"So where is Esmé?" I hadn't noticed her Amazonian profile anywhere about.

"In New York. She'd committed to personally overseeing the details for a movie premiere, but she made the arrangements and sent half her senior staff to us for Ev," Frankie explained.

Smart girl; that way she got two commissions, because if the gossip about Esmé was true, she charged ferociously for anything last-minute.

We were all silent for a moment. Frankie seemed lost in her own thoughts; Chip and Jake were probably running the numbers in their heads, estimating if there'd been any cost overruns they would have to fight with Esmé about later.

Jake's voice broke the brief silence. "Heard you-all had to talk with the police in L.A. They finally have any idea about the cause of death?"

Paul and I studiously refrained from looking at each other.

"Actually," Paul said, "the medical reports aren't all back yet, but there's some question that Ev's death might not have been accidental."

Frankie grew noticably paler.

"You mean," she asked weakly, "they think he did it *on purpose*?" Her eyes were starting to tear again.

"No, I mean they think somebody *else* might have done it. On purpose."

I handed Frankie my lace hanky, the emergency one all mothers insist we carry, although I must confess this was the first time it had ever been needed.

"As a matter of fact," Paul said, "we've been asked if we knew anyone who might have been angry enough with Ev to want him—well, you know."

"*Dead*," Chip volunteered impatiently. Plain talk from the publisher of *Aspire*.

"Yes. And actually, we've—Alex and I, that is—been asked to look around a bit and do some preliminary research for the detective in charge. Truth be told, your perspectives would be appreciated. Any thoughts or suggestions you have would be useful. Can we come see you in the next couple of days?"

"Be my guest." Chip shrugged. "But you'll have to travel to the Vineyard. We're leaving tomorrow and won't be back until the Wednesday after Labor Day." *Nyah, nyah, try and catch me!*

"Fine," I lied. "Let's make it Saturday. We'd planned to spend the weekend up there anyway."

"Really?" Chip looked surprised. Obviously, I didn't look like the type who had people on the Vineyard. And he didn't know I knew (from my people on the Vineyard, of course) that this was only his second summer there.

Chip brought out a monogrammed leather card holder, shuffled through a stack of different cards, all with his name on them, and handed one to Paul. I glanced at it.

CHARLES MITCHELL WILEY III
Greywing
West Tisbury, Martha's Vineyard
(508) 953-1110

I hate people who name their houses. Like an address isn't good enough. Or is superfluous.

"Call when you get there," Chip offered. "Someone will be there to take the message. I'll get back to you about the time."

Frankie silently handed me her card. "I'm in the office all next week. We're finishing up the Christmas issue, so I'll be around. I'd be happy to talk with you." She didn't *look* very happy, but who was I to question her?

"And I'll be in the office too, as usual," Jake said, giving us each a card. "I rarely take vacations." He looked pointedly at Chip as if to say, Unlike *some* people.

"Great. Well, it looks as if we'll be on the road soon. Thanks again for agreeing to do this. Everybody will feel better when they know the police are being overly suspicious about this."

"As usual." Jake harrumphed.

"They have a job to do," Chip snapped. "We're not *all* members of the criminal element—though you wouldn't know it to read the paper." And he looked at me sternly.

I couldn't agree with him more. My white folks *did* seem to focus a lot on negative black images; trying to counter them with positive stories was like bailing out a leaky boat with a berry spoon. But I wasn't ready to plow that particular field this afternoon.

"Well, the party was lovely," I offered. "Thank you, for Ev. He would have said as much, I'm sure, if he could have been here himself."

"If the nigger could've been here himself, he'd have paid his *own* bill!" Jake barked, and he and Chip burst into laughter, which they quickly stifled when several pairs of eyes turned disapprovingly toward them.

A *New York Times* person motioned Paul over to a group of men.

"Editors," he explained, excusing himself. "Be back in a few."

I excused myself soon after, looked around to see if there was anyone else I hadn't said hello to, and found myself staring straight into the amber eyes of Eileen Stevens.

I was again taken with how very pretty she was. I'd never seen such a dazzling combination: skin that was deep cocoa brown and flawless, clear amber eyes, and that strange-colored hair, too red to be brown, too brown to be truly red, lighter than auburn. She tilted her head, silently encouraging me to speak. Most folks were too busy socializing with each other to notice us. They'd sized her up and dismissed her or were busy gossiping about her among themselves. It didn't seem to faze her. She looked as serene here as she had at the service. I walked over to introduce myself.

"Hi, I'm Alex Powell. I worked with Ev at *Diaspora* about six years ago, and I've been a contributing editor ever since. I just wanted you to know how sorry I am about his death. He was a good friend, and I'm going to miss him."

She nodded slowly. "Thank you. I think a lot of people will, though it might take awhile for them to realize it."

I must have had that *huh* look on my face. Eileen smiled. The twins' dimples could have come from her as easily as from Ev.

"Look, you worked with him, so you know as well as I do that Everett was a demanding and often difficult man. Some days he was no walk in the park, as M'Dear would say."

We paused—and then grinned widely, wondering which one of us was going to tell the truth first. She won.

"Okay." She chuckled. "*Most* days he wasn't a walk in the park. But as impossible as he could be, a lot of people put up with him because *Diaspora* was doing something important, something other black magazines weren't. Not often, anyway. He was actually addressing world issues as they affect African Americans. He was making us see how interconnected our lives are with the African continent. And I think people will miss that, once they realize the impact of its absence."

She made eye contact with a passing waiter, who glided over and offered us each fresh champagne.

"To Ev." She raised her glass and gently touched the rim of mine.

"To Ev," I echoed. "How did you-all meet, if you don't mind my asking?" And even if you do, I hope you'll tell.

She smiled again, and her eyes had the faraway focus that tells you the person you're speaking to has retreated to a pleasant private memory.

"It was in Côte d'Ivoire about seven years ago. I was finishing field research for my master's degree."

"In . . . ?"

"Developmental psychology. I was actually at a UN conference on children's welfare. I'd been asked, as junior member of a research team, to present a paper on how perception of race and racial bias affects black children. Ev was there to interview the first lady of Ghana, who was the keynote speaker. We met at a reception during the conference."

"Love at first sight?" I teased.

"Let's call it significant interest at first sight." She smiled. "When I returned home, about ten days later, he called me. We started seeing each other—over coffee, over dinner—and one thing led to another. . . ."

As if by mutual consent, we'd been walking toward a quiet atrium away from the hum of the main reception. A marble sculpture by a contemporary Senegalese artist was set on a pedestal in the center of a shallow pool that gleamed silent and wet. Eileen motioned for us to sit on the bronze bench that faced the sculpture and the open doors that led to the main hall. I was glad we were away from alert ears, because I had to know something.

"Eileen, would you mind sharing why you and Ev broke up?"

She smiled slyly, not at all like the other open smiles.

"Why, what have you heard?"

I toyed with the remainder of my now-lukewarm champagne and decided to tell the truth. "Nothing, really. Remember, we didn't even know you existed until a few hours ago."

"Oh, I can just *imagine* what they're saying in there right now!" But her voice was playful, even teasing. "I'll tell you something, Alex—it wasn't for the reason most people would suspect."

"And that would be?"

She waved a hand impatiently. I noticed a ring with a good-sized clear yellow stone of some sort, set in white gold or platinum, and a big gold bracelet made of panels that interlocked in a design I'd never seen before.

"Girl, please. How dumb would I have to be not to know Ev was a major player? Most people probably think we ended for the same reason most of his other relationships did."

"Commitment anxiety? Isn't that what you mental health professionals call it?"

She looked at me closely to determine whether or not I was

needling her. "I specialize in *children*, Alex, so don't quote me—but yes, that's what I think Ev's problem was."

"But not with you?"

She played with her ring, twisting it around for a moment before answering.

"No, not with me," she said quietly, firmly. "We had other differences. Like the fact that he was so paranoid about other people knowing his business he would hardly bring me out in public. I felt like a mistress, and I was going with a single man!"

Ev did have a penchant for privacy; I used to wonder whether it was old-fashioned paranoia or whether he got a thrill out of sneaking around—even when he didn't have to.

"Then, when I found out I was pregnant, it was like living with the Fetus Police: he'd call at ten P.M. every night and ask when I was going to bed. Didn't want me to continue with my casework and interviews. He said," she noted dryly, " 'You can't ever be too safe. You know poor rugrats got the most germs.' "

She rolled her eyes and I smiled. Good Ev imitation.

"Did you ever talk about getting married?"

"For about five minutes. I didn't especially want to be a single mother, but I couldn't see a happily-ever-after for us if we were married, either."

"Too *overwhelming*?"

She blushed. "I see you've been speaking to M'Dear. I thought it was easier to tell her that and let her wonder about me than to get into the other reasons, because as far as M'Dear is concerned, no woman in her right mind would refuse to marry her Everett if he asked."

I nodded. Black men and their mamas—or mama substitutes—form an inviolable bond. Only death is stronger. Another thought occurred to me.

"Did he go into the delivery room with you?"

She nodded. "He did. Stayed through the whole thing, cut the umbilical cords, took photos, the whole nine yards. At first I was worried he was going to pass out: I had a last-minute C-section, and he hadn't planned on watching surgery. A regular delivery would have been more than enough. But he wanted to see those babies born, and he did."

"Boy, he must have been crazy in love," I blurted. "Ev didn't even like to see blood in the *movies*, let alone real blood. And from someone he knows?"

Curiouser and curiouser.

"Yes," she said softly, watching Henry Adams making his way toward us. "I loved him, too—for a long time. But I didn't think I could live with him." Henry was now almost upon us.

"One more question: Was he a good father? Did he see the boys often?"

"He was wonderful. He usually came out to spend the weekend with us a couple of times a month. And when they were older, he'd come and stay at my house and I would leave the three of them alone—I'd go away with girlfriends for a long weekend, just reconnect, you know? In the summers, he'd take them down to M'Dear's and bring them back three or four weeks later. Twice I used that time to do field work in Africa. The boys are going to miss him terribly."

Henry had now reached us with a message from her almost mother-in-law: It was time to leave.

Like M'Dear, Eileen gave me a warm hug. "I hope we'll meet again," she said, when we stepped back from each other.

"Next time under happier circumstances," I promised.

She nodded. "It would have to be, wouldn't it?"

She waved good-bye and started to walk away, her pale silk suit glowing in the late afternoon light. Then she came back.

"Alex—I just remembered something. You know what Ev used to call you?"

"I'm afraid to ask."

"Wells Fargo."

I had that *huh?* look going again. She laughed.

"He said sending you out on a story was like sending the Pony Express—you got through, usually in record time."

"What's that got to do with a mega-bank?"

"Where were you in history class, honey?" she chided. "Remember? The Pony Express turned into the Wells Fargo Bank over a hundred years ago."

And she was gone.

I thought how ironic it was that he named me for a bank. Ev didn't pay much money, and his checks *never* came in record time. Oh, well. I went to find Signe.

The party was breaking up. Waiters were pick-ing up empty glasses. People were deciding if they wanted to continue their conversations over dinner. Ev's family had already quietly taken their leave, as had Signe and Ellen, who were trying to catch a six-o'clock Metro back to New York.

"Time to get to work," Paul said. "And you know, I do some of my best thinking on a full stomach. Let's get some dinner."

So we took our leave.

9

Even though it was close to six when we finally
emerged from the air-conditioned museum, it had barely cooled off.
In summer, Washington moving toward sunset feels as saunalike as
Washington at noon. Before air-conditioning was widespread, foreign diplomats assigned to D.C. were given a hardship bonus, the
same pay they would have received for being posted to muggy Cal-
cutta or the scorching Cameroons.

But tonight there was a cool breeze blowing off the Potomac, and
I was wearing comfortable shoes, so we decided to walk down the
Mall a bit. We wove through after-work joggers thundering down
the Mall's close-cropped grass and passed a knot of exuberantly
screaming volleyball players—two teams from different government
departments, to judge from the lettering on their sweat-saturated
T-shirts. A gaggle of elementary-school children were having a fight
with Supersoakers. We got spritzed in the crossfire, but it felt good.

A little farther down the way, a lone man was flying a nylon kite
with absolute concentration. We stopped and watched as his odd
two-line contraption dipped, swirled, and careened crazily on
unseen thermals.

Commuters whizzed through the edges of Rock Creek Park on
their way over the Memorial Bridge to bedroom communities in
northern Virginia. The Potomac sparkled in the near distance, and

the marble buildings that housed several cabinet offices of the United States government glowed like incandescent wedding cakes across the Mall.

"You miss it, don't you?"

I looked at Paul and shrugged. "Do I look like I do?"

"You do to me."

"Yeah . . . well." I sighed, giving up. "I do miss some parts: the greenness of it. How beautiful many of the neighborhoods are. I even miss the humidity sometimes." Los Angeles was so dry. When I first moved there, the insides of my nose had hurt for weeks.

"You could always come back," Paul said, looking at me closely.

"And do what, work as a beat reporter at the *Post*? I don't think so. Write about where to find the best frozen latte for the *Washingtonian*? *Nyet*. Do work I love while starving at NPR? Uh-uh. I don't miss it *that* much."

It was true. I might have missed the physicality of Washington—the greenery, seeing large numbers of well-educated professional black folks every day in nearly every part of the city, the interest in the arts and international affairs—but there were lots of things I wouldn't miss. Washington is a one-industry town, and if you aren't fascinated by government—its inner workings, the minutiae of its daily administration, the ever-changing cast of players—it doesn't pay to hang around. Even the ancillary industries, like journalism, hinge on government. In contrast, the entertainment industry drives much of Los Angeles, but there is a thriving garment industry, lots of international trade, and a local government that makes the slugfests on *Jerry Springer* look positively sedate.

Sure, I missed Washington, but I think I'd made the right decision to leave. Standing on the Mall, looking at the setting sun, I was satisfied I'd done the right thing.

We'd walked farther than either of us realized, for we were standing at the edge of seventeenth and Constitution, near the Daughters of the American Revolution Hall. When I lived here, I'd always blown a Bronx cheer at the place as I went past; Marian Anderson might have forgiven them for not letting her sing in their funky old building, but *I* never would.

In mute agreement we stepped to the curb to hail a cab. After several tries, we got one.

"Dinner somewhere in the neighborhood?" Paul asked, after giving his address to the cabbie. "Or do you want to stay dressed and go somewhere fancy? You look very nice, by the way."

"Neighborhood. We've been dressed up long enough. Let's get real."

Paul lived in the 2000 block of Kalorama Road, just over the DMZ that straddles Yuppie D.C. and truly multicultural D.C. If you exit his house and turn right, a short walk will take you past the limestone and Georgian mansions of Embassy Row, on Massachussetts Avenue. The neighborhood's fluidly looping streets, with stately trees and private security services, signal that you are in the coveted territory of the power elite, international division. Robert McNamara lives there. Several ambassadors from First World countries do too, as well as liaisons from countries that allegedly deplore this way of life. Go figure. Several big cheeses from the World Bank and the International Monetary Fund call Kalorama home, as do a half-dozen former cabinet members and a smattering of former presidential candidates. It's that kind of neighborhood.

If you turn in the other direction, a few blocks will bring you into immediate contact with what *really* makes Washington international. Nearby Columbia Road, where I'd lived, might have condominiums that housed culturally tolerant lawyers and journalists who'd not yet escaped uptown to Cleveland Park, but Eighteenth Street, one block farther east, was the 'hood. The streets throbbed with life: Ethiopian and Eritrean refugee entrepreneurs ran restaurants specializing in their native cuisines. Salvadorans, Guatemalans, and Cubans chattered to their families while squeezing the produce offered by Cambodian merchants. Aging hippies produced organic meals a few doors down. Two brothers from New Orleans who'd become struck with Potomac fever offered shrimp étouffée and jazz nightly at their little spot. And French expatriates ran one of the best bistros in town.

I had lived here when I worked in D.C., and I loved this neighborhood. It was everything Los Angeles, with its huge grab bag of immigrants, domestic and foreign, should have been and didn't want to be. And unlike Los Angeles, where people were Balkanized in enclaves dotting the sprawling city, here everyone was jammed shoulder-to-shoulder, working and taking Rodney King's advice, just getting along. There's something to be said about the upside of high-density populations.

We turned right off Connecticut onto Kalorama. Two brownstones in, on the left-hand side, I recognized Paul's gray stone townhouse.

"Remember, it's on the second floor. Think you can make it?"

"Oh, please. I live in L.A. We're all physically fit." Doesn't he watch any of those nighttime soaps where they all wear bikinis or micro-minis?

Paul had bought his apartment several years ago, when real estate was still cheap in Washington and his block was considered too close to Eighteenth Street to be as desirable as it is now. About five years ago, the apartment above him became vacant, and with a little financial rearrangement he bought that too. It turned out to have been one of the smartest things he'd ever done. For a nominal fee, he got twice the space and a roof for barbecueing.

I followed him into the foyer and up the staircase.

"No elevator," he called over his shoulder, cheerfully. "Land of tofu burgers and organic produce made you soft, Powell?"

"Shaddup."

I was determined I wouldn't fall out, at least not until I could collapse, in private, on the bathroom floor. I *had* gotten soft in the five years I'd been in L.A. When I lived in D.C., I walked three miles every day, rain, snow, or shine, to and from work. In L.A., land of perfect weather, I walked through the neighborhood or ran on a treadmill maybe three times a week.

He stuck two keys into two locks. I heard a deadbolt turn. Then he opened the door, deactivated the alarm, and waved me in. The air was hot and still; I heard him snap on the air conditioner. Then he grabbed my bag, which I'd left by the door with things spilling out of it.

"I'm going up to change. I'll be ready in a minute."

Upstairs, Paul had knocked out several walls to make two large bedrooms. His faced the street and had a green-marble master bath attached, courtesy of the previous owner, a gay man from one of Virginia's first families who had been a computer technician during the week and a decorator on weekends. When someone in his family died, the technician took his inheritance and became a full-time decorator; he bought a house in Georgetown with his banker companion and sold his apartment to Paul at a very decent price.

The room I'd been assigned overlooked the garden that probably belonged to the tenant on the first floor. It had a simple pine daybed pushed against one wall and looked like a combination extra bedroom and TV room. A door opened from this room to the hallway bath (gray granite, brushed-steel fixtures). I left my toothbrush on the sink's edge and quickly shucked my funeral suit and pumps in exchange for a loose cotton sundress and a pair of flat sandals.

Downstairs, a bottle of Sancerre was open and partly empty. Two thick green wineglasses were about each half full.

"I thought we could have a drink while I look through the mail and return a few calls. Make yourself at home."

I took a glass and sipped; cold and faintly fruity. Then I walked over to a big chair in the living room and plumped down.

"Tired?"

"Sort of. I've never been able to do that coast-to-coast thing without its catching up with me. I left L.A. in the dark and twelve hours later here I am."

"Yes," he said quietly. "Here you are."

We stared at each other for a minute, saying nothing.

"And you're probably hungry."

"Getting there." I should have been stuffed with hors d'oeuvres from Ev's reception, but Mrs. Weeks was right: That little-bitty food didn't make a meal for anyone with a normal appetite.

"Then let's do 'that dinner thing,'" he said, mocking my description of transcontinental travel. "Don't you people speak English out there?" He put the bills in one basket, the other envelopes in another basket, and tossed a handful of catalogs and circulars in the trash.

"Next to *nobody* speaks English out there. That's why my acquaintance with it is dwindling daily."

"Okay, then: ¡*Vamanos, esta hambre!*"

"That means 'Haul it up, I'm starving' or something, doesn't it?"

"¡*Muy bueno, chica!*"

"Whatever." I couldn't do Berlitz on an empty stomach.

A five-minute walk later, we found ourselves on the corner of Kalaroma and Eighteenth in a little neighborhood bistro that was well-known for its use of fresh ingredients in innovative combinations.

Over plates of grilled chicken breasts and *spaghetti di checca*, we talked about lots of things and carefully avoided any mention of why I was in D.C. or why we were leaving the next morning.

Out of the orbit of Charming Tim, whose charm, I belatedly realized, made him seem much better looking than he actually was, it occurred to me that Paul was truly attractive. His proximity to Tim had pretty much blinded me to what he really looked like, but it was becoming clearer: broad chest, nicely sinewy arms, long fingers with neat squared-off nails, even white teeth, and good cheekbones. When I'd been with Tim, Paul was just an extra hunk of protoplasm, an annoyance to be dealt with or eliminated, if possible. Now I found myself wondering why I hadn't noticed the real him before.

I heard he had a busy social calendar. His brief marriage had finished years ago, and a single man—especially one with a prestigious job and a decent profile—was still, at only forty-two, a hot commodity in D.C. At least that seemed to be the case, judging from the interested looks he got from some of the female diners when we entered the little restaurant. Was he truly clueless about the discreet looks or just pretending to be? And did he, I wondered, miss being married?

"You have such a nice kitchen, do you ever cook at home?" I asked.

"Not much. No time."

"How's your mom?"

Paul sighed. "Clara's good. Still telling me, at least once a week, she's *so* sorry she'll die before she's a grandmother."

I laughed. "Did you tell her you practice all the time?"

"Jesus, no. Sometimes I wonder if she even thought I had sex when I was married!"

"Did you?"

He grinned crookedly. "Depends on which year. Lots in the beginning. By the end. . . ." He was quiet. "Well, it's hard to do the nasty with someone who's always pissed at you."

We let the silence grow. The waiter discreetly removed our plates and left a dessert menu for us to share

"You pick," I said. "As long as it's anything lemon or chocolate."

"Yassum."

I watched Paul as he read the menu. The softly lit restaurant brought out the planes in his face. Candles on the table bounced off his reading glasses

"Do you miss your ex-wife?" I asked softly.

He looked up from the menu. "You know what, Powell? I feel sorry that I don't. I miss the *idea* of her, but I don't miss Cheryl at all."

The waiter reappeared. Paul gave him our order and asked for two decafs, "one Americano, one latte."

"The idea of her?"

The smell of freshly brewed French roast was starting to waft from the kitchen. I could hear the espresso machine snorting.

"Yeah. It would be nice to bring the same person to the office Christmas party every year and know what she liked—and didn't—in jewelry and clothes and books. I'd say I miss having someone to share private jokes with, except the things that cracked me up didn't move her at all. We didn't like the same music. Had different tastes in art."

"What *was* this, an arranged marriage? Why were you even together?"

He shrugged. "To be painfully honest, I can't tell you. I thought I loved her. I thought she loved me."

"You know what Signe says? She says men get married on impulse. They just wake up one morning, decide it's time to do it, and marry the first woman who crosses their path."

He smiled. "Would explain a lot of marriages I'm familiar with. Of people our age, anyway."

"Do you think she's right?" I took a bite of the flourless chocolate cake we were ostensibly sharing; it was excellent. Paul had better get cracking if he wanted his half.

"Actually, I don't remember deciding. Cheryl and I went out for a while, and everybody just sort of *assumed* it was going to happen. And frankly, we seemed to get along well."

"What, so one bride's as good as another? This one had been road-tested, found sturdy, and the price was right?"

He smiled sheepishly over the rim of the coffee cup filled with decaf Americano. "All of the above, I guess. A little, anyway."

"Do you think she misses you?" I was curious. I took a cautious sip of the steaming latte. It's really a breakfast drink and it was gauche of me to order it, but I wanted one. Sue me.

"I doubt it. I think she's happy being in the suburbs. They have a nice big house with a pool. Living out there would've made me eat a gun. And she seems to love being a mother. Brian willingly goes to all those functions I couldn't stand—the garden club dance, the cotillion, the annual luncheon for at-risk teens—and he's happy with someone who wants to run the house while he earns the money. It's a good arrangement."

"Arrangement. Ugh. That's why I'm never getting married."

He looked at me and laughed. " 'Never' is a long time. Powell. You're still young."

"Thirty-five is pretty old in California, pal. In L.A. years, thirty-five is about sixty. The Everready in my bio clock will have given up."

"Pity." He sipped, finally speared a good-sized chunk of our rapidly diminishing "shared" dessert, and smeared it with the whipped cream I'd virtuously been ignoring. "You'd have made a superb mother."

"Oh, I intend to, one day," I assured him. "I'm going to adopt a little girl. Probably sometime in the next two years. I've always wanted to, and there's no reason why not."

"No reason for me, either, except the fact that my mother hasn't given up hoping I'll grow my own."

"You know what? She'd rather have adopted grandchildren than *no* grandchildren, believe me," I assured Paul. "I have lots of men friends who don't seem to be in any hurry. But men can wait forever. I had an uncle who remarried late in life and had a second family at sixty-two."

"That's indecent. You can't even live long enough to see them grow up."

I shrugged. "Who says you will if you have them when you're forty, either?"

"True. But barring a terminal disease or an out-of-control bus with your name on it, you have a lot better chance living to see them grow up if you have kids in your forties. Or before."

He paid the bill and thanked the waiter, who looked pretty happy with his tip, and we walked out into the cooler but still-steamy D.C. night. Moist halos glowed around each streetlight, and the maples overhead whispered and rustled as we walked under the dark canopy formed by their arching branches. After we crossed Columbia Road, the streets were silent, except for the tinkle of wind chimes on some-one's porch.

"Anyway, there are lots of lovely little black children out there who need a mom, and one of them, maybe two of them, has my name on her. Or him."

Paul opened the door to the foyer and gestured me in. "You could do both. In fact, you *should* do both."

"Do *what* both?"

"Have a child and adopt a child. Best of both worlds."

We walked up the stairs and into his foyer. The bare wood floors gleamed in the soft light of the hall table.

"I don't know how to break this to you, my brother, but the world is not teeming with men who are interested in being married for the rest of their natural lives to independent women with opinions. Not teeming with *black* ones, anyway, and I'm not ready to go multicultural quite yet. And there are even fewer who will jump at the idea of adoption. Has to be *their* genes, you know?"

He snorted. "Men who think that way are knuckleheads."

He lowered the air conditioner and turned on the alarm system.

"It would be a real waste not to share what you have with someone who deserves you, Alex."

I shook my head and laughed. "I'll make you a deal, sweetie: You scare up the men you think deserve me—all one point five of them—and I'll take care of the rest."

He gave me a peculiar smile. "I'll get to work on it right away. Meanwhile, Boston in the morning, so you'd better get some sleep. You must be whipped."

I was. It had been a long day, and fatigue had caught up with me with a vengeance. Morning would be here before I knew it.

We turned off the lights downstairs. The streetlights shining through the trees made lace patterns on the living room walls. I followed Paul up the stairs, wished him good night, and was in bed ten minutes later with a paperback I'd started on the plane. Since we had to be up at six-thirty, I knew I should turn out the lights, but unless I'm sick, I can't go to sleep unless I've read a couple of pages first.

An hour later, I looked at the clock: twelve-thirty. Reluctantly, I closed the book and placed it on the floor. In the dark, I listened to the click of Paul's keyboard across the hall. I fell asleep to the clicks and, softly floating beneath our closed doors, the lush mournful sound of Jimmy Scott's voice urging me to "dream, when you're feeling blue."

I wasn't blue, but dreaming sounded like just the ticket, and I was soon taking Mr. Scott's advice.

10

"Toto, I don't think we're in Chocolate City any-
more," Paul whispered to me next day, at Logan International.

Duh. Can't imagine what gave that secret away—unless it was all
those beefy pink-faced white guys wearing Celtics caps. The well-to-
do ones wore them with pleated khaki Bermudas and pastel polo
shirts; the shirts had little emblems on the left breast: polo players,
crocodiles, or sheep dangling from some sort of bunting. Some of the
old well-to-do guys wore Madras button-downs. No socks, of course,
just Topsiders or loafers. Their women, with their bright A-line
dresses, pearl earrings, and headbands, were straight out of Talbot's
summer catalog.

The less affluent guys wore jeans with baggy butts and T-shirts
with words on them that advertised the local Y, Sam Adams beer,
and, in one case, a distinctly antifeminist sentiment. Instead of Topsiders, they wore athletic shoes (teen sons in high-end pneumatic-
type high-tops, their dads in classic canvas sneakers). And unlike the
rich guys, they always wore socks. The young girls, regardless of
class, all wore the same thing: shorts or denim jumpers, dangly earrings, and nail polish guaranteed to creep Mom out: baby blue,
putrid green, and red so dark it was black.

Lobsters moved sluggishly in plexiglass tanks, waiting to be
packed in aerated cardboard boxes as edible souvenirs. Unlike
National Airport, which in addition to the requisite burgers and

doughnuts had concession stands with buffalo wings and barbecued ribs, here in the "town of the bean and the cod" there was not a barbecued rib in sight. I couldn't wait to get on the Vineyard and see some color.

The problem was getting there from here. There are several ways to get to the Vineyard from Boston, but we'd eliminated two of them en route. Even if we'd wanted to spend the money and rent a car to drive to Woods Hole, there was no guarantee that we'd be able to book a spot on the ferry that left—packed—every hour or so. The closer to Labor Day, the less the likelihood that last-minute drivers would be able to secure a space. And for Paul, helicopters were absolutely a last resort ("maybe . . . if they needed to bring me out by medevac").

After a bit of bickering, we'd decided the smart thing to do was to take a puddle jumper straight to the island. We were in luck, the local commuter line had a few seats left, so we paid for our one-way tickets and hopped aboard. Less than twenty minutes later we touched down at the island's handkerchief-sized airport, walked across the tarmac, and hopped into a cab for Oak Bluffs and my Uncle Webb's house.

Webster Barnes had been my dad's first cousin, the closest thing Daddy had had to a brother. He and Daddy had grown up down the street from each other and, as adults, had remained close. I saw less of him after Daddy died, but he remains one of my favorite relatives.

For many years, Webb and his wife, Ruth, had been Vineyard staples. Each summer, their tiny gingerbread Victorian on Narragansett was in the thick of Oak Bluffs' social whirl. ("Really," I told my mother when she described a particularly arduous weekend with them a few years ago, "I don't see how you old folks can keep that up. It can't be good for your health!") It wore me out just thinking of their schedule.

Last summer, for the first time, their normally abuzz house was quiet; Ruthie had died suddenly the winter before, and we wondered whether Webb would even open the house again. It seemed so much a reflection of the two of them and their happy married life, many people thought it would have been perfectly logical for Webb to sell the house or leave it to his son and daughter.

Time and habit had helped a little, though. That and the fact, as Webb told me on the phone, that maybe Ruthie would have encouraged him to go. After all, they had spent thirtysomething summers there. I could almost hear her. "Webb, don't be a knucklehead! We've always had a ball on the Vineyard. Now you'll have to party for both of us, sweetheart."

And it looked like he was trying his best to do that. When Webb returned to the island this year, their old running buddies embraced him and tugged him into their tonic-scented orbit, and in a few weeks things were almost the same again. All the Cottagers referred to Ruthie as if she were sitting among them, something that would have pleased her deeply. They also set about fixing up Webb with what I maliciously called the Casserole Brigade. (Which, of course, is something they never would have contemplated if Ruthie had been living. Cottager loyalty is about on par with the Mafia's.)

"It's amazing," he'd confided. "Who'd have thought anybody'd be interested in a broken-down old widower like me? You should see the women who stop by just to see how I'm doing."

I'd laughed. "Webb, Webb, Webb. You're an *available* broken-down old widower. And there's a lot more manless older black women than you can imagine out here."

"No kidding!" Webb had exhaled in true wonderment. "And they keep themselves up, too."

"Well, don't question it," I'd told him, envisioning the thought that went into the perfectly coiffed dos, the carefully chosen "casual" summer outfits, and the elaborately choreographed, ostensibly spontaneous moments to which he was, in all likelihood, being treated. "Have some fun."

He'd taken my advice. Since his official retirement, Webb divided his time between doing pro bono cases for a New York community legal center near his home in Brooklyn, private work on a client-by-client basis (mostly probate things), and moonlighting as— of all things—a cocktail pianist.

An only child, he'd played classical piano since he was five. He worked his way through law school by providing elegant background music for Main Line Philadelphians' evening affairs. Rodgers and Hammerstein, Cole Porter, you name it. But as he got older, Webb had a hankering for jazz. So he took some classes and, in the winter, played Oscar Peterson and Ahmad Jamal and Bill Evans at a small bistro in Brooklyn Heights.

"I get paid for it!" he'd crowed. I went to hear him once when I was in New York. He was good.

When I called Webb to ask if he'd mind having company for the weekend, he'd said, "Come on up. I've got to go to Boston overnight, but you can pick up the key at Jenny's. You know her place, don't you?"

Everybody knew Jenny Evans. If you were looking for someone on the island, all you had to do was look in at Jenny's or leave her a message. So by one-thirty we were on the way to Siblings, the gallery Jenny owned with her sister, Judy. Jenny, Judy, and Webb had been friends for years, and he often left his key—or legal documents or the gardener's check—at Sib's. It was a convenient dropoff point. And he and Judy and Jenny got to engage in their favorite sport: They were all, Webb included, world-class gossips.

"Hey, stranger! Finally got you to come back for a little bit!" Jenny said, giving me a big hug. She looked over my shoulder at Paul and smiled a warm welcome. "Is this the fiancé Webb was telling me about?"

We both choked. "Jenny, Webb's been stirring the pot again. This is my friend Paul Butler. Paul, Jenny Evans."

"Pleased to meet you, *friend*." Jenny winked. She cocked her head in blatant assessment. "Pity, though. . . ."

I groaned. "Jenny, don't you start too! Before you have me drifting down the aisle in one of those stupid Cinderella dresses, could I have Webb's key? He said he'd leave it here."

Judy came out from the back. "He did, honey. And don't pay any mind to my sister. You know she's terminally romantic."

With her close-cropped natural hair, batik caftan, and big gold earrings, Judy was a larger version of her little sister. "Come here and gimme some sugar, girl."

More hugs all around. "Hi. You must be the un-fiancé," Judy said, perfectly straight-faced, while offering her hand for a shake. We all laughed.

"That's me," Paul admitted cheerfully. Relief must've been making him positively giddy.

"Webb left his car, too. Said to tell you the keys are in the piano seat, and to remind you, Alex, not to give yourself a concussion with the power brakes." She and Judy burst out laughing.

"We should tell Paul," Jenny said, looking at her sister.

"Would be rude not to, since we've referred to it right in front of him," Judy deadpanned.

I sighed. "Have your fun, ladies. But payback might be in your future."

"I feel lucky." Jenny grinned. "I'll risk it. You see," she continued, "several summers ago, Alex was up here on vacation to go to a wedding. The Carter girl's, wasn't it? Webb and Ruthie had gone on ahead with a neighbor, and they'd left Webb's car for Alex so she could follow when she was ready."

"It's a Thunderbird," Judy said, picking up the narrative, "a nice silver one, fully loaded. Power everything. Including brakes." The two looked at me meaningfully.

I stuck out my tongue.

"She was okay going. On the way back, Webb and Ruthie went with Alex and let her drive. Everything was fine until she was going at a nice clip down Edgartown Pike and a rabbit shot across the road."

"Alex *slammed* on the brakes, honey! Ruthie was in the back seat, so no harm done. And Webb braced himself. But Alex knocked herself silly." Judy hooted.

"Had a big purple bump the size of a hen's egg," Jenny agreed. "Looked like hell the rest of the week."

Paul was looking at me with a huge grin. "Surprised that hard head didn't shatter the windshield," he murmured.

The sisters looked at him in amazement. "Get out! How did you know?"

Paul looked at me in genuine shock. "Your head actually broke the glass?"

I shrugged. "It *cracked* the glass, okay? Nothing broke."

Jenny's smart-ass remark notwithstanding, I actually had had a hairline concussion, but the way they'd been having yuks at my expense, wild horses couldn't have dragged that out of me.

"Jesus. Although I suppose that explains a lot about your mangled thought processes."

The three of them just hee-hawed.

"Okay, enough already. Let's not forget, Paul, I have the key to my uncle's house. You need to show a little respect."

"Oh, shoot." Judy flipped her hand, like Sally, my landlady, likes to. "If she won't let you in, Paul, here's our number. You can come stay with us. Our house is just across the street." She gave me a triumphant I-told-you-so look.

Without a word, I put the keys in my pocket, grabbed my overnight bag, and turned on my heel. Webb's place was only two blocks away, and I could make it just fine by myself, thank you. I heard Paul swiftly saying his good-byes and scrambling to catch up with me. I knew, as soon as he left, Judy and Jenny would start planning for our nonexistent wedding. They were like that.

Webb's house looked just the same. The old ebony upright was still opposite the stairs. The dining room table looked as if it was being used as his desk: law journals, a calculator, letterhead stationery, and some manila folders were neatly arranged at one oval end. The small sunny kitchen had a note on the refrigerator door:

Alex—Back tomorrow on the noon ferry. Don't meet me; I can use the exercise. You know where everything is. Louise Howard (major general in the C.B.) left a lot of lobster salad last night. Thought you kids might finish it off for me, it's very good. See

you tomorrow. I put you both in the guest room; don't tell your
mother. Stay out of trouble. W.
P.S.: Boston number, if emergency: 617-555-0000. Major
Hamilton, on Rutledge Place. Major is his first name, not his
rank. He's not in the C.B.

I poured from a chilled bottle of fumé blanc Webb had left
behind. He'd scribbled DRINK! GOOD! across the label in black felt-
tip marker. We drank. It *was* good. He was right about the lobster
salad, too. Major general Howard had outdone herself; it was terrific.

"What's the C.B.?" Paul asked, hopefully peering into the empty
bowl we'd all but licked clean.

"The Casserole Brigade. You know, the single ladies who drop
off casseroles after your wife dies, getting their early dibs in on the
newly freed spouse?"

He laughed. "Works in cases other than death, too. I could've
eaten like a king practically every night after Cheryl and I split. If I
had taken up every invitation that was extended to me, I'd look like
George Foreman."

"So it was fear of fat that made you decline?" I asked, as I rinsed
our luncheon dishes.

"Nah. Price was too high. The last thing I wanted to do was get
married again. And certainly not after having just gotten divorced.
And that's *exactly* what those gorgeous cooks had on their minds. So
I turned down the invitations to all the gourmet meals and ate a lot
of takeout."

I shrugged. "Guess it looks different when you're almost seventy."

"Yup. When you're almost seventy, even *you* might consider getting hooked up, Alex."

I thought for a minute; I had about thirty-five years to change my
mind. Not that I was going to.

The drive to Greywing Saturday afternoon took
less than ten minutes. Chip lived almost directly across from the airport, at the end of a long private road that reminded you of its pri-

vateness every hundred feet or so: PRIVATE PROPERTY! RESIDENTS AND THEIR GUESTS ONLY! ABSOLUTELY NO TRESPASSING!

Most of the island was pretty friendly. Millionaires' Row, as this was sometimes informally referred to, was different. The road was unnamed, not even a county numeral to mark it. The rooflines of what appeared to be large frame houses peeked over the top of thick hedges. We could hear the *thwack!* of tennis balls from behind some properties. At the end of the road was a private beach accessible via a private road open only to residents. Lesser mortals, if they were determined enough, could get there by canoe. Few nonresidents bothered.

This was Chip's second summer on the Vineyard. Before that, his family owned a good-sized house in Sag Harbor on Long Island Sound. They'd been there for almost fifteen years, but Chip had been heard to complain: "Sag is getting a little common, you know? It may be time." And shortly after that, he and Evelyn had begun looking on the island.

But not in Oak Bluffs. Before recent presidents decided to make the Vineyard their watering hole, real estate in the prime part of the Bluffs turned over quietly and slowly. It often stayed in the same family for generations, passed down from father to son to grandson — or daughter. And for the most part, long-time Oak Bluffs residents knew one another's families and friends well. While the community is certainly more elastic than some people have depicted it, the circle of friends is still, in many subtle ways, fairly insular. And Chip, with his bluster, his emphasis on money and status, his consistent need to have the biggest and best, would have fared badly there among people who didn't feel obligated to talk about such things. In a place where the unspoken question is Do We Know Your People? Chip would not have had an answer that made him comfortable.

Then too, Chip, for all his talk about strengthening black institutions, was also a firm believer in integration, especially when he was doing the integrating. So to be the only black resident of Millionaires' Row was a first of which he was very proud. He and Evelyn threw an annual party on Illumination Night for the neighbors, most of whom came out of genuine curiosity about the rich colored family that lived in their midst. Most of them didn't know any black folks personally, so this was their chance to get up-close and personal and acquire their Vicarious Negro Experience.

From the road, Greywing loomed above a neat lawn of closely clipped Bermuda grass. It stretched out in three different directions, rather like a post-modern Y. The gray clapboard contrasted richly with the blue sky and whitewashed window frames. A large porch ran the length of the front wing. When we walked up the steps, we could see, through the front door's glass panels, that the back of the house was almost completely glass. We could hear the ocean pounding not too far away.

A small brown-skinned woman in a pale gray uniform opened the door.

"Please come in. Mr. Wiley is expecting you," she said politely. The maid's accent indicated Caribbean ancestry. She gave us a very discreet once-over and seemed to approve of our neatly pressed shorts and shirts. She led us through a stone foyer and through the large open living room. The cathedral ceilings were double height; generous sofas and chairs were upholstered in a cheerful yellow, green, and, white banana-leaf pattern.

Recessed glass bookshelves held family photos and media clippings in silver frames of varyingly degrees of ornateness: Chip and Evelyn in evening clothes at a recent gala; Evelyn and Chipper in front of 1947 Hall at Princeton, he in graduation robes with an orange-and-black hood; Chip and half a dozen other middle-aged brothers in flight suits before a needle-nosed airplane—clearly a reunion of some sort. There was a clipping from W of Evelyn with Annette de la Renta and Brooke Astor, all three in big hats, gardenia corsages, and slight variations of the same pink Chanel suits, at some fund-raiser for, according to the caption, the Central Park Conservatory Gardens. And a huge picture of daughter Meredith by one of the Madison Avenue firms that specializes in tasteful wedding portraits.

It looked familiar—until I realized I'd seen it a few years earlier in the weddings section of the *Times*. Meredith was smiling and holding a cascade of tiny white orchids; her bare shoulders emerged from a froth of lace and intricate pearl beading that must have given a whole roomful of Third World seamstresses carpal tunnel syndrome. A garland of orange blossoms and stephanotis encircled her head, and a tulle veil flowed down her back.

"Quarter of a million dollars—not counting the dress, of course. Worth every penny."

I jumped like a guilty person who'd been caught in the act, which was stupid. I mean, it wasn't as if I were poking through Chip's drawers or anything. Still, he'd spooked me, sneaking up on me like that.

"She was a beautiful bride," I said quickly.

Chip strode forward, hand outstretched. "Thanks. *I* thought so. 'Course her mother cried through the entire ceremony." He rolled his eyes at Paul, who laughed. "Still don't know why. I kept telling her, 'Woman, she's only going to be three blocks away!' It's why we bought them the damn duplex in the first place."

"Well, you know us babes," I said lightly. "We're like Asians: totally inscrutable."

Chip gave me a look that let me know my insolence wasn't appreciated. "Actually, I find Asians much more scrutable than women. I *know* what Asians want, they want to beat the pants off us in business and take over the world."

"*All* Asians?" I asked innocently.

"The ones that count. Filipinos are about as shiftless as some of our people."

It was an opinion voiced with his usual absolute certainty.

"It's a nice day. How about something cool on the deck?" Chip opened the large glass doors and walked through them like a man accustomed to giving orders and having them obeyed. He gestured to a round glass table surrounded by canvas and steel chairs—"Have a seat"—and pressed an intercom button. "Beverly, would you bring iced tea for three, please?"

"Yes, Mr. Wiley," said the unseen Beverly.

"So. About this business with Everett. What does any of it have to do with me?"

Paul and I exchanged glances. "You the man," I said sweetly. "You start. Please."

"Well"—his look clearly said, I will settle with you later—"as we said in Washington, we're just really asking some elementary questions on behalf of the police."

"The police already asked me questions. By phone. Why is this any of *your* business?"

"Chip, aren't you the teensiest bit embarrassed that this happened at, of all places, an NABJ conference? I mean, think of how it looks." Hey, if you couldn't appeal to his morality, I'd appeal to his vanity.

Chip grunted. "Why should *I* be embarrassed? It wasn't me who was caught dead with my pants down."

Well, that was true enough.

Beverly materialized with a large glass pitcher and three heavily iced glasses. A small glass bowl of lemon slices, long spoons, and a silver pot with packets of sugar and sugar substitute were carefully arranged on the tray. She deftly poured tea into the glasses and passed them around.

"Although I must say, I'm not a bit surprised," Chip added.

Paul and I looked at each other, startled.

"You weren't?"

"Hell, no! Carson's always had trouble keeping it zipped. I told him time and again, *Do* your thinking with your *big* head, Everett. But he obviously didn't listen."

I shrugged. "The magazine got out on time. And he was single. Which meant he was entitled to a social life, if he wanted one."

"Perhaps." Chip took a judicious sip of his tea and added more lemon. "But his judgment in partners left much to be desired."

"How so?" Paul asked.

"He ran around with a lot of . . . oh, hell, with women who were barely removed from being whores. And he treated the nice women who were interested in him extremely poorly. Extremely."

It was unusual for Chip to be so emphatic about something that didn't affect him directly. So unusual I was suspicious.

"You know someone he treated badly?" I asked timidly. I could see Paul's wildly gesturing eyebrows: Do you really want to know the answer to that question? Maybe not. What if it was his wife?

Chip looked at us strangely and began, uncharacteristically, to fiddle nervously with his slender silver teaspoon. We waited while he waged his internal struggle.

"I might as well tell you," he said finally. "You could find out easily enough anyway." He looked through the patio doors into the living room. "Yes, that bastard hurt someone close to me. He damn near broke my daughter's heart."

"Meredith?"

We followed his gaze to the large photograph on the glass shelf.

"I don't *have* any other daughters," Chip snapped.

"It never would have occurred to me," Paul said quietly.

"Me either. But she was crazy about him. They met in Philadelphia when she came to a seminar for minority publishers at Wharton with me. In case you don't know this, he can be charming, in his country-boy fashion. Nobody asked me whether or not I approved, but I suppose my opinion was beside the point. Meredith was twenty-four, old enough to make up her own mind about such things. Before I knew it, they were an item."

He paused, clearly groping for the right words.

"And then, before I knew it, they weren't. I had no idea Meredith was so attached to him. She's not a baby; I knew she'd—uh, lived her life as a woman for a while. But she flipped, absolutely flipped out, when they broke up."

I hesitated. "You mean *flipped* flipped?"

He slammed down his glass. The noise on the glass tabletop was firecracker-loud; we all jumped. "I mean Whitely Pavilion flipped, all right? We were so worried something was going to happen—"

"Wow. You institutionalized her?"

"Only for a weekend. Still, I can't begin to describe to you how worried we were. To see your little girl in a room that only locks from the outside. To see her in so much pain, wanting to die, because some . . . some *nigger* decided one woman at a time wasn't nearly enough. . . . I was so angry I could have killed him with my bare hands. I have the expertise, too. Uncle Sam's a good teacher." His fist gripped his empty glass until the knuckles were white. Then he exhaled loudly.

"But that was three years ago."

We sat in silence for a moment. I could feel the salt from the ocean air on my lips. Chip stared out toward the surf, his heavy brows drawn together, fingers absently caressing that stupid mustache. He looked away from the ocean and seemed to give himself an almost imperceptible shake.

"As I said, that was three years ago. Water under the bridge. She met Royce—her husband—about six months after . . . well, after Carson broke it off. At first, Evelyn and I were relieved she was seeing someone more suitable. Royce is only a few years older than Meredith. His father went to Lincoln. Royce, of course, went to Harvard."

"Of course." I could see Paul lift an eyebrow—again—in warning.

"And to the Business School."

As if there were only one. But I was a good girl and stayed quiet.

"Then, when they started to become serious, we got worried."

"I don't get it. I thought you liked him. Dad went to Lincoln and all that."

"Oh, we *did* like him. We *do*, I mean. But Evelyn started to worry that Meredith was becoming involved with Royce because of the other thing."

"Everett?"

"Yes." Chip sighed. "She thought Royce might be a . . . what do they call it when you date somebody on the rebound?" He turned to me, waiting for the phrase.

"Recovery man?"

"Exactly. Turned out it was the real thing. They seem quite happy. And"—a very un-Chip-like little smile played below his mustache—"I'm going to be a grandfather in February."

"Hey! Congratulations!"

Paul clapped Chip on the shoulder and they beamed at each other. As if either of *them* would have anything to do with bringing this baby into the world. Men.

"Oh, I see he's finally decided to share his news with the outside world!"

We turned. Standing framed in the open doorway was Mrs.

Charles Mitchell Wiley III, looking every bit as pretty as she did in her pictures in a navy linen sundress that looked as expensive as it was chic.

And she smelled heavenly, an elegant floral with a hint of oriental undernotes. Classy.

Chip actually ducked his head like a little boy. "How could you tell?"

"You were smiling. There are only a few things that bring on that smile."

"One of them best not discussed in company." Chip laughed, patting the arm she'd thrown around his shoulders.

We were flabbergasted. Chip, human?

"Evelyn, meet my colleagues, Paul Butler and Alex Powell." Paul stood and pulled out a chair for Chip's wife. She waved him down.

"No, darling, sit, please. I just wanted to remind my husband that we're due at Katherine's house in about forty minutes. He forgets about time when we're up here."

"Katherine Graham," Chip said helpfully, for us hoi polloi who weren't on a first-name basis with the empress of the *Washington Post*.

"Wow," I breathed, so Chip would know how impressed I was. "Don't forget to eat something first."

Chip looked at me as if this admonition confirmed his initial suspicion: I was gauche. Untraveled. Coun-*tree*.

"Why on earth would I eat *before* going to a cocktail party?" he asked, rising from his chair. He was probably trying to figure out if it was worth it to explain the concept of horse-doovers—oops, hors d'oeuvres—to me.

Paul laughed. "Because that party will probably be critically Caucasian, and you know what the peeples say about white parties. White folks' hospitality is usually limited to—"

"—a mayonnaise sandwich and a glass of ice water!" Three of us said it in chorus. Only Evelyn looked puzzled.

"I don't get it," she said hesitantly.

"Of course you don't, sweetheart. You're Jamaican. It's different down there." Chip actually winked at us. "Say good-bye to our guests, Evelyn, and let's go figure out exactly what I should wear so I won't embarrass you."

We shook hands and offered to see ourselves out. Our last glimpse of Chip was the back of him, walking Evelyn up the stairs with an arm around her waist. His head was bent down close to hers, and he was saying something that was making her laugh.

"Ready?" Paul had opened the door before Beverly could get to it.

"Amazing. Almost makes me like the man."

I went out on the veranda just as a sleek navy Town Car was pulling up the drive. The driver—in full livery—let the engine idle so the car would remain air-conditioned. *That* was more like the real Chip.

"Okay, I feel better. I don't have to like him anymore," I said cheerfully, as we approached Webb's T-bird.

As small and informal as the island was, nobody who was able-bodied—no matter how pretentious—had a driver. And even those few folks kept simple cars. The general rule among long-time islanders was, the richer the person, the more decrepit the auto. The few people who kept drivers sat up front, next to them. Even with the Vineyard's recent higher profile (and resultant dreadful traffic), it was routine to see network anchors driving their kids to the beach, movie stars browsing in the Safeway, or, on Saturdays, the governor and both senators from the Commonwealth of Massachussets loading up their own Jeeps and Explorers at the Farmer's Market in West Tisbury. Even Jackie O had driven herself around (way too fast, some locals grumbled) in an old BMW.

But not Chip.

"Poor Chip." I sighed. "He's never going to get being Negro gentry exactly right, is he?"

"Nope. But since the people he's going to see wouldn't know Negro gentry if it bit them on the ass, he's safe. . . . Somebody ought to write a primer," he added thoughtfully.

I grunted. "The way publishers are paying for the Negro Experience, somebody probably will. They'll be white—and get it wrong."

"Or black—and get it wrong." Paul took the keys from me.

"*You* want to drive? You don't even know where you're going."

"True," Paul admitted, opening the passenger door for me. I slid in. "But I *do* know how to stop for rabbits. Where to now, Miss Daisy?"

We ended up at Patsy Dotson's and spent a very pleasant late afternoon watching the sun sink toward the horizon as we sank into a couple of Pimm's Cups. We sat with our feet on her railings and waved at everybody we knew. Patsy, a writer, does this every day she's up here.

"I can make all my calls without ever leaving the porch." She grinned.

She had a point. I said hi to almost everybody I was planning to call, just sitting and drinking with Patsy. And Paul caught up with some former *Post* colleagues—from other bureaus, yet.

"What you doing out here, Barkley?"

"Man, I'm Northwest bureau chief. It's in *Seattle*. Need I say more?"

We agreed to return for brunch before leaving on Sunday. Brunch at Patsy's mother's house was legendary; besides the wonderful food (both Patsy and her mom, Geneva, were great cooks), there was an ever-changing cast of characters that wandered through.

And brunch just might prove to be fertile ground that, planted with the right inquiries, would yield some useful information as to what had really happened to Ev.

11

We could smell the food and hear the folks well before we got to Patsy's house. Paul sniffed the air appreciatively and began rubbing his hands together in greedy anticipation.

"Yes, yes, *yes*—we gonna be fed well this afternoon, children!"

"Anybody ever tell you you're spending too much time watching the Christian Broadcasting System?" His imitation of one of the few black ministers on "the other CBS" was uncanny.

"Geneva Dotson's cooking is enough to make anybody get religion. I hope she made crab cakes."

According to Patsy, who had called just before we left, Geneva had. And Grand Marnier crêpes, and two kinds of bacon—"turkey for the wimps and pork for the real bacon eaters!"—and home fries and grits and buttered English muffins and a basketful of pastries from the Black Dog, with at least a half-dozen pots of homemade preserves of fruit that had come from Vineyard gardens and orchards.

Geneva saw us through the big living room window and came running down the walkway. Her outstretched arms indicated it was Big Hug time.

"Girl, it's been too long! How's your mama? Why're you so skinny? You like Patsy, always on some kind of crazy diet, like those bony white girls? I hope you're gonna be black and eat today!"

I hugged Gee back. Patsy's mother had a raspy voice that reflected her lifetime cigarette habit. At the nagging of her children, she'd switched from Camels to Virginia Slims and now sucked on her cancer sticks through an elegant tortoiseshell holder her oldest son, Virgil, had brought back from a trip to London. She was a tall woman with hair that had turned platinum in her early thirties. She'd never bothered to tint it, and now it was part of her persona — so much so that the *Amsterdam News* had once dubbed her the Silver Fox. A half-dozen gold bangles from the Indies clattered on her right arm, an interesting foil to the man's gold watch that was clasped around her left wrist. She smelled like an intoxicating combination of l'Air du Temps, suntan oil, cigarette smoke, and vodka tonics.

"Gee, I'd like for you to meet my friend Paul Butler. He was just rhapsodizing about your crab cakes. He happened to have been in New York last March when you sent some to one of Patsy's dinner parties, so if he dies this afternoon —"

"—I'll die happy." Paul laughed, not in the least ashamed. He made a little mock bow and handed a large bouquet to Gee. "For our elegant hostess."

Gee took the lilies and sniffed deeply, while caressing the tails of the white satin ribbon that were wrapped around the stems. "Any man who can find fresh Casablancas on a Sunday morning in this cow town is all right in my book. Thank you, sweetie." She took his arm and walked him toward the deck. "I love a black man who treats black women right!" She tossed the flowered skirt of her sundress girlishly and grinned her famous red-lipstick grin. Paul grinned back.

Jesus. I'd be lucky if I got a crab *crumb*.

"Yo, girl, you out here letting my mother flirt with your man?" Patsy laughed, kissing me lightly. I held up the bottle of (unribboned) Moët, which had gone unnoticed in all the fuss about the flowers, and shrugged.

"He's not 'my' man. And what can I say? She likes Casablancas."

"Yeah? Well *I* like a nice *appellation contrôllée* myself. Thanks for being classy enough to bring a good bottle. You can't *believe* what some of these Negroes dragged in the door!" she whispered, as we slipped into a side door that led to the mud room.

No laundry folded in neat piles today. Instead, the washer and dryer tops had been pressed into service as an extra table, and both held an assortment of bottles. Some of them were quite nice. Two of them had screw tops. One you could buy for three dollars at the drugstore, if you caught the right sale.

"That particular one came from someone our age who should know better."

She pointed through the window to a lanky guy dressed in khaki shorts and tasseled loafers, no socks. "He's a corporate lawyer, makes more than you and me put together. One of your bottles could've bought *eight* of his, and you'd have had change left over." We snickered. Too tacky for words.

"Go get you a plate. I'll bring a cold bottle out in a minute."

Paul, of course, was already eating. There was a space where his first helping of crab cakes had been, and he was happily plowing through a pile of home fries and fruit salad. He was deep in conversation with two lawyers, one of them a distinguished-looking older man. The other, Patsy's screw-top-bottle guy, was speaking about the likelihood of Everett Carson's killer ever coming to justice.

I nodded and sat down and began eating while they continued.

"He's black and this is still America—or have things changed overnight?" asked the older man, who was, in fact, a judge on the Second Circuit Court of Appeals. Laughter and applause broke out all around us, as eavesdroppers registered their agreement.

"Watch it now, Lester!" someone called out. "You know you're talking to a reporter!"

"Uh-huh," Hizzoner said, pointing his fork, which had a shrimp impaled on the end, at my chest. "That was strictly off the record, young lady. You *do* know what off the record means, don't you?"

"Oh, yes, sir—and so do you. So you know you have to give that caveat *before* you say your piece."

"*Oooooh.*" It was the sound of playground observers gleefully looking forward to a butt-whipping contest. Conversation had stopped.

The judge laughed. "Girl, I used to change your diapers, right along with Woody's; don't start with me!" He angled his smooth cheek for a kiss, which I happily gave. The nosey parkers went back to their assorted conversations.

"Hey, Judge Williams, long time no see. How is Woody, anyway?"

"Still using a Columbia law degree to sell bean pies, honey. Nothing's changed."

He made light of it, but the one consistent pain in Lester Williams's life was that his eldest son, Lester Wood Williams III, had turned his back on his middle-class roots and decided to Do For Self with the Nation of Islam. Woody wasn't really selling bean pies, he was a valued legal adviser to the Nation. But to most mainstream black parents, he might as well have been offering to wash windshields with a spray bottle and a squeegee near the Triborough Bridge; to them, what he was doing Just Wasn't Respectable. Big Lester and his wife, Mora, had hoped Woody was just going through a stage — but it was a stage that had lasted more than two decades so far. They saw him once or twice a year, and it was always politely strained.

Woody, now married to a dutiful Muslim wife and the father of two children, saw his father as an idealistic cog in a racist system; his father saw the son as hopelessly deluded. As if to make up for their older brother's rebelliousness, the two younger Williams boys had finished law school and were practicing in private firms. One was on his way to becoming a premier civil rights attorney. The other was a corporate lawyer specializing in environmental litigation.

"But seriously, if it had been S. I. Newhouse instead of Everett Carson, don't you think they'd have been farther along than they are in this thing?" Screw-Top asked condescendingly.

Shows how much he knew magazine publishing; *everybody* in the industry has wanted to kill S. I. Newhouse at some point in his career.

"Maybe," I conceded, "but it would still be hard. It happened at a convention. Everybody left the next day. No one knows what the motive might have been—"

"So race doesn't matter? You the new PR gal for the cops?" Screw-Top asked archly. The conversation around us had stopped again.

"Of course it matters, but it's probably not central to this particular case. After all, it happened at a convention of mostly black people." Fuck you, cheapskate.

The brunch crowd thought that over for a minute, and the murmurs of several different conversations began again. I was relieved to see Patsy walking my way with a cold bottle of good Champagne, the kind that's legally entitled to its capital C.

Screw-Top put down his empty plate and held out his hand. "Patsy, let a man do that for you. If it makes a big pop when you open it, that means you've bruised the wine." He turned to me. "I hate it when that happens."

"Oh, is *that* why you brought those screw-top bottles, so the wine wouldn't be bruised by the inexperienced among us?" I asked, sweetly.

Out of the corner of my eye, I saw Paul grin.

The ooooh sound started up again.

Laughing silently, Patsy handed me the bottle. I swiftly took the dish towel she offered and wrapped it around the bottle to tighten my grip. Then I pulled the bottle away from the cork a few times and tugged gently. The silent deck heard a tiny *pop!*, an almost-imperceptible sigh, then nothing. I tipped the sweating bottle toward Screw-Top.

"Champagne?"

Pissed but not stupid, Screw-Top extended his flute and I filled it.

"You know"—he leered at me—"when they're properly opened, Champagne bottles should always sound like the sigh of a contented woman."

Jeez, this fool just wouldn't give up.

"Depends on the bottle. And the woman. Nice meeting you."

I went on to fill the glasses of the folks around me. That boy had more nerve than Carter had pills! I've never ever sounded like a champagne bottle being opened—and I've had a few contentment-inducing experiences. (None recently, but he didn't need to know that.)

A long brown arm presented itself to me, an empty flute attached to the hand at the end. "Well done, Alex. It's about time someone gave that one a taste of his own medicine."

The woman was striking: maybe five-ten, large-boned but athletic looking. She wore her wavy hair natural and short, brushed straight back. Her white capri pants hugged well-toned thighs and ended in the middle of a pair of extremely nice calves. She wore a blue-and-white striped shirt with the tails knotted at her waist and navy espadrilles; one ankle was encircled with a dainty gold chain dangling tiny bells. I'd been brought up to consider ankle bracelets, like tattoos and inch-long fingernails, tawdry. (But nobody would have accused my mother, then or now, of living on fashion's cutting edge.) Somehow, on this woman, it looked right.

I must have been staring at the ankle thingie longer than I'd realized, because the woman laughed. "I've wanted one for years, but you know what our mamas would have said." She paused.

"Nice girls don't do that?"

"Yeah. But that was before rap and punk rock and all these people who feel free to show up in public without hardly covering their 'possibles.' " She paused, grinning wickedly. "You don't know who I am, do you?"

I was mortified but figured I'd been peeped, so I might as well confess. "Actually, it's been bugging the hell out of me, because you look like somebody I should know, but I'm sure we haven't met before."

She giggled. "Oh, we have, Alex—but I looked completely different. I'll give you a hint: It was at Tony Shepperd's L.A. premiere of *Romp!*"

I remembered the movie. It hadn't been worth the half-hour wait to get out of the parking lot afterward, but I'd interviewed Tony Sheppherd once for *Radiance* and had ended up on the press mail-

ing list ever since. It was a slow night and I didn't have anything better to do, so I went. But this babe's face wasn't ringing a bell. I must
have looked as puzzled as I felt.

"Remember the woman who was screaming at the caterers and
trying to position the photographers?"

Sure. A big chunky woman with too much fussy jewelry and a
muumuu made of African-inspired cloth, with more extensions than
Patti LaBelle in her heyday. She was rumored to be the most power-
ful black publicist in New York. . . .

"Esmé?"

"Ta-da!" She actually pirouetted in delight.

"Wow! Where's the rest of you? Oh, God, that didn't come out
right. I mean you look . . . you look . . . *fabulous!*"

And she did. Esmé Marshall had lost a ton of weight and had
changed her style, too. Gone were the extensions, the power nails,
and the over-the-top jewelry. The new Esmé looked like an ad for an
American couturier: sleek, streamlined, and expensive, even in play
clothes. Losing the weight and cutting her hair had made her look
years younger; so had trading the dragon claws for short nails in
sheer polish.

"Guess how much I lost? Guess!"

"Oh, gee. . . ."

I hate doing that. Guess too much and it sounds like you're saying, Wow, were you a pig before or what? Guess too little and you
diminish the dieter's sense of accomplishment. Shit.

"Seventy-five pounds! I still weigh a lot, but it's all muscle." She
pinched the back of her upper arm. No middle-aged wobble. I was
impressed. "Fourteen percent body fat," she proclaimed, with well-
deserved pride.

"G'on, girl! How'd you do it?"

"Going to the gym every day for an hour. Eating three meals a
day, instead of skipping two and then eating a whole refrigerator's
worth of food at night, 'cause I was so starved by that time. Learning
to meditate. Using homeopathic remedies to increase my energy
and strengthen my immune system. Getting my life in order. Stop-

ping the search for Mr. Right, starting to be responsible for my own happiness."

It sounded like a *Radiance* article—"10 Ways to Take Charge of Your Life"—but it obviously worked for her.

"Congratulations, Esmé. I wouldn't have known who you were if you hadn't told me."

She laughed. "Yeah, that's why I didn't get to NABJ until the Awards Dinner; I wanted to unveil the new me when they announced the Humanitas Award. We organized the AfriCare fundraiser that received the award. Even though I was working, I had such a good time—I kept passing all these people and greeting them by name, and none of them knew who I was!"

Well, at least I wasn't alone in my cluelessness. Then something occurred to me.

"Didn't you organize the stuff for Ev's service, too?"

Esmé's face immediately lost its party gaiety.

"Yes, that was us. Frankie Harper called and asked me to pull something together. It was hard, because I'd already committed to doing Ashley Austin's premiere in New York, but I couldn't say no."

Ashley Austin was a thirtysomething singer with a five-octave range and enough lung power to blow out a kerosene lantern at fifty paces. She had an impressive voice, but she was a first-class diva who required constant hand-holding from an extensive entourage of old friends, family, and newly acquired leeches, all of whom were on her payroll. No wonder Esmé had stayed in New York to supervise the post-premiere party: To leave Miss Austin (as she insisted on being addressed) in the hands of anyone other than Esmé's own would have made her life hell for months to come, and Miss Austin was one of Esmé's most famous clients.

"But all Ashley's stuff must have been arranged months earlier. Wouldn't she have understood if you slipped away for an old friend's memorial service?"

"She understands that she's a client who keeps me on retainer," Esmé said tightly. "She expects *her* needs to come first, whatever else happens. I bill her accordingly."

"Well, a girl's gotta eat. But your staff did a great job. The reception at the museum was truly lovely. Even Chip Wiley was impressed."

Esme rolled her eyes upward. "Oh, well, now I can sleep nights."

We grinned, bonding over our non-fondness for Chip. Then she broke the bond.

"Uh, Alex, I've been meaning to ask you: Who was that brother you were talking to with that knucklehead Walter Edsel and Judge Williams?" (Walter Edsel—a perfect name for Screw-Top!)

"You mean Paul Butler? He's in the Washington Bureau of the *Times.*"

Her eyebrows arched in comprehension. "Oh, *that's* why I hadn't met him before. Is he yours?"

That was Esmé, cutting to the chase.

"He's my *friend*, Esmé, nothing more. We've known each other for years."

"Hmmm. In that case, would you mind if I—you know— checked him out?"

Guess the search for Mr. Right was on again. Change that to Nine Ways to Take Charge of Your Life.

"Be my guest." I shrugged. "Everybody's grown."

I looked over to a corner of the deck where Paul was laughing with Patsy and two other New Yorkers. His chambray shirt was rolled up on his forearms and opened to mid-chest. The deep blue was a nice contrast to his faded jeans and brown ankles in their battered Topsiders. In the sun his teeth flashed even and white. Maybe I minded more than I thought. But I'd been cutting off my metaphorical nose to spite my face for so long, I was starting to look like Michael Jackson. Old habits die hard, though; I wasn't hardly going to let Esmé know Paul was looking more attractive every hour we were thrown together. I took a deep breath and began to conduct my own rhinoplasty, sans anesthesia, of course.

"Want me to introduce you?"

"No, I think I'd rather introduce myself. See ya."

So I watched as Esmé sauntered over to the quartet, her ankle bracelet tinkling ever so faintly.

But before she got to introduce herself, Geneva intervened.

"Esmé, I want you to meet somebody," Gee cooed, drawing an obviously annoyed Esmé in the opposite direction from Paul and Patsy. He never even noticed.

Patsy discreetly circled her thumb and forefinger, Buckwheat shorthand for Oh-Tay! She and Geneva must have had a discussion at some point, because, between the two of them, Esmé never got within striking distance of Paul during brunch.

As we helped Patsy and Geneva clean up around three o'clock, I cataloged aloud what we'd accomplished in the last forty-eight hours. We'd learned that Chip had an alibi for his whereabouts the night Ev was killed—and also a motive. Figured out Webb was indeed the hot date of choice this summer. Discovered why Esmé hadn't been to Ev's funeral (I made a mental note to check the New York paper's party pages to see if she was in any of the pictures at the Austin premiere). And (a note of individual accomplishment) through the generosity of one of Patsy's good friends whom I knew slightly, I'd found us a way to get down to New York, even if it made Paul's stomach do flip-flops.

"You said yes to *what*? Without even asking me?" Paul was livid.

"Well, we only had a one-way on Cape Air and they don't have any seats out till tomorrow. We could go standby on the ferry, but we might have to wait a few hours to get on, and by the time we took the bus from Woods Hole to Logan for a flight to New York, the last shuttle might have left. And we'd miss our appointment with Frankie."

Paul looked at me in undisguised annoyance. "You're going to enjoy this, aren't you?"

"Enjoy what?" I asked innocently.

"Watching me white-knuckle it for an hour."

"Look, if you can catch a ride back with someone from New York who's leaving, do. But whoever it is probably won't have room for both of us, and it will take you six hours to get home. I just thought this was more efficient. I know how you admire efficiency."

"Fine. Tell him we'll meet him at the airport whenever he says. Do we know anything about this guy's flying ability?"

It was a legitimate question, since during the previous year, a number of self-piloting celebrities had killed themselves by overestimating their airborne expertise.

"Only that he's been doing it since he was fourteen, owns his own plane, flies up here almost every weekend, and pilots himself to Black Ski every year. I figure if he can land in Denver's suicide-strip airport, he can land almost anywhere."

I had a point; Denver's private airport is known as an airplane-eater.

Paul sighed. A direct flight did seem to be the simplest way to get home, even if it was on a dreaded four-seater.

"Okay, I'll do it."

"Cheer up, honey." Gee laughed, taking his damp dish towel away and kissing him lightly. "I flew in one of those in Alaska with Patsy's father one year. At first I didn't want to do it, but when I got up there in that little plane, swooping over those glaciers, it was like previewing heaven."

"Gee," Paul said, hugging her good-bye, "I don't *want* to know what it's like before I get there."

"*If* you get there," Patsy pointed out. "You are, after all, a journalist. Me, I'm not bucking for heaven. All the truly interesting people are going to be somewhere else."

That's Patsy, always interested in a good party.

So we kissed the Dotson ladies and went home to spend the rest of the afternoon with Webb. My socialite uncle had been up and out before we'd left for Patsy's. According to the note he left under the magnet on the refrigerator, he had a hole between brunch somewhere in Edgartown (a polo-shirt-and-blazer meal with his contemporaries) and dinner with a group of friends at a Oak Bluffs restaurant (a small birthday party for—surprise—a comely divorcée).

We spent the rest of the afternoon playing tonk, gossiping, and sipping mimosas on the front porch. At six o'clock, resplendent in white ducks and a navy linen blazer, Webb drove us to the airport, where I introduced him to Thad Gordon.

• • •

"Not John's boy?" Webb asked, looking in amaze- ment at the handsome six-foot-three-inch young man before him.

Thad grinned. "Yes, sir."

"Damn! How old are you now? Aren't you still in grad school or something?"

"Almost thirty. I'm a partner at Towne and Crain."

"God!" Webb gasped, genuinely amazed. "How'd you get to be so old so *quick*?"

Thad laughed. "Time flew while you and Dad were making a living, I guess."

Webb looked at him admiringly. "Yes, indeed, it certainly did. Well, take good care of my niece and her friend here. I know your dad taught you well, so I'm not worried about you-all getting back in one piece."

He turned to us.

"Before he retired, Thad's father was one of the first brothers to fly for the commercial airlines. He's much younger than I am, but I know him as a frat brother. Alpha man."

Thad grinned and spread his hands wide, palms skyward. "Is there any other kind?" They shook hands in what I guessed was a tribal Greek shake.

"Okay, I'm off. The champagne's getting warm while I'm standing round jawing with you young folks. Don't want to keep the birthday girl waiting!"

Webb gave me a hug, shook hands with Paul, clapped Thad on the shoulder, and was gone.

Thad took my bag and indicated we should follow him out a glass door to the far end of the tarmac. Several small planes painted in bright colors were tethered to what looked like iron blocks by taut wire ropes.

"Ever been in one of these before?" he asked.

"Only on the way out here," Paul muttered.

I'll bet he was already regretting having eaten so many crab cakes. I'd squirreled a couple of garbage bags into my tote, just in case the flight got choppy and he had to heave. But I didn't think I should tell him unless he showed signs of needing them. Packing barf bags doesn't inspire confidence in anxious flyers.

Thad laughed. "This is a Cessna. It's a little smaller than the twelve-seaters they fly on and off the island."

I thought I heard Paul mutter "Oh, great," but I wasn't sure.

"But it's a sweet ride. I think if you don't mind, Paul, I'm going to sit you in back to balance us out. Alex, you'll ride shotgun next to me."

We climbed into the small cabin. Paul immediately buckled himself into his seat belt. Thad looked amused but didn't say anything.

"Alex, I'm going to give you some co-pilot duties: I need you to check off the things I call out right after I say them, okay?"

He handed me a clipboard with a grid on it and room for checks. For the next ten minutes we ran through the list—oil and fuel pressure, brakes, wheel release, wipers—till we were done. Then he put on headphones and began to speak to the control tower.

When the tower gave permission, we taxied out onto the runway and got in line behind two other similarly sized planes. About ten minutes later, we were rushing down the runway, faster and faster and a little bumpily. I felt a twinge of guilt—maybe this *was* a mean thing to do to Paul—

And then we were aloft. Almost instantly the ride got smoother, although the drone of the engines seemed louder without the road noise. I looked down and could see the outlines of the Vineyard become apparent. Due east, there was Chappaquiddick on the "hook," the chalk cliffs of Gay Head at the western end, its lighthouse part of the island quartet (the others were on points of the Chops, West and East, and near Chappaquiddick). We could see the frothy wakes of the ferries from Vineyard Haven and the sunset sailors off Squibnocket and Menemsha heading back to port. The lowering sun gilded the waters surrounding the island until the landmass floated black on a sea of molten coppery-gold. It was so beautiful no one talked for several minutes. Paul seemed to be as enthralled with the view as I was. Geneva was right. It *was* a preview of heaven.

We didn't talk a whole lot for the rest of the ride because we had to shout above the engine noise. We chatted just enough to learn that Thad was single and lived on the Upper West Side. Had a girlfriend with an MBA who worked for the international division of a large consulting firm. Was "starting to think about" getting married—which elicited the longest conversation from Paul yet. (Basically he advised Thad to "be really, really sure. You don't want to get divorced if you don't have to.") Thad's dad had, indeed, taught him to fly when he was fourteen, and he'd soloed at sixteen. "Dad used to talk to me about how beautiful it was, up in the air alone. He flew a bunch of missions when he was Vietnam. Got a Distinguished Flying Cross before he stopped."

New York didn't exactly appear out of nowhere— we'd been following the coast all the way since Rhode Island—but it was impressive, nonetheless. We flew over Yankee Stadium, which was dark—either a no-game night, or the home team was playing away. But the major thoroughfares and the local highways were streamers of pulsing white light. Our approach pattern took us past the FDR, where the squat housing projects of Spanish Harlem gave way to the Upper East Side's glittering high-rises. Sticking out at the edge was Carl Schurz Park and Gracie Mansion; the park's walkways were studded with necklaces of streetlamps.

We floated past Stuyvesant Oval, around City Hall, its Beaux-Arts architecture artfully lit, and past the Brooklyn Bridge, its Gothic arches highlighted with floodlights. The Brooklyn-Queens Expressway flowed white (incoming headlights) and red (outgoing taillights). The plane followed the BQE to the Queens outback.

In the distance, we could see the Statue of Liberty planted firmly on star-shaped Liberty Island. The lady faced impassively eastward, her right arm raising the celebrated torch into the evening sky. Thad spoke softly into his mouthpiece as the tower relayed its final instructions, and then we were looping down in big spirals, past the suburban tract houses in farthest Queens, past the big airfield at Kennedy, to the commuter field nearby.

The runway rushed up to greet us, and after a good-sized bump ("Sorry about that") we were earthbound once more. I felt a profound sense of disappointment. Looking back, I was amazed to discover that Paul seemed downcast, too.

Thad looked at us and laughed. "Don't feel bad. Everyone who does this for the first time and likes it feels like a kid when the merry-go-round stops. I still kinda feel that way every time I have to turn out the lights and lock her up till next time."

Reluctantly, the three of us undid our harnesses. We handed the bags out while Thad ran through his checklist again, left a note for his mechanic, and tucked the flight manifest under his arm. Then he passed an open palm in a half-arc at chest level.

"A dee buh dee buh dee—that's all, folks!"

"Thanks, Porky. Since you gave us a ride home, can we give you a ride into the city and maybe some dinner?" It was only eight-thirty.

Towne & Crain's youngest partner ducked his head like a sixteen-year-old. "Thanks, but Genna got back in town last night, and I think she might come out to meet me."

When we stepped through the doors into the waiting room, a petite pretty woman with a broad smile and dark shoulder-length hair was the only black person there. Her caramel skin gleamed against the deep V-neck of her cream silk sweater. A pastel Hermès scarf was casually knotted around one handle of her Italian leather handbag. She was a perfect hybrid: American casual and European elegant.

"Genna?" I asked.

"Definitely."

From the way he was looking at her, they'd probably be married sooner rather than later.

"What up, cap'n?" she teased.

Thad gave her a chaste peck and introduced us. She graciously offered to drive us into the city, but we told her Thad had taken us far enough, and we didn't want to intrude on their time. We exchanged cards and promised to get together when they got out to the West Coast in a couple of months. The handsome couple disappeared into Genna's green Saab convertible; I could see Thad through the window, giving her the kiss he would have if we hadn't been with him when he first saw her, and was glad we hadn't taken Genna up on her offer.

Almost before I could finish that thought, a hand pulled me away. "C'mon, nosy, our cab is here. You can pick out their silver pattern and name the babies on the way into the city. And what is this?" One of the plastic bags had slithered out of the tote's open top and was flapping in the breeze like a ragged shutter in a windstorm.

"Oh . . . insurance. In case you got airsick."

He was horrified. "You thought I was gonna be a punk and *puke*?"

"Well, my grandmother always used to say, 'Better to have it and not need it.' "

"Just for that," Paul warned, dumping the bags in the cab's already opened trunk, "you're buying dinner. Plan on spending lots of money. I'm suddenly *very* hungry."

12

I thought we'd had reservations at one of the nicer chain hotels in midtown, but when the taxi headed for the East Side after we crossed the Triborough, I'd looked at Paul.

"Just shut up and ride. We changed hotels."

"Why? We got a good deal at the other one and you finally got what you wanted—twin beds!"

The cabbie, a middle-aged Indian gentleman, looked at us both with interest in his rear-view mirror.

"The Titanium people messed up. There's a convention of orthopedists in town, about four thousand of them, apparently, and somehow our room got lost in the shuffle."

That had happened to me before, too—and I'd ended up in the hotel equivalent of bad fast food in a Third World country. I thought the Titanium people *never* messed up—that's why members paid them the big bucks. Now, however, was probably not the time to point that out.

"Uh oh. So where'd they put us—or do we have to sleep on a bench in Grand Central?"

"I had to jump up and down a bit, but I got us a room at a small hotel. I thought nobody would be in the city over Labor Day weekend, but it just goes to show what I know." I let that pass, too.

The taxi had turned off Madison down 64th Street and stopped before a glass awning.

"The Plaza Athenée? You've gone certifiably insane, haven't you?" I'd thought the chain price of $275 per night was bad enough—this was going to be *much* worse.

Paul had paid the driver, who'd handed our bags to a handsome young bellman. I stared at the small trees in front of the hotel, they were threaded with hundreds of tiny white lights. I guess for some people, it was Christmas every day. Women in Serious Jewelry were emerging from brass-edged revolving doors. They were on the arms of men in well-cut summer suits, and they got into waiting Town Cars. By staying there, we were probably lowering the median age of the place by about ten years.

Paul walked directly over to registration as if he'd spent time here before. While he gave them his card and filled out the forms, I looked around. The lobby was a beautiful little jewel of a room, done in tones of gold, black, and celadon. Gilt Louis Seize chairs with black leather upholstery flanked ebony tables with vases of fresh flowers. The chairs' fluted legs were placed firmly upon twin Aubussons in celadon, cream, and rust. Down a few steps, black marble cherubs holding aloft candelabra of gold bouquets with ivory tapers silently pointed the way to the elevators. Elevators with brushed-brass doors opened soundlessly to disgorge more well-dressed people carrying $2,000 handbags and briefcases of marginally endangered species, with wristwatches that cost more than I make in several months. They murmured to each other in many languages other than English as they walked into the balmy night to wait for their cars. Oh yeah—definitely our kind of place. When they find out what kind of money we don't have, they'll have a bouncer show us the door, *très vite*.

"Madame Butler? You will come and sign the register, please?"

A willowy blonde in a navy uniform with an ethereal smile held a pen toward me and gestured to the space in the big leather book where I should scribble my name.

"Madame Butler will probably use her maiden name to register," Paul said straight-faced. "She seems to use mine only for correspondence—and of course, the bills." Take my husband—please.

I signed—my own name—and the young woman closed the register. "*Voilà!* I am so sorry we did not have the two beds—Mr. Butler explained about his back—but I believe you will find your room— and your bed—quite *confortable*. My name is Nancy, and I will be here until eleven this evening. Please do not hesitate to call if we can do anything for you." She sounded like a commercial for Air France: "my name is Non-cee. Pleese do not 'esitate to call eef we can do ann-ee-sing for yew . . ."

Non-cee signaled the bellman we were ready to go up, and he took us to the third floor. The room had a cream pile rug you could get lost in, a bed big enough to play volleyball on—framed in a Louis Something-or-Other gilded headboard—a tapestry love seat and a couple of arm chairs. On the dresser (more Louis Whoever) was a good-sized bronze box of Godiva chocolates and a signed note from the manager wishing us a pleasant stay. La-di-da.

The bathroom was black and cream marble, with a telephone, a television, and one of those French magnifying mirrors that cost $300. My shiny, suntanned face was magnified about a zillion times. Looking at my pores, I didn't know whether I'd want one of these even if I could afford to buy one. With a cheaper mirror, I could remain blissfully ignorant of my many imperfections.

"Everything is to your satisfaction?" the young bellman asked. He seemed genuinely interested in our answer.

"You may have to call the police to make me leave," I assured him. He smiled. He thought I was kidding.

Paul tipped him and the door closed softly. "He thought you were kidding, you know."

I grinned, looking in the refrigerator in the closet-sized kitchenette.

"Yeah. Wait'll he finds out I wasn't. How did we end up here, anyway?"

"I told you, our original room was given away . . ."

". . . No, no, I know that part of the story. How did we end up *here*?" I waved my arms to indicate our specific location.

"Oh. Well . . . when the Titanium people messed up, I told them they had to make it right, and the only thing that would make it right for me was a room as good as or better than the one that was given away—for the same price. I had a choice of here and someplace else, and since this was French and I know how you like French, here we are."

Voilà, as Non-cee would say.

I looked at him in undisguised admiration. "Damn, you're good! This room is so cute, let's just forget about seeing Frankie. Let's just stay in and order room service, eat chocolates, and pretend we're rich."

"Get a grip. We have dinner reservations in a half-hour. You'll want to wear a dress—if you've got one in that bag."

Of course I'd brought one, I'd brought two. It was just going to take a jolt from an industrial-strength steam iron to unscrunch them. I picked up the phone to see what the valet could do. Then I called home to check my messages.

In the days since Ev died, Henry Adams and I had become a regular item. It seemed I got a call from him just about every other day. It was always some *Diaspora*-related business. Usually it was related to his anxiety over who might be competing with him for Everett's position as *Diaspora*'s editor in chief.

Sure enough, this evening there was another message from Henry.

"Alex, I thought you should know that the board has added four new members: here are the names . . . do you know them? Can you put in a good word for me? Call me immediately, please."

Stop the world—Henry wants something. Curious, I called. Turned out I knew two of the contenders, and knew of the other two. One was the head of the journalism department at Northwestern, one had a seat on the N.Y. Stock Exchange, one was a nationally-prominent civil rights activist, and one was a D.C. mover-and-shaker type. Looks like big changes were going to be underway soon. And Henry was, predictably, anxious.

"Why would my word mean anything to them Henry—and why do you need a good word put in for you, anyway?"

Henry was audibly annoyed.

"Well, it seems that *someone* on the board—one of the new people—thinks it's a good idea to look at an array of candidates for Everett's position. I'm just to keep things running until they make up their minds," he said bitterly, "and perhaps be rewarded with the position permanently—and perhaps not."

"Hmmm . . . Frankie Harper was in that same position, remember, and it worked out well for her. She now heads *Radiance*."

"Begging your pardon, Alex, but *Radiance* is not on the same level with *Diaspora* . . . it's a women's magazine."

Oh no he didn't, either!

"Oh I'm sorry Henry—I didn't mean to insult your masculine sensibilities. But frankly, *Radiance* has a much higher circulation, a subscription base that's three times larger than *Diaspora*'s, and it's been around for twenty years. So maybe you're right—maybe I *shouldn't* be comparing the two."

Snotty little bastard—no wonder the board is considering other people!

Henry took a deep, cleansing breath; or maybe he was counting to ten.

"Anyway, Alex, I just wanted to let you know that according to what I've heard—not that anyone will tell *me* anything—a list is being drawn up and board members will be calling contributing editors, consultants, and some outside people in publishing with the names of the half-dozen candidates they'd like to consider."

"Okay, Henry." Your point being?

"My point is," he continued patiently in that "haven't-you-got-it-yet-stupid" monotone he liked to affect. "I would appreciate your vote of confidence. You know I've practically run the magazine for Everett these past two years, since he's been so much in demand as a speaker and panelist on those TV news shows."

"Henry, I have no idea who's on the list at this point, and I have no idea that the board would ever consult with the likes of me, but if they do, I will take your request very seriously. I know how hard you've worked to run *Diaspora* in Everett's absence."

I also knew that Everett had tired of so much traveling and had expressed, to me, anyway, a resolution to stick closer to home in the coming months. Which meant that Henry's run as overseer might have been about to come to an end.

There was a brief silence.

"Does that mean you can't promise me your vote?"

I hedged. "I don't have a vote, and if I did, I wouldn't want to foreclose my options this early in the game—but frankly, I can't really see anyone running *Diaspora* other than you at this point." I couldn't envision anyone really *wanting* the job other than Henry, but who new who was on that list?

"Well." He sighed. "I guess I'll just have to hope that you're in that frame of mind when you get the call. Thanks for your time, Alex."

He clearly was disappointed, but I couldn't lie to him. What if Signe had been on that list?

Since her name had come up, I called her to let her know we'd arrived, and, before I hung up, asked if someone had offered her the top job at *Diaspora*.

"Leave the *Times*—for *Diaspora*?" She'd giggled. "I ain't *that* tired of my white people yet!" Then more seriously: "Frankly, someone should slap me if I ever want to be an editor in chief anywhere other than a magazine I start from scratch. And probably even then."

"Why would that be such a horrible idea?"

"You, of all people, shouldn't have to ask. Too much administrative bs, honey. I'm a writer—I want to *write*. Not edit someone else's writing. Remember, that's why I turned down the assistant Metro editor at the *Miami Herald*."

"That, and the fact that you hate Miami."

She'd shrugged. "That too."

Having dealt with Signe's ambitions—or lack thereof, as far as *Diaspora* went—we left for dinner.

It is amazing how much some people can stuff into their bodies without exploding. For instance, you would think that a *civilized* person, having single-handedly consumed the brunch equivalent of Thanksgiving dinner, would have been con-

tent to have a light supper on the evening of the same day, but
nooooo. Pig Boy, as we were leaving the room, cheerfully announced
that he intended to eat me into bankruptcy, and by God, he made
an impressive effort. Actually, it hadn't been that much of a feat,
considering the restaurant he chose.

When we stepped outside it was clear we weren't going to someplace nearby because he hailed a cab. And since we were going
downtown, and not towards Harlem, one actually stopped. Then he
told the driver to take us to Brooklyn.

"Brooklyn! You made me put on a dress and heels so we could go
eat in *Brooklyn?* You're losing it. And if I have to pay for a cab to
Brooklyn *and* dinner, you might as well ask brother here to pull over
to the nearest bodega when we get over the bridge, 'cause all I'll be
able to feed you is saltines . . ."

"Alex, listen to yourself—you're raving. Clearly in need of a stiff
martini. And of course I'm paying for the taxi. I'm not a complete
cretin."

Mollified, I settled down and watched the scenery glide by till we
got to our destination.

We'd ended up on the waterfront, in Brooklyn Heights, one of
the most beautiful parts of New York City. Even as I was gladdened
by the shimmering lights of the converted river barge before us, my
heart sank: I knew dinner was going to cost a pretty penny.

"The River Café," I said weakly. "What a nice surprise."

Paul held the door as we walked into the restaurant's cool dim-
ness. All around us, couples smiled at each other over cloth-draped
tables lit with candles. Beyond them, through seamless plate-glass
windows, Manhattan's magnificent skyline twinkled and blinked
like a sophisticated Oz, while the famous Gothic bridge soared just
above us.

I sighed inwardly. All the money I'd saved by hitching a ride back
with Thad was going to be spent—and then some—on dinner. But
it would be worth it, I knew. The one previous time I'd eaten here
(on someone else's expense account), the food had been as good as
the view. I was glad he'd suggested we change. In my simple silk
sheath and black lizard sandals, I looked like everyone else.

"Oh, well, in for a penny, in for a pound." Maybe I could find a second job when I got home. I was going to need one—Paul had that Hungry Man look in his eye.

We ate smoked fois gras (well, I did; Pig Boy had gravlax), grilled sturgeon, and one of the best roast chickens I'd ever had. Paul insisted we order different things, so we could share. We chatted about nothing in particular, and our hands kept crisscrossing the table for another forkful of this, another taste of that. I ate so much I knew I would have to go back to the gym—if, after paying for dinner, I could afford the monthly membership.

When the check came, I took a deep breath and reached for it, but Paul slapped my hand. He took out his Titanium card and placed it in the little leatherette folder, and a waiter quickly appeared and whisked it away.

"I'm confused. Wasn't *I* supposed to take *you* to dinner to make up for something?"

"Yeah, to make up for shanghaiing me onto Thad's plane. But I actually had a pretty good time—once I relaxed and realized he was a good pilot."

I swirled the last of my Calvados in the snifter and looked at him. The weekend had turned him a burnished-copper color, and his eyes danced in the soft light.

"If you had doubts, why'd you agree to come?"

"They weren't exactly doubts," he clarified, sipping a bit of his cognac, "they were more like *concerns*. But they weren't serious concerns, and I couldn't let you fly with him by yourself. God forbid something had happened and I'd have had to explain why I was still breathing and you weren't—to Webb, your mother, and my mother."

True. Clara is very fond of me. So, for that matter, is my mother. And Webb.

"Anyway"—he laughed, pocketing the card and coming around to pull out my chair—"I got my money's worth watching you squirm. When I ordered the Château d'Yquem with dessert you almost passed out! Worth every penny." Maybe I should just hire myself out for bar mitzvahs and birthday parties, I'm so damn amusing.

Dinner must've cost a bundle, and Paul must have been extraordinarily generous with the tip—our waiter practically wept to see us leave.

After we arrived back in our upgraded hotel room, I rummaged through the Godiva box while Paul channel-surfed. A split of Taittinger had magically appeared in the mini-refrigerator (*Compliments of the Titanium Card*, the note around its neck read), so we opened and drank it.

It was strange how comfortable I was getting, sharing a room with this man; we each were starting to know what the other was going to do before he did it. He plopped down and watched the news so I could have the shower first. I took the side of the bed closer to the window, because I knew he'd rather sleep closer to the door. Little routines just seemed to have fallen into place without either of us making any conscious decisions. We were almost beginning to feel like an old married couple—not that I'd know what being married really felt like.

Monday morning, Paul cheerfully ate an inde-cently large breakfast in the hotel's beautiful little restaurant, while I had my usual melon and *grande crème*. Then we left our keys with the concierge and went up to *Radiance*'s offices.

I'd successfully appealed to Paul's common sense and revulsion for tardiness, so we were, to my great joy, going downtown on the subway. It was only the Lexington Avenue line, but that was better than nothing. Paul watched with amusement as I stood in line and plunked down several dollars for a few tokens. He turned his token over and over, squinting, while people streamed around us, impatient to get to jobs they hated. I pulled him out of the main flow of traffic.

"What are you looking for?"

"The slots. Didn't the Y in NYC used to be slotted?" He held the token up for me to see; the famous stylized initials on the coin's face were solid.

"Urbanite, they stopped minting slotted tokens in Ronald Reagan's first term, almost twenty years ago. Cheaper to mint them solid. Don't you ever ride the subway when you're up here?" I dropped my coin in the box and pushed the heavy metal turnstile, which thrust me onto the platform for the downtown train.

"Hell, no." Paul snorted. "These things are unpredictable and"—he wrinkled his nose—"they *smell*." I did suddenly notice the pungent aroma of *eau de pee-pee*. Given the prediction for the day's heat, by evening rush hour it should really be ripe down here.

"If you're lucky enough to live in a city with public transportation you should support it," I said loftily, as I looked for the lights that signal an oncoming train.

So far, nothing. Just a swirl of litter in the wake of the newly departed uptown train, across the platform, and the plaintive wail of a distant saxophone playing a very respectable rendition of John Coltrane's interpretation of "My Favorite Things." The musician's case was open, but it only had a few coins—and a crumpled bag that judging by the label had once held doughnuts.

"When I'm here, I support public transportation by taking taxis. But give a brother a little credit—I do use buses and the Metro at home. Which are cleaner. Air-conditioned. And excuse me—but do *you* take the train in L.A.?"

"It doesn't *go* anywhere. It's the most expensive underground system in the world that doesn't go anywhere. But if it did, I would."

I could feel his eyes rolling in disbelief behind his shades.

Our non-air-conditioned train thundered into sight and screeched to a stop before us. A stream of already bored-looking people—lots of suits but a fair percentage of artsy-looking types too—poured out the double doors, shoving their way through the incoming passengers, who, per tradition, refused to give way so the outgoing could leave first. Just in case someone who doesn't play by the rules tries to slip in in front of them. Noo Yawkers.

I reveled in the ride downtown. I always love people-watching on the train. This was the first official day of the new school year for the public and parochial schools, so our car had a gaggle of Dominican girls in navy sweaters and plaid pleated skirts (with the waists rolled up to make them minis, of course), clutching the pole and giggling hysterically each time the swaying train pushed them up against an adult. Lots of Hugo Boss–wearing young executives, pointedly ignoring everyone in favor of their neatly quartered *New York Times*es. Several West Indian ladies in blue scrubs that seemed to indicate they were going all the way to Bellevue or to St. Vincent's in the Village. And there were lots of parents who, clearly, were escorting their backpack-wearing youngsters to school. Everyone was in his or her own little floating world. No man is an island—unless he's on the IRT at rush hour.

We took the Times Square Shuttle to the West Side ("from bad to worse," Paul grumbled), and when we emerged at 42nd and Broadway, a young man was playing Kenny G tunes on the sidewalk. His upturned cap was already half filled, as exiting customers continued to show appreciation for his tedious music by dropping coins—even dollars—into the cap. The Coltrane guy gets empty Krispy Kreme bags, while this schmo gets rich before 10 A.M. John Kennedy was right: Life is not fair.

Radiance was located in a building that is supposed to be emblematic of what the Convention & Visitors Bureau emphatically insists on calling the New Times Square. The gray Beaux-Arts facades of the square's older buildings were reflected in the new ones' dark-tinted glass. Movie houses that had shown girlie flicks were giving way to new office and restaurant complexes. Two major publishing houses had plopped themselves down scant feet away from doorways where beer-bellied hawkers used to entice visiting rubes into dark caverns to watch pneumatically enhanced women perform barely simulated sex acts, solo and with each other. The shops that sold overpriced cameras and tacky souvenirs to tourists were losing ground to mega-shops that sold overpriced theme merchandise from the Happiest Place on Earth and its competitors. The theater industry had received a shot in the arm as the economy improved, and banners advertising plays and musicals floated every-where, bright spots of color against the canyons of stone, steel, and glass.

As we stepped from Broadway into the frosty stillness of the lobby, Paul whistled. "Maybe they use it for ice-skating after hours."

The lobby did, as we say out on the Left Coast, give off that vibe; it was huge, glistening, and chilly. Partly from the incredibly effi-cient air-conditioning system, partly because every surface—vertical and horizontal—seemed to be composed of marble, glass, or chrome. We glided across a few acres of highly polished floor to the security desk. It was on a platform. The uniformed officer looked down at us like he was a hanging judge and we were convicted felons awaiting sentencing.

"Help you folks?" he asked neutrally.

You just knew if you gave the wrong answer a hidden door would open and uniformed guys with guns would escort you off the prem-ises—or worse.

We told him where we were going, and it must have been the right answer, because he directed us to the elevator bank and instructed us to take the middle set. Apparently each bank served a different series of floors. *Radiance*'s offices were not in the low-rent tier, but they weren't in the top third either. We checked ourselves in the shiny chrome doors, then shot upward to the twenty-second floor.

The receptionist, a startlingly pretty young woman with a regal arrangement of cornrows and a British accent, nodded when we told her Frankie expected us. "Have a seat, please, and her assistant will be out to fetch you in just one moment," she cooed. "They're finish-ing up a story conference."

Sure enough, a few moments later, another pretty woman swiveled in to greet us and show us back to Frankie's offices. This one wore a severely tailored taupe suit and chocolate high-heeled ankle straps with steel spikes. She introduced herself as Dinitra.

"Have you ever been here before?" she asked pleasantly, as we shook hands. I noticed she was wearing one of the world's biggest diamond engagement rings. Emerald-cut, set in platinum.

"Believe me, if I had, I'd remember." Paul grinned.

"Then let me take a moment to give you a quick tour. Frankie's finishing up with her editors, so we have a little time."

Dinitra walked us around the editorial floor. We met the Fashion & Style editor, who looked as if she did exactly that for a living, with her chignon of braids, black body-hugging dress, and geometric sterling bangles. The Books editor wore an aqua linen miniskirted suit, a short natural, and European-looking horn-rimmed specs. We couldn't tell how the the Food & Living editor was dressed, because she was wearing a lab jacket. "Recipe testing," she said cheerfully, offering us bites of mini salmon-and-wild-rice cakes she was preparing to share with the staff. (They were great.) The Poetry editor looked suitably ethereal in flowing lavender voile and a cascade of blond dreadlocks. And the managing editor was a tiny wraith of a woman in black leather pants and an antique beaded cashmere cardigan; she had a gamine haircut, a big smile, and a huge desktop that probably hadn't been clear for the last couple of years.

Paul was like a sugar junkie who has died and gone to chocolate heaven. Everywhere we looked there were attractive black women, in flavors that ran the gamut from milk to dark chocolate.

"Don't you hire any ugly women—or do you just hide them when you give the tour?"

Dinitra dimpled. "Why, Mr. Butler, I do believe you're giving us a compliment!"

"*Oh, yeah.*"

His eyes lingered once more on Dinitra's high metal heels. Pathetic.

"Careful you don't slip on his drool, honey." Falling off those stainless-steel stilettos could critically injure a girl.

Dinitra deposited us in Frankie's still-vacant office and, after we assured her that we were fine, no coffee, tea, or anything else was necessary, she let herself out and gently closed the door.

For my money, you can tell a lot about a person from his office. For instance, according to the photos published in

Chip's magazine, *Aspire* (and to Signe, who had profiled him for the *Times*), the furniture in Chip's office was all dark polished wood that was at least a hundred and fifty years old. His walls were covered in testimonials to himself: honorary degrees, service awards, and mahogany-framed photos with people like Donald Trump, Reginald Lewis, Felix Rohatyn, several Democratic presidents, and every New York mayor from Abe Beame through the current occupant of Gracie Mansion. Jake's would probably look pretty much the same: the Big Man school of interior design.

Frankie's space, on the other hand, was intensely personal. Her walls were covered too, but not with photos of herself with the rich and famous. Her desk, which looked like a plain pine table you could find in a farmhouse kitchen, was placed catty-corner at the end of the room. Behind it, to my right, was a large quilt on a frame, a beautiful fabric picture of black angels hovering near a golden ladder with a silver-bearded brown-skinned God smiling benignly from a throne of clouds. The adjoining wall held a grouping of simply framed paintings and drawings that looked as if a fifth-grader could have made them. In one, brown children in pastel clothes played ring-around-a-rosy in front of a little red schoolhouse. Another one showed workers bent over cotton plants, the sacks slung over their backs bulging with white blossoms. A black-and-white drawing of a chicken running across the yard made me gasp; it was done by a once-obscure Outsider artist named Bill Traylor. I had seen one like it years before in Washington and wanted it desperately, but at the time I couldn't square spending almost a thousand dollars of my meager reporter's salary.

"If you don't you'll be sorry," the gallery owner had warned me. Seeing it on Frankie's wall, I knew he'd been right.

There were several small tables scattered throughout the room that looked as if they were handmade by Shakers or by someone who admired Shaker work. Their tops held small African carvings, antique silver cups and bowls, some filled with a spicy potpourri, and old books with battered leather covers. I sneaked a look; they were autobiographies written by escaped slaves (*Martha Jackson: My Life As a Slave Girl, My Escape to Freedom*, published by the Society of Friends, Cambridge, Massachusetts, 1831). One table featured a small wire replica of the Eiffel Tower.

Above a round oak table that served as a sort of mini-conference area, Erzulie, the Haitian goddess of love and forgiveness, smiled serenely from the spangled surface of a *voudou* flag. On the windowsill nearest Frankie's desk were a few photos: Frankie and her husband, Neil Grayson, embracing on a beach somewhere, smiling, cheek to cheek, into the lens; the *Radiance* senior staff at what looked to be a country retreat (everyone was wearing cutoffs and sunglasses and sitting in Adirondack chairs in front of a small lake); Frankie and a young woman with an Angela Davis–style Afro, lounging at a sidewalk café on the Left Bank. They were wearing the obscenely short skirts that were the fashion back then and making a great show of being suitably blasé for the photographer. ("Look, Ma, we're drinking wine in the middle of the day! We're reading the newspaper—in *French*! We're soooooo sophisticated!") I have a few photos of myself like that too, taken in approximately the same place at about the same time.

Most prominently placed was a heavy silver frame with an old black-and-white snapshot of a lanky man and a woman holding the hands of the young girl who stood in front of and between them. They were standing in front of a cinder-block house with a corrugated tin roof.

The man, in khakis and a white short-sleeved shirt, was squinting and smiling. His arm was around his wife's waist. The woman, also in slacks and a camp shirt, was smiling too. The little girl, in a striped T-shirt, baggy shorts, and cap-toed sneakers, stood on prepubescent, coltish legs between her parents; she was smiling like her mother and squinting like her father. She held each parent's free hand, and a fuzzy aureole of hair glowed around her thin face. They all looked happy.

"That was taken a few years before my parents died. I was maybe nine or ten."

Frankie had slipped into the room as we—or I—tried to read her history on its walls.

"It's a great picture. I love your artwork too. Especially this Traylor. I almost bought one like it in Washington, about ten years ago. Seeing it on your wall, I'm kicking myself."

Frankie looked at the painting fondly. "Yes, I got that on the installment plan; I couldn't even think about buying it today if it was for sale. Or the others, either. They're Clementine Hunters, but I bought them from an American when I was in Paris, for very little. They weren't considered collectible then."

"Well, they are now," Paul pointed out. "I hope you've insured them well."

Frankie crossed over to the sofa and patted its white cotton cushion. "Very. Although if something happened to them, the money would be beside the point. I bought them because I loved them; they're like family to me. They remind me of Louisiana. I was born there, but my family moved away soon afterward. But I don't think you two came to see me to discuss my art collection, such as it is. So why don't we sit and talk about how you think I can help you out."

She wore a pale yellow silk suit and ropes of creamy pearls. Pearl earrings shone from her lobes, and her russet hair was piled on top of her head. Beneath her light tan, she looked drawn. Dark circles accented the deep blue of her eyes. Either she was working very hard or she still hadn't recovered from the shock of Everett's death.

"You know, I just can't seem to pull myself out of this hole I've been in since . . . since last week," Frankie began, as if she had read my mind.

"It's been a shock for everyone," I assured her.

She took a deep breath and seemed to calm herself; then she looked at Paul. "What do the police say? I keep thinking about poison, and how horrible that must have been."

"Jim Marron says the toxicology reports aren't back yet, but he's pretty sure they'll confirm what the coroner's office found in the autopsy. Basically, someone put something in his echinacea that gave him heart failure."

"And," I continued, "it probably had a cumulative effect. He might just have been feeling crummy—like you'd feel if you had a low-grade infection or a lingering case of the flu."

I looked around anxiously; maybe I'd scuttled the barf bags a couple of days too soon. Frankie definitely looked green around the gills. And the woven basket she was using for trash wouldn't recover if she had to hurl into it.

"God, of all people. Poor Ev! And those children, without a father. Did *you* know about them?"

Paul lowered himself into an armchair opposite us on the sofa; he passed a white handkerchief to Frankie, who dabbed at her eyes delicately.

"Thank you. You never see men with real handkerchiefs anymore."

Paul smiled. "I'm an old-fashioned kind of guy," he said gently. "And no, we didn't know about the twins. Until the funeral, of course."

"It's so *odd* he never mentioned them. He talked a lot about Nathan," Frankie mused.

"But remember, Nathan was a *friend's* child," I pointed out. "There was no entanglement with Nathan's mother—I guess."

"I'd bet there wasn't. Men tend to stay away from their best friends' wives," Paul said firmly.

Frankie and I looked at him skeptically. We'd both seen too many stories in the colored press about love triangles that had involved exactly that, and had ended in homicides. Or at the very least, attempteds.

"Well, *right-thinking* men tend to stay away," Paul amended.

Uh-huh. Maybe that explained why he'd never made a scintilla of a move the whole time we'd been sharing a room. Even though we'd split ages ago, in his mind I was still Tim's property, and Tim was his boy. Annoying as hell.

"Anyway, it looks as if Eileen was the one who wanted out of that relationship." I shrugged. "She told Ev's great-aunt that she found Everett *too overwhelming* and thought marrying him would be a bigger mistake than being a single mother."

"So you don't think it was Eileen," Frankie concluded. "Then who would be angry enough with Ev to want to—well . . . ?"

"Kill him? You tell us, Frankie."

She began to look a little green again. "What do you mean? I was very fond of Ev; I couldn't imagine hurting him!"

Paul leaned forward and placed a placating hand on Frankie's wrist. "Alex is letting the reporter in her go a little crazy right now, *aren't you, Alex?*"

"I guess. I mean, I don't think you're a suspect, Frankie—but Ev *was* beginning to include more style stories and celebrity interviews. It's not much of a secret that you weren't very happy about it."

"But only because they were never originally part of his magazine! When he started out, we all were assured—Chip, Jake, and I— that there would be minimal overlap. It was the primary reason we agreed not to stand in his way. It would have been *much* harder for him to start *Diaspora* if we had."

I thought about the appeals he could have made to big advertisers and well-known writers; that was probably true.

"And then he changed his mind, and the overlap became considerable."

I took one of the little silver bowls off the table nearest me and sniffed appreciatively. Cinnamon, orange rind, and clove scents wafted up to me. "Considerable enough that you had to speak to him?"

"Well, yes. We went to lunch. La Cloche."

Paul laughed out loud. *"That's* something I would like to have seen! Doesn't sound like Ev's kind of place at all."

Frankie smiled wryly. "It's not, but it was near Condé Nast, and he had meetings there right up to lunch, so it seemed simplest. Actually, the food was lovely, as always, but we had to search a minute for something that appealed to Ev."

"Let me guess: He complained that the menu was all in French."

"He did." Frankie laughed.

"And he ended up eating steak and fries or roast chicken and fries," Paul guessed.

"Steak frites." Frankie chuckled. "You know him well."

Ev was famous for having scant tolerance for fancy food. "Gimme something honest," he'd grump. Before he went to *Diaspora*, he worked for the *Atlanta Constitution* as a national correspondent. When the president of France visited Atlanta to open a show on French Modernists loaned to the High Museum by the Musée d'Orsay, Ev was invited to a fancy dinner afterward by Rosamonde "Bitsy" Coombes, heir to a vast newspaper fortune, thrice widowed, and as pleasant as a hornet trapped in a Mason jar, who decided to show her racial tolerance by asking Ev to escort her. It was the first time a French president had visited Atlanta, so the guest list was triple-A. Everybody at the paper was dying to be chosen by Bitsy—everybody except Ev.

But when he was asked, he said, "It was easier to go with the old bat than say no and have to explain why I didn't for the next three years. And what was I going to say anyway? 'Bitsy, I do a lot of things, but I don't do white women'?"

So he went. He was seated at a prime table. Normally they'd have been across the room from each other, but Bitsy'd been stupid enough to confide, on the way over, that she'd asked for him to be seated nearby "because I know this can be uncomfortable if you haven't been in this situation before." So of course he repaid her condescension by shaking his head every time a course was placed before him and refusing, to her intense mortification, even to sample the morsels of haute cuisine everyone else was gobbling up.

"What's this?" he'd ask suspiciously, as a savory little dish was gently placed in front of him.

"Sweetbreads *en glace*," Miss Coombes, resplendent in Dior and diamonds, would hiss. "They're lovely."

"And what part of the pig or cow or whatever do these things come from?" Ev would ask, in a normal voice, as he poked a lightly sauced bundle.

"They are baby calves' thymus glands, Everett Carson, and they are delicious!" Miss Coombes's crepey neck shook with indignation. "Now eat then and hush up!"

According to legend, Everett put down his fork and stared straight ahead. That had happened with the *moules au saffron* too ("I don't eat nothin' out of a shell").

Finally, as everyone's *homard à Picasso, neige des tomates* was being served, a sympathetic waiter placed a different plate before Ev.

"Amen!" he'd exulted. "Food a brother can recognize. Thank you!"

"Monsieur is entirely welcome," the waiter whispered, smiling.

There on the Limoges plate sat a gorgeous grilled filet mignon, nestled in a golden wreath of crisp, skinny fries.

"If you even *think* of asking for ketchup, I'll fire you on the spot, so help me God!"

Ev was actually insulted. "Ketchup—on steak this fine? I ain't a barbarian, Miss Coombes!"

Shortly afterward, the position at *Diaspora* became available, and Ev packed his bags and left Atlanta. And Bitsy Coombes, tart-tongued enough to make Fortune 500 CEOs feel like little boys in short pants, heaved a huge sigh of relief.

We laughed, remembering how everyone had whispered about the incident for weeks afterward. It had made Ev into something of a legend in publishing circles—and it had cured Bitsy Coombes of her experiment in racial uplift. The next time I saw her in W, it was for a reception for the Olympic Organizing Committee. By her side was Bradford Bondurant Coombes II. He didn't look all that happy to be there, but his trust fund hadn't kicked in yet, so when Granny requested an escort, he knew what to do.

But that was back when Ev was still breathing.

"Okay, so you could live with the new arrange-ment. What about Chip? Or Jake?"

Frankie shook her head, hugging an embroidered pillow to her chest. "Each of us would have too much to lose to put ourselves in jeopardy over Everett. Our magazines have been around four times—in Jake's case, ten times—as long as *Diaspora*. We've got enough on our plates."

"What about women?" Paul asked.

Frankie furrowed her brow. "What *about* them?"

"Well, the brother was known as something of a connoisseur."

Frankie got up, walked over to her windows, and gazed for a moment down into the New Times Square. The blare of taxi horns stuck in crosstown gridlock could be heard just above the air-conditioning's whispery hum.

"Everett did like women, all kinds of women. But I don't know of any in particular he felt strongly about. You know he had commitment anxiety. None of his affairs ever lasted very long. And he was almost always the one to break them off." She turned and looked at us squarely. "That's what the rumors say, anyway."

Paul and I looked at each other. We had heard those rumors.

The door opened and Dinitra's sleek head popped in. "Sorry to interrupt, but you're expected at Arcadia in twenty minutes. Your car will be downstairs in five." Frankie looked like a man on death row who's received a hoped-for phone call from the governor.

"Thank you, Dinitra. I have to make one phone call; then I'm gone."

We didn't need telling twice. "Thank you, Frankie, for seeing us," Paul began.

"I'm sorry. I'm afraid I wasn't much help, but I don't know much more than what I told the police."

"It's okay," I assured her, shaking hands. "Sometimes it just helps for a different set of ears to hear the same information. It's like having five people trying to find Waldo."

We laughed, Paul shook her hand too, and, after he drooled over Dinitra (and her shoes) one last time, we glided downstairs to the icy lobby.

"So," I said, as we emerged into the sunny warmth of Broadway at lunchtime, "where are we off to? MoMA? TKTS, to see if we can get some cheap seats for something good?" The discount booth was only a few blocks away.

"Neither. The museums're closed and Broadway's dark. It's Monday, remember?"

"Damn! In New York, and we can't do two of the things this city does best! This was very poor planning on somebody's part."

"*Yours*, Einstein. And since we've got time, let's see about getting some lunch. I'm not going to last till we meet Signe at seven."

"Well, since it's my fault, I'll pick—and you pay."

"What a novel arrangement. How about that restaurant in Rockefeller Center?"

"The food's good, but it's so touristy."

"Alex, we *are* tourists."

"We are not. We're people from out of town who are here on business."

"Whatever. Let's walk over; it's a nice day, and as you can see, crosstown traffic is moving even more slowly than you do."

"Ha-ha, Jesse Owens. Let's go, then."

He forgot I was wearing my city shoes, and he had to hustle to keep up with me. By the time we got to Rockefeller Center, he was breathing hard—and looking at me with new respect. My feet were starting to hurt—I hadn't broken in my city shoes quite as much as I'd thought—but that would be my little secret. Thank God I didn't share Dinitra's taste in foot gear.

On the other hand, if I *had* worn Dinitra's high metal heels, he might have carried me the whole fourteen long blocks.

Life is a series of trade-offs.

13

By the time we had waited for a table, were
seated, and ate lunch, it was after two-thirty. We weren't supposed to
meet Signe until seven; she was going to leave a message at the hotel
by four-thirty and tell us where.

"So Frankie told us nothing particularly useful. Which means
we've wasted time and money coming down here," I said, as I
reached for the check.

It wasn't bad, for lunch. The sun streamed through the restaurant's heavy plate glass, raising the air-conditioning a few degrees.
Around us, business types from the nearby banks, law offices, and
media houses were finishing up and preparing to go back to their
jobs—which, from the look of their clothes and haircuts, paid quite
handsomely. Outside, golden Prometheus, with bowls of fire bal-
anced on his open palms, hovered above them, wistfully watching
mere mortals enjoying themselves. Looking at him, people who
remembered their mythology probably didn't order liver when it was
on the menu. For that matter, if the restaurant was smart, it wouldn't
serve liver in the first place.

"Powell, wake up. Are you suffering from Colored People's Post-
prandial Disease?"

I snapped to. "Actually, I was thinking about Prometheus getting
his liver picked out by eagles every couple of hours." The waiter

appeared with my receipt, thanked us both, and beat a hasty retreat after overhearing that picked-liver remark.

Paul just looked at me blankly. "You're a sick specimen, know that?"

"Um-hm. Anyway, we didn't waste time and money, because we didn't know for sure what Frankie was going to say. Call it woman's intuition or something, but I think she's holding out on us. There's something she doesn't want us to know. I just wonder if we can find out what it is in time."

He raised an eyebrow. "Woman's intuition? Do feminists believe in that stuff?"

"This one does. Let's use up some time while we wait to meet Signe."

"Uh-uh. I am *not* trailing behind you while you go shopping."

"I wasn't talking about shopping. I don't have any money anyway. And neither should you, after dinner last night."

"Dinner, Einstein, was *prix fixe*. You were hyperventilating so hard you didn't notice the fine print when you opened the menu. It was pretty reasonable."

Oh, man. I felt like the woman in the story who stayed in her room during the cruise she'd spent her lifetime saving for because she'd spent all her money on the tickets and couldn't afford to eat. She didn't know meals were included in the price of her passage.

His laughter made me wince. "That expression is priceless. So what are we going to do with the next few hours? Too bad it's so hot. I'd go back to the hotel, change clothes, and run for an hour or so."

"You can run when you're back home. We need to find out more about Frankie. Don't you think it's strange that we're all about the same age, give or take five years, yet *nobody* I know knows anything about her?"

"That's not so strange. She grew up abroad, went to school in France. Why *would* anybody know her?"

Around us, tables had been cleared pretty quickly. There were only a few isolated groups of diners remaining. The waiters weren't hurrying any of us away.

"Because that saying 'It's a small colored world' didn't spring up from nowhere, it's true. Think about the black people you've run into when *you* were abroad. Didn't everyone know someone who knew someone?"

"Or was related to someone. Yeah, you might have a point."

"So how come everybody we ask only knows the same few facts about Frankie—orphaned, convent, Sorbonne, Neil? It's like she's handed out a press release or something with Frequently Asked Questions about Frankie Harper on one side of one page and then . . . *nada*."

A couple appeared at the front desk and were offered a late lunch at the bar. They seemed to be pressing for seats near the window, but it looked as if the maître d' was explaining that those tables were being set up for dinner. The couple turned away.

"So what do you want to do, call Interpol?" Paul joked, as he came around to pull out my chair. He was, as he said, an old-fashioned kind of guy.

"Better. Aunt Edith. Let's go see her, if she's home."

"Oooh. Bringing out the big guns!"

"Yep. If anybody knows anything about Frankie Harper, Edith does. Or she can hook us up with someone who can tell us something."

Aunt Edith was really a cousin, but she was the same age as my aunts, so "Aunt" was what I'd always called her. Considering the rest of my family structure, which was mostly educators (from university presidents to kindergarten teachers), Edith was a bit bohemian: she'd been the first black executive to work at the Ford Foundation, years ago, and had retired in the mid-eighties. "Now that they have a black president," she'd chortled, "my work here is done." Since then, she'd spent her time volunteering all over the place, traveling and lunching with the other members of what her husband, Uncle Harmon, cheerfully called the Old Biddy Society.

"Darling, you're in town! Come up and see your aunt Edith."

I explained that I wasn't alone and would be bringing a friend.

"Wonderful. See you within the hour. I'll put tea on."

We walked over to Broadway and took the bus (Paul refused to get on the subway again) up the West Side to 102nd Street. Edith lived in a brownstone on the corner of West End and 102nd, one of the few buildings in the immediate neighborhood that wasn't a pre-war apartment house. She and Harmon had bought it in the early sixties, when that part of West End wasn't nearly as chic as it is now, and they'd rehabbed it themselves. It took the better part of ten years, but when they were done, it was the perfect showcase for the Hamiltons' extensive collection of Afro-American and Afro-Caribbean art. Their home had been the site of several parties and receptions for starving artists and writers who started out as family friends and ended up as cultural icons. When I lived on the East Coast, I often stayed with Edith and Harmon when I came to New York and enjoyed being treated as their errant child. In some ways, I had more in common with her than I did with my mother, in that I had a greater tolerance for what my mother would view as their "frou-frou social activities." I didn't mind going from time to time—as long as I didn't have to join the frou-frou organizations that sponsored them.

There was a short stack of buttons by the heav-ily carved double doors. I turned the big brass knob and pushed hard. The door gave way to a small tiled foyer and a set of stairs that led to the two upper floors that were used as rental units. The smaller door before us flew open and Edith burst out.

"Darling! It's so good to see you! Let me look at you! And who's this?"

I was enveloped in the warm, heady scent of 1000 de Patou, Edith's eternal perfume. She was a head shorter than I, pale café au lait, with silvery hair piled up in a lopsided little bun. Gold hoops swung from her pierced ears, and she was wearing a caftan—something else she'd been wearing since the sixties—made of deep green batik. Heavy gold bracelets from her annual winter trips to Montego Bay jangled up and down one arm.

"Hi, Aunt Edith. Good to see you too. This is my friend Paul Butler. Paul, my aunt, Edith Hamilton."

"My, aren't you the handsome one!"

Edith held out her hand, and Paul bent over it, kissing the air above the back of her palm.

"Oh, and gallant too—Alex, this one's a keeper!" She winked broadly to show she was kidding. Kind of.

"Hmmmm." Paul grinned as Edith tucked her little arm into his lanky one and ushered him through the door. "I want to hear about the ones she's thrown away."

"Oh, my dear, don't get me started!" Edith rolled her carefully made-up eyes. "And call me Edith, sweetheart. Everyone does."

Paul smiled wickedly. "Oh, I couldn't. You know you-all didn't let us call adults by their first names when we were coming up. It's a hard habit to break. But may I call you *Aunt* Edith?"

She'd died and gone to heaven. "Certainly you may. And who's your mother, darling? Do I know her?"

My luck being what it was, of course Edith knew Clara. It *is* a small colored world.

"Oh, my God, Alex, why didn't you tell me he was Clara Butler's son? Of course I know Clara! We're Gay Northeasterners, you know. I see her every year at our convention." (The group had changed its name years ago—probably when "gay" started to mean something other than merry—but Edith still insisted on using the original name.)

I hope my look said *Now see what you've done*? We were probably going to have to spend an hour on who-knows-whom-from-where. Dammit.

Edith and Paul chatted animatedly while she set out the tea things. A plate of homemade-looking brownies was placed on the kitchen table.

"Sarabeth's," Edith whispered, when Paul was off in a far corner examining a Hale Woodruff woodcut. "You know I don't bake, now that Harrison is grown and out of the house."

So she hadn't baked for—what, almost twenty years? Harrison Harmon Hamilton was only a year younger than I am. And where's the shame in store-brought brownies, if they're good ones? I never did understand women who won't 'fess up to takeout.

We watched as she swirled hot water into a silver teapot ("Alex's great-great-aunt Sally's") and then dumped it out, spooned several teaspoons of Darjeeling into the bottom, and followed with a cascade of scalding water.

"Let's let that sit for a moment; then we're ready." A china saucer of lemon slices and a Depression-glass creamer and sugar bowl were placed next to the brownies.

"This is like being in a private museum," Paul marveled. "You must have begun collecting when you were pretty young."

"Graduate school," Edith said proudly. "And the things on that wall over there"—two large Beardens, a Jacob Lawrence, and a Loïs Mailou Jones of a Montmartre street—"were a steal before the white folks validated the artists. Of course *we* always knew they were masters." She shrugged, pouring tea through a silver strainer into three warmed cups. "But the market value doesn't reflect what we know until those *other* people confirm it. White man's ice."

Oh, God. Let's don't get into that again, we'll be here forever. How often had I heard Edith disparage black folks "who think that, just because it belongs to the white man, his ice is always colder?" I cut to the chase, before it got too late.

"Aunt Edith, do you know Frankie Harper?"

"The editor?" Edith asked, as she placed two brownies on Paul's plate. Then she passed the brownies to me. Clearly, *I* was supposed to help myself; no brownskin service for me. What is it with him and old ladies, anyway?

"Yes. The editor. Do you?"

"Well, only a little. She's not social, you know."

"Not social" in Edith's lexicon meant Frankie wasn't a Link, a Girl Friend, a soror, or a Gay Northeasterner.

"How'd you meet her then—since you are? Social, I mean."

The brownies, store-bought or not, were excellent. Edith was already pressing seconds on Paul, who was, of course, taking them.

"Oh, well, that's easy. Frankie Harper's not social but she is *professional*; we're in the Coalition, you know. And we were both trustees of the Studio Museum at the same time."

Hmm. So Frankie was a member of the Coalition of 100 Black

Women. That was interesting. And given her passion for black art and crafts, the Studio Museum made perfect sense.

"Do you know anything about her personally? Who her family was, that sort of thing?" Paul asked. He bit into his third brownie and sighed deeply. Such round heels for sugar.

Edith pursed her lips and stared at the ceiling. "Well, let's see." The bangles jingled softly.

"Her father went to Dillard. He was a doctor. Harmy and I used to see them from time to time at the NMA conventions. But that was decades ago. You know they went as missionaries to the Belgian Congo and were killed in that civil war. Very sad."

"So what happened to Frankie?" I reached for half a brownie before Paul killed the plate.

"Her parents' parents were deceased, and both her parents were only children, so there was no aunt or grandmother to take her when she was orphaned. But Dr. Harper knew that the Belgian Congo could be dangerous, and he'd made provisions in his will that if anything happened to them she was to be sent to the best possible boarding school, here or abroad. That was back in 'sixty-one, so the ones in the States, of course, were still segregated for all practical purposes. And really, Frankie had lived all her conscious life in a French-speaking country—I think they moved there when she was about one—so she went to convent school in Provence and then to the Sorbonne."

"That's interesting, but who *arranged* all this? Someone had to decide where and how long and all that," I pressed.

"If I remember correctly, her father's best friend was also a medical missionary, and he did the research. He was single and unable to take her in because he was always volunteering to doctor in some war or another. It wouldn't have been suitable, a single man. *And* he was white."

"Ironic, isn't it?" Paul asked. "Now the taboo's been lifted, so many white folks—even single ones—are adopting black kids."

Edith banged a newly replenished plate of brownies on the table. "Don't get me started on *that*," she warned. "I get sick every time I open *People* magazine and see that someone in Hollywood has taken on a new black child. It's like those poor children are the flavor of the month! Pets! Like Michael Jackson's monkey. What's its name, the one he dresses up all the time?"

I stifled a giggle. "Bubbles. Aunt Edith aren't you being a bit harsh?"

Edith bit into a brownie and put it down. "Not at all. If they made the laws more flexible, more of us could adopt our own. They're only taking ours because *white* babies are in such short supply. And you'll notice they only want the *best* black babies, not the ones with problems. Skimming."

"Yeah, but if the system is preventing black kids from getting into black homes, isn't living with white people—even rich ones—better than languishing in a public institution for years and years?" We'd had this argument before, Edith and I.

Paul lifted his eyebrows. "Alex, don't upset your aunt."

Edith patted him on the forearm. "Don't worry, darling. Your girlfriend likes to stir the pot."

I let the "girlfriend" pass; lately I'd been letting a lot pass. Maybe I was maturing.

"She's always been that way. No respect for the black middle class. It's a form of rebellion," Edith went on. "Or self-hatred."

"Jesus, Edith, I was asking about Frankie Harper and I get the Negro Manifesto! Calm down. Do you know anything about her husband or his people?"

"No, Alexa, I do not. They're not social, either."

"Or . . ."

"*Or* professional. They just *are*. They're different from us."

"Different how?" Paul was genuinely curious.

"I mean he was a good-looking guy with a football scholarship to a no-name university and he lucked up: He discovered a talent for acting and met an accomplished woman who fell in love with him!"

Hey, tell us how you really feel, Edith. I forgot to mention my Aunt Edith is a bit of a snob.

"So no one you know would be likely to know much about him?"

"Not really." Edith had calmed down a bit. "There are a few charities he's attached to, children's clubs and a literacy program and so forth. He spends about as much time in Los Angeles as he does here.

And don't get me wrong. I know as soon as she's out the door Alex is going to give you chapter and verse on what a snob I am."

I looked at her and lifted my eyebrows: Who, me?

"I'm just saying that because our milieu is so small, it's fairly easy to get the 911—or whatever you young people call it—on people you may not know but whom you know *of*."

Paul's mouth puckered as he took his last sips of tea.

"It's 411, Aunt Edith, 411. You know, like Information Please?"

"Whatever. Paul, would you like to see some of Alex's ancestors? I have a little gallery in the hall back here you might find interesting. She likes to pretend she has no people, but of course that's part of her rebellious act."

"Gee, Aunt Edith, we'd love to stay, but we have another appointment downtown and we'd better hustle."

"No, we don't," Paul protested, laughing in my face, "we're clear until six o'clock. And yes, I'd *love* to see Alex's relatives." He leaned forward to Edith and stage-whispered, "She always acts like they found her in a basket on the library steps."

"They most certainly did not. Alex is a Powell, a Wheatley, and a Roberts! Let me show you, quickly, who some of her people are— before she pushes you out the door to another nonexistent appointment."

So there.

Edith's high-heeled sandals *click-clicked* across the shiny parquet floor to the long hallway that connected the front of the house to her master bedroom suite. On both walls were old sepia tones, copies of daguerreotypes, and black-and-whites of her family and mine. There was even a small photo of me, taken at some Jack and Jill Christmas party, years and years ago. My hair is in long pigtails anchored by velvet bows, and I'm reading a poem in front of a Christmas tree. My navy velvet jumper is fluffed up with about a hundred layers of crinoline, and I'm wearing, if I remember correctly, black velveteen Mary Janes. Nauseating.

"Coming?" Paul grinned.

"Not hardly. Been there, done that. Try not to laugh *too* loudly; Edith's under the delusion you're refined."

It didn't do any good. I could hear them both hee-hawing conspiratorily as I put the tea things away. I tried to ignore them, but it was hard. When Edith brought Paul back, she kissed him soundly and made him promise to visit the next time he came to New York, "whether Miss Black America over there is with you or not."

Ungawa.

"I promise," Paul said, raising his hand like a Boy Scout.

"And," Edith stage-whispered, "if you call me I'll fill you in on her Revolutionary Phase. Has she told you about the boyfriend from Baltimore with the gold teeth?"

"I promise to call *soon.*"

" 'Bye, darling. Kiss Signe for me. Tell her she *could* come up and see me sometime—we're practically neighbors, you know."

Right. Signe lived on Riverside Drive, twenty blocks to the south. In Manhattan, twenty blocks away is like living in another galaxy.

" 'Bye, Auntie."

The door closed. Paul looked at me, waiting.

"It was only *one* gold tooth, okay? And it was on the side, not the front."

He was in such a good mood we took the Broadway local down to Seventy-second Street. The crosstown bus was crowded, so we sat across the aisle from each other. Every now and then, he'd look at me, bare his perfect uncapped teeth in a big cheese-eating grin, and burst into silent laughter. The prim Puerto Rican woman in a pale gray maid's uniform edged nervously away from him.

I looked at her sympathetically and tapped my temple. "*Loco, pero no peligroso.*"

She nodded and relaxed. If he was crazy but harmless, she could live with it. This was, after all, New York.

14

After we got off at Madison, I convinced the King of Comedy to stop at one of the neighborhood wine boutiques (no liquor stores here) for a couple of good bottles of wine. Considering what I'd just gone through, I needed a drink. After a brief consultation with one of the sales staff, we found what we wanted and walked the block back to the hotel.

Non-cee was on duty this evening, too, and welcomed us. " 'Allo, Monsieur Butler, Madame Butler-Powell." Hmmm. I'd been hyphenated in my absence—and backward at that. Oh, well. It's not every day a girl gets a new hyphen.

When we got upstairs, we saw we had voice mail, too. One was from Signe:

> Hey, I'd come and meet y'all so I could see what a five-hundred-dollar-a-night room looks like, but the WP are working me hard today. I'ma go to the restaurant straight from the plantation, so y'all meet me at Café Beulah. It on East Nineteenth, between Broadway and Park. Come on Caucasian People's Time, not Colored People's Time, 'cause I be hon-gree! Overseer worked me so hard I only had yogurt for lunch. Pitiful. 'Bye!

'Bye sounded exactly like bah. As in black sheep. Or humbug.

The other message was garbled and in French and sounded like a bad connection from an international call. I just shrugged and erased it. It was probably for another guest. If it was for either of us, whoever it was would call again if it was important.

"Where we going?" Paul asked, as he turned on the shower. I knew he was getting in first because he assumed I would take longer to get ready.

"Café Beulah. Downtown. Nineteenth and Park. You could take a leisurely shower and we could take the Lex down," I offered. I am nothing if not selfless.

"Let me see: subway at rush hour, jammed next to lots of unwashed bodies after a hard day's work . . . why am I not seeing the attraction in this?" He had to shout, because the news was blaring from the bathroom TV.

"It was just a thought."

"Not a good one. Think about opening that bottle of Vigonier, Einstein. Now *that's* a good thought."

He was right. After a somewhat heroic struggle with the hotel's cheapo corkscrew, I managed to open the bottle. I filled two water tumblers halfway and stuck my arm around the corner of the bathroom door. "Here."

"You can come in. I don't take as long as *some* people I know."

Paul was at the sink; he had a towel wrapped around his taut waist while he vigorously scrubbed his hair dry with a smaller towel. His muscles glistened wetly. Cute. Peter Jennings was giving us gloom and doom about something in his plummy, affected baritone.

"Of course"—he sipped the wine—"I'm not as *dirty* as some people, either."

"Get out. My turn."

"Is that any way to speak to someone who is *loco, pero no peligroso?*"

I slammed the door. I could hear him laughing from the other side.

We got to Café Beulah on the stroke of seven; Signe wasn't even there yet. We gave the maître d' Signe's name and immediately got Big Respect. "Oh," the slender young man breathed, "you're Miss Tucker's friends! Let me seat you right this minute. She should be along in a few." We followed as he wound his way through a large yellow room hung with old family portraits, hand-stitched samplers, and sepia photographs in ornate mahogany frames. He pointed to a cozy table for three and pulled out ladder-back chairs with chintz pads for us.

"Here you are. What can we bring you from the bar? On the house, of course."

Jeez. How often did Signe eat here, anyway?

"Lillet, please."

"Blonde or rouge? Rocks or straight?"

You go, girl. "Blonde, rocks, twist."

"Very good. And you, sir?"

"Iced tea would be fine, thanks." The maître d' looked disappointed. "Back in a sec. Oh, here's our girl!"

It was hard to say who was dimpling more, Signe or the maître d'. "Hey, Miss Tucker! You look fabulous, as always. Come sit down and join your friends." Kiss, kiss.

"Hey, James. Thanks for looking out for them. These are my ooooold friends, Alex Powell and Paul Butler. I dragged them all the way from the Upper East Side, 'cause I thought they needed a touch of Beulah this evening. God knows I do!"

"Pleased to meet you both. Welcome to Café Beulah." James pulled out Signe's chair and took her briefcase. "If you don't need anything in here, I'll place it up front."

Signe turned to us, beaming. "See why I love it here? Everybody's so civilized, you almost forget you're in New York. James, honey, I'll have the usual."

"Very good, Miss Tucker. I'll send Roberto over with menus and a list of the evening's specials."

Shortly after that, Roberto appeared with our drinks and the menus and recited the evening's specials. Paul actually listened to him. Signe and I just stared. In his white wing-collared shirt and pleated black trousers, he looked just like that brother in the Polo ads: shaved head, granite cheekbones, wide shoulders, narrow waist.

"And a *very* nice butt." Signe sighed, watching that particular part of his anatomy disappear toward the kitchen.

"Yeah, buddy," I seconded. We were not alone; every woman in the room—and maybe a third of the men—were watching Roberto's retreat with mute appreciation.

He must be used to it, because his serene manner never wavered throughout dinner. When we ordered, Signe informed him to feel free to guide our choices: "They're Yankees, honey, so they're not used to good southern cooking. What do *you* think they should eat? Oh, and that one"—pointing at Paul—"doesn't eat meat."

Roberto gazed at us speculatively for a moment. I felt that gave me license to stare right on back.

Finally Golden Boy spoke. "I'd say shrimp pilau for the gentleman, barbecued duck for the lady, and maybe, for you, fried chicken fillets with corn pudding?"

"Okay with y'all?" We nodded.

"Whip it on us, then, Roberto."

He nodded and walked away, and we got to admire the view again.

"You know, you're both about old enough to be his mother."

"Get out! Are not!" Signe and I howled in outrage as Paul's shoulders shook with laughter.

"Okay, you're *almost* old enough to be his mother—if you'd been fast girls with too much time on your hands and too little parental supervision. Better?"

"Boy, don't you be playin' that stuff with me. You don't know how old I am!"

"Signe, darlin', I can do the math. You and Alex both graduated from the same school in the same year, so my guess is you're her age. And she's going to be thirty-six in about a minute and a half." True. I had a birthday coming up in about a week.

"Well, you know what old folk say about what happens when you assume. I'm in the same class as Alex, but I skipped two grades in elementary school and graduated from high school a year early."

I looked at her and smirked. "This story gets better every year.

Now you're Signe Tucker, child prodigy? Keep rolling back your age, girlfriend, and soon *I'll* be old enough to be your mother."

"Hey, don't start no stuff, won't be none. Take a biscuit out this basket and shut up."

She passed a small basket of heavenly homemade biscuits and deep-yellow corn bread. I was happy to obey.

"So, tell. What did y'all find out about Frankie when you went to see her today?"

Paul buttered his biscuit, slathered honey on it for good measure, and looked up. "Nuttin', honey."

Signe took a deep draught of her kir and frowned. "What do you mean, nothing?"

I shrugged. "Basically, just that. We heard a little bit about her childhood and got some background on why she and Chip and Jake decided to let Ev see if he could get *Diaspora* off the ground without arranging to have him strangled, financially speaking. Of course, now they're sorry they didn't squish him when they had the chance, since he stepped all over their carefully agreed-upon territory."

"Oh, that stuff." Roberto was walking toward us with a big tray. Behind him was another waiter. He wasn't as handsome, and his butt probably wasn't as nice.

The plates were set before us, and after we'd oohed and aahed, Roberto left to get the wine we'd ordered.

"Is there something else we should have asked her? You're looking like you know something we don't." Paul had finished his biscuit and was giving Signe his full attention.

Signe squirmed a little. I have only known her to do this maybe three times in the whole time we'd been friends, so I knew something was up, something deep.

"Signe, you *do* know something! What is it?"

She indicated that we should wait while Roberto served the wine. He poured a small amount in a glass and placed it before Paul. Paul drank it straight down, nodded, and Roberto filled my glass, then Signe's, then Paul's.

"Everything is good? Can I bring you anything else?"

"Everything's excellent," I assured him, "and we've got every-thing we need right here, thanks." Roberto nodded and withdrew. I didn't even look at his butt this time.

"So what's the deal, Signe?" Paul asked.

"Okay. You remember about two years ago, when Frankie had been in her job for about six months, spending every waking moment pouring herself into that magazine?"

"Of course." Frankie's non-life was legendary. Nobody had seen anybody work as hard as she had to pull *Radiance* into shape. Mostly she was admired for spending so much time on it, but Frankie was also ridiculed by those who assumed she was working so hard because she had nothing else to do.

"So girlfriend was working like crazy: coming in early, leaving late, and taking work home with her at night and on weekends. Then all of a sudden, she still came in early, but she wasn't staying as late. And she was glowing. You know what *that* means."

"Good makeover?" Paul asked.

Signe laughed. "You know as well as I do that when a woman starts looking like that there's only one reason—a man."

"So? She was single; it wasn't against the law."

"Good thing you aren't an *investigative* reporter, Alex, you haven't been putting the pieces together. Honey, the new man was Ev. Close your mouth, darlin'."

Paul and I were speechless. Everett had always been consistent in his choice of women. They may have varied in height and shape, they may have had naturals or straightened or naturally straight hair, but they were *always* medium brown at the very least. And, despite Ev's joking boast that he liked his women "in a plain brown wrap-per," they were always beautiful. Frankie, alabaster-skinned Frankie, only filled half that bill. My mind was fighting to accept this new information even as, at some level, I knew Signe might be right. He would have seen her as a challenge. And he liked smart women—especially smart women who found him attractive.

"Ev has railed about light-skinned women and pigment privilege all his life! We've never seen him with anyone even *approaching* light. Are you sure?"

"I'm sure. They mostly met in each other's apartments. They'd have dinner delivered, work side by side on their respective magazines, then hop into bed around eleven o'clock and screw like crazed weasels all night." I envisioned them in Frankie's Gramercy Park apartment, laptops at opposite ends of the dining room table, pausing every now and then in stepping on some writer's deathless prose to grin at each other. Wow-ee.

"Signe, you amaze me! How did you find this out? And why did none of the rest of us ever discover it?" Paul wondered.

"Well, you're a man, honey. No offense, but y'all ain't always too swift on the uptake, you know? And you"—nodding at me—"are on the West Coast—you-all find out *everything* last."

Well, we don't, but it does feel like that sometimes.

"But really, I had lunch with Frankie one afternoon and you know how it is: You're in love, and it's supposed to be a secret, but you just *have* to tell somebody? Well, I just happened to be sitting across from her when the dam broke. So I got the four-one-one straight from the filly's mouth." Or the 911, if you were Edith.

I thought back, mentally counting on my fingers. "But she's been married to Neil for almost two years. She must have been with Ev just before she met him."

"Basically. She and Ev went out for about four months. It was *major* hot and heavy. But then Ev walked in one day and told Frankie it was over." She snapped her fingers. "Just like that."

"But why? Didn't he love her?"

"He did, in his own Ev-ish way. But he loved his public image more. And it was getting to him that he couldn't take her out in public without generating a whole bunch of flak from busybodies who'd figure he was colorstruck and had really wanted a white-looking woman all along."

"So he dumped her because she was . . ."

". . . too pale. And *told* her that's why she had to go. Needless to say, girlfriend was devastated. I mean, one week he's talking about having kids with her, which is something she said she wants desperately, and the next week he's telling her 'Never mind, I don't want you anymore. And for reasons you cannot control.'"

We were silent, imagining how hurt Frankie must have been at Ev's brusque rejection. Roberto returned to retrieve our practically licked-clean plates. "Dessert?"

"*Always* dessert," Paul assured him. "And"—he looked at us— "none of this one-plate-three-forks business. Women always say they only want 'a bite'—they never warn you it's a gorilla-sized bite."

We ordered three different desserts and coffee and promised to share. Paul snorted.

"Did she marry Neil on the rebound?" I asked Signe.

"Some people think so. I think she really loved him then and she certainly loves him now. But she hates Ev—mostly because he insisted on conducting their affair underground and, when it was over, would barely acknowledge her in public. It made her feel stupid for ever having been with him in the first place. And demeaned."

"But why *kill* him? Nobody knew he'd dumped her except her— and you—so there could be no gossip. It's not enough motivation."

"It is if you spent your childhood being looked upon as a freak and your young-adult years being lambasted because you look exactly like the 'white devil.' Having women who can no more help being brown than you can help being light sneer at you because of your skin color and give you big-time attitude because they assume you think like every yellow gal who's ever snubbed them because of *their* color. Maybe Ev's rejection—and the reason for it—was the final straw."

"Maybe." I thought back. Frankie *hadn't* been on the dais when the dinner began. Maybe there was an explanation for that.

"Why didn't you tell us before?" Paul asked, as he placed a steaming spoonful of apple cobbler on the extra plates Signe had requested.

"Don't forget the ice cream, honey," Signe instructed. Bossy, bossy.

Then she answered his question.

"She told me in confidence, way before Ev was killed. But that was two years ago, and murder kind of changes the weight of my promise. I've been wrestling with myself since Ev died; I decided to say something tonight if she didn't tell y'all today. She didn't, so I'm telling you now."

"Wow. You know, Paul, if we hustle tomorrow morning, we could go back and ask her about Ev before we leave for San Francisco. Just mention that we'd heard about her and Ev somewhere. We wouldn't have to give Signe up; if they were in public at any point, chances are somebody saw them, even if they didn't know they were being noticed. This news is something we have to pass on to Marron, anyway."

"Yeah. Probably we should just go on up there. Something tells me Dinitra isn't going to shoehorn us in if we call ahead of time."

"Not even for you, appreciator of fine black women?"

Roberto laid the bill down next to Paul. Guess he was an old-fashioned kind of guy, too.

Signe moved to take it, but Paul blocked her outstretched arm. "Don't even ask. Anybody want anything else?" He took out his Titanium card again.

Roberto picked up the leather folder, walked toward the desk, and stopped halfway. Then he turned around and came back.

"I'm so sorry," he said, "but we don't take Titanium. Just Diner's Club, MasterCard, and Visa. And cash, of course."

Heh-heh. "Gee, someplace *else* your Titanium card isn't welcome. Good thing I didn't leave home without my Visa." I placed the lowly card on the folder, and Roberto took it.

Paul looked at me in exasperation. "I'm going to hear about this forever, aren't I?"

"Nah. Just till I get tired of pointing it out. Coupla years, max."

"Come on, y'all. I want to go back with you and see what your room looks like. One of our travel editors says y'all might be the first Negroes ever to stay there. *American* Negroes, anyway."

So we went uptown and Signe got the full treatment: doorman, Non-cee, brass elevators, Godivas, the works. Paul opened the bottle of Perrier Jouet he'd chilled before we left, and the three of us laughed and drank champagne until about eleven o'clock.

"Ooohh, the flower bottle!" Signe'd squealed. "Don't y'all just love this champagne? The bottle's so pretty!"

"If I say nobody but a woman would buy wine because of the bottle will I sound like a total sexist?"

"Damn skippy."

Finally, Signe stood and smoothed her suit skirt. "I love y'all," she announced, "but I gotta go downstairs and let that white man get me a cab. Me and Ted got a standing date at eleven-thirty *every* night."

"Who's Ted?" Paul asked. "What happened to Otha?"

"Koppel, honey. He and Otha do two entirely different things for me, and they're both *very* good at their respective jobs."

She's incorrigible, that girl.

Laughing, she hugged me good-bye and made us promise to call from San Francisco the next night and tell her how our talks with Frankie and Jake went.

"I'll walk you down and make sure they get you a cab," Paul said, throwing Signe's shawl around her shoulders. "The Yankee Barbarian here can walk us to the elevator."

"I thought 'Yankee' and 'barbarian' were synonymous," Signe murmured.

I give her a digital signal that's synonymous with something else, just as their elevator doors closed. Before I could retract my finger, a dead ringer for Rex Harrison and a significantly younger miniskirted "niece" appeared as the second elevator's doors parted.

"Oh, my!" He blinked.

How veddy, veddy rude of me. His blond trophy giggled. He was not amused.

"Americans!" he hissed with disapproval, after they went around the corner.

It probably wasn't the finger he was mad about. It probably was that nasty skirmish over the Colonies. Long memories, the British.

15

We settled up the bill after breakfast and left
our bags with the concierge. The staff seemed genuinely sad to see
us go. But then, they'd looked sad to see each couple checking out.

"*Un autre jour, un autre dol-laire.*" I grinned. Head 'em up,
moooove 'em out.

Paul frowned, perusing the bill. I guess the Titanium people had
done what they'd promised, because he wasn't having a heart attack,
or anything, at the bottom line. Which, from my upside-down per-
spective, looked considerable.

"Mr. Butler, everything is correct?"

This accent belonged to a thirtyish man with closely cropped
brown hair. I'd guess German or maybe Austrian, but he could have
been Swiss. I looked at the name plate on his navy blazer. It said
HEINRICH. *Ja*, German.

"The Titanium Card alerted us that they would be paying the
balance of your bill, which is what the subtotal means, right here."
An immaculate fingertip pointed to the line in question.

Paul nodded, closed the pages, and placed them in an envelope
with the hotel's crested logo. "Everything's fine. If you'd just stow
these two bags for us, we'd appreciate it. And we'd like a taxi at
eleven-thirty for Kennedy."

I swear, Heinrich actually bowed. Maybe he even clicked his

heels together. We couldn't see behind the desk to know for sure, but I wouldn't be surprised.

"It will be done."

I resisted—only just—intoning, I'll be back, in response. Hasta la vista, Heinie.

The traffic gods were with us. Even though it was rush hour, we caught a cab right away. From the looks of it, somebody was coming to have a late power breakfast at La Regence. We'd decided last night to do it Paul's way and go with no advance warning.

"Either she'll see us and fill us in on the real deal or she'll have us kicked out, in which case we'll have to get to Marron right away."

"I guess. . . ."

"What? Your woman's intuition working overtime again?"

"Maybe. I just have this feeling that whatever she's scared of isn't that the cops like her for killing Ev. It might have something to do with Ev, but it's not that."

The taxi pulled up to *Radiance*'s building. We got out and managed to merge into the flow of incoming pedestrian traffic. This was not one of those lobbies that has to sign you in and buzz you up, but you never know. If Frankie even suspected we might be coming back, she could have left instructions that we were not to be let up. Assuming security could identify us.

The cornrowed receptionist was at the phone again, crisply picking up line after line.

"Good morning, *Radiance*. Will you hold?"

"Good morning, *Radiance*. May I ask you to hold, please?"

And on and on. She motioned to us she'd be right with us and, after she'd transferred the first batch of calls, she was.

"Good morning." She beamed. "Here for Frankie again? She just got in."

"We are. Just some cleanup stuff. It'll only take a minute."

"Fine. I'll tell Dinitra you're here. Please have a seat, Miss . . ." She frowned prettily. So many people to remember.

"Powell. Alex Powell and Paul Butler."

"Of course. Just a sec."

She turned away to buzz Dinitra and spoke into her headphone.

Through the half-glass, I could see her giving us a puzzled look. She gestured to me, all the while transferring calls.

"Dinitra checked with Frankie, and she says you're not expected. Frankie apologizes, but she says she simply cannot see you this morning. She's swamped. They're closing the Christmas issue."

Of course they were. All lifestyle-type magazines published during the Christmas holidays were actually finished as much as six months in advance. Heaven help us if some *real* news intervened at the last moment. But closing or no, Frankie was going to have to talk with us.

The door swung open and two *Radiance* staff members emerged, chattering away, with two big brown rag dolls in their hands. One doll was swathed in kente, the other in a full skirt, billowy white blouse, and starched headcloth. Both dolls were faceless, with large golden hoops where their ears should have been. We'd met the women yesterday, but I couldn't remember their names.

I didn't know he could move that quickly. One minute Paul was next to me, hearing about how terribly busy Frankie was. The next, he was across the room, holding the door for the two chattering sisters, who flashed him plenty teeth as they passed.

"Oh, *thank* you!"

From the fervor, it was obvious that *Radiance* didn't get a whole bunch of male visitors. Or maybe they didn't get a whole bunch of *attractive* male visitors.

"My pleasure."

Paul made a little bow that would have done Heinrich proud. Then he jerked his head toward the door. "Einstein, are you waiting for a personal invitation?"

I blinked and followed, as the receptionist furiously phoned back to Dinitra.

Tattletale.

We quickly wove our way through the thicket of desks and room partitions. It was still early, and people were continuing to drift in. If it was a closing day, they might be here till nine or ten this evening.

"Back again?"

"Hey, welcome back!"

They were a lot friendlier than Dinitra was going to be when she caught up with us.

Which happened in the next twenty seconds. She stood before us, plenty pissed off, in an olive linen pantsuit with safari pockets and a belt. All she needed was a pith helmet, a large-game rifle, and some heads on the walls. She was looking as if she wished they were ours.

"I believe I indicated Frankie would be unavailable this morning," she began. Veerrrry frosty.

I noticed Paul looking sadly at Dinitra's feet. Today she was wearing glossy brown high-heeled loafers with a thin silver bit across the top. Not a stainless stiletto in sight. No-nonsense shoes for a no-nonsense babe. Not an easy nut to crack. But I gave it a try.

"She did. But this is an emergency, and frankly, Dinitra, it can't wait."

The girl wasn't moved. "What sort of emergency, hers—or yours?" Ouch.

"Hers. And believe me when I tell you this is something she'll want to hear *privately*, not out in the hall. But please tell her if we have to do it that way, we will. We'll wait here for her answer." *Two* can be no-nonsense, missy.

Dinitra left.

Paul was looking at me as if I'd sprouted horns and a tail. Or maybe it was new respect. "Whew! You can be one cold-blooded sister, can't you?"

I shrugged. "If I have to."

Dinitra returned. She was much less frosty, almost uncertain. Frankie's reaction must have been swift and intense.

"Follow me, please, she can only spare a few minutes, but if it's an emergency . . . ?" She gestured us through Frankie's door and shut it softly.

Frankie Harper looked as if she'd aged overnight. Her skin was papery-pale, and her eyes were red-rimmed. She was wearing a navy pantsuit so dark it could easily have been mistaken for black. Her chestnut hair was pulled back from her face and fastened with a sim-

ple tortoise barrette. No apparent makeup. She hadn't looked this
funereal at Ev's service.

She stood, keeping the big desk between her and us, almost as if
she needed its protection. We fidgeted—I did, anyway. If Paul was
feeling as uncomfortable as I was, he didn't look it.

"Frankie," he began gently, "we're sorry to intrude upon your
personal life; we don't want to cause you any pain or embarrassment. But last night we discovered you had what could be a strong
motive for wanting Ev dead, and we have to ask you about it."

"What we say here will remain between us three," I promised.

"If possible," Mr. Responsibility amended. He was probably
keeping in mind that pesky statute about witholding pertinent evidence in a murder investigation.

Frankie drew a hiccupy breath. "I don't even know where to
begin. . . ."

"Begin where you want to, and we can go forward or backward
from there."

Another hiccup. "Okay."

She sat, and indicated we should take the fauteuils before the
desk.

"I'm adopted, you know. I've always known I was. My parents
were very frank about that, from the time I was old enough to understand. I'm sure it cost them something in personal pride—back in
the fifties, people didn't talk about infertility the way they do now.
Babies just appeared and everybody pretended they'd always been
there. But not my parents. They always told me, 'We chose you
because we loved you, and we knew God wanted us to have you. You
were meant to be our child.' Every year on July fifteenth they'd tell
me the story about how the nuns at Sacre Coeur heard, through a
parishioner, that a nice couple over in Thibodaux was longing for a
baby. My mother went to meet the Mother Superior, who told her
the baby would be born in two months or so. My parents agreed to
take the child, whatever its sex.

"Almost two months to the day, I was delivered in the parish hospital's colored wing, a long skinny baby with blue eyes and rosy

cheeks. The nuns called, and my parents were at the hospital within two hours. They never met the mother, but they were told she was a sweet girl who desperately wanted to keep her baby. And her parents were equally adamant that the baby be given away."

"Because she—you, I mean—was born out of wedlock?"

Frankie gazed at the angels flying up and down the heavenly ladder on her quilt. God still looked on benignly, the way God is supposed to when all's right with the world.

"That—and the fact that the baby was colored and the girl was not."

Oh. That would make perfect sense. Illegitimate births were bad enough in the fifties, but to white people an illegitimate birth that resulted in a biracial child was beyond taboo, especially in the pre-integrated South, where laws against miscegenation were severe. It would also explain Frankie's fine hair and blue eyes—although, God knows, enough of us "pure" coloreds have united purposefully over the years to achieve the same effect.

"So your parents, who were pretty fair themselves, if that photo over there is accurate, took you and you became a family."

"Yes. The only family I ever knew. And as is the case in a lot of adoptions, I grew up looking like the people I loved, even though I had no biological connection to them. I had my father's sandy hair, my mother's blue eyes. She said he and I shared the same capacity for tracking down a Hershey bar in a sandstorm." Her eyes crinkled in fond memory. "We moved to the Congo when I was almost one; I learned to walk there. I have a very funny photo of me, around age two, on the deck of someone's house. I am sitting on a chamber pot, being potty-trained, and a little spider monkey is sitting right next to me—with my ABC book on his lap!"

We all smiled, imagining a fat-legged toddler and her simian buddy.

"We were Catholic, so I went to convent school not far from what was then Léopoldville. It took boarding and day students. Before the war, I was a day student. My father was one of the first black medical volunteers in the country, sort of a precursor to

Médecins sans Frontières. We call them Doctors Without Borders here. We'd been in the Congo for almost a dozen years when the war broke out."

"The civil war, in 'sixty-one?'"

I remember seeing photos in *Life* of the murdered rebel leader, Patrice Lumumba, lying stiff and dead in the capitol's streets. Raging against decades of brutally racist rule by the Belgian colonials, furious Congolese had gone on a retributative rampage, often killing anyone associated with the status quo. Horror stories of nuns being bayoneted and white children's heads being smashed in were splashed across the major papers in Europe and America. Of course, these same papers chose not to illustrate the Belgian atrocities that had sent the Congolese over the edge in the first place.

"Yes, that war. My parents lost their lives in it because they refused to leave when the State Department advised all American citizens to vacate the country. They couldn't, you see; they'd lived there for over ten years, and the people they'd come to know felt like family. My father, especially, knew doctors would be needed badly. So he wouldn't go."

I thought back to how my parents would have reacted to an impending crisis like that. Daddy would have wanted Mother to take me and leave, and she wouldn't have gone. Although she probably would have tried to get me out, over my protests.

"Your mother wouldn't leave, either, would she?" I asked gently.

Frankie turned away from the window and looked directly at me for the first time. "Exactly, Alex. She refused to go. When things were getting really bad, and rumors flying all around about when the rebels would reach Léopoldville, I remember being kept up by their arguments several nights in a row; then, one night, nothing. Just a big family dinner the next evening, with friends.

"There were even presents. I was given my mother's gold heart locket, something I'd coveted ever since I could remember. It had *More than yesterday, less than tomorrow* engraved on both sides— one side in French, one in English—in fancy script. My father had given it to her on their wedding day. She always used to laugh and tell me, 'I'll leave it to you, when I die or when you marry, whichever comes first.' That was a joke between us, because I'd always vowed I'd never marry. I was going to be a nun, like the sisters who taught me.

"It was a fine party. But at the end, they spoiled it by telling me they'd decided to send me away, for my own safety. I was leaving in the morning, on one of the last planes out. I would be going to the Ivory Coast to stay with friends of my parents, people I'd never met who would meet me at the airport. And when it was safe, I would come back."

I imagined a ten-year-old Frankie, wide-eyed with fear, not wanting to get on a plane and not wanting to leave her parents. Worrying that, if she let them out of her sight, she might never see them again.

"That's what was *supposed* to happen—but that's not what happened. My parents, you see, were twenty-four hours too late in coming to their agreement. That morning, about six o'clock, a band of rebels came through our neighborhood and began slaughtering foreigners. The cook's screams woke us up."

Frankie paused, eyes unfocused, clearly envisioning a past horror that we, mercifully, could not.

"My mother shoved me under their big bed and kissed me hard. 'Stay here—don't move. Always remember that we love you, sweetie.'

Then she was gone. I didn't know it then, but those were the last words I'd ever hear from her. I stayed under the bed, shivering with fear, while I heard big boots stomp throughout the house. And loud voices in a language I didn't know, some tribal dialect."

It was very quiet in Frankie's office. I had a strange feeling of déjà vu. Like yesterday, she was standing at the window, looking out but not seeing. Like yesterday, the cacophony of traffic was audible, but filtered up through the distance of twenty-two floors.

"Then there was a lot of shouting, and the soldiers left. Something approaching scared them off. You could hear their voices fading away, and as they did, the wails of the people left behind became louder. After what felt like hours, I got out from under the bed.

"The door to my parents' room, where I'd been hiding, had been closed. When I opened it . . . when I opened it—"

Frankie stopped to collect herself. Her eyes filled, but she went on.

"When I opened it, my mother rolled across my feet. Her skirt was above her head, her panties were ripped half off, and there was blood everywhere. I pulled her skirt down and saw that a lot of the blood came from the back of her head, where someone had bashed her skull in. Her blue eyes were wide open. I touched her lids to close them, as I'd seen the nuns do in the hospital. She was still warm. There was a smear of blood from the doorknob to the ground where she'd fallen. Obviously she'd died blocking the way so they didn't find me. She distracted them by allowing them to rape her. To save me."

Jesus. What could anyone possibly say after a story like that?

"What about your father, Frankie?" Paul prompted, in a low whisper.

Frankie wiped her eyes and sighed.

"I found Papa in the kitchen, his body hunched over Desirée's two children. Desirée was our cook. She was already dead. They'd killed her—probably severed an artery—with a machete; it was still in her neck, where it meets the shoulder. Someone had carved *putain* on her belly. She was five months pregnant."

Putain. Whore. Because they assumed the cook was dishing out favors to the foreign devils, or just whore because she chose to work for them? At this point, it made no difference.

"Papa, too, had been smashed on the head, then shot in the back. Still, he'd not moved; he'd stayed hunched over those children. I turned him over. From the front, he looked perfectly normal. Except his eyes were open too. I closed them.

"Then I saw a foot move. I thought I did, anyway. I wanted to leave, to get out of that horrible house. But if Desirée's children were still alive, at least Papa would not have died for nothing. I had to think: If I were three and four, what would I do? Play dead, of course, and hope no one noticed me."

I looked at Paul. He made a "let her go on" motion with his

hand. Guess we were going to miss the plane, but that didn't seem very important. Not compared to what was happening here.

"Know what I did?" She smiled to herself. "I tickled that little foot, and it jerked! That's when I knew Papa had done what he'd set out to do. So I gently moved his body and called them the way their mother always did: *Émile! Henri! Come here, my two bad boys!* They came up, saw all the blood and their dead mother, and began screaming and crying. I hustled them out the kitchen door, thinking we would never go back to that house, never.

"The neighborhood was just as bad as the house: blood everywhere. Everywhere bodies of the dead and dying, most of them white, but many household and office staff to the missionary community, too. We had one grand Requiem Mass the next evening—"

She stopped and looked at us. "In many parts of Africa, it's too hot to wait any longer. So the dead are put to rest almost immediately."

We nodded.

"And that"—she sighed—"is the end of my childhood story. Pretty much the end of my childhood. Papa's friend, Dr. Morris, found a good school for me in Provence, and I went. I was glad to leave Africa. The nuns were very nice to me. I spent holidays with my friends. Then I graduated and went to the Sorbonne and came to New York after working a few years in Paris, as a gofer for the Fairchild Publications bureau there. I worked mostly for W."

"So how does Ev fit into all of this?"

"Well, he was threatening to tell everyone . . . you know."

"And it would have been embarrassing?" Paul asked.

"Worse. As soon as *Radiance* finds out I'm white, my job is history. Which is so unfair. I didn't *know* I was white until three months ago. And I'm good at this job! I worked hard to get here!"

We were staring at her as if she was speaking another language. I'm sure our chins were on our chests, and our eyebrows were all the way up into out hairlines. Frankie, white? Say what?

Frankie looked from Paul to me and back again; then she slowly crumpled into her seat.

"Oh my God, oh my God!" she wailed, pounding her desk in impotent fury. *"You didn't know, did you?"*

Paul closed his mouth. "Maybe we'd better start from the beginning—again."

16

It was very quiet in Frankie's office. We could hear the phone ringing on the other side of the door and Dinitra answering it in low, unhurried tones. On Broadway, horns continued to bleat, distantly. Somebody yelled "Ya-hoo!" down the hall, to a lot of answering laughter. We could hear the faint *click, click* that marked each second's passage on her quartz desk clock. Several clicks went by.

Finally Frankie spoke.

"About two months ago, a young woman sent me a letter, here at the office. It was marked PERSONAL AND CONFIDENTIAL and certified, bonded, registered, everything, so Dinitra left it unopened on the desk. When I opened it, I discovered a letter with a Louisiana postmark and a brief note, written by a woman named Jacqueline Metoyer, saying she had reason to believe she had information about my birth mother and would be willing to share it if I contacted her.

"I'd never really thought about my birth mother; I'd belonged to my parents since I was a couple of days old. I even looked like them, so unlike a lot of adoptees, I wasn't plagued with agonies of wondering. My parents were the people who raised me. Period. Then, out of the blue, comes a chance to find out something about my past. Initially, I wasn't interested. Then, because I knew I wanted children, I thought it might be a good thing to ask—for the medical information, you see. So I called Jacqueline Metoyer at the number she'd given me.

"Turned out it was a New Orleans number. She works for the Convention and Visitors Bureau as a public relations person. She told me her mother was very ill and, because of that, had decided to reveal that she had had another child. Until then, Jacqueline had lived and thought as an only child. Until then, I'd thought the same about myself. Apparently Jacqueline's mother felt it might be important for us to have each other after she died."

"What happened to Jacqueline's father?" I asked.

"Jacques-Yves Metoyer had died ten years before, of the same disease that was killing his widow—cancer. Liver, though, not breast."

"So Jacqueline's mother . . ."

I wasn't sure I should call her Frankie's too, since Frankie hadn't yet referred to her that way.

"Juliette Marie Metoyer, née Baptiste."

"Yes. Mrs. Metoyer thought you might want to know you had a sister in the world, after all this time?"

"I think it was more that she wanted Jacqueline to know *she* had a sister in the world," Frankie said, with no apparent rancor. "After all, I'd been an orphan for more than thirty years."

Paul leaned forward, intrigued. "What did you do? Did you meet her?"

"I met Jacqueline first. She has dark hair and dark eyes, but we favor each other somewhat. She was going to be in New York on business—something about how to get more New Yorkers to New Orleans for visits—and asked if I'd consider a brief meeting. We met for tea at the Palace."

"And?"

"I liked her. She came with old family photos and one of Juliette, who looks quite a lot like me. She could tell me my birth date, the convent where I was born, the Mother Superior's name at the time, and a bunch of other information that would not have appeared in publicity files. She didn't know my adoptive parents' names, but she knew that a baby girl had left Sacre Coeur convent two days after I was born. Only one infant was there that summer. It had to have been me."

Something wasn't adding up, though.

"I thought you said you were born in the *colored* ward of that hospital."

"I was. Everyone assumed I was black because Juliette had been sent to the convent because she'd had a—well, a *friendship* with a black boy who lived down the road, on the colored side of town. He looked about as white as Jacqueline, but you know how that goes. One drop, and there you are."

"But the baby wasn't his?"

"No. Big irony; they'd never had sex! She loved him, but he was too terrified to even *think* about that. Emmett Till wasn't the first, you know, just the best publicized. When Juliette was young, black men disappeared all over Mississippi and Louisiana by the dozens every year. He'd never even *kissed* her, but if he stayed to defend himself, he could end up losing his life, if for no other reason than to intimidate other black boys who didn't scare so easily. So his family shipped him to Chicago to make sure he didn't decorate one of their hometown trees."

"Then who got her . . . ?" Paul was thrashing around for a delicate way to say "knocked up."

"The boy who delivered croissants to the nuns every morning! Soon after Antoine Dumas left town, Juliette's parents practically imprisoned her. They used to let her out rarely, almost never without some sort of chaperone, her mother or a brother or an aunt. Her one unescorted excursion was to town for bread."

According to Frankie, the Baptistes ate freshly made bread daily, like most of their neighbors. The boy behind the counter found Juliette beautiful, and Juliette, angry with her parents and on the rebound from Antoine, found him irresistible. She probably allowed him liberties she wouldn't have under normal circumstances.

The inevitable happened. She hid her pregnancy for as long as she could, but when her parents found out they immediately sent her to the convent.

"Jacqueline said, '*Gran'père* told the sisters to take my mother or he'd kill her himself and they'd have her blood on their hands. He was furious! Pregnant—and by a black boy?' They assumed that a black man's raging hormones would immediately make the pure Juliette pregnant."

"The pure Juliette's natural fecundity at that age probably helped," I murmured.

"True."

"Why didn't she tell them Antoine wasn't the father?" Paul wondered.

"She told them, but they didn't believe her. She said, 'They'd not seen me with the baker's boy, and 'Toine had conveniently disappeared—although I didn't find out why until much later. So why would they believe me?' In those days a colored baby had to be born in the colored wing. Juliette had to switch beds when her labor started, to make sure I was born in the right place."

This was too much.

"So when you were born—"

"When I was born, my real parents—Juliette is my biological mother, but my *parents* raised me—were already waiting for me. They were scheduled to go abroad within the year. As I said earlier, the sisters called Thibodaux the morning of my birth, and they drove up two days later. My father said he was so excited he had to keep his hands on the steering wheel to steady them . . . Juliette, by the way, was sent to Lake Charles, to live with an aunt for two years."

Paul straightened up and shook his head, as if that would make any of this less confusing. For the first time, Frankie laughed.

"You're wondering how I got from colored to white, right?"

"Well, yeah. If it's not too much trouble."

"Well, here's the deal. The boy behind the counter wasn't afraid to have sex with Juliette, because he was white! And later he married her. Jacques-Yves Metoyer was Creole, just like Juliette!"

Jeez Louise.

"So you're saying *both* your parents were white, but because nobody would listen to your mother, you were born in the colored section of the hospital—"

"And," Paul continued, "of course your birth certificate said COL-ORED, so that was that."

"And it was," Frankie agreed, "until Jacqueline called me. I've been raised colored, schooled colored, churched colored, and dated colored all my life."

Wow. In one fell swoop, Frankie's world must have been turned upside down. The face she saw in the mirror was the same, the experiences that had shaped her were the same, but now they'd been put in a different context altogether. That'd be a real Maalox moment for most people.

"How are you dealing with this?" I wondered.

Frankie got out of her chair again and began to pace her office. "How do you *think* I'm dealing with this? I'm freaked! I've worked at a magazine for fifteen years that's devoted to the beauty and well-being of black women, thinking I was one of them. I've suffered all the predictable slings and arrows someone my color would bear during a period of black nationalism. Don't think I didn't know they were making 'ghost' jokes when I first came, or referring to me as 'Miss Anne' or 'Annie' behind my back. All the work I've done to bring this magazine to its present market position—do you think that's going to mean squat when they find out who I really am?"

"When are you going to tell them?" Paul asked quietly.

She sat down on the sofa and hugged a pillow to her middle.

"I don't know." She sighed softly. "Any suggestions? *Good staff meeting, everybody. Oh, one last teensy detail: I'm white.* Think that'd do it?" She laughed again, bitterly.

I could see her point. It was going to be a toughie. Then I thought of something else.

"Frankie, have you told Neil?"

"You know, I considered saying nothing to anyone *except* Neil, he had a right to know. He's not one of those people who always go around pointing fingers saying 'the *white* man,' blah blah blah. But he deserved to know. Even if it meant he walked away."

"I gathered he didn't?" I asked cautiously.

She smiled.

"No. Initially, it threw him for a loop, but he recovered almost immediately. You know what he said?"

Something noble, probably: I-love-you-for-what's-on-the-inside, or some similar shit.

"He said, 'Cheer up, girl—your *kids* are still gonna be black!' "

She was chortling like it really amused her. Actually, it *was* pretty funny. We grinned back.

"Well, he's the one who counts most, so if you're okay with it and he's okay with it, everybody else will have to make the adjustment. I don't guess *Radiance* is going to be open-minded enough to keep you on, though."

"Not hardly. I'm not going to suggest it, anyway. But there are a few major articles I'd like to have well under way before I pull the covers off myself. Do you think you could give me a couple of weeks?"

Paul and I looked at each other and shrugged.

"As long as it doesn't have any bearing on this business with Ev, when you enlighten them is your business," he said.

"Thank you. Thank you very much."

Frankie stood and came around the desk. She offered her hand to Paul, who shook it. I offered her my hand, but she surprised me by enveloping me in a fragrant hug. The scent flipped some switch deep in memory.

"Frankie, that's a very distinctive perfume you have on. What's it called?"

She smiled. "Vingt-et-Un. A little parfumier on the Left Bank made it for me when I turned twenty-one. He's one of those men who only has private clients, and he keeps all their formulas in a little safe. They say Grace Kelly had her scent done by him, too. And Marie-Hélène Rothschild.

"All I know is, a perfume made just for me was something I'd always wanted. So when I turned twenty-one, I took the discretionary money I made as a part-time shop assistant my senior year, and about twenty percent of the money my parents had left for me, and treated myself. It's an odd way for a young person to spend money, I know, but I think my mother would have understood. I've worn it ever since. No matter how poor I am, I have two bottles shipped to me annually. I love the fact that no one else, no one, can get this exact scent. Now Neil keeps me in supply. Why?"

I hated to burst her bubble, but I supposed I had to.

"Ev's room smelled a lot like your perfume when I came in to find him. Why weren't you on the dais when I left to go up to his room?"

"Ah."

Frankie sat down on the sofa. We did, too.

"Everett knew. Or he guessed, anyway. And he was getting ready to put a not-so-blind item in *Diaspora*'s "Talkin' Loud" column. If it ran, things would go downhill from there pretty quickly. I wanted to appeal to his sense of decency. Or at least to our past relationship, if it meant anything to him.

"But when I got there, he was rushing around like a crazy person. Said he was expecting someone, and we'd have to talk later."

"So did he say he wouldn't tell?"

"No, he said he'd *think* about it. I told him to think hard; then I left. No one was there when I closed the door and went back downstairs to the awards dinner."

Assuming she was telling the truth, someone else had come in after her.

But who?

17

Our ad hoc meeting with Frankie meant we'd cut getting to Kennedy pretty close. As it was, Paul used a lobby phone (the battery on his cell was dead, as mine had long been, and nobody felt like going the Dinitra route again) to call the hotel and ask that our bags be taken out *immédiatement*, and they were waiting, with Heinrich, at the curb when our taxi screeched to a halt minutes later. As soon as the driver popped the trunk, Heinrich swiftly placed both bags into the car. Paul had just enough time to tip him before the young German—or Austrian or Swiss, whatever—bowed (this time I *did* hear heels clicking), shut the door, and sharply rapped the cab's flank with the flat of his hand, twice. I guess that's German for "Step on it."

Not that it mattered in the end. After the mad dash to the airport, we discovered the plane had been delayed forty-five minutes, a lucky break for us, since we were able to check our bags and sprint through the airport to the gate, which was almost empty because everyone else had boarded. Since we had practically missed the plane, our original seats had been given away to a family with small children.

"I'm sorry I can't seat you together," the gate attendant said, handing us our boarding passes, "but I do have two seats left in first class." And we were happy to take them, even if it did mean sitting two rows apart.

Frankly, some time apart wasn't such a bad idea. We'd been traveling like the Gold Dust Twins for several days now, and it was nice to feel single again. Paul was too polite to say so, but I know he was thinking the same thing. I could tell by the way he sighed when he opened his *Fortune* and stretched out his legs.

I'd always promised myself I would fully enjoy flying first class whenever I had the chance—which happened rarely enough—and I'd done pretty well about keeping that vow. Today, though, I was so drained by our morning session with Frankie that shortly after take-off, and well before dinner, I fell asleep. Missed the chicken tarragon and the nice white burgundy they offered with it. Missed the special showing of Alfred Hitchcock's restored classic, *Rear Window*. Missed the chocolates and cordials. Instead, I was dreaming.

Ev was at Frankie's good-bye dinner, held in the Congo so long ago. He was, as usual, refusing to eat what was put in front of him. Frankie wasn't Little Frankie but Grown Frankie, and she was wearing the locket her mother had given her the evening before she was killed. Frankie's husband, Neil, was there, explaining to her father, "I didn't know Frankie was white when I married her, but that's okay. It's what's inside that counts." And there was a *thump, thump, thump!* Which could only mean one thing: the rebels were trying to break down the doors and kill us all. Nobody else at the dinner party was paying much attention. Incredulous, I ran to jam my back against the door to delay the inevitable, but the thumps were hard, I was shaking with their reverberations. . . .

"Alex, wake up. You're having a bad dream."

I opened my eyes. Paul had been shaking me. So much for rebels with battering rams. The seat next to my window seat was vacant.

"Are we there yet?"

"In about an hour. I walked back to go to the head, and you looked like you were having a stroke. What were you dreaming about, anyway?"

"Frankie. Frankie's mother getting killed. Everett at dinner. It was crazy."

I shook my head violently to clear the cobwebs.

He nodded seriously. "That story could give anyone nightmares."

Then my seatmate, a handsome software designer, returned from his leg-stretching stroll, so Paul made ready to go back to his seat. "By the way, you might want to catch that drool before we hit the terminal."

Oh, no! My hand flew to the corners of my mouth—which were dry. My seatmate had opened a copy of GQ, but I could see him looking furtively at me when he thought I wouldn't notice.

Damn Paul! It was definitely time for us to wrap this trip up.

We'd chosen to use our frequent-flyer miles on a nonstop flight, which meant we'd be flying into San Francisco and would have to figure out how to get to Oakland to see Jake in the morning. Paul had booked us a room at Campton Place, just off Union Square. I'd often passed it when I'd stayed in the considerably more modest hotel I usually used when in the city. Now *I* was going to get to be one of the people being ushered inside by the smiling help for tea in the lobby. Goody.

When we checked in, we discovered that the staff, helpful people that they were, had upgraded us, "Courtesy of the Titanium Card, Mr. Butler." Paul couldn't figure out how to tell them gracefully we'd like separate beds, so we meekly followed the bellman to see what we'd been given.

The upgrade meant we'd been moved from a room with two queen-sized beds into a suite that had the biggest four-poster I'd ever seen outside a palace. Had to be bigger than king-size; must've been *emperor*-size.

"This is getting to be funny, isn't it?" I grinned, as the bellman quietly shut the door.

"Side-splitting, Powell. Goddamn knee-slapping hilarious."

"My, we're grumpy when we need a meal! Let's dump the bags and take a walk, see what we can find."

It was about four o'clock—too early for dinner—so we walked through Union Square, then down south of Market. Stopped in the Museum of Contemporary Art, had tea, and split a sandwich (which I mostly ate, since I'd slept through the meal on the plane). Then we took the trolley back up to Washington Square for an Irish coffee and, having gotten our second wind, walked down Stockton back to the hotel.

Of course we window-shopped along the way.

"Powell, have you *ever* met a store you didn't like?"

"Oh, sure. Hardware store. Car-parts store. Athletic equipment store."

San Franciscans and tourists alike hurried past us, walking purposefully in the late-afternoon light, knees thumping large shopping bags emblazoned with the names of local and chain emporiums: Crate & Barrel, Cable Car Clothiers, Nordstrom, Williams-Sonoma. The cool air already held a hint of autumn. The deliciously smoky tang of a pretzel vendor wafted over us, as the *clang-clang* of trolley bells intermittently filled the air.

"This is better than L.A.," Paul said, stopping to look at a display of fifteenth-century Chinese pottery in a gallery window.

"Better how? Cleaner? Richer? Whiter?"

To most L.A. residents—even indifferent transplants—Bay Area condescension was an invitation to the verbal equivalent of a fist fight.

"More like the cilvilized East Coast."

"Cleaner. Richer. Whiter."

Before we could get into a serious discussion about that, we were at the hotel, where we bumped—literally—into a friend of Paul's.

"Boy, I can run, but I can't hide, huh?" Paul said. The two men clasped hands at the elbow in the standard brothaman greeting.

"Who you calling *boy*, boy? What you doing up here, anyway? Last I heard, you were talking the cops out of arresting you in L.A. And"—turning to me—"this must be your accomplice. I heard she was fine." He held out a neatly manicured paw. "Byron Campbell."

"Careful—'she' doesn't like being talked to as if she's not in the room."

"Alex Powell."

We shook, but not the elbow grab.

"And we were nowhere *near* being arrested."

Byron grinned. He was a smooth café-au-lait, with eyes that crinkled at the corners when he laughed. Nice teeth. He was shortish, stocky, and impeccably dressed, a TV network anchor who had been elected to the Best Dressed Hall of Fame by not one but two men's magazines. In addition to his reputation as a fashion plate, he also had a reputation as being something of a player, although I couldn't see it. Maybe the Staple Singers knew what they were talking about when they wrote that song; maybe heavy *does* make some people happy.

"Well, you know the folks; we like to exaggerate every now and then." Crinkle, crinkle.

"You working or on vacation?" Paul asked.

"Working. Definitely. Have a quick interview on the hill, but I should be back by seven. Whyn't you guys meet us for dinner, here in the hotel, at seven-thirty?"

Paul looked at me. The hotel had a great restaurant. I nodded.

"Sure. See you then."

A slim young brother in jeans and a windbreaker came up to us. "Sorry to interrupt, Byron, but the car's here and we're all loaded."

"Gotta go; see y'all at dinner."

Which is how we found ourselves in Campton Place Restaurant a few hours later in an interesting group: Besides us and Byron, there was Walter Choice, a columnist for the *Bay Area Guardian*; Shelley Mixon, an on-air reporter for the ABC affiliate; and Lauren DeGroot, the culture editor for *San Francisco* magazine, who, despite her Dutch last name, was black.

Through dinner, Byron regaled us with the story he'd finished yesterday, an interview of the city's African American mayor, a guy with such charisma—and *cojones*—he was a national political figure. They'd spent the downtime between takes comparison-shopping:

which Hong Kong tailor was best, where each went for shoes when they were in London, why nobody will ever make a tie like Charvet . . . important things like that.

Oh, and white girls.

"Honest," he told me, "never be afraid of being an equal opportunity dater, but don't let them think you have a jones for Miss Anne exclusively. Even *white* people think that's pathetic in a black man."

"Amazing." Lauren hooted, shaking her mahogany mane. "The mayor gave *you* dating advice?"

"Straight up."

We all laughed, although we sisters laughed a little less loudly. It is tiresome to have so many publicly prominent black men hooked on that White Thighs thing. I thought back to Frankie and how often she must have heard this—and how hard it must have been for her to listen.

By the time the dessert menus were being passed, we'd moved on to other things. Like why Paul and I were in town.

"So . . . anybody know anything about Jake besides the stuff that's usually printed?" Paul asked hopefully.

"Did you know he's a philanthropist?" Shelley asked casually, twisting the gold bracelet on her wrist.

"Jake?" I was truly surprised. I'd heard he donated a fair amount to the United Negro College Fund, but I thought that was mostly corporate money, contributed from *Onyx*'s profits and strong-armed from *Onyx* advertisers.

"Yup. He personally endowed a chair for A.C. Coleman at Berkeley's journalism school. Very low-key."

Strange. Jake and A.C. had clashed over several issues over the years. A.C. had been a columnist for the New York *Daily News* before he moved to San Francisco, where he wrote twice weekly for the *Examiner*. Jake was old-line civil rights, while A.C. was more of an ideological loose cannon. Like the *Village Voice*'s Stanley Crouch, you just couldn't predict what he would think about anything on any given day.

A.C. died suddenly a couple of years ago, and people were

intrigued when Berkeley announced the A.C. Coleman Chair for the Study of Media and Society. At the time, we figured the *Examiner* had funded it, something the paper neither denied nor confirmed.

"Why would Jake spend his own money endowing a chair to honor anyone other than himself? I didn't even know he and A.C. were close."

Shelley blew on the foam of her nonfat latté to cool it, then sipped delicately at the brew beneath.

"They were closer than most folks knew. Fellow Southerners. Veterans of the civil rights movement. And Jake felt the work A.C. was doing with the Institute—providing well-trained black journalists for papers across the country—was about the most important thing anyone could do."

Paul looked up from his plate. "Even though most of them were going to the mainstream press?"

"Jake thought the only way to reform the white press was to get more of us in it." Walter chuckled. "He figures it's better to conquer from the inside out."

"And," Lauren added, "don't forget, he has a few of A.C.'s graduates in his *own* empire. So he must have been impressed with the quality of the product A.C. was turning out. Rumor has it one may actually succeed him when he retires in about five years."

"Get out! I thought Jake had kids. None of them wants to run *Onyx*?"

I put my spoon in Paul's plate while I waited for someone to answer. Tarte tatin with cinnamon ice cream. Heavenly.

"His daughters aren't interested," Walter said thoughtfully, crunching an almond tuile. "The youngest child, Louise, is an aspiring opera singer. She lives in Switzerland and only comes home about once a year. Totally into a white life. The middle child, Charlotte, has two children of her own. She lives in Dallas with a husband who's some sort of big-deal doctor. Heads an institute at Baylor or something. She's big into community stuff, the bullshit kind and the sho'nuff kind. So neither of the girls, even if they had an interest—which they don't—are in a position to come out here and run Daddy's company."

"What about the third child? You've just mentioned the youngest and the middle one. Isn't there a third?"

"Jacob Julius Jackson, Junior. Hasn't spoken to his daddy in years."

We all looked at each other. There was definitely a story behind this piece of information.

"How old is he? What's he do? Where's he live?"

"About forty-one, forty-two, somewhere in there. He's the West Coast editor of *Vibe*. Lives here in the city. Uses his mama's maiden name. Masthead says J. J. Thornton."

Damn. I'd seen that name on the masthead and knew the editor was black, but I had no idea that J. J. Thornton was really Jake's namesake—which apparently was exactly why Thornton had chosen to use his mother's family name.

"What did he and his dad fall out about?" I asked.

Walter grinned, swirling his cognac and enjoying the fumes that wafted up from the glass.

"The fact that his only son and namesake is gay."

"Jake Junior is gay? Is this just rumor, or has he said he is?"

Walter shrugged. "A lot of people don't feel the need to send out announcements, Alex. He just *is*. I've seen him out and about. He doesn't make a big deal of it, but our circles often overlap. If you think it's a small *colored* world, imagine how small the world is if you're colored *and* gay."

I could imagine. Walter was, as he liked to say, "gay and *political* about it." But not every gay brother chose that route. Especially if choosing that route was going to give you a whole lot of grief.

According to Walter, who'd gotten this news from someone who'd once gone out with Jake Junior's old boyfriend, Jake was becoming worried about what would happen to his life's work after he died. According to Walter's source, Jake had had some very tentative conversations with Everett about perhaps merging the two magazines at some point. But Ev, while interested, had made the mistake of telling Jake what changes he'd make in the magazine immediately ("A lot of those lists? Most Important this and that? Best Dressed whatever? We'd have to get rid of them"). And that was that. Jake had no more interest tethering *Onyx*'s future to *Diaspora*'s.

The waiter unobtrusively removed plates, refreshed coffees, and brought more cognacs for those who were drinking them. The check had arrived—in another of those suitcase things, which meant it was going to be expensive, even split six ways.

As we pulled out our wallets, Byron waved us back. "Oh, no, no, no. This is my treat. I insist. You all have been rechristened: You are the Sources."

Huh?

"Mr. and Mrs. Reliable Source." He nodded to Paul and me.

"Their children, Impeccable and Usual." Lauren and Shelley blew movie-star kisses.

"And Reliable's brother, Highly Placed." Walter saluted.

Byron signed the bill, closed the folder, and beckoned to the waiter.

"After the network dicked me by passing me over for the Denny Freeman interview, I figure they owe me. They must agree, because they keep signing off on all my expense accounts. And I ain't fin-ished being mad yet."

Former NBA all-star Dennis Freeman had gone on to spend his life in prison after murdering his blond wife, her two sisters, and their parents after a Thanksgiving dinner argument two years ago. Although his trial had polarized Miami and drawn squads of reporters—from representatives of the *New York Times* and *Der Speigel* to the *National Enquirer* and the Brazilian equivalent of *People*—he was old news now, a year after the trial's conclusion. But while he was *new* news, Byron, who'd golfed with him from time to time, pre-homicides, had gotten Freeman's lawyers to agree to an interview.

It was a huge coup. Everyone wanted Denny Freeman, but Byron managed to get him—and Byron's network promptly handed the job to its bass-voiced anchor, explaining they needed to "keep things objective." The inference was that a black correspondent couldn't possibly maintain his journalistic remove while interviewing a black subject if critical questions needed to be asked.

Till then, Byron had been known as one of the toughest interviewers in the business; his hold-no-punches probes had pissed off many an elected official and made one former Miss America cry on-camera. So to be passed over as not tough enough—especially when he'd snagged the interview—was a true insult. Byron had been furious. He hadn't bitten his tongue about it to other media, and he'd staged a two-week walkout on his morning news show that made it abundantly clear how pissed he was. Apparently, Byron's ire had very long legs. The better for us; we had a terrific free dinner.

Lauren and Shelley left to share a taxi.

"Workday tomorrow, darlings." Lauren laughed. "You know Shel has to get home so she won't have those unsightly bags on-air tomorrow."

"What's your excuse?" Paul laughed. "You're print, not electronic."

"Gym at six A.M. You don't think these hips stay this slim with no work, do you?" She grinned and slapped a lanky flank. Paul gazed back in frank admiration. I must be invisible or something.

I said good night and went upstairs as they were all exchanging cards. Walter and Paul stayed behind, drinking and talking, until who knows when. I watched local news, had a satisfying tryst with Signe's other man, Ted Koppel, and eased into the big bed. It was so big I never knew when Paul finally came in.

18

We checked out after breakfast, left our bags
with the concierge, and took BART across the bay to Oakland.

"If there's a subway to hop on, you'll be first in line," Paul muttered.

But he couldn't complain: Bay Area Rapid Transport actually is
pretty rapid—during rush hour, anyway—and it gives commuters a
great view of both cities, coming and going.

The *Onyx* empire was located in prime territory, on the shores of
Lake Merritt, a large manmade lake near downtown. Jake's magazines—*Onyx*, *OT* (for *Onyx Teen*), *Onyx Man*, *Lady Onyx*, and
Midnight, the weekly tabloid that started Jake's publishing business—were located in a set of sleek modern buildings all fronted in
dark glass and connected by walkways. The buildings—a rectangle,
an ellipse, and a square—were surrounded by parklike spaces liber-
ally laced with shallow reflecting pools.

Jake's secretary ushered us in promptly at ten, and he offered us
coffee—"plain ol' American, not that stuff they charge three dollars
a cup for, across the way." But just as he was about to pour himself a
cup, he was called away on some editorial emergency.

"Make yourself at home. I'll be back in a few minutes."

The few stretched to twenty, which gave me time for a leisurely
inspection of his premises. By this time, Paul knew better than to tell
me not to snoop.

"Remember, Einstein, there *are* privacy laws. If Jake catches you, he *will* press charges. And I *don't* have the dough to bail you out. Not after this week, anyway." Killjoy.

Paul took his cup of plain ol' American and retreated to the leather sofa, where he proceeded to become engrossed in the *Wall Street Journal*.

I'd assumed Jake's private offices would be as formal as traditional as Chip's were reputed to be, with lots of dark glossy furniture from previous centuries, but I was wrong. Way wrong. Jake Jackson, who looked like he was born to be a 1940s undertaker, had an office that was flooded with light and filled with the kind of cutting-edge design New York and Milan were noted for.

His desk was a large thick glass rectangle set on four stainless-steel legs. The end closest to him had a black matte telephone that looked like the user would need a Ph.D. to operate it. At the far end from the telephone was a swoop of black metal that apparently was some sort of desk light. A silver julep cup held a fistful of ink pens and a carved wooden mail opener that had, perhaps, come from West Africa. Tiny halogen task lights with glass halos dangled from the ceiling on gently undulating wires.

To Jake's right was a sleek credenza that looked like dark Italian marble but, on closer inspection, actually seemed to be wood painted to look like marble: barely detectable seams delineated where the drawers and storage areas were. To open one, you probably had to exert some pressure on a specific corner or something. I tentatively reached out my hand. . . .

"Don't even *think* about it!" Paul admonished from behind the paper.

Damn.

The top of the credenza held two Lucite trays. One was full of a pile that said *needs signature* on sticky notes, the other had a few signed letters in it. Guess that was outgoing. Besides the trays there were a few African carvings and a small bronze by Constantin Brancusi. Who'd ever have figured Jake for a modernist?

The walls held tastefully framed pieces by contemporary African American masters—Jacob Lawrence, Betye Saar, Romare Bearden, and Sam Gilliam—all the walls except one. That was obviously Jake's braggin' wall; it held photographs of him and Mavis at every presidential inauguration from Truman on. There were three with the Kennedys alone: one at the inauguration, Mavis in navy satin next to Jacqueline Kennedy's white ensemble; one with the President and First Lady a few years later at the White House dinner that celebrated the hundredth anniversary of the Emancipation Proclamation (the invitation was displayed directly beneath it, matted in the same frame); and the last with the First Couple and President and Mme. Félix Houphouët-Boigny of the Ivory Coast. The black ladies looked as elegant as Mrs. Kennedy, although Mme. Houphouët-Boigny, a new bride in head-to-toe Givenchy, was clearly the star of this particular photo. Jake had the same cheese-eating grin in each picture, and the corresponding smiles of each president varied in sincerity. The Kennedys, Johnsons, Reagans, Bushes, and Clintons looked relaxed and easy. Eisenhower looked resigned. Richard Nixon looked positively pained but dutiful.

There were also photos of historic significance: Jake on the steps of the Supreme Court the day the country's ultimate lawmakers made de jure educational segregation illegal; Jake, Thurgood Marshall, and Roy Wilkins, in shirtsleeves and loosened dark ties, hours after the March on Washington was successfully concluded; Jake with Senator Edward Brooke on the latter's boat off the coast of Martha's Vineyard. In a proud column were a half-dozen framed honorary doctorates from some of the country's most prestigious learning institutions, black and white.

Finally, a steel console behind his desk held family photos. A glorious black-and-white of Mavis that was taken probably twenty years ago by a photographer of well known socialites sat in a simple sterling frame. There were photos of Jake walking Charlotte down the aisle in what clearly had been a mini-coronation, and a charming photo of his three granddaughters catching butterflies in white linen dresses. There was a dramatic one of Louise, in costume, on the steps of the Staathaus Opera in Vienna. There was no evidence of Jake Junior anywhere about.

Before I could mention this to Paul, the door opened and Jake walked back in.

"How's everybody?" he asked heartily, shaking Paul's hand first, then mine. "What's the word? You people find out who did Carson in?"

"Not yet," I admitted.

"Huh." He grunted, scanning the contents of the IN box and rapidly signing several letters, still standing. "How many dozens a folks said *they'da* done him in first if they could have?" He chuckled at his own joke.

We just looked at him.

He rolled his eyes and shook his head in weary disgust. "Oh, please. Don't tell me you've found out everybody loved him, he visited the old folks' home on Sunday, and there's an orphanage named after him! Integration might've broke the back of black business and made our kids behave as bad as the white ones, but it *did* place enough of us in the room at one time that we don't have to like every single colored person just *because* he's colored. Or African American. Whatever the hell we're calling ourselves this month." He stalked to the ironwood box that served as a coffee table and poured himself a cup of plain ol' American.

"I take it Everett was one of those folks in the room you could afford not to like?" Paul asked mildly.

Jake nodded. "No secret. Me and Carson got along like oil and water. Thought his poop didn't smell. Thought he'd *invented* the black newsmagazine. Shoot, I was publishing *Midnight* while he was still sucking at his mama's . . . oh, never mind."

He stopped and looked at me, slightly abashed. "Excuse me. But you know what I'm saying. I been in this business way before he was born, but that doesn't count to people like him."

Jake walked over to the braggin' wall and silently surveyed it. He was right. There was a lot of history there, and he was the person responsible for it. He moved to the framed degrees and read aloud where they'd come from with considerable satisfaction: "Harvard. Yale. Howard. Morehouse. Berkeley. Hampton."

"Nothing from Princeton?" I asked innocently.

Jake grunted. "That big orange P on those sweaters stands for Peckerwood. Always has, probably always will. Peckerwood U don't give no honorary degrees to Negroes—unless," he added thoughtfully, "they're *foreign* Negroes."

He shrugged and gave the six degrees one last glance. "Never went to college myself," he said casually, stirring his coffee. "Came straight out the army, took my mustering-out pay, and went home to see my mama and tell her what I was going to do. Know what she did?"

I shook my head.

"She gave me the papers on her house—made the bank take a second so I'd have enough money to start *Midnight*. I know everybody laughs about me bein' a mama's boy, and I don't care. I *love* my mama." He didn't use the past tense, even though we all knew Marietta Jackson had been dead for a decade. "Took good care of her while she was alive. She lived like a queen—didn't want for nuthin'." He nodded at a small photo on the corner of his desk, a wallet-sized black-and-white in a silver frame, of a smiling dark-skinned woman with a pleasant face and the same hooded eyes of her much-photographed son.

"That looks like an old picture," Paul said. "Taken maybe in the forties?"

"Just before I went in the war, 1942. Mama said she wanted me to have something of her to take with me, to keep me safe. Worked, too. It's my favorite picture of her."

It was the only one peering directly at him, not on display for visitors' perusal.

He pointed a finger at us. "*Always* take care of your mama." Then he looked back to the framed degrees. "Where'd *you* go to school, baby girl?"

"Wellesley."

"How many black in your class?"

"Well, the class was a large one—maybe four hundred and fifty. There were probably forty-five of us."

Jake nodded in satisfaction. "The government-mandated ten percent. Don't ever get over that, does it?"

"Not by much," I conceded.

"You think you coulda gone there forty years ago?" He knew the answer to that.

"Probably not," I said. "They only had two or three to a class forty years ago."

He harrumphed in satisfaction. "Same with magazines. Wasn't nobody doing this when I started. Come straight out of Itta Bena, Mississippi, straight from the arms of my Uncle Sam, right after I'd been in the South Pacific, getting shot at by Japs."

"They're Japanese now," I reminded him gently.

"Uh-huh. Some of my best business associates are Japanese. But in 1944, when they were tryin' to shoot my ass off just for makin' sure our supplies got through, they were *Japs*." He paused. "I'll tell you this. You young ones, it's hard now, but you have no idea"—pronounced like Signe did, *eye*-deah—"what it was like back then. Where I came from, anyway. Black men being snatched off the streets and beaten just 'cause the crackers didn't think they were humble enough. Women and children bein' leered at—or worse— by trash, and if you tried to act like a man and protect your family, you ended up looking like a bad piece of barbecue. It was *bad*. . . ."

He'd drifted off in a reverie, but we didn't want to disturb him. You take your oral history where and when you can get it.

"Right then and there, getting grenades lobbed at me on Tarawa, I made myself a promise: If the goddam Japs—excuse me, *Japanese*—didn't kill me, I promised myself that when Sam let me go, I was gonna do something to keep black people connected with one another, to be like the drums were in African villages: something just for *us*. The white folks wouldn't understand it and wouldn't want it."

"I'm curious," Paul said, after a pause. "Did you know you had a gold mine then? Or did that happen later?"

Jake smiled, pleased with his own prescience. "Oh, I always knew I'd at least break even. One thing we *will* do—three things, actually: Pay to dress right, pay to keep our hair up, and pay to see ourselves anywhere—print, movies, wherever—to remind us that we *do* exist. So I knew nobody would mind givin' ten cents for *Mid-*

night — that's what it cost in 1945, when it first came out — and later on I knew they wouldn't mind payin' sixty-five cents for *Onyx*. Where else you gonna see us at the White House? *Eisenhower* sure wasn't sendin' them pictures to the *New York Times!*"

He laughed, but without mirth, and looked around the room. It reflected his travels, his struggles, his rise to prominence. Jake had a right to be proud.

"For a long time, it worked. Then" — he sighed — "we started *specializin'*."

"But you still have a core audience," Paul pointed out. "Lots of people buy both *Onyx* and, say, *Radiance*."

"Yes, they do, thank the Lord, but that's changing. Magazines are mergin' and bein' taken over left and right. I have to look to the future to protect *Onyx*, if there is gonna *be* an *Onyx* after the dust settles. And I'm seventy-two. I'm not gonna be around forever. And Mavis is determined that I won't die at this desk."

He tapped the thick desk lightly.

"So you're looking for a possible successor, or partner?"

"Oh, yeah, and let me tell you, children, the pickings are slim, very slim."

He paused for a moment, running his hands lightly over the small Brancusi sculpture. It looked like a bronze feather.

"You know who came to see me? The editor of that rap magazine, what's it called?"

"*Whazzup?*"

"Uh-huh. And that cow over at *Black Women Today*."

"Alice Mann-Davis?" Like I didn't know.

"Yeah. Two hundred pounds of bad attitude and an itty-bitty subscriber base! I couldn't even *believe* she was suggestin' that match!"

He seemed still indignant that this mouthy Sistahmagazine, as *BWT* liked to refer to itself, would dare to expect consideration for a merger with the likes of *Onyx*. I almost laughed; he was like the outraged father of a debutante being courted by an upstart boy from the wrong end of town.

"Who else?" Paul asked. "Did you and Chip ever have a conversation?"

"*That* lasted about five minutes." Jake laughed. "We had lunch out here when he was in town. Some Eye-talian place over across the Bay." Shades of Ev! "We had a nice lunch I paid way too much for. And after the first few minutes, I could see it wouldn't work."

He stopped and looked at our faces, which had "how come?" written all over them.

"Wiley is basically interested in one thing," Jake explained patiently. "Money. Or maybe two things; money, and being seen as a player in the white world. Now, he'd continue to make money with *Onyx* if he took it over, but his prestige level would dip—he thought so, anyway—if he merged *Aspire* with us and we stayed the same. Which is where my problem with him came in."

"Too many changes?" Paul asked.

Jake nodded. "So many of 'em that, if I'da done what Wiley wanted, it wouldn't have been *Onyx* anymore, and what would have been the point of that? My mama didn't take a second on her house so *Onyx* could impress the white folks. The white folks are not our crowd."

"That's what Chip wanted to do?"

"He didn't say so, honey, but that was exactly his plan. No more of the annual Single and Available issue; people love that! Wanted to cut the Gospel Report and any mention of church news. And the worst part, he wasn't gonna make advertisers use black models in every single ad. I sweated *blood* to make that happen in the late forties, wouldn't take advertising that didn't have black folk in the photos! And here, in one fell swoop, he was gonna cut it out." He shook his head at such craziness.

"Did Chip say why?" Paul asked.

Jake went over and stood in front of him. "Yeah. Three words: 'Times have changed.' Didn't think it was *necessary* anymore, since even white companies used black folks in their ads now. I told him times *had* changed—but not as much as he thought."

Paul shook his head in an I-hear-you gesture. "So it became clear to you that this wasn't something that would work for you or your readers."

"Oh, yeah." Quietly.

I looked at a photo of Jake, Chip, and Everett taken at the Homeboy Golf Tournament a couple of years ago. Traditionally a fundraiser for a local foundation, the "homeboys" were movers and shakers, mostly from the East Coast, who had gathered in suburban New York for several years for a weekend of shit-talking golf-playing. A lot of business got done there too.

"What was the barrier to merging with *Diaspora*?"

"Too political, little girl, too political. My crowd understands the need for political action, don't get me wrong. Remember, these are the people who did the postcard campaign that got the Greenville Boys freed in fifty-one. Eisenhower, with his sleepy do-nothin self, even *he* sat up and paid attention to the three million postcards that people ripped out the magazine and sent to the White House. If he wanted to be reelected, some justice was gonna have to get done.

"Anyway, like I say, I'm as political as the next person, but I ain't no fool: I know if the average reader is faced with two covers—one with Denzel or Vanessa Williams on the cover and the other with somebody like Mumia Abu-Jamal—well, which one do *you* think is gonna sell better?"

Good point.

"I kept tryin' to tell Carson: lure'em in with a pretty face, *then* educate 'em while they're turning the pages. He wouldn't consider it. And, like Wiley, he wanted to do away with what he called the "old-timey stuff" my core *Onyx* readers think is important. Boy didn't even have the good grace not to sneer when he said it. So no, that was not a match, most definitely."

The room was quiet. We could hear soft voices in his assistant's office next door, and the muted electronic bleeping of phones somewhere. His own space-age box on the desk merely blinked, no sound.

"I guess your children aren't interested?"

"No, baby girl"—he sighed—"no interest there. And it's just as well. Charlotte is a mother in Dallas, with three little girls to raise and a husband to look after. She sits on the *Lady Onyx* Fashion Board, so we can bring her in four times a year. Her mother likes to work with her, but we understand her obligations are elsewhere."

"What about the other one?"

He looked through his large windows at Lake Merritt, twinkling in the distance. "Louise is off in Europe, doin' her own thing," he said slowly. He paused, as if he was considering sharing something. "Louise is a different kind of girl. She's probably spent as much of her life outa the country as in it at this point. . . ."

"Like Frankie?" I offered.

He looked back to me. "*Not* like Frankie. If she was, I'd have a chance. See, Frankie, for all she looks like a white girl, she has her heart in the right place. She works at *Radiance*, yes, but she also sits on the boards of several black nonprofits, like Alvin Ailey, the Studio Museum, the United Negro College Fund. I think she's on the Coalition, too."

"That would be the Coalition of One Hundred Black Women?" Paul asked.

"Yeah, that's the one. Frankie might have grown up in Europe, but she knows where home is and she lets you *know* she knows."

"Louise, on the other hand—?"

"Honey, I can talk straight to you, so I will: Louise is one of them people who enjoy being the only colored in the room. Over there in Europe, they're making a big fuss over her. They love her voice. They think she's so . . . so . . ." He searched for a word, frustrated.

"Exotic?"

"Yeah, that's it! Like she's some strange pretty bird sitting in their living rooms."

I smiled grimly. "So cultured, so refined—they almost forget they're talking to a—"

"You got it. I see you know the drill."

Paul went over to the braggin' wall and casually scanned the photos. Then he turned.

"What about your son?" he asked quietly.

"I *had* a son; I don't anymore," Jake said levelly. The way he looked at Paul almost dared him to say more.

"Of course you do. He lives just across the Bay and he works in publishing. Why not him?"

"I told you: he's dead. To *me*, anyway."

"Does Mavis feel the same way?" I asked.

Jake gave me a *what, you too?* look. "What Mavis does with that boy is Mavis's business. We don't discuss it."

This time there was definitely a long silence, as if Jake was daring either of us to ask a follow-up question about Jake Junior. We had overstayed our reluctant welcome; Jake's glances at his watch weren't even subtle anymore.

"So what are you going to do, Jake?" Paul asked.

"Dunno yet. Maybe a partner from outside the country. All the publishing houses seem to have them, don't they? There's one guy I've been talking to who gets the point. We don't know if we can work it out, but maybe. Anyway, since my kids aren't interested and the others—Wiley and Carson—didn't see it my way, maybe this one will."

"Who is it?" I asked.

Jake stood, indicating our time with him was indeed finished. Paul immediately rose and gave me the eye to do the same.

"You're good reporters." Jake smirked as he opened the door for us. "Try to find out."

19

Of course Sally saw us when the taxi dropped us off in front of her guest house, and of course the phone rang about two minutes later, with Guess Who on the other end.

"Oh, Alex, you've finally caught one—good for you!" she trilled, as Paul made a leisurely inspection of the premises.

"Sally," I hissed, "first off, I did not 'catch' one; Paul is a friend. *Just* a friend."

"Well, honey, you're going to have to work on him, because he's much too handsome to pass along to someone else," Sally said cheerfully. "He needs to go from being a friend to being a *boy*friend."

I rolled my eyes and was intensely grateful I wasn't on the speakerphone.

"Second of all, if I may be allowed to finish, what makes you think I would have to catch a man, anyway?"

"Well, dear, I assume if you had any *skill* in that department, I would have seen one over there before now."

I sighed. I couldn't exactly argue with her there.

Paul was walking back into the living room and opening the armoire that held my stereo and my collection of old vinyl and CDs. As Sally continued to prattle on, I could see him flipping through the piles, alternately nodding approval (Jimmy Scott, Etta James,

Carmen McRae, Oscar Peterson, and Bill Evans) and shuddering in disgust (Barbra Streisand in a weak moment).

"So, Sally, is there anything I can do for you?"

"Well, actually, I wanted to invite you two over in a little while for drinks. I'm an old woman, and I don't want to take up too much of your time, but I thought cocktails might be nice. Aren't you going to show your young man some of Los Angeles?"

Paul was standing rigid as a cement pole; clutched to his chest were a few CDs, but I couldn't see what they were. I raised my eyebrows in question, and he staggered around like Fred Sanford: *Elizabeth, I'm comin' ta meet ya, honey!*

"Alex?"

Sally was waiting for an answer, more patiently than I would have if the circumstances had been reversed.

"Drinks? Well, actually . . . uh . . ."

No way was I going to bring this boy by for general inspection. For one thing, I'd already seen the effect he has on old ladies. For another, we could have drinks wherever we ended up for dinner without having to socialize first.

"Drinks?" Paul boomed, knowing Sally could hear him from across the room. "Great—tell her we'd love to! Can she make a good martini?"

"Oh, my dear, a martini man! You children hurry on over, and I'll have Josefina chill the glasses and get the shaker out."

I sighed. Now that Charming Billy had indicated an interest, I knew I *had* to take him over. Her feelings would be terribly hurt if I just "forgot." Not smart to piss off the landlady—and even if I could have, I didn't want to. I was genuinely fond of Sally.

So we'd go to damn drinks. But *only* drinks.

"We are *not* staying for dinner, you hear me? We're going someplace nearby, in the neighborhood."

"Bet. You're probably anxious to get back to the farm, anyway."

"What?"

He snorted and waved the CD aloft. He'd found my collection of Broadway show tunes and was picking on *Oklahoma!* He was warbling a stanza from "Oh, What a Beautiful Morning," serenading me with a smarmy imitation of Gordon MacRae's classic rendition.

"I'm going to put a bright golden haze on your *forehead* if you don't put down my CD," I growled.

He just hooted and continued to itemize my stuff, holding it tantalizingly out of reach as I impotently tried to grab it. He held me off easily; he was stronger than I thought.

"*The King and I? Camelot? South Pacific?*"

"Yes, dammit. I *like* those musicals. So what?"

"Bet you know all the words by heart, don't you, Einstein?"

I paused and considered. Oh, what the hell.

"Yeah, I do. What's it to you?"

He continued to run through the list: "*Carousel. Guys and Dolls. West Side Story*—actually, that one was pretty cool."

"Like you'd know cool if it was in the same room with you! This is modern American history, knucklehead."

Paul put his bag in the closet and laughed. "Oh, yeah. I'll bet they teach *The Wiz* in Modern American History at fine educational institutions all across the country."

I could hear his chuckles echoing in the little closet.

I took a deep breath and considered letting it pass, then decided a little guilt never hurt anybody. Especially smart-ass people like "my" young man.

"Not that it's any of your cretinous business, but I grew up listening to this stuff. My dad worked at night a lot, and when he was gone, my mother would entertain me by putting on her old records of Broadway shows. She knew all the words to all the songs, so I learned them by osmosis from the time I was really little. I like having those reminders around."

Just me and Mother, singing at the tops of our lungs, while we dusted the dining room, or washed and dried the dishes. "Oddly enough, love of show tunes is one of the few things we have in common."

He looked at me more kindly and gently placed the stack of CDs back in the armoire. "That's how I got into Sinatra. Who I see you also have."

" 'Cause your mother loved him?"

"The old man. *Big* Sinatra fan. One of the few things *we* had in common."

Huh. Go figure. We stared at each other for a moment. Either he was getting better the more time I spent with him, or I was becoming susceptible to Sally's silly suggestion. Paul waited, velvet-brown eyes calmly assessing me, refusing to break contact first.

Enough of this silly game. I moved my eyes away.

"Well, let's go. We'll make Sally happy for a few minutes. Then we'll walk down the street to Prado for dinner."

"What's Prado?"

"Kind of pan-Hispanic with a Caribbean twist: chicken with mango salsa, shrimp in black-pepper sauce, paella—"

"Excellent. Let's get that martini first. I want to meet your land-lady."

So we walked across the court for a visit that should have been about twenty minutes and turned into maybe an hour. Sally fell in love with Paul, just as Aunt Edith had, and like Aunt Edith felt compelled to give him the 911 on me.

"I'm so glad you're here, she'll have some fun for once! Alexa works too hard."

This said while walking him into the library, with her arm tucked companionably into the crook of his, just as Edith had.

"Come, Paul, I'll show you my first editions from the Harlem Renaissance."

I tried not to be miffed that she'd never shown *me* the damn first editions, but that's Paul's effect on old ladies again.

Way past our intended twenty minutes, Sally sat up, startled.

"Oh, dear, I'm afraid I've kept you past time to go."

"What's the matter?" Paul winked. "Commandant over there giving you the eye?"

Hell, no, I was giving *him* the eye, and he damn well knew it.

"Well, *I did* say I wouldn't keep you from dinner. . . ."

"Why don't you join us? We're just going to Prado. Have you eaten yet?"

Sally beamed. "Isn't she the *sweetest* girl, Paul?"

"Um-hmm," he murmured. Mr. Noncommittal.

"Thank you, dear, but I want you two young people to go out and enjoy each other without an old lady present. Maybe another time. Anyway," she added, "I have an engagement: I'm going down the street to audition the string quartet for the annual Windsor Square Garden Party. God knows who they'll pick if I don't oversee the process! So you all run along."

So we did—but not before Sally made Paul promise to return "for a *real* meal, very soon." Food 'ho that he was, of course he promised to do just that.

Although we'd initially intended to walk, I decided to drive. I hadn't really had anything but mineral water at Sally's house and wasn't planning to drink more than a glass of wine at dinner.

"Good. Then I can have two glasses," Paul said, reaching for his jacket.

"You've already had two martinis," I pointed out.

"Yup. This is the last couple of days of vacation, and I'm going to make the most of it."

"Some vacation."

"Oh, come on. Part of it was fun. You got to do what you like to do best."

"That being?"

Paul ticked off his list on three fingers. "Traveling, staying in nice hotels, and getting into everybody's business."

"Yeah, but we didn't find the one piece of business that would have been helpful in finding out about Everett."

"We said we'd try. We've done our best. Let's go eat."

Before we left, however, we got into a brief argument about who got to sleep where.

"You'll stay in my room; the bed's longer and the bathroom's closer. I'll sleep on the sofa."

"No way I'm kicking you out of your own bed. And the sofa opens up, so I'll be fine. I'll sleep there."

"Etiquette books say the good guest sleeps where his host asks him to, and the good host always puts the guest in the most comfortable place. And the good guest is gracious and *takes* it."

"Well, I read a different book, the one that says you don't sleep in a woman's bed unless the woman's in it with you."

Whoa! Who wrote *that* book?

"Really?"

"Really."

"Is that a backhanded invitation, or did I not understand what you just said?"

He shook his head in frustration. "I don't know that *I* even understand what I just said. Forget I said it. The week is starting to get to me, I think. Or maybe it's the martinis."

We both laughed, but it was edgy laughter. It's true. We'd never seriously considered each other as anything but acquaintances. And even if I'd been Halle Berry, I don't think Paul would have laid a hand on me. As I said, I was still Tainted by Tim. Men are funny about that.

On the other hand, Tim was ancient history. And Signe says he and Paul were nowhere near as close as they had been when Tim and I dated. Maybe distance had something to do with it: Tim was in London, doing God only knows what.

And we were here. Intriguing.

"Let's argue about this later," I offered. "You probably need some food to soak up those martinis."

I turned off the lights and turned on the alarm system, and we left. In the side yard, the pool glowed aquamarine, like a cabochon jewel.

We had a pleasant dinner at Prado, a unpreten-tious neighborhood restaurant with mismatched chairs and a trompe-l'oeil ceiling painted with cherubs. Toribio Prado, the owner, was an impossibly good-looking young Cuban émigré who had become a casual friend over the years. Tonight he hovered over us, assuming (wrongly) that this was a Big Date night.

"So," he said, looking at me meaningfully, black eyes dancing, "how was everything?" He looked at Paul and all but winked.

"Great. Better than great. The shrimp were incredible." Paul grinned.

The host laughed. "I'll tell Mama when I talk to her tomorrow; it's her recipe. The recipes were about the only thing we were able to take when we left Cuba, but they turned out to be better than money."

No kidding. He and his brothers had brokered Mama Prado's recipes into several successful restaurants, all of them good.

"Do you talk to your mother often, Toribio?"

"Every day, Alex."

"Really?"

"You don't?" he asked, genuinely shocked.

Paul made *tsk tsk* sounds and shook his head mournfully at Toribio, who was shaking his ponytailed head.

"You need to work on her, man. We only have one mother, right?"

"Absolutely!" Paul agreed, emphatically.

"I'll play The O'Jays for you later. Toribio, may I have the check, please?"

"No, Toribio, give the check to me," Paul said firmly.

"Actually, I'm not giving it to either of you. There's no charge."

"Toribio," I began warningly, "you know you can't comp me; the paper has rules about that."

We'd argued about this over the years. He didn't see the harm since I wasn't a restaurant reviewer, and although I'd explained our fairly stringent conflict-of-interest clause many, many times, he often showed how little he thought of it by sending over a lovely glass of wine or a plate of dessert.

"It's just a sip, just a taste—I want to know what you think," he'd cajole.

But a meal—two meals—was different. Accepting meals could land a reporter in deep doo-doo and was exactly the kind of documentable transgression they'd hang over your head when they were ready to get rid of you. So I began protesting again, but Toribio held up his hand, palm outward, like a school crossing guard.

"I didn't say *I* was paying for it, Miss Integrity," he sniffed.

We both looked at him, waiting for an explanation.

"Mrs. Ferguson, she paid for it. She calls up and says, 'Send me their bill, Toribio. Dinner's on me tonight.' I ask was it a special occasion, and you know what she said?"

We shrugged.

"She said, 'Maybe . . . we'll see. Make sure they have a nice bottle of wine.'"

We were still laughing about that when I drove home through the winding dark streets toward Sally's house, discussing whether it was too late to ring her bell and thank her in person.

The car came out of nowhere.

Paul had been saying "Maybe she can come to breakfast, or to lunch tomorrow," when I barely had time to register a blur of lights from my left. Streaking across Beachwood Drive, a sedan ran right across our path. I heard a thud, then a sickening crunch of metal and a squeal of tires. We'd hardly had time to assess what had hit us when it was gone.

"Are you all right?"

Paul was rubbing his right shoulder, where the seat belt had yanked him back.

"I think so . . . You?"

"Fine. Let's see what kind of damage that asshole did."

A significant amount, as it turned out. The entire front bumper lay twisted in the street. One headlight hung from its socket, swinging crazily from an almost-severed wire. The other was totally crushed, but the signal light, for some reason, still worked. It blinked on and off like an amber strobe. Bits of glass and other unidentifiable parts littered the area.

Even though there had been a squeal of tires, no one had poked his head out to see if we were okay. Life in the big city.

"You didn't see who it was who ran the stop sign, did you?" Paul was tucking the bumper under his arm; he opened his door, slid his seat forward, and with some difficulty placed the bumper across the back seat.

"Nope. One minute he wasn't there, and the next minute he was."

Paul sighed and looked at the skid marks. "Nobody's hurt, nobody saw anything. It's going to be an uninsured driver claim, unless we can give them some more information about who it might have been."

"Which means my rates go up?"

"Probably. We might as well see if we can drive the rest of the way home, because cops usually won't come out for a no-injury collision."

True. They only do that here if you have a no-injury accident on the freeway at rush hour. If it's only *your* day that's screwed up, that's between you, your God—and your insurance company.

I climbed back in and started the car, which rumbled to life immediately.

"Home, Jamesina," Paul muttered.

In less than two minutes we were cranking and wheezing into the motor court. I coaxed the car around back, because I didn't want Sally to have a heart attack if she got up before we did and saw it.

I was glad we'd left a few lights on in the living room; it wasn't cold out, but the warm glow made things feel safer indoors.

"Your message light is blinking." Paul pointed to the machine on the kitchen counter.

"Hit it. It's probably Sally, wanting a recap of our terribly romantic evening," I teased.

He smiled and pressed the button.

"You have two messages," the mechanical woman's voice informed me silkily. "Message one . . ."

A hang-up. The dial tone echoed in the room for a few minutes, then silence.

"Message two . . ."

That wasn't an accident—and the next time, you won't walk away.

20

"Call Marron," Paul instructed tersely.

"You're kidding, aren't you? It's past ten o'clock. We can wait till morning."

"Fuck morning. You pay taxes—and he wants to be kept up to speed. If you don't call him, I will."

In the end, it wasn't his challenge that made me call, it was the F-word. Unlike me, Paul didn't sprinkle his conversation with it casually, so the fact that he'd used it—and the tone in which he had used it—was a good indication of how upset he was.

While he walked through the house, checking the locks on the windows and French doors, I dug into my purse, found my wallet, and fished out Marron's number. The voice mail told callers to have the watch desk page him in case of emergency. I thought about it for a moment, then called.

"Homicide, Radin," a no-nonsense voice said. It sounded like it belonged to a woman you wouldn't want to tick off if you didn't have to.

I told her my name, said Marron had instructed me to call if something came up, and gave her my number.

"I'll try to reach him now for you, ma'am," the brusque voice said.

Three minutes later, Marron called back.

"S'up? Where are you?"

"Home. Got back a couple hours ago. Was going to call and let you know tomorrow, but something happened a few minutes ago and Paul wanted to call you now."

Briefly I told him what had happened.

"You were right to call. Stay there. I'm coming over. Give me directions."

"Where are you coming from?"

"Boys Town, around the corner from the station."

This was Marron's politically incorrect way of saying he was in West Hollywood, which had been gifted with the nickname because of its large gay and sometimes flamboyantly out population. I started to point out that plenty of lesbians and seriously artsy types lived in West Hollywood too, then skipped it and just gave him directions.

Fifteen minutes later he was at the door.

"Boy, when they say 'plainclothes officer,' they must've had you in mind."

He ignored the comment and pushed past me. He was all in beige linen, but his oatmeal-colored jacket and slacks were as austere as a Quaker's—if Quakers shop at the Gap.

"Tell me again what happened."

So we did. Then he made us play the tape for him, several times.

"You have another tape for this machine?"

"Sure, I have spares in the drawer. Do you need one?"

"Nope. You're gonna need one, though."

He flipped open the machine and popped the tape out of its holder. "I'll send this to the guys in voice analysis in the morning."

"Don't you want to put in a Baggie or something?" I asked.

He rolled his eyes at Paul. "She should maybe stop watching so much *Law and Order*, don't you think?" Then he turned back to me. "No, actually, I don't need a plastic bag. The message came in over the phone, remember? He didn't walk in here and leave it, whoever he is. If you have an old envelope, that would be fine."

I gave him a *Standard* envelope, part of my office supply that it was technically illegal for me to keep at home; Marron ignored my flouting the "no-company-property-for-personal-use" rule, put the minicassette in, sealed the envelope, and dropped it in his pocket.

"Anybody hurt?"

"Nah, just a little sore where the seat belts saved our lives." Paul rubbed his sternum gingerly.

"Or," Marron pointed out, "more likely, your faces. Lot of people who go through the windshield don't die—but the way they look afterward, they wish they had."

"I'll keep that in mind if I'm ever tempted to drive without my seat belt."

He looked closely to see if I was being a smart-ass, but I wasn't; I don't even back out of the driveway without buckling up. "You-all might want to consider staying somewhere else tonight. Are there friends you can call?"

"Not at eleven o'clock at night, there aren't. And I'm not leaving my house—I just got back!"

"You're worried that someone will try to come back this evening?" Paul asked, frowning.

"Well, let's look at what we've got. Someone comes out of nowhere, speeds up, and almost rips your car in half. Allegedly you were just in the wrong place at the wrong time and got smashed up. Except when you get home, that same somebody—or one of his pals—has left you a nasty voice mail telling you it could happen again." He turned to me. "Is you number listed?"

"No," I said slowly, "it's not."

That's standard procedure at newspapers. Many reporters and virtually all columnists and editorial-page writers have unlisted numbers. It's a safety precaution to ensure that when people get wildly unhappy about the way you cover the school board meeting or a local gang's activity, there's some insulation between the writer and the general public. As it is, enough of them show up ranting and raving in the lobby every day to warrant two armed security guards.

"So whoever this asshole is, he's found out where you live and what your telephone number is. He only needs one to get the other."

I knew that well from my days on the Metro staff back east. The good ol' Reverse Phone Directory can give you anybody's address if you have their phone number. And there were a lot of Internet phone guides that could give you a phone number if you could input an address. But still—

"Okay, you just got home. How about staying in the big house across the way? Didn't you say the owner is your landlady?"

"She is, and I'm sure she'd let me if I asked, but I don't want to worry her."

"That's nice," Marron mocked. "How worried do you think she'll be when the EMTs come to put you back together after this psycho comes for you? Don't you have *any* common sense?"

I just shrugged at him. I wasn't leaving, and that was that.

"How about if we stay in the same room?" Paul offered. "It wouldn't necessarily stop an attack—if there's going to be one—but it might make whoever it was think twice about trying to get through one of these windows."

"Oh, please. It wasn't even a specific death threat, he just said *next* time. . . . What?"

Marron was looking at both of us oddly. "Actually, I'd assumed you were *already* sleeping together. When I first met you—"

Paul laughed at Marron's confusion.

"When you first met us, you asked where we were staying, and we both told you 'in the hotel.' "

"But we never said we were staying in the same *room!*" I tittered.

Marron exhaled in annoyance. "Yeah, I should have remembered what my mom taught me about what happens when you make assumptions."

"Yup." I was trying to wipe the grin off my face.

"Anyway"—Marron had regrouped—"if you could be in the same room, that would be helpful. I'd send a squad over, but right now we're stretched tight as hell. About twenty percent of the force is doing some kind of cockamamie diversity-training thing, and a bunch of guys are out with some flu that's going around."

"In the summer?"

"What can I tell you? It's a summer flu."

Or Blue Flu, but I certainly wasn't having that discussion at this hour.

"So the windows and doors have been checked, we'll put the

alarm on, and we'll stay up all night and stare at each other. Satisfied?"

Marron heaved himself up out of his chair and looked at me
balefully.

"You know, I can fully understand why someone would want to
put a hit on *you*, but you could have some compassion for my man,
over here." He gestured to Paul. "He was just along for the ride to
keep you out of trouble, and now he's stuck in a bad remake of *The
Bodyguard*."

"Well, he can leave with you if he wants; it's a free country. You
can drop him off at the Millennium on your way back to Boys
Town."

Marron shook his head. "Uh-uh. I'm going home, which is not,
and will never be, in Boys Town. And if he doesn't stay—"

"I'm staying! *You* go!" Being stuck up under me was finally making Paul edgy.

"I know you are, I was just ribbing Miss Daisy, over here. You
guys get some sleep, if you can. Somebody will probably call to get
the exact place the accident occurred, so they can estimate how fast
the asshole was going."

He opened the door.

"I'll talk to you tomorrow. Keep the door locked."

"Yessir." I shut it, practically in his face. I could hear him laughing on the other side. He knew I'd done that on purpose.

"Take some Tylenol, you're going to be sore in the morning. And
put on the alarm—now."

"*Go home!*"

"I am. Right now. And I think I'll put on some Whitney when I
get there."

We heard him mangling the theme song from *The Bodyguard* as
he walked down the driveway: "*A*nd *eye-eee will always love
yeeeewww . . .*"

It was my turn to laugh. I turned around to see Paul looking at
me like he was trying to figure something out.

"What?"

"I'm trying to remember how that movie ended. They showed it once when I was coming back from San Francisco, but I fell asleep before the end."

"She doesn't sleep with him. She meets him on the runway as her private plane is getting to leave, and she gives him one long deep kiss."

"Oh, man!" He threw up his hands. "I'da been totally pissed!"

"Why? Even *I* have to admit it was romantic."

"He took a *bullet* for that whiny self-centered bitch and all he got was a kiss?"

"Hey, they could chop your head off and you'd get doodly from me, so he did better than you would have."

"Don't flatter yourself. That wasn't an invitation. Where do you want to sleep, out here or in there?"

"I want me to sleep out here and you to sleep in there."

"Nice try. I promised to look after you, and I'm going to. So out here or in there?"

The bedroom had a larger bed, but it was too . . . bedroomy.

"Can you sleep on a pullout?"

"I can if you can."

"Then let's sleep here."

And we did, for several uninterrupted hours, until the phone rang at eight the next morning.

"Hi, this is Alex Powell. Sorry I missed your call—"

I swung out of bed, thinking I could race to the kitchen counter and turn the machine off, but I hadn't realized how sore I would be—even with the Tylenol I took before we crashed.

"Ooooohh!" I gasped.

"You okay?" Paul asked, squinting. When I nodded weakly, he crammed the pillow over his head to block out the sunlight that was pouring through the windows and promptly went back to sleep.

I caught the damn machine just as Henry Adams's voice started to come through it.

"Oh, Alex, hi. I hope I didn't awaken you."

I grunted.

"But I remembered what an early riser you are, so I thought I'd try."

"What can I do for you, Henry?"

"Someone called here trying to reach you, but he's actually in Los Angeles, so I thought, since you were in the same time zone, I'd leave you the message."

I grabbed a pencil and poised it over the note pad I always leave on the counter.

"Okay, shoot."

"His name is Benjamin Soyinka, and he'll be at the Peninsula for the next couple of days. Room thirty-twelve."

"Did he say what he wanted?"

"Not exactly. He called asking to speak to someone who could tell him something about the investigation he understood was going on about Ev. He knew enough to know that some civilians were asking questions, and he wanted to speak with whoever it was. I wouldn't give him your home number, but I promised to pass the message along immediately."

"Thanks, Henry. Do you know anything about him?"

"Just that he's rich, rich, rich, kind of like an African Ted Turner, and he wanted to speak to you."

"Hmmm."

"And one other thing. Apparently he's one of the people the board is consulting with about *Diaspora*'s future."

Ah, *now* it became clear why Henry had been so assiduous about passing along the message!

"So if he happens to ask about the line of succession, it wouldn't be out of line for me to sing your praises, right, Henry?"

"Well, only if you think that's merited, of course." His tone indicated that there could be no doubt whatsoever about *that*.

"*If* he wants to meet and *if* we have that conversation, Henry, I'll keep it in mind. Gotta go."

Paul was still sleeping, facedown. He'd run out of clean T-shirts, so he'd simply slept in his drawstring pajama bottoms. The sheets had been thrown back, and I could inspect his back, slim but with well-defined muscles, as it rose and fell with his even breathing. His sinewy arms were still cradling the pillow that was jammed over his head. Sally might be right—maybe he *was* too handsome to pass along. But if he was even a smidgen interested, he hadn't given any indication of it in the days we'd been together. Just the same kind of offhand affection my good male friends showed me. And while I did consider myself a feminist, I was still a *black* feminist—which meant that if he didn't make the first move there would be no movement.

I turned back to the phone, wondered if it was too early to phone Ben Soyinka, decided it was, and walked to the shower.

21

Paul left as I was getting into the shower, but by the time I was dressed he was back again. I'd thought he'd been running, since he had on ratty shorts and sneakers, but he had a bag under his arm that indicated he'd been in to the Village.

"What's in there?"

"Coffee. Bagels. Your refrigerator had a bottle of champagne, forty watts, and a lot of cold air. Figured if a brother was going to get a cup of coffee, he'd have to provide it himself."

"I don't make coffee at home anymore. I just get it on the way to work."

"What about weekends?"

"I walk over to the Village and drink it there."

He shook his head in amazement. "And you call yourself a civilized human being."

While he talked, he was taking stuff out of the bag. A pound of coffee. A bag of bagels. Two kinds of cream cheese—"real and that other low-calorie stuff"—and a small French press.

"What on earth?" I looked at the press. I'd wanted one for years but had been too cheap to invest in one.

"Belated housewarming present."

"Seriously belated—I've been living here for five years."

"Okay, then, the truth. It was on the clearance shelf—it only holds four cups. But a small press is better than no press."

"There's usually nobody here but me anyway."

"No wonder. Why would anyone stay if there's no coffee? Put the kettle on, will you?"

I wanted to point out that I had charms other than providing coffee, but he wouldn't have heard. He was busy measuring grounds into the pot's glass chamber; then he looked around for plates for the bagels.

"Third cabinet, first shelf."

The plates came down and the kettle began to rumble, preparatory to the choo-choo-train sound it made when the water boiled. I'd bought it because it had a little harmonica instead of a whistle in the cap.

"*Whooo-whooo!*"

Paul, slathering a bagel with cream cheese (the real kind), jumped. "What the hell is that?"

I told him about the kettle and he laughed. "You've got a burglar alarm you don't use and a kettle that sounds like a burglar alarm—this house is as crazy as you are!"

"Yeah, but we're *consistent.*"

I watched as he poured the hot water over the grounds, releasing a cloud of fragrant steam. He placed the cap with the little pump handle on top.

"Now what?"

"Now we wait about five minutes and then press this thing down"—he touched the handle of the press's pump—"and: coffee. With milk, because I remembered to get some."

He reached into the bag and removed a quart of milk. It was whole milk, not one percent, but I could live with it.

Over coffee (which, I am happy to admit, was very good), we discussed whether it was still too early to call Benjamin Soyinka to find out what he wanted.

"It's a little after nine. If he's the go-getter Henry thinks he is, he's been up and has made calls back to New York and the Continent and any other place that's hours ahead of us."

He was probably right. I went to find the number I'd written down, picked up the phone, and called. The hotel put me through immediately.

"Soyinka here." The voice was richly masculine, heavy with overtones of expensive education and lots of money.

"Mr. Soyinka, this is Alex Powell, you—"

"Oh, Miss Powell! I'm so glad my message reached you. It's very kind of you to return my call."

"I hope it's not too early, if it is, my apologies."

"No, no—please: I've been up for hours. When I'm traveling, I try to speak to my office twice a day. Here that means I'm often awake at extremely bizarre hours."

Paul had been right. Again.

"What can I do for you, Mr. Soyinka?"

"It's a matter of . . . some sensitivity, Miss Powell. It concerns Everett Carson's death. As you may know, I'd been consulting with him on *Diaspora*."

That was news.

"Actually, I'd been led to believe that you were consulting with the magazine *after* Everett's death. I didn't know you and he had had contact before."

"Phone and e-mail. We were to have met on this trip, but obviously that's not going to happen."

Not unless you believe in channeling, bub. "I'm sorry, but I still don't understand. What can *I* do for you?"

"I'm wondering if it would be possible for you to meet me here, at the Peninsula, for tea. You see, Mr. Carson's death has affected a joint enterprise we were about to embark upon that has economic repercussions in both your country and mine. I'd like to discover what you've found—and share with you what little I know—and to tell you what he and I were beginning to work on."

What the hell. We didn't know anything particularly useful, but it would be nice to have tea.

"I'd be happy to meet you later this afternoon. You're aware that I've been asking questions with a colleague, Paul Butler?"

"So I've been told."

"Would it be all right if he accompanied me?"

"Oh, by all means. He's more than welcome."

"Good. What time did you have in mind?"

"Four o'clock?"

"Fine. I'll look forward to meeting you then."

"Thank you, Miss Powell. The pleasure will be mine, I'm sure."

Paul was not happy. "Tea? At the Peninsula? Four o'clock?"

"Yup."

"Damn. That blows a hole through the rest of the day, doesn't it? I was planning to rent a car and hit the beach."

"It's only nine. Nobody stays at the beach all day here. We could rent a car, and you could head back around two and still have plenty of time to get ready. Or—"

I looked outside. The day promised to be lovely, and the pool beckoned invitingly, mere feet away.

Paul followed my gaze and slapped his hand on his forehead.

"I forgot. All you granola heads have pools, don't you?"

I shrugged. "Gotta be *some* advantage to being a granola head."

"This'll work just fine."

By the time we'd called a rental company and they'd delivered a car, the sun was full up. Paul spent a few hours alternately swimming laps and sunbathing. I took the car and went to the grocery store for a few odds and ends for lunch. When I got back, he was in the water again.

"You're going to be a prune, you keep that up."

"I don't care; it feels great. You're not coming in?" He looked at my shorts and T-shirt.

"I don't know how to swim."

He gazed at me in undisguised horror. "You're kidding, aren't you?"

"Nope. Don't know how. Never learned. I just splash around in the shallow end."

Truth be told, I was afraid of swimming pools. I'd almost drowned in one as a child when an overzealous instructor decided the best way to teach kids to swim was just to throw them in. Luckily for me, a teacher with a different philosophy came by and dragged me out, sputtering and half dead. I'd had to take lessons in college, but I'd never totally learned to shake the fear. It didn't stop me from sailing or doing anything else in or near the water, but pools gave me the creeps.

"Well, get on your suit and splash around in the shallow end, then. Maybe I could teach you a couple of strokes—"

"I'll come in, but not for a lesson. Just to keep you company."

"*Everybody* should know how to swim."

"You're probably right, but this body isn't going to learn this afternoon, so if you want company, skip the lecture."

He shrugged, gave me an *I tried* look, and went back to his laps.

"I have to confess," **Paul said, as we signaled to** enter the Peninsula's driveway, "I'm sorry your little car got hit, but I'm glad we're riding in this one."

The car in question was a Mustang convertible; the rent-a-car guys didn't have much to offer between a teeny subcompact and a Lincoln Continental. As we'd discussed the merits of looking like impoverished grad students versus looking like a pimp and his hooker, the Mustang had been returned, so we took it.

"Wanted to be seen in the archetypical California car, did you?"

"Nope. *Didn't* want to be seen in your rolling shit box—charming though it is. And if your car worked, I know we'd have been in it; you get perverse pleasure out of pulling up to a place like this in a car like that."

"Just for that, I'm glad I made you keep the top up."

"Only till we leave. My concession to your vanity can be stretched only so far." I touched my hair, satisfied that it wouldn't look like a rat's nest in the hotel at least. Benjamin Soyinka had sounded interesting on the phone. Interesting enough to merit a coral silk dress and my favorite silver bracelet, a cuff shaped to follow my wristbone. He probably had three wives and sixteen children between them, but you never knew. . . .

Paul had been thoroughly amused. "My, my. Getting totally laid out for Africa's Ted Turner!" He'd chuckled.

"Well, it's this or shorts—everything else is dirty or at the cleaner. And a suit seemed a little over the top."

"Well, to *some* people, maybe."

Paul was, in fact, wearing a suit—but with an open-collared shirt beneath it. Maybe a tie was a little over the top for him.

I don't know whether it was the dress or the fact that we were going to tea, but whatever the reason, I was starting to feel a little special. At the Peninsula, one valet opened Paul's door, while another handed me out on the passenger side. A smiling doorman opened the lobby doors for us, and Paul, his hand on the small of my back, guided me through.

We walked through the foyer to what the hotel called its Living Room, a broad sunny expanse dotted with invitingly comfortable chairs and low tables. After telling the maître d'hotel (who, I guess was a *maîtresse d'hotel*, since the position was occupied, this afternoon anyway, by a woman) who we were here to see, she brightened.

"Oh, yes, Mr. Soyinka is expecting you. Please come this way."

She led us across the shiny wood floors to an alcove with a love seat and two club chairs. One of them was occupied by someone in a suit reading a paper. The hands holding the *Wall Street Journal* were very brown and neatly groomed. Pale blue cuffs showed inches above a tropical-worsted sleeve, and a hint of gold winked beneath the fine fabric. The long legs were crossed and ended in black cap-toed oxfords that looked for all the world as if they'd had their soles polished.

"Mr. Soyinka? Your guests."

Immediately the paper came down and Soyinka stood up. If the hostess hadn't been standing directly behind me, I might have fallen down from the shock.

Benjamin Soyinka was the spitting image of Everett Carson.

Ev's doppelgänger extended his hand to each of us for a firm English shake. "Benjamin Soyinka. Miss Powell, I presume, and Mr. Butler?"

"Um . . . yes. Pleased to—um, meet you."

I sat down with a thump. Even Paul looked startled.

"Is something wrong? Are you feeling unwell, Miss Powell? It's very warm here today. Perhaps the heat. . . . ?"

I shook my head.

"No, thank you. I'm fine. I was just taken aback. You could be Everett Carson's identical twin!"

"Well," Paul amended, "his identical twin in bespoke clothing, with better posture."

Soyinka smiled faintly. "I've been told there's a resemblance, but frankly I don't see it. And since Mr. Carson and I never got to meet, it would be impossible for me to say. Although I must admit, the photos gathered by the people who put his dossier together don't show much of a likeness." He offered a folder with some photos in the back.

In addition to Ev's curriculum vitae and several articles by and on him, there were a few photos. And I saw immediately why the resemblance wasn't that strong. Ben Soyinka looked like the *after* part of a before-and-after ad: Not only was he impeccably tailored, he was considerably lighter and leaner than Ev used to be. The New Ev, like the new Esmé Marshall, had been unveiled at NABJ. It was the New Ev, with revamped eating habits and a recently acquired fondness for a daily date with the treadmill, who looked an awful lot like Ben Soyinka. The old one could have been their chubby brother.

"Please, shall we have tea now? My mother says 'Good food restores the soul.' I hear the tea here is very good."

A waiter had appeared out of thin air. "Tea, Mr. Soyinka?"

"Thank you."

"Your mother is in Nigeria, then, Mr. Soyinka? Soyinka is a Nigerian name, isn't it?"

He laughed, delighted that I'd gotten it right. "It most certainly is, Miss Powell. Either you know Nigeria or you've read my celebrated countryman."

"I have been to Nigeria twice, and I'm quite fond of Wole Soyinka, yes."

Tea things began arriving, and we chatted about this and that as the waiters—there were two of them—placed a three-tiered plate laden with small sandwiches, cream scones, and pastries on the table. One passed around plates and napkins while the other prepared the teapot, rinsing it with hot water, spooning loose tea into the pot, and pouring scalding water over all. A heavenly scent drifted up.

"Earl Grey?"

"Earl Grey," he confirmed.

"So, Mr. Soyinka—"

"So formal! Please, call me Ben. I've spent so much time in the United States, I've learned to use first names very quickly. Do you mind?"

"Not if you'll call us Paul and Alex."

He turned to me. "Short for what, Alexandra? Alexis?"

"Alexa."

He looked at me with naked appraisal. "Alexa. It suits you. I shall use it, unless you'd rather I didn't."

"I don't mind." Just keep talking, your voice is sooo seductive.

"Um, I wonder if we could get down to why we're here?" Paul asked coolly, as he swirled a scant teaspoon of sugar into his tea. Soyinka, I noticed, took nothing but a little milk. Maybe, like Georgie, he thought sugared tea was for children.

"Yes, of course. As you know, I am in communications in Africa. My family had some business holdings in oil that grew after Independence—"

"Nigerian independence?" Paul clarified.

"Exactly. In the early 1970s, before we joined OPEC, oil was doing marginally well, but not as well as it has since. Wishing to hedge his bets, my father asked me to take some of the refinery's profits and begin a publishing empire. I had been away for several years, first at Cambridge, then at the London School of Economics, where I'd concentrated on communications management. I'd been planning to start a publication of my own, for blacks living in Great Britain—rather like *Diaspora*, actually. My father knew of that intention and asked me to transfer my interest closer to home, for the sake of the family's well-being. So I returned home to establish—and run—a new part of the family business."

I bit into a cream scone I'd smeared with jam and tried not to moan aloud.

"That part of the family business being?" I asked, with my mouth still partially full.

"Two magazines. *Afrique Noir* is distributed in much of French-speaking West and Central Africa, and *Black Africa Review* is an English-language newsmagazine that is published biweekly throughout much of the sub-Saharan continent. In the past ten years, I've added a Francophone radio network, Radio Publique d'Afrique, and negotiations for a bilingual television network devoted to news throughout the Diaspora are in the process of being finalized."

"You cover a lot of ground," Paul observed, reluctantly impressed. "Must spend a lot of time in the air."

Soyinka smiled. "Yes. Enough to merit a company plane. Commercial flights are sometimes unreliable in the places I travel."

"Corporate headquarters are in Lagos, then?"

"No, no. Right now they're in Abidjan, on Avenue de la République. Do you know it?"

"I do," I said. "It's where the American embassy is, isn't it?"

"Correct."

"I'm confused about something, though," Paul pressed. "You're Nigerian, but your business headquarters is in Côte d'Ivoire. Won't your government take a dim view of that?"

"Under normal circumstances, yes."

Soyinka put a few pastries on a clean plate for each of us and passed them to us.

"But my circumstances are slightly abnormal. You see, my father is Nigerian, but my *mother* is Ivorian. And as the eldest male descendant in her family, I am responsible for the economic well-being of them as well. So I live in Abidjan and maintain a residence in Lagos, but most of my "down time," as you might say here, is spent in Abidjan."

Anyone who's visited both cities knows what a no-brainer *that* decision must've been. But the Nigerian half of him probably would have been offended if I'd pointed it out.

"So even though the base for your fortune came from Nigeria, the Nigerian government is okay with your living out of the country?" I asked. "Seems odd. You must be one of the country's first families."

"I get away with it, Alexa, precisely *because* I'm from one of the country's so-called first families. And because I hold a dual passport, thanks to my mother. And because I've—shall we say—made it *worthwhile* for certain people in decision-making positions in Lagos to see the wisdom of this arrangement."

Ah, graft, the fuel that runs much of the Third World's engine.

"Where does Everett come into all this?" Paul asked, wiping his mouth with a tiny linen napkin.

"My second in command is a young Nigerian man named Jeremy Opoko. He's been the key man in our preliminary discussions with Mr. Carson. Both Jeremy and Mr. Carson had been very interested in creating a globe-spanning communications empire that would address the needs and interests of all peoples of the African Diaspora. We all of us agree that it's far past time that Africans and African-descended people have a more intimate relationship. Both men were convinced that cable TV and, perhaps, the Internet were the answer to doing this.

"We'd hammered out an initial agreement that Mr. Carson would supervise the United States and the Caribbean, while our people would oversee the Continent—the African continent, of course—and parts of Europe, mostly, at this point, France and England. We planned for the cable network to be bilingual, and Carson and I would jointly choose the new president of DNN, the Diasporan News Network.

"Had you been approached by anyone else regarding a similar merger?" Paul asked.

"Ah, I assume you're speaking of Jacob Jackson. Yes, I was planning to investigate whether *Onyx* might be interested in participating in this joint venture, but it would be one of several publications.

From the initial conversations we've had, I'm not sure he is interested in being one of several *anything*. So I am hoping to move forward with the *Diaspora* merger and perhaps add *Onyx* later on, if
Mr. Jackson is amenable."

"Does he know you and *Diaspora* had a deal in the works?"

"Oh, yes. I'd informed him of that several days ago. I gather he
wanted an exclusive agreement. But *Diaspora* fit more immediately
into our overall plans; I couldn't see not including it. Jacob Jackson
wasn't terribly happy about that."

"I would imagine not. *Onyx* is still the more prestigious of the
two publications."

"In some people's eyes, yes. But *Diaspora* is the more relevant of
the two—another reason for uniting with it first."

"When," Paul asked, eating the last chocolate tart, "were you
going public with all this?"

"Carson was to have announced it with a flourish on the evening
he received his award; he was insistent that the news be broken to, as
he liked to put it, *the family* first. I believed it amused him to think
of people *outside* the family scrambling to catch up. . . . But of
course, because of his sudden death, that never happened. So now
we—what do you people say over here?—regroup?"

"Yes."

Paul's next question went right to the point. "With the way things
were set up, if something happened to either of you, would the other
be free to start over again from scratch, or were you bound by the
agreement to keep moving forward?"

Soyinka's eyes sparkled appreciatively. "I see you're a reporter
with a businessman's mind. Interesting."

Paul acknowledged the compliment with a nod of thanks.

"Actually, both of us were interested in a contingency plan, and
the idea was to do just that. If something happened to me, Mr. Carson was free to continue to work with my people or to seek a merger
elsewhere, if that suited him. If something happened to him, I had
the same leeway. We were comfortable with the arrangement because
we were each convinced that our—oh, let's call it product—was

unique enough that if something happened to one, the other would want to move forward with the same people."

"But you're not sure that's the case now?" I'd taken off the bracelet and was running my fingers over its bumps and curves, keeping my hands busy so I wouldn't make a total pig of myself.

"I'm not sure that it's *not*; we'll have to see. I don't know that Mr. Carson's second-in-command is as equipped to replace him as Jeremy Opoko would be to take my place."

Uh-oh. Bad news for Henry.

Paul leaned forward and tapped Soyinka's *Wall Street Journal*.

"Henry's not Mr. Personality, but he's run *Diaspora* competently for the past couple of years, when Everett's been traveling around the country speaking and lecturing. Why don't you think he'd be able to do the job permanently?"

Soyinka sighed and stretched out his arms. As he did, I saw a flash of gold at each cuff, an interesting design I'd seen somewhere before, but I couldn't remember where.

"The problem, Paul, is this: While *Diaspora* remains only a magazine, I'm sure Mr. Carson's editor is perfectly competent to run it. But if the two businesses come together, *Diaspora* will be more than a magazine. It will be part of a worldwide communications system, and as such would require greater oversight and greater business knowledge than I think the editor—"

"His name is Henry Adams."

"Of course. Sorry. Than Mr. Adams may be capable of. Ideally, I'd want someone who has an MBA, is bilingual or even trilingual, and who has lived for at least a bit in Africa and the Caribbean."

I was skeptical. "Are there people—besides you, I mean—who actually possess those credentials?" I wondered.

"Arthur French," Paul said thoughtfully.

I had forgotten about Arthur French.

"Yes, you know him?" Soyinka asked with interest.

"We went to law school together, but we each decided that law was about the most boring thing you could do with your life, so we started working for newspapers. He was the *Times* man in West and Central Africa for about six years. Then he went to Johannesburg as bureau chief for four more years. Now he's running the Paris bureau."

Poor Henry. He couldn't hope to compete.

"So you see, Alex, it's nothing personal against Mr. Adams, it's just that there are people who may be a better fit for the job. Mr. French seems a particularly attractive prospect, because he's contributed to *Diaspora* over the years, so he's not a complete stranger."

He turned to Paul again. "You were both at Yale law? When?"

Paul told him.

Soyinka gave a short bark of laughter. "The same class as Laddie Ndukwe!"

"Who's Laddie Ndukwe?" I asked.

"A complete fool." Ben Soyinka chortled.

"*Total* and complete." Paul grinned, finally warming up to Soyinka. "He used to wear a fur coat to class and pay some kids in New Haven to deliver his books to his rooms at the end of the day because, as he always used to say—"

"Fetching is for retrievers, not Ndukwes!" roared Soyinka.

"Do you know where he is now?" Paul asked. "I always suspected he'd end up somewhere being fabulously rich—richer even than he'd been when he came to Yale."

"Oh, yes," Soyinka said dryly, "he's somewhere that doesn't have an extradition policy with Nigeria, and, yes, he's sinfully rich."

They spent the next twenty minutes having old home week. Turned out, between reporters and ex-classmates, they knew a bunch of people in common. Small colored diaspora.

I was about to give Paul my *can't we wrap it up* look when I stopped midway: I'd suddenly realized where I'd seen the design of Ben Soyinka's cuff links.

"Ben, your cuff links—they're a very interesting design. Did you have them made?"

He looked fondly down at them. "Someone had them made for me: my fiancée. The symbols are Adinkra, a sort of pictograph that began in Ghana with the Ashanti, but it spread throughout the West Coast. It's even become popular here in the States, with so many African Americans going back and forth."

He removed a link and passed it to me. The rounded square glinted in the late-afternoon sun, just as it had a few days ago, on another arm, in Washington.

"You're marrying Eileen Stevens, aren't you?"

Now it was Soyinka's turn to be surprised. "How could you know?" he wondered. "We've said nothing to anyone yet, not even our families."

"She has a bracelet with this design on it. She wore it to Everett's memorial service."

"Ah, yes." He nodded. "She probably assumed most people there would have no idea what it meant."

"She was right. I didn't make the connection until I saw your cuff links. What do the symbols mean?"

"Loosely translated, they mean *fidelity*. The whole phrase is 'love does not get lost on its way home.'"

"Congratulations." Paul lifted his teacup.

"Thank you. I'm glad someone other than Eileen and I now know the news. In fact I think we should celebrate with something a little stronger than tea. Could I convince you both to share a little champagne?"

Champagne? My arm *would* have to be twisted. "That would be a lovely way to toast your engagement," I agreed.

Soyinka raised an eyebrow and a waiter came scurrying. After a whispered consultation, a bottle of Billecart-Salmon appeared in a pedestal bucket of ice. The pale pink liquid foamed into the tall glasses. After the waiter had passed them around, we held ours aloft.

"To you and to Eileen: much happiness for many years," Paul proposed.

We touched rims and drank.

"Where did you meet? Where will you live? Did Everett know about your relationship?"

Soyinka laughed, holding up his hands as if to stop my avalanche of questions. "I'll answer, but one question at a time!" he protested.

"You know you don't have to," Paul advised him.

"I know—but I don't mind."

So we heard the story. They'd met last summer, in Ghana, when Eileen had gone to do a follow-up study to the one she'd done while finishing her master's. A friend of Soyinka's who is an airline flight attendant introduced them. It was, apparently, love at first sight, or something close. He'd been to New Jersey and met the children, had spent a couple of vacations with Eileen and the boys. And they didn't see the point in a commuting relationship.

"If all goes well, she'll receive her Ph.D. late this year, and we'll marry quietly in London—or wherever she wishes—soon after."

"Will you live here or there?"

"My business being what it is, we'll probably live in Abidjan at least part of the time. But we'll make sure the boys get back to the States frequently, and we're hoping to convince their grandmother to come and stay for long stretches of time."

"You've not yet told M'Dear, then?"

He looked uncomfortable. "No. We wanted to iron out all the logistics before we made an announcement. We don't want to upset Mrs. Weeks; we know she'll be distressed at the notion of the children moving an ocean away, but we're trying to arrange things so that she'll see them the same amount of time, if not more."

"How do you think Everett would have reacted to this news?" Paul wondered.

Soyinka blew out loudly, an exhalation that said *oh, boy!* better than words could have. "He would not have been happy," Soyinka admitted.

"Do you think he'd have pressed his case in court?" I asked.

"Quite possibly. Although Eileen, as sole custodial parent, would have had the right to take her children wherever she wanted. She was hoping that with the merger, Carson would have been traveling back and forth to Africa and would have had ample access to the boys. No one wanted to deny him that."

Paul scratched his cheek and looked out over the Living Room's expanse. Tea drinkers had given way to sleek entertainment execs in dark clothes drinking cocktails. Almost time for us to beat it.

"I would imagine that it was dicey, balancing a personal relationship with Eileen with your business relationship with Ev. Would he even have entertained working with you if he knew you were going to marry the love of his life?"

"That, as you Americans say, is the sixty-four-thousand-dollar question. In a way, I'm happy I didn't have to find out."

Happy enough to have eliminated Everett as a complication, I wondered?

Shortly afterward, we left Benjamin Soyinka where we found him, sipping the last of the Champagne and making calls to his overseas offices on his cell phone.

"Love does not get lost on its way home," the Adinka symbol promised. But what would Ben Soyinka be willing to do in order to make sure it didn't make a detour en route?

22

While we were waiting for the car to be brought around, it occurred to me I might want to check messages. Marron's people hadn't come by before we left, and I'd totally forgotten they might have questions about our "accident" last night. I pulled out the cell phone, reached out, and touched my mechanical self.

Sure enough, some guy named, of all things, Brisket, had left a slightly irate message, promising to call back in the early evening.

Henry had called, wanting an update.

A.S.'s secretary, Francyne, had left a rather cryptic message.

Alex, this is Francyne. A.S. says to remind you that you're a day overdue; you haven't checked in and he's not happy about it. Make my life easier, girlfriend, and leave him a voice mail, please. He'll be out from three-thirty to five-thirty; then he's back in for an editorial board dinner. If you hurry, you can let him know what's up while he's out. Might buy you some more time.

Good old Francyne. She knew how to work the system. I went on to the next message.

Yo, Shorty: your overseer is looking for you hard. He called me to ask if I'd seen or heard from you! I told him it wasn't my job to

*keep up with his colored staff. Guess I shouldn't have; he was not
amused! Anyway, call him. Or call me and I'll call him. Oh—
one of Ev's old girlfriends is in town and you might want to see
what she knows. I had dinner with Esmé Marshall last night.
She's in town to hold somebody's hand for the Soul Train
Awards. She's staying at the Metropolitan. Ciao.*

"What? You have that look on your face that says uh-oh."

"Where do I start? I missed the appointment with the po-leece,
'cause they came after we left. A.S. can count and has decided I've
been off the plantation two days too long. And Georgie just told me
something I should have found out when we were on the Vineyard:
Esmé Marshall was involved with Everett."

"Man, turn your back for one *minute*," he teased. A car stopped,
and the valet held the doors open. "Einstein, this is us."

I had totally forgotten because I was waiting for my orange car,
which of course wasn't coming.

"Want me to drive while you call Georgie back, see what's up?"

"I don't know that it will make a difference. I'll have to spend half
of my time telling you what to do."

"Like you don't try to anyway, car or no car. Get in, I'm driving."

The doorman, grinning, carefully shut my door as Paul tipped
the valet.

"Where to? Left, right? And give a brother some warning if you
want a turn, okay?"

This was getting to be tedious, and we hadn't even gotten out of
the parking lot yet.

"Turn right. We're going to go on this street for about three or
four miles. I'll tell you when to turn, and it'll be another right when
I do."

Paul swung smoothly out into traffic, using his signal (a sure sign
he was a visitor—who else in L.A. bothers to do that but people from
someplace else?), and continued on down Little Santa Monica. I hit
Georgie's number on my speed-dial.

"Save that accent for the WPs. Whazzup?"

"About time! When are you coming back? You know they have your picture on milk cartons down in the cafeteria, don't you?"

"Get out—turn right three blocks, at the light—I'm barely over-due. A.S. is so *anal*."

"As befits him, the little asshole. But he's a little asshole who's your *boss*, Alex, and he's viewing your non-checking-in as an act of gross insubordination. Especially since his colleagues are teasing him about it."

Oh, fabulous. Now my life *would* be hell.

"Are you on the cell? Who are you talking to, anyway, besides me?"

"Paul. Who is going to bear to the left at this juncture, right, Hoke?"

"Yassum, Miss Daisy."

"Oh, the Wicked Ex's Best Friend. Interesting." I'd once told Georgie about the ex and the Last Supper I'd fashioned for him, al fresco. And the fact that there'd been more than just him on the doorstep. She has a good memory.

"Not really."

"Alex, don't tell me you've been with that man for practically a week and nothing's happened! Esmé says he's gorgeous, in—what did she say?—an offbeat kind of way."

" 'Pends on what you like, Georgina, 'pends on what you like."

I looked over at Paul, who was comfortably jockeying himself through early evening rush-hour traffic, using some inner com-pass in his head to get him toward the house. He *was* a good-look-ing man—but apparently not interested in *moi*. Just as well. I guess.

"What?"

"Nothing. You're doing fine. If you want, we can stop and pick up some stuff for dinner; I'll cook. Take the next left, and we'll use the grocery store on Museum Row."

"Oooohhh . . . cooking dinner for the man. Don't tell me you're not interested, Alex. You don't rattle pots and pans unless you're hav-ing a party or trying to get your groove on."

"Georgie, it's been so long since that's happened, I probably couldn't even find it with a search party. You're overreaching."

"I don't think so, little one. Well, go grab your dinner makings, but chew on this: I told you I had to go to a big dinner last night, and your friend Esmé was very talkative."

"What was the dinner for?"

"Oh, the usual: letting the advertisers mingle with the stars. Basically, it's stroking the fashion advertisers, so I had to go. Your Ms. Marshall was there with La Diva—all in Armani, of course—and while the advertisers were sucking up to the Diva, she and I chatted. Your name came up."

Paul had pulled into the store parking lot and gotten out. He'd walked over to a railing that faced the street, pulled out his cell phone, and begun checking his e-mails over the wireless. He motioned for me to continue with what I was doing.

"Why would my name come up? Esmé barely knows me."

"I'd complimented her on her weight loss, and she said she'd freaked out a *Standard* reporter on the Vineyard when she hadn't recognized her. It gave her a real kick."

I'd like to give her a real kick, all right.

"Anyway, while we were talking about how she'd dropped that lard, she told me about these vitamin supplements and her whole regimen. Says she not only did it for herself but guided an ex-boyfriend through the process too, and he'd lost a ton of weight, looked better than ever."

Ev had lost a ton of weight, couldn't stop bragging about it at the convention.

"She hadn't been—"

"Yes, she had. I asked. I'm very smooth, a skill *you* could learn, by the way."

"Shut up. What'd you say?"

"Just 'Oh, are *you* responsible for Everett Carson's weight loss? I hear he looked fabulous—everybody was marveling at how fit and trim he was.' Then the floodgates opened."

Paul was writing in a little notebook as he talked on the phone.

Looked like I had a couple of minutes before he came back this way.

"How'd she say she did it?"

"Oh the usual blather—lots of protein, daily exercise. Vitamins. But here's the thing. She swears part of what helped her slim down was a boosted immune system."

"*She* was taking echinacea tincture too?"

"Not only that, she turned Ev on to the source. Something expensive and hard to get, that's made up in small batches."

"Well, well. Guess I'll have to ask her about this source."

"Well, well. Guess you'd better. The show doesn't start till nine, and dinner is a midnight supper afterward, so you'll probably be able to catch her at the hotel if you hurry over there."

"Thanks, Georgie. I owe you one."

"You owe me many, girlfriend. Just do me two little favors, in exchange for the one big one I just did for you."

"And those are?"

"One: call your white boy, so I don't have to deal with him again. He has no manners, and you know how I hate that."

"Done. What's two?"

"Call out that search party and find your groove, please. And then see if Mr. Smoothie's needle fits."

She was still laughing when she hung up.

"Everything okay?" Paul opened my door. "Are we stopping here or not?"

I sighed. I really had been looking forward to a quiet dinner at home.

"Not. We're presentable enough. We have to go over to the Metropolitan. I'll tell you how to get there. Then I'll take you to dinner, okay?"

He shrugged. "Fine with me. Although it would have been interesting to see if you had any competence in the kitchen." He looked at me and grinned.

"I'm competent enough, just uninterested. And we have something more important to do."

"What," he asked, starting the car and carefully backing out of the space, "is more important than a good meal? You skinny people have your priorities all screwed up."

We were back on Wilshire, going in precisely the direction we'd just come.

"In this case, catching up with your admirer, Esmé Marshall, before she disappears. Georgie saw her last night at dinner and found out something very interesting."

Westbound traffic was hellishly slow, one long string of stop-and-gos. The setting sun bounced off the windshields of the commuters trying to reach their homes in Beverly Hills, the Pacific Palisades, and Santa Monica. Many people were yakking on their phones—despite a statewide ordinance requiring drivers to have a hands-free device if they were using their phones while the motor was running. A motorcycle cop wove between cars, impassively glancing at the chatty drivers but citing no one. Maybe because nobody was moving, so what kind of trouble could they be in?

"What did Miss Marple unearth?"

"Esmé turned Ev on to the echinacea that she swears helped them both lose all that weight. She had a source somewhere that shipped it to her and, I guess, to him too. But we don't know that, and we need to find out. Could make a difference."

He nodded.

Then I called A.S. and left a blatantly false but plausible excuse as to why I wasn't back yet and promised to call and speak with him personally tomorrow. (Notice I did not promise to go back to *work* tomorrow.)

We could barely turn into the Metropolitan's circular drive, it was so cluttered with stretch limos. Somebody—probably a rapper—had ordered a white stretch Hummer, a gleefully over-the-top touch that would be talked about afterward for weeks. Thanks to the Hummer's length, we were stuck out on Sunset, causing a huge backup. We idled, waiting our turn, as driver after driver pulled around us, saluting us with the Universal Digit to indicate their annoyance.

I could relate. I'd be mad at me too, if I wasn't me already.

23

It took us ten minutes to get an elevator up to the eleventh floor. Apparently, people in the suites above were making their way downstairs in droves, and many of them were holding the elevators for stragglers. I briefly contemplated walking up and decided I didn't have to see Esmé that badly.

When we finally stepped off on the eleventh floor, we followed the handsome rug down to Esmé's room. The door was cracked a little, and Dinah Washington, in a bad mood, was spilling out.

"Uh-oh," Paul said. "It's gonna be bad."

" 'Cause she's playing Dinah Washington?"

" 'Cause she's playing *that* Dinah Washington. I have never met a black woman who played that song, that loud, when she wasn't pissed off."

He pushed the door wider, and we stepped in.

Esmé, as befitting the head of The Marshall Plan, had a suite, not a room. The mauve furniture was draped with clothes that had been tried on and discarded. The gray-carpeted floor was littered with expensive shoes. Four different newspapers and a trade daily were stacked sloppily in one corner. Her laptop was up and running, but we couldn't see what was on the screen. A CD hidden in the armoire was playing "This Bitter Earth"—again. And an apparently empty bottle of Veuve Clicquot was dripping condensation on the rosewood dresser, while its full mate was nestled in what had been the first bottle's bucket of ice.

"I'm coming—y'all make yourselves at home. I'm struggling with my contact lenses," Esmé shouted from the bathroom.

I grabbed a napkin, blotted the dresser top, and wiped down the bottle. Paul went to the armoire that held the mini CD system and looked through the selections.

"Esmé, may I play one of your CDs?" Paul called.

Her head peered around the door. She was fully and skillfully made up. Big diamond studs winked in her earlobes, and her shoulders were smooth and bare.

"Fine man, you can do anything you *want* around here," she purred. Then, laughing, she disappeared again. "Back in a sex. I mean sec!" More laughter.

Smiling to himself and shaking his head, Paul slipped something out of the jacket. Etta James poured out, backed by a lush set of strings. Unlike Dinah, this girl was way happy. At last, her love had come along.

"Good choice. I love that song. Don't you love that song, Alex?"

"I do. And you look great, Esmé."

"Stunning," Paul agreed. "*Way* too classy for where you're going tonight."

She giggled, pleased. She was in pale pink satin, a simple dress that showed off her newly trim figure to its best advantage. A diamond bracelet and a pair of pink satin spike-heeled mules with crystal beading across the throat finished the outfit beautifully.

"Well, you know what they say—sometimes you have to lead by example. Handsome Boyfriend, there are some empty glasses over there, would you do the honors?"

"Happily."

Esmé watched appreciatively as Paul expertly opened and poured three tall flutes and passed two of them to Esmé and me.

"What shall we drink to?"

"To us making enough money that we can afford to drink this

shit!" Esmé said gleefully. Then she attempted a more somber note. "No, no . . . let's drink to Everett."

"Works for me." Paul shrugged. "To Everett."

"To Ev," I echoed.

We all took a sip, as Etta, on a new track, went on to insist that she didn't want any weak-ass explanations from the pathetic excuse for a man she was now singing about.

"Esmé, I understand you met a friend of mine last night."

"Oh, yeah, Maggie. Very cool girl. We had a good time. *Long* drinka water, I tell you!"

"Uh, Georgie. Georgie Marks."

"Georgie, Maggie, whatever."

She was inspecting herself in the room's large Deco mirror, making sure that her eyeliner was straight and her individual eyelashes had been applied properly.

"Yeah. Well, Georgie says you told her the big secret to your weight loss—and Everett's—was the brand of echinacea you were taking. Can you tell me something about that?"

She looked at me archly. "Nope."

"I beg your pardon?"

"Silly, it's a secret. A skinny girl like you doesn't have to lose weight. It would be wasted on *you*."

I sighed. Great. It's gonna be like that, is it? I looked over at Paul, who'd been listening to this exchange silently.

He got up and went over to Esmé and held out his hand. "May I?"

"May you *what*, cutie?"

"May I refill your glass, Esmé?"

"Oh. Oh, well. Sure." She handed the flute to Paul and allowed her hands to graze his for a moment. "He's *so* damn cute, Alex," she stage-whispered. "How do you stand it?"

"I bite the insides of my cheeks a lot. Listen, Esmé, what if I wanted to take echinacea not for the weight thing but to keep healthy? Where would I go to find the best? What would I have to do?"

She smiled thinly. "Act like Dorothy." She burped, startling us both. "Oops, sorry!" She giggled.

"Who's Dorothy, and why would acting like her get me great herbs?"

"You know, *Dorothy*," she said, clearly annoyed at my density.

"Red slippers? Blue and white dress? That Dorothy?"

"*Wizard of Oz* Dorothy," Paul said helpfully.

"See why I keep him around, Esmé? He's cute *and* smart."

Paul lifted his still mostly full glass in silent salute.

"Uh-huh," she agreed, looking over at him with boozy approval. "Any more like you at home?"

"Sorry. I'm an only child."

She pouted. "Cousins?"

"Lots. So tell us about this Dorothy business. Your echinacea came from a farm in Kansas? It's made from sunflowers? What? I'm not following you very well."

Esmé leaned against the open casement window, through which we could just barely see the city's most famous billboard. The studly cowboy who'd always ridden down Sunset, cigarette tucked raffishly in a corner of his mouth, had been erased as part of a tobacco industry settlement designed to discourage smoking. So instead of his manly magnificence, five young white kids from a dreadful Gen-X network sitcom stared, wide-eyed, over Esmé's shoulder.

"Silly. What did Dorothy find out? That what she was looking for was right under her nose. *There's no place like home, there's no place like home* — remember?"

Of course we remembered. Anyone our approximate age remembered. Those flying monkeys scared the crap out of me.

"So you're saying the stuff is made in your home or someone else's?"

She sighed in disappointment, walked shakily over to a pink satin evening bag, rooted through it, and exhaled in frustration.

"Dammit, when I need to smoke I always forget I don't smoke anymore! I don't suppose either of you . . . ?"

We shook our heads no.

"Why am I not surprised?" She sighed. "Anyway, what was I saying?"

"You were saying where the echinacea was made."

"No, no, no, Skinny Girl, I was not *saying* where it was made. I was *hinting* where it was made. You wouldn't win any money on those game shows."

She looked in annoyance at the armoire with the CD.

"Paul, honey, would you put on something else? That bitch is starting to get on my nerves." Evidently, Etta's version of "Embraceable You" was not to Esmé's liking.

Paul immediately got up, riffled quickly through the CD cases, and put on a Billie Holiday. In very quick order, stars were falling on Alabama.

"Alabama . . . that's where Everett was from," she said dreamily.

"Not South Carolina?" Paul asked. "I thought that's where they were burying him."

She waved a hand in loopy dismissal. "Oh, yeah. Well, South Carolina, Alabama. Same diff. South. Country."

I guess to some people it's all the same.

"Where are *you* from, Esmé?"

"Philly. Born and bred. Went to Penn on full scholarship. Majored in math—ain't that a hoot?" She leaned forward and pointed a gleaming rosy-nailed finger at me. "Know how many parties I went to while I was at Penn?"

"How many?" I asked obligingly.

"Maybe a dozen. That's about three a year, in case nobody else here was a math major. Three fuckin' parties a year—in the seventies!"

That *is* pathetic. Everybody black knows the seventies—especially the early seventies—had been *the* decade for college parties. I'd missed out completely but never failed to hear the stories.

"So you were bustin' it while a bunch of other folks were having a good time," Paul sympathized.

"Had to," she said shortly. "Had to keep my eyes on the prize, like my grandma usta say. Little Esmé. Going places." Her speech was becoming slurred. Had she consumed the entire first bottle by herself?

"You were more focused than the rest of us."

"Hadta be, Skinny Girl. I knew I was gonna do something big when I got out, and I knew, to do it, a woman has to be five times better than a man just to get in the door."

The champagne definitely was having its effect.

"So you worked hard . . ." I prompted.

"Oh, girl, you have no *idea*! I had *no* life for about five years. Then just a li'l bit of a life, once I opened the agency. So now, you want a black person in PR, I'm the man. Well, the girl. And guess what I found out?"

"What?"

She turned to Paul. " 'Member *Mahogany*?"

"That Diana Ross movie?"

"Yup. Know what my favorite scene was?"

Jeez. First the *Wizard of Oz* and now this. Unlike the *Wizard of Oz*, though, *Mahogany* had been a piece of shit. I was too young to have seen it on first run, but I'd caught it in film retrospectives and on BET's old movie nights. I know it was hard to make black movies back then (still is), and Berry Gordy had pushed this one through, but it was *still* a piece of shit, a vanity project with lots of awful clothes. If Esmé had a special place in her heart for it, now was probably not the time to bring that up.

"I'll bite. What was your favorite scene?"

"When Billy Dee tells her, 'Success is *nothing* unless you have someone you love to share it with.' Well, that movie was a piece of shit"—Esmé's film connoisseurship rose a notch in my estimation—"but the boy was right. I mean, *lookit* me: fine, plenty money, good professional rep—and no one to share it with."

Paul looked at me, kind of like *here goes*, and said, "So you couldn't share it with Ev?"

She didn't even blink. "Oh. I see you know about that. No, I couldn't. I was gonna, but he fucked up, big time." The three glasses she'd had since we'd arrived seemed to be catching up with her. Quickly.

This time Billie wasn't in sync. She was singing about how her love was here to stay.

I'd wondered if Esmé would even deign to discuss Ev, but since she brought it up . . . Paul must have been thinking the same thing, because he leaned forward and said quietly. "You and Ev were pretty friendly for a while, weren't you, Esmé?"

In the background, Billie was telling Joe the bartender to set up one more for the road.

She nodded her head in appreciative time to the music. "Yup. Good friends. *Dear* friends. For a while."

"Intimate friends?" I asked carefully.

"Oooh, yes," Esmé said bitterly. "We were gonna build a communications empire together."

"Really?"

"Yup. *Diaspora International*. We were gonna do an African version of the magazine. Maybe some television, eventually."

I blinked in surprise. Paul's look clearly said, *Shut up, stupid*.

"It sounds like a good idea," he said blandly. "What happened?"

"He *fucked* me is what happened! We were three-quarters of the way through the planning, and he changed his mind."

"Why, Esmé?" I asked. "Doesn't sound like Ev."

"Oh, yes, it does." She seethed. "He got a better offer and he left. Just told me he'd had a better offer . . . and *left*."

"That was kind of rude. Where'd the offer come from?"

"Some African motherfucker. Had a buncha his daddy's money and was planning to go international—from the *other* end." She snorted, bitterly amused. "I guess, to Africans, *we* look like the international part, huh?"

"Did you know who the African in question was?" Paul asked.

She shook her head. "He wouldn't tell. Probably thought I might find whoever it was and tell him what a dog his new partner was gonna be. And I might have, too . . . if I had known who to tell."

"Esmé, if you and Ev were thinking of going into Africa, and neither of you had done business there before, who were you going to use as your African point of contact?"

"Everett thought about Arthur French. Do you know him?"

"I do."

"Yeah. He useta live in Africa. Still has a lot of friends there.

Everett useta say he was okay—for a yella guy." She looked at me. "Sorry."

I shrugged. Price of the ticket.

"So, okay, you guys were going to speak to Arthur about hooking you up with some continental contacts, and I guess he would have had a piece of the pie eventually."

Esmé nodded. She was looking loopier by the minute.

"But where was the money coming from? Start-ups like that take a boatload of money, don't they?"

She smiled thinly. "I'd mortaged the Marshall Plan to the hilt. You know I'm the sole owner and partner, built my stuff up from nothing. Just me. It's the way I like it. So I didn't have to ask anybody but me if I could do it. And I told me yes. Hell, yes!"

"But Esmé, if you'd invested a good chunk of the money, and Everett then decided the deal wouldn't work or he didn't want to go through with it, shouldn't he have repaid you? He was legally obligated to really, wasn't he?"

"Well, yes, he was, *really*." She mocked me, then stopped. "I'm sorry, Alex. It's nothing personal, but I'm still mad."

"I would be too, good and mad."

"He was going to give me back some of the money, but there was a big chunk of it he *wasn't* giving back. We'd already spent a lot on doing a dummy issue, a prospectus, some stuff for a portfolio. Thousands and thousands of dollars."

"Wouldn't he have shared that cost with you?" Paul frowned, swirling his still mostly full glass.

Esmé looked a bit embarrassed. "Well, we did it kinda different. Because I know PR and marketing, I prepared all the materials and paid for the costs out of pocket. Ev was going to pay for the second stage out of pocket: the editorial meetings, the transcontinental travel, whatever we were going to need to do to woo the Africans."

"Was it on paper?" Paul pressed.

"You know Ev—'How long we been knowin' each other, girl? I don't need no paper to tell me you're all right or to tell me what to do.'"

"Uh-oh." I couldn't help it, it slipped out.

"You're damn skippy, uh-oh! Soon's the Prince of Africa came along, I was forgotten. Li'l Esmé. Going *no* places."

"Is that when you stopped seeing each other altogether?"

"That woulda been about when, all right."

Something still didn't add up. I walked to the window to clear my head. Taking a deep breath of L.A.'s night air wasn't going to be a big help, but it would be better than nothing. Esmé was beside me, her back still to the window, looking up at the ceiling. A single tear coursed down her beautifully made-up cheek, dribbled off her skin, and skittered down the front of her pink satin dress.

"You really loved him, Esmé?"

She turned to look at me full on, and that's when I realized what I should have known before: Esmé's room smelled like Ev's had the night he died. Or almost like it.

"I did, Alex. My own damn fault. I always pick the wrong man."

"You're wearing Fracas."

"What?"

"Your perfume . . . you're wearing Fracas, aren't you?"

She smiled crookedly. "Good nose, Skinny Girl. Now you're a perfume detective?"

I smiled in what I hoped was a natural way. "Nah. But it's a very distinctive smell. Most women can't wear it."

"Most women don't *know* about it."

True. Robert Piguet's white-flower fragrance, heavy on gardenias, had been introduced in the 1930s and was all the rage among fashionable women on at least two continents for a few decades. Then it was all but withdrawn from the market, which made it even more prized for the tribe of devotees who knew where to go to find its signature black-glass bottle. And they jealously guarded their secret; they didn't want Just Anybody smelling like them.

I skipped the "I-Like-to-Think-of-Myself-as-Not-Just-Any-Woman" speech and cut to the quick. "You were in Everett's room the night he died, weren't you, Esmé?"

She looked genuinely startled. "Who told you?"

"Your perfume. It's so unusual it's a fair guess that most of the women there never even heard of it, let alone wore it." Combined with Frankie's scent, it smelled exactly as Ev's room had.

She looked at me hard for a minute, then relaxed and shrugged. "Yeah, I was up there. I wanted to ask Everett, one more time, to give me that money back. People think you have a bunch of money when you work for yourself, but let me tell you, Skinny Girl, you don't. You have a payroll to meet, *every* week. People depend on my ass. And after spending that money on the dummy and those other materials, I'd had to rob Peter to pay Paul. That thirty-five thousand might not have meant a lot to Everett, but it meant a lot to me." She sounded sober now. And angry.

"I can see that." Paul nodded. "So really you just wanted to get back to where you were before: financially solvent."

She nodded, beginning to cry again.

"What'd he say when you told him this?" Paul asked.

"He said something like 'It was all a big misunderstanding, and there are risks as well as rewards in any new venture, and unfortunately for me I'd had the risk part first,' some shit like that."

"Did you tell him you were considering legal action?" I asked.

She gave me one of those *what do you think I am, stupid?* looks and said, with exaggerated patience, "Why, yes, Alex, as a matter of fact I did. Or I was *planning* to, when I saw something."

"Which was?"

"Back in a sec."

She returned almost immediately with a big brown-and-white striped cosmetics bag, the kind you pack your face cream and stuff in when you travel. After picking through it, she grabbed something out and threw it in my direction.

"*That.*"

It was a palm-sized leather notebook in *Radiance*'s signature hyacinth color, embossed with the magazine's logo and with gold-stamped initials that read FWH.

Frankie. She knew Frankie had been in Ev's room too.

"I'm *not* stupid, Alex. I figured Ev pulling out of the deal was only part of why he'd stopped seeing me. It made things convenient for him. But I also knew Ev well enough to know if he was getting cold feet it wasn't just about money. I figured there was probably another woman involved, and there was."

"Actually, Esmé, I think you have the wrong idea about this—"

"Actually, Alex, I think I *don't*. You don't think he told me about having been with Frankie a couple of years ago?"

Now it was our turn to look surprised.

"Oh, yeah." She smirked. "She thought that was such a big *secret*. Well, it was—until Ev shared it. I didn't believe it at first, 'cause I'd never seen him with anyone who looked like Frankie. He'd always chosen brown girls. But it figures. Even a race man like Everett Carson is not immune to Yellow Fever."

I started to interrupt again, to set her straight, but she thought I was offended. She held up her hand to stop me:

"No offense, Alex, but some brothers are never gonna outgrow the need to have women who look like you on their arms. Doesn't matter how brilliant or interesting a sister is, she can be out in the cold in a minute if the right woman walks by. Funny how the right woman is always the same color, with the same kind of hair . . . ever notice that?"

I deemed it prudent not to answer and looked over to Paul.

"So you thought he'd gone back to Frankie?" he asked.

"Of course. You come into a man's room and it smells like another woman and her stuff is on his coffee table, what *else* are you supposed to think?"

"That maybe she had some unfinished *un*romantic business to discuss with him," I said softly.

"Oh, yeah? And what might that be?" Esmé sneered. "Everybody always sympathizes with poor little Frankie. So sweet. So considerate. So hard-working. She makes me *sick*." Esmé was pacing the room now, truly agitated. "And you know what pissed me off most of all? I lost a baby because I thought I had a future with Everett—and he didn't want one, not under any circumstances. If I'd known then what I know now, I'd have kept that baby and kept on steppin'."

Oh my God. "Esmé, were you . . . ?" I couldn't even say the word. Everett was like the Everready Bunny.

"Yes, damn you, I *was*. And I wanted it, too. But nooo, Everett wouldn't even discuss having a child. I brought it up once or twice and he said, 'No way I'd ever have a child with you, honey. If that's what you want, you want another man.' I thought I'd found the man, so I had to make a choice. So I took that walk to the clinic. Hardest thing I've ever done. And I shouldn't have," she said miserably, "I wanted that baby."

"Oh, Esmé," I murmured.

She walked over to the cosmetics bag, withdrew a tissue, and wiped her face. "Yeah, joke's on me, huh, Skinny Girl? How you think I felt when half a dozen people who were at the funeral told me he already *had* two crumb snatchers? He meant it when he said he didn't want to have a kid with me—he'd already *done* it with that rusty bitch from New Jersey!" Her face was streaming tears now.

"You never told him?"

She looked at me as if I'd lost my mind. "What would have been the point? He'd been real clear about what he didn't want. I knew what I had to do. Least, I *thought* I did."

She threw down the crumpled tissue and went back for more.

But she didn't come up with tissue this time. This time she came up with a gun.

24

The gun looked sleek, elegant, and lethal from where I stood. It glimmered in the room's flattering light. I know nothing about guns, so I couldn't tell what kind it was, or even whether or not it was real. At that moment, it looked real enough.

"Esmé, I like a woman who's full of surprises, but this is a bad idea," Paul said calmly. "Why don't you let me have that?"

She smiled coyly. "Noooo, cute man. You'd just take it and call the police. I don't like police."

"Maybe I'd just take it and keep you safe."

Please God, let his rap work. I'll be good. I'll start going to church again, I'll—Oh, what the hell. Either He was gonna help me out or not. God knew better than to expect radical behavior modification from me after all these years.

"Esmé, if you were in Ev's room and had a gun, how come you didn't just shoot him?" I asked.

"I hadda leave to go *get* it," she said coldly. "When I came back—couldna been more than ten minutes—he was naked and asleep. Or I *thought* he was asleep. Maybe he was already dead. Anyway, the walk back to his room gave me enough time to cool down, so I just left. *With* my gun. Unfired.

"Anyway," she added, "shooting him woulda been bad publicity."

Could explain why Donald Trump is still walking among us—nobody wants the bad press.

"Did you drink anything the first time you were up there?" Paul asked, keeping an eye on the gun.

"Somma that." She gestured to the Veuve bottles. "Said he wanted to toast our futures, make sure there were no hard feelings."

"Was the bottle already opened?"

"Yeah, the bottle was already opened. That's what room service *does*."

Maybe it wasn't the echinacea, maybe it was the Champagne. But no, she would have had some too and keeled over.

"Stop thinkin' so hard, Skinny Girl, you're gonna bust something." She laughed loudly at her own joke and finished with a hiccupy sob.

"Esmé, you really *should* put down that gun—" Paul began.

"I will," she said calmly. "But I've just been listenin' to myself. Pathetic. And know what? I can't stand to have another person know how pathetic that was. Not the Ev business. Not the baby business. And not the business business. So I'm afraid we're all going to have to keep quiet about this."

"Works for me," I said hastily.

"Only works for me this way."

And she swung around, aimed, and fired at us—just like that.

Only she missed. The bullet hit the Deco mirror just behind us—which promptly broke into about a hundred sharp pieces and rained down upon us.

I didn't see all this while it was happening, because Paul threw himself over me and we hit the floor hard. There was noise all around: from the gunfire—they tell you gunshots sound like firecrackers, but that one didn't, not to me, anyway; it sounded like a little cannon—from pieces of the mirror hitting the furniture and the floor, from the windows rattling. It was amazingly noisy in there.

I heard Paul grunt as we went down behind the sofa, and when it was quiet we looked at each other.

"You okay, Einstein?" he whispered. The left side of his face was reddening rapidly. He must have hit the walnut console as we were going down.

"Yeah . . . thanks. But where's the blood coming from?"

There was lots of it, and it turned out to be coming from a flap in my upper arm, the left one, courtesy of one of the flying pieces of glass. We had been lucky.

"Stay down."

I stayed down, looked around and grabbed a soggy napkin and flapped it to get any slivers out, and then slapped it on my bleeding arm, which was now throbbing hotly. Its wet coolness felt great.

"Esmé?" Paul called out cautiously.

Esmé was walking back and forth in front of the windows, keening. She seemed to be repeating the same thing over and over. I listened hard and figured out what it was: oh-shit-oh-shit-oh-shit-oh-shit.

Paul's voice startled her. She jumped, the gun still in her hand.

"I fucked *this* up, too! I'm so sorry, you guys, I didn't mean to hurt you! I just cannot stand this anymore. My business, my every-thing, is just . . . *shit*."

I peeped above the sofa's back in time to see Paul walk slowly, deliberately, toward Esmé, arm outstretched to take the gun.

"C'mon, Esmé. You don't want to do this. Give me the gun, and we'll figure things out from there."

Then we all jumped because the door seemed to explode.

"Ms. Marshall! Security! Open the door, please!"

Somebody must have reported the gunshots. Thank God. The door banged loudly again.

"Open up, ma'am! LAPD!"

"Oh, God, oh, God!" Esmé screamed. Then she looked us dead in the eye and said, "Be fair when you write about this."

And before Paul could reach her, she jumped through the case-ment windows. She didn't even scream going down.

'Course, it would have been a short scream. Little Esmé, going places, intent on the upward trajectory at all times, had never bothered to look down, just out. Otherwise she'd have seen there was a lovely terrace one floor below her. Instead of breaking her neck, she broke her leg. And her pelvis. And, from the angle of how she was lying there, an arm. It occurred to me, fleetingly, that before her diet she would never have been able to slip through the tall thin casements to take that plunge.

We were hanging out the window, listening to her moans and preparing to open the door, when the it burst open.

"LAPD!" a familiar voice barked. Then: "Oh, man."

There, bracketed by a beefy hotel security guard and the night manager, stood Jim Marron and a couple of uniformed police officers.

"Esmé tried to shoot us and then she jumped out the window!" Sorry, but some days I just cannot keep a secret.

"She's alive, but she's hurting. She hit the terrace," Paul said.

Marron looked out, rolled his eyes, and jerked his chin to the uniforms. "You guys know the drill. Be down in a minute. Don't forget to—"

"We know: Mirandize her."

I wanted to point out that Mirandize wasn't really a verb but thought better of it. My increasing capacity for self-censorship was starting to worry me.

Marron turned to the distraught hotel manager. "Calling 911 would be a good idea right around now, don't you think?"

"Yes, sir!" the night manager, who looked to be all of thirty, gasped.

Marron looked at us both—me bloody and pale and Paul with a major shiner, both bristling with glass—and grinned.

"You," he said to Paul, "look like you've been on the wrong end of Leon Spinks."

Paul grinned back. Pride over a black eye must be a Y-chromosome thing.

"And *you!*" He shook his head. "How bad is it?"

Gingerly, I removed the napkin, and the flap started spurting again. All of a sudden, I didn't feel so good.

"Sit," Marron commanded, and pushed me on the sofa. "Put your head between your knees." I did, and hoped all the nice things I'd eaten for tea wouldn't end up in an ugly splat on the floor.

Someone took a towel, dunked it in the champagne bucket, and slapped it on the back of my neck. Its icy wetness made me shiver, but I felt better almost instantly.

"May I sit up now?"

"Only if you lie down, keep your feet up, and put this across your forehead."

No argument from me. Paul swung my feet into his lap, and Marron moved the towel that had been on the back of my neck to my forehead. He probed a little, to make sure my wound wasn't serious. Then he had the manager call for an ambulance. He and Paul would follow in his car.

"Why can't he just drive me to Cedars in our car?" I whined. I didn't want to miss the party.

"Rules. And Hertz probably don't want you bleeding all over their rental."

"That's why we used Avis—they try harder. Why can't *you* drive us?"

"Hard as I worked for that Lexus, and I'm gonna let you soak the backseats, Powell? They're leather. Get real."

I forgot. I live in Southern California, where they take their cars seriously. Oh, well. I'd never ridden in an ambulance before.

"I gotta go down and check on your friend. We'll see you at the hospital. And don't worry about your car. Nelson here says it's on the house till you can get back to pick it up."

Whew. At least it wouldn't cost a hundred bucks to get out. I guess management was happy that we didn't look like litigious types.

"Isn't this funny?" Marron mused, as he went out the door.

"Funny ha-ha? Funny peculiar? Funny what?" I wondered.

"Funny ironic. All these hard-assed rappers here tonight, you'da thought if there was gonna be trouble it would have come from one of them. Not from a member of the black bougie-woogie."

"Oh, you did *not* say that to me. I know you didn't."

"Hey, with the drugs they're gonna give you when they stitch you up, you'd better believe you won't remember even if I did."

• • •

The drugs were good. Almost as good as the ambulance ride. I especially liked the sirens. But Marron was wrong about one thing. The drugs might have made me a little fuzzy around the edges, but I did remember almost everything.

For instance, I remember giving a statement—in a separate part of the ER from Paul—before I was given any pain medication. And the pain medication was da bomb.

I remember being stitched up by an incredibly cute doctor who said he was a plastic surgeon.

"Are you any good?" I asked him. Miss Snippy, even on drugs.

"Remember what happened to Sammy Wilson's nose?"

Everybody remembered what happened to Sammy Wilson's nose—it had been covered by *Entertainment Tonight*, *Extra*, and *Access Hollywood*, along with gossip columnists across the country. And two full pages in *Jet*, of course.

Sammy Wilson was a world-renowned pop singer whose bride of three months had opened his nose with a carving knife after she discovered him in bed with his bodyguard. One of the tabs had caught him as he was walked into the Cedars ER, in the ten seconds he'd lowered his blood-soaked handkerchief. He'd looked like a "before" picture for cleft-palate reconstruction.

"I fixed *that*," my terminally cute doctor was saying confidently, "so *this* is a piece of cake."

Damn. He *was* good. Despite the grisly photos. Sammy was back onstage, his pretty-boy face seemingly unscathed by Marissa Jeter-Wilson's assault.

For my money, the boy shoulda known better. Marissa's dad, Jerry Jeter, was one of the most famous R & B musicians ever born; his temper and prowess with a knife were almost as legendary as his musical genius. He and Marissa's mom, Melinda, had been notorious for leaving blood-splattered hotel rooms in their wake while on tour. Melinda was no slouch herself in the battery department; she'd been reputed to match Jerry blow for blow. ("I'm from Detroit," she'd said in a *Rolling Stone* interview. "We don't fuck around.") They'd both calmed down in their old age, but clearly Marissa was a chip off the old chopping block.

I remember being shot up with tetanus and antibiotics afterward and being given scrubs to wear home, because my poor coral dress was finished. They stuck it in a red plastic bag marked HAZARDOUS WASTE and let me take it. The nurse who helped me into the scrubs explained. "We usually have clear bags for our patients' effects, but I didn't think you'd want anyone to see those bloody undies."

She was right. I was leaving without underwear; let's hope nobody tells my mother. I wasn't so much peeved about the panties, but a good bra—and mine had been a good one, fairly new too—can set a girl back at least thirty bucks, dammit.

I remember walking out carefully between Paul and Marron (who had been kind enough to carry my purse), so nobody would know I wasn't wearing a bra.

And I remember, on the way, seeing a very dapper black man coming down the corridor straight at me. He was wearing a collarless white silk shirt, black trousers, and the most startling grape blazer I'd ever seen.

"This is *not* good news," Marron muttered. "Oh, well. Might as well be civil."

The man was right up on us. In my drug-induced haze, I was beginning to think I knew him.

"Paul Butler, Alex Powell, I'd like to introduce you to—"

"Rupert Washington Junior," the dapper man said smoothly. "So good to meet you both. And good to see you again too, Detective Marron."

"Right," Marron muttered.

No wonder he looked familiar! Anyone who had seen even ten minutes of Denny Freeman's trial knew who Rupert Washington Jr. was: the best defense money could buy. Esmé must have *big* juice to get Washington himself on such short order. I carefully placed my hand into his extended one to shake. Instead, he patted it gently. Then he smiled widely, his pearly whites bracketed by a lush mustache.

"Miss Marshall has just engaged me to represent her, which means of course we won't be speaking to any members of the LAPD—even those as sensitive as Detective Marron, here—without my specific authorization and presence. And I'll need to speak with you both, Mr. Butler, Ms. Powell, to get your version of events."

"Which of course won't be done without *my* prior notification and approval," Marron emphasized.

Washington dipped his head in a courtly bow. "Of course. I wouldn't dream of it. Washington and Associates respects the work of the LAPD."

Marron looked like he was going to throw up, right there.

"In any event," Washington went on, dimples in his chiseled mocha cheeks flashing, "I'd appreciate being able to speak with you both in the next twenty-four hours. Do you mind if I call tomorrow, say ten-ish?" He turned to Marron. "Do I have approval for that?"

"Yeah, of course."

"Ten o'clock then, or thereabouts?"

We looked at each other, nodded our heads, and said, "I guess." Marron wrote my number on the back of one of his cards and handed it to the defense attorney, who slipped it into the pocket of his loud jacket.

"Good, good. I'm sure we'll all feel better when this is straightened out. Oh, and Miss Powell?"

"Yes?"

"You won't be writing anything about this before I speak to you, will you?"

I could hear A.S. grinding his molars from here. Tell the press what to do? Heavens!

"Probably not, Mr. Washington. I have a bad habit of gathering as many facts as possible before I sit down to do a column. And I have the feeling there are still some facts outstanding in this case."

Broad, mustache-y grin. "Indeed, indeed. It's why I've always enjoyed reading you—you're fair."

"But not easy," I warned. "And don't let's forget one teensy salient point: I was *there.*"

I remember his grin fading just a little bit. "Yes, well . . . all we're asking for is fair, which I'm sure you were going to be anyway."

"Bet on it. May we go now?"

"Oh, certainly. I'm sure you're anxious to get home and into something more . . . *comfortable*. Good evening to you all."

I remember thinking he somehow knew I wasn't wearing any underwear but found that less worrisome than having my mother find out. And I didn't have to worry about her finding out from him. It might be a small colored world, but it wasn't *that* small.

Yet.

25

Marron drove us home and even came in with us and looked around. I heard his stomach grumble and realized it was almost ten-thirty. None of us had had anything to eat for hours.

"Anybody hungry?"

Marron looked at me strangely. "Can you cook?"

"When I have to. And since everything is closed, just about, looks like I have to."

He looked at Paul for guidance.

"Can't be any worse than a stale burger would have been, right?" Paul asked.

"Okay." Marron nodded. "You may cook. If you feel like it."

I didn't even bother to roll my eyes, just headed straight for the kitchen. I boiled some farfalle, melted a half stick of unsalted butter in a sauté pan, threw in a few chopped scallions and the rest of the lox from breakfast, added a little cream, and tossed the whole thing together with half a package of peas I found in the freezer and defrosted in the microwave.

Marron came to the pass-through to look.

"Smells good," he noted.

"I'm not even going to be offended that you sound so surprised."

I threw leftover bagels in the toaster. They'd have to do for bread. There was a bag of salad greens, the prewashed kind, I'd never gotten around to eating. I opened the bag and sniffed—not totally fresh, but not slimy either. I decided we'd chance it; I rinsed the greens in cold water, patted them dry, and tossed them in a vinaigrette. My arm was beginning to hurt for real, but Dr. Cutie and his nurse had told me not to mix the pain meds, if I took them, with alcohol. Considering the amount of Champagne I'd consumed earlier, aspirin would have to do. If I had any.

After the first bite, Marron looked at me with new respect. "Damn, you *do* have some social utility after all. This is excellent."

"Gee, thanks. I think."

As we ate dinner, we asked Marron what he thought would happen to Esmé.

He shrugged. "Rupie will probably get her off with probation."

Paul frowned. "Even though she used a gun, one that probably wasn't registered to her?"

"Well, she didn't actually shoot you, she shot *at* you, so that may get her some leniency. And if Rupie runs true to form, he'll claim extreme emotional distress. Maybe she was taking something, like Prozac or Zoloft, that she can blame it on. He'll probably go for something like diminished capacity.

"Speaking of which," he continued, as he divided the last of the pasta between Paul and himself—"You don't want any more, do you?"—"you'll need a lawyer if you're going to talk to him tomorrow. It's just prudent—and standard. I called a friend of mine before we left the Metropolitan, and she's agreed to represent you if you want. Here's her number."

He scribbled a name and number on a napkin and pushed it across the table.

"Gisele Martin? *The* Gisele Martin I see on CNN? The one who eats prosecutors for breakfast?"

"That's the one."

"Wow. How do you know her?"

"We went to Boalt Hall together for a couple of years."

That certainly merited a sip of wine. "*You* have a law degree?"

"Part of one." He poured more wine into my glass. "I dropped out at the end of my second year. By then, I knew myself well enough to know I wasn't going to enjoy lawyering. That had been the old man's idea. He's a lawyer. Me, I needed to be on the street, not behind a desk."

Well, well. Wonders never cease. "So you and Ms. Martin became friends back then—"

"—and have remained friends ever since. Despite our political differences. Sometimes we do each other favors, for old times' sake."

"And why would she be wanting to do you *this* favor?" Paul asked.

"She hates Rupert," Marron said cheerfully. "He made the mistake of being condescending to her at a press conference once, and she told me later she decided, then and there, that whenever she could take a chunk out of his ass, she was gonna do it. Here's an irresistible opportunity. She hates him so much, she's offered to do this pro bono. And"—he sighed—"because she's a big Powell fan. Of Powell's column, anyway."

"Really? I like her already."

"Yeah, you-all remind me of each other: too damn smart and vindictive for your own good."

"I am not either vindictive!"

He pushed back his chair and rose. "I'd love to stay and have this argument, but I'm on call tomorrow at seven, so I'm going home. Don't forget to call Gisele in the morning, early. Her office will be expecting to hear from you. And don't forget to put on the alarm."

"Hasn't everything that's going to happen already happened?"

"Who knows?" Marron sighed. "Why tempt fate? Lock up."

He left, and I did.

Paul had quickly rinsed the dishes and shoved them in the dishwasher. I pushed the chairs back under the table, corked what was left of the wine, and stuck it in the fridge. I was hoping to sleep till at least seven, so I turned down the answering machine too. I knew my nosy friends would be calling as soon as the news of our adventure at the Metropolitan got out.

Now that we weren't all talking at once, the house seemed very quiet. I sighed loudly—probably more loudly than I'd thought.

Paul came up behind me and took my injured arm in his hands carefully. "Hurt?"

"Yeah. Feels like little guys with red-hot hammers are taking turns slamming it."

"Well, let's get you something for it. What did the hospital give you to take at home?"

"Stuff you shouldn't take when you're drinking. I needed the wine worse than I needed the drugs. I *thought* I did, anyway."

"Well, take two of these, then." He handed me some aspirin and half a glass of wine, which I obediently swallowed. He continued to stare at me.

"What?"

"You've had a hard day, Einstein."

"This from somebody who looks like he pissed off Evander Holyfield." I laughed.

"My black eye will be gone in a couple of weeks. What about your scar?"

He was standing behind me and had begun to knead my shoulders. It felt heavenly.

"Your're stiff as a board," he *tsk*ed, as he continued to press just the right spots. "Does this hurt?"

"Nooo . . . feels good."

He continued in silence for a few more moments. Then he stopped. I felt a pair of cool lips on the top of my shoulder, right where the bandage ended.

"Shoulder still hurt?"

"Not as much as before."

"Should I continue the alternative therapy?" He kissed my collarbone, then the hollow of my throat.

I shivered with pleasure. "Couldn't hurt."

He ran his nose along the side of my neck and inhaled deeply. "Smells good," he breathed. Then he nibbled my earlobe. I shivered again. "Cold?"

"Confused."

"Really? Why?" The nibbling, sniffing—everything—stopped.

"Well, I mean, we've been together for a week. We've shared the same bed for that long, and never once, not *once*, have you ever given any indication that you were interested in me in that way."

"And I wasn't going to, Einstein, until I had some indication that the interest was mutual."

"So what indication did I give?"

"I figured I might stand a ghost of a chance when we were up in Esmé's room. You looked daggers at her a couple of times when she was flirting with me."

I thought I'd been rather low key about it. Just goes to show you what I know.

"She's a very annoying person, Esmé, but I feel bad for her."

He chuckled. "I don't. She almost killed us!"

"Well, not really. Her aim wasn't all that great."

He sighed. "I am going to miss your impossible logic when I go back to D.C., Einstein. Everybody's logical in D.C."

"Yeah. I always think how very logical those white boys who make up Congress are, every time I watch one of them on C-Span. And that's another thing. I live here; you live there. What's the point?"

"What do you mean, what's the point?" He slid his hands up my neck again and gently massaged my scalp. It felt so good I went limp.

"Well . . . it's hard, dating long distance."

The massaging stopped. He turned me around to face him. "I'm not after a *date*, Einstein. I can get plenty of those in Washington."

"Well, what then? What do you want?"

He pressed his lips together for a moment, exhaled gently, and squeezed my shoulders. "I want something else. Something serious. I just turned forty-two; you're practically—"

"I can do the math, thank you!"

He smiled. "See what I mean? What I want is a decision from you to take me seriously." He kissed the underside of my neck.

I closed my eyes and sighed. It was a physical version of déjà vu—as if I'd done it before. And liked it. Lots.

"I want you to be serious about taking me seriously." He brushed my warm lips with his cool ones. They were slightly parted. "And I want," he murmured, "to take you to bed. Finally. What do you want?"

He stopped and looked at me. The CD had stopped, and it was very, very quiet in the room.

"I want what you want," I said simply.

He drew me closer and placed his mouth over mine. Kissing him felt like eating a ripe peach. I could feel him, rigid, against me. We broke away after a moment. He wasn't smiling anymore, he was looking at me intently. Then, as he had when we were in the Millennium, he picked me up, walked through the living room to the bedroom, and kicked the door shut with his foot.

The CD may have stopped, but the sound track in my head went on and on that night: Aretha, singing "Dr. Feelgood" over and over. And the sister was right: The man sure was making me feel real.

26

I should have gotten up early the next morning, called A.S., and explained, in the humblest tones possible, why I wouldn't be in until much later. Say, a day or two later. But let's face it: When you haven't had sex in a long time and then you do, and you're suddenly given the opportunity to have a little more (okay, a *lot* more), if you're smart, having seconds (or, in this case, fifths) is what you do.

So the choice of leaving a warm bed and an aroused man who was doing an excellent job of arousing me reciprocally to call my already pissed-off editor or staying happily where I was seemed like a no-brainer to me. By the time I finally staggered into the kitchen to squint at the clock on the wall, it was practically the crack of noon.

The night before I had turned my answering machine all the way down; now it was blinking furiously. Sighing, I hit the PLAY button.

Alex, this is Henry. I'm trying to learn what the upshot of your meeting with Benjamin Soyinka was. Another board member, Bill Preston, called with some disturbing news; seems they've almost decided to replace Everett with someone else. Someone who isn't, obviously, me. What did Soyinka say? I need to know immediately. Please call, no matter how late you get in.

Damn. In all the excitement, we hadn't even checked for messages last night! Poor Henry must be worried sick. I'd have to call him with the bad news later on. The next message was starting up:

Good morning, Ms. Powell. This is Marie in Gisele Martin's office. Detective Marron spoke with our Ms. Fraizer last night, and she wanted me to remind you to refer Mr. Washington's calls to her, should he attempt to contact you. Please call her at this number when you have a moment.

Then:

Alex, this is A.S. I see you're still being the Invisible Woman, and I assume you have some explanation for your disappearing act, or we're going to have to decide the terms of your probation, I don't give a shit what the Guild says.

Because of an arcane arrangement from a previous owner from whom the Hansons had bought the paper decades ago, reporters and correspondents at the *Standard* were West Coast members of the Newspaper Guild of New York. Thanks to the Guild, there are very specific rules about how management can go about firing us. Usually three written warnings come first (they might be in my in-box, for all I knew), *then* probation, but A.S. sounded so angry he might be able to get away with skipping step one.

Miss Powell, Rupert Washington here. I'd understood you and Mr. Butler would be available at ten this morning, but perhaps something happened. Please call my office as quickly as possible; ask for Sherri, my personal assistant. The number here is. . . .

His smooth baritone was a mixture of disappointment, probably fake, and annoyance, probably not fake at all.

Alex, darling, it's Sally. Come up for brunch, won't you? I thought Paul might want to sample Josefina's huevos rancheros, and the strawberries and mangoes this morning at the farmer's

market are to die for, so we'll have a big bowl of those. About
twelve-thirty, all right? See you then!

And finally, some news I could use.

Yo, Shorty: Saw the shooting thing on the news this morning
while I was doing my Tae Bo—that was you-all, wasn't it? I
figured if you were seriously hurt, somebody would have called me
by now to pick you out a decent burial outfit. How 'bout I stop by
around four with a couple of bottles of Champagne and you can
catch me up? And I'll get a chance to meet the Wicked Ex's Best
Friend. Unless I get a message from you saying don't come, I'll
assume I should. As you probably have already. Multiple times, if
you're lucky.

There was a gale of laughter before she hung up. So amusing, my
friend Georgie Marks.

"Lots of calls?" Paul, still damp from the shower, bent over and
kissed the back of my neck. His lips felt wet and cool.

"Lots. A.S., pissed off. Rupert Washington, sorry he didn't reach
us when we said we were going to be there. Jim's friend Gisele,
telling us don't talk to Rupert without talking to her first. Henry—"

"Always Henry."

"True—saying he'd heard he wasn't going to get the job and
what did I know about that."

"Uh-oh."

"Tell me about it. Sally invited us over for brunch in a few minutes, and Georgie wants to come by later in the afternoon to have
drinks, catch up, and, I'm sure, meet you."

"Oh, good. I've never met anyone who keeps Queen Elizabeth
in the library."

"That's at her mother's house. Not that it matters."

"Not one bit."

I sighed. "I'd better call A.S."

Paul leaned against the counter. His torso glistened, the wetness
outlining the sinews in his upper arms. I tried to concentrate on listening to him.

"What are you going to tell him?"

"I dunno. Guess I'll make it up as I go along."

He grinned broadly. "This should be good. I've never heard you grovel."

"I'm sorry to disappoint you, but today ain't the day, my brother."

That's what I said—but I was talking a lot braver than I felt. As I punched the number, I didn't relish the prospect of job hunting unless I was doing it of my own volition.

Francyne picked up the phone immediately.

"Oh, *hi*, Alex." I could tell by the way she emphasized the *hi* that A.S. was within earshot. "So that *was* you on the news? Are you all right? . . . I'm glad it wasn't worse. . . . Yes, A.S. is right here, he's anxious to speak with you. Hold on."

I hadn't yet said a word; Francyne had primed the pump for me. Maybe it was the aromatherapy kit I'd given her for Christmas. Or the big bouquet during Secretaries' Week. I didn't have time to pat myself on the back, because A.S. came right on the line.

"Powell, are you okay?"

"Good morning, A.S. I'm fine, nothing a few hundred stitches couldn't fix. Sorry I didn't call earlier; the pain pills must have knocked me out."

Paul rolled his eyes in the kitchen as he ground coffee and filled the press.

"Don't worry about it. Jim Marron called this morning and filled me in. And Keith Stansfield was on night cops last night and told me he'd heard about the shooting at the Metropolitan. When he got there, they told him a couple of reporters had been involved, one of them from the *Standard*, but they wouldn't say who. Marron wanted to let me know you were all right." He paused. "I'm glad."

"I'll bet." I couldn't resist: "If I'd been killed on the job, you'd have had to send three times my annual salary to my poor bereaved mom. My annual salary *is* kind of a pittance, but still."

Paul was standing, open-mouthed, as the water started to boil. Grovel *that*, Cute Man.

A.S., however, was far from speechless. "You know. Anybody else would have been happy not to have been fired. Anybody else would have—"

"Allan." I cut him off, using the first name nobody ever called him. "You hired me precisely because I'm *not* anybody else. Too late for this leopard to change spots now."

There was a brief silence; then he yelped with laughter. "You're right. What *was* I thinking? I am, after all, only your employer. So tell me this: Do the pills work well enough to allow you to file for tomorrow's paper?"

"I need more time. It's past noon now. Even if I started immediately, I don't think I'd be done by four. Why don't you run a brief item about the shooting and let me file for the day after? That way I can get you everything."

"Not only does she want an extension, she's telling me how to do my job."

"No, I'm *suggesting* a logical way to manage this. Nobody else has all the pieces to the puzzle, and I want to put them together properly. It's not like the *New York Times* is going to scoop us or anything."

I looked over at Paul, who was placidly drinking his coffee and pretending not to hear me.

"Okay, fine. File by one P.M. tomorrow latest; I'll have them save the space."

"Front page?"

"Yes, dammit, front page."

"Above the fold?"

"Goddammit, Powell!"

"See ya, A.S. I gotta call my lawyer."

And I hung up.

Paul whistled. "So *that's* what that strange noise was last night."

"What noise?" I could't remember anything but the whisper of the pool sweeper and the assorted noises the two of us made. Which I won't go into here.

"Your big brass ones, clanking together."

"I didn't hear any complaints last night."

He came over and took me in his arms. "I didn't *see* them last night. Calls for another inspection." He began to unknot the sash to my bathrobe.

And I was on my way to letting him, too, till I remembered. "Sally's expecting us."

He stopped his preliminary inspection. "So she is. You'd better get some clothes on."

"And you're going in a towel?"

"Men are always ready quicker than women. It's an immutable law of nature."

"Kinda like 'What goes up must come down'?" I teased, pulling the edge of the towel, which was no longer poking out like a tent in front.

"Yeah, but I'm like the Old South." His black eye winked. "I, too, shall rise again."

Good. I was planning on it.

27

Sally was in her element at brunch. She'd in-vited a few of the neighbors over, and of course we were pumped for details as to what had happened the night before. She was a little disappointed to find out we couldn't really discuss it any detail, but she was fascinated to hear we'd met Rupert Washington Jr.

"He's quite dishy, isn't he?" she whispered. "I used to watch him all the time during the Denny Freeman trial. Come to think of it, that's probably why most women watched."

Paul choked on his margarita. "Went down the wrong way," he apologized, wiping his eyes. I could see the smile beneath the napkin he held up to his mouth.

"Oh, darling, don't worry," Sally hastened to say. "He's not nearly as dishy as you are. *You're* the sophisticated woman's choice."

Now it was my torn to snort into my drink. "Sorry."

Sally frowned. "Maybe Josefina made them too strong?"

Nah. After Josefina's great eggs, a platter of chorizos and grilled prawns, and a sublime bowl of fresh fruit, we carried the dishes back to the kitchen (over Josefina's protests) and excused ourselves, explaining I had editorial duties to attend to. And Paul had to pick up the rental car. We probably owed a zillion dollars on it by now.

· · ·

I called Henry at home when I got in, planning to fill him on what I knew about Ben Soyinka's plan for *Diaspora*, but no one was home. Just his answering machine with a prissy message:

> *You have reached Henry Adams, managing editor of* Diaspora. *If this is editorial business, please press one. For all other messages, please press two. Thank you for calling.*

Guess he wasn't a *have a nice day* kind of guy.

I was momentarily flummoxed: This was an editorial call, but it was personal too. I finally chose two and left him a quick message:

"Henry it's me, Alex. I'm sorry I didn't call you last night, but we had a couple of emergencies around here, some of which relate to you, so call me when you have a moment."

I took out a legal pad and a bunch of pens and started to outline what had happened last night. When I had that in order, I'd take out my laptop and start writing.

Paul had jumped into a cab half an hour ago and was on his way over to the Metropolitan to retrieve the car. He said he might stop in and speak with the people in the *Times* L.A. bureau on the way back, so I didn't expect to see him for another couple of hours. Finally, after all this time, I was alone.

It felt nice. All I heard was the gurgle of the pool sweeper, the distant drone of a neighboring gardener's lawn mower, and the rasp of my rollerball on the legal pad.

I wrote quick fragments of what had happened: the conference, Ev's death. Meeting three of the biggest black publishers in the business. Why each of them might have had their own reasons for wanting Ev gone. (In Frankie's case, I had to commit a sin of omission, but I'd rectify that soon enough when she'd told the board and staff at *Radiance*. She had one more week before she dropped the bomb, and I intended to keep my promise to her.)

I wrote about Esmé's transformation and her discovery that Ev had dumped her, not only personally but in business as well.

It was a good story, but I didn't have an end. So far, my outline read like a whodunit with the last few pages removed.

I went back over my notes and realized I hadn't fully explained about the tainted echinacea. I picked up the phone and, after Information gave me the number, called the Herb Garden on Melrose.

"The Garden," a cultivated male voice intoned.

"This is Alex Powell at the *Standard*. I wonder if the owner might be available?"

"Padgett? Of course. Please hold." The line was immediately filled with a Windom Hill New Age kind of symphony. Figures.

"This is Padgett Ross," an even smoother voice said.

I told him who I was and what I wanted to know and why.

"Who is the client?"

"There are two, Everett Carson and Esmé Marshall. Apparently they order the same thing, some kind of echinacea."

"We don't give out that information under normal circumstances," Ross demurred.

"I know you don't, but these aren't normal circumstances. You can check with Detective Jim Marron in the West Hollywood division if you'd like. Here's the number . . ."

"Let me make the call and get back to you in a few moments." Two minutes later, Ross was back on the line. "Okay, I'll give that info to you now. Sorry I couldn't give it straight off, but we have a lot of A-listers who take their privacy very seriously, so we have to, too."

"I understand." Megastars were rabid about keeping their private lives private, and were fiercely loyal to establishments that helped them do it. Ross would have needed a good reason to speak to me.

"Hang on for a sec, I've got to go online. . . ." Now it was Peruvian flute music.

"Okay . . . yes, Esmé Marshall is a regular. Tincture of echinacea, shipped once a month. But not to her."

"You mean, not to her office or her home?"

"Not even her home *state*. It was shipped to Washington, D.C., to the offices of *Diaspora* magazine. I remember because it's a special order: Ms. Marshall buys a lot at one time, but she always asks for an extra dropper bottle. Apparently she splits it with someone. Maybe your Mr. Carson, maybe someone else."

"Why would she go to the trouble? Why not just order two smaller bottles?"

"Well, I don't like to offer this as an option, but I'll do it for some of my regulars. Ordering in one big bottle is like getting a forty percent discount. It's significantly less expensive."

"Does it compromise the quality of the product?"

"Not if it's done correctly. We ship an extra clean bottle, and she probably fills it using a standard pharmacist's funnel. They save about fifty dollars by doing it that way."

I was astonished. I'd heard of echinacea before and figured it couldn't cost more than a couple of bucks.

"Is it normally so expensive?"

"Oh, you can buy generic stuff at the drugstore for twelve to twenty dollars a bottle, depending on who makes it. But this is special; it's grown in New Mexico and formulated by Benedictine monks. I have a waiting list. Half of Hollywood insists on using it."

Really. I smiled to myself, imagining Sly, Vanessa, Madonna, and whoever chugging down thick liquid from brown squeeze-drop bottles.

"Mr. Ross, one last question—"

"Padgett, please." He laughed. "Mr. Ross is my father."

"Okay: Padgett. What does it taste like and why do people take it?"

"That's actually two questions, Alex, but I'll be glad to answer both. It tastes like weed killer—and despite that, people take it because it keeps them healthier than they've ever been in their lives. Come see me; I'll get you started with some samples. See if you don't feel better within a week."

I promised I would, as soon as things calmed down. If the idea of drinking something that tastes like weed killer didn't put me off, the idea of finding a parking space on Melrose certainly would.

After I hung up, there wasn't much time to ponder what else could have gotten into the echinacea, because a series of sharp knocks startled me. Three-thirty. Georgie must have gotten away early.

But when I opened the door, it wasn't Georgie at all. It was Henry Adams.

"No wonder you weren't home when I called you earlier today. What are you doing here, Henry?"

28

Henry smiled thinly. He was dressed as he al-
ways was — like someone who'd scarfed down a Ralph Lauren catalog and had a little trouble digesting it — navy blue blazer with a
crest over a white open-necked polo shirt, khaki trousers, and (here's
where the sartorial burp comes in) black oxfords. Not white Keds.
Or navy espadrilles. Or brown fisherman sandals. Black wingtips
like the kind Richard Nixon wore when he walked the beach at San
Clemente. Henry's getup had the same unfortunate effect.

"Kind of you to finally return my call. But I got tired of waiting.
Desperate times do indeed call for desperate measures. So here I
am. May I come in?"

I shrugged, still confused — "Of course" — and stepped aside to
allow him to pass me. I could see him assessing everything in the
room. *Not bad,* his glance seemed to say. *Better than I might have
thought.*

He seemed a little nervous and was pacing fitfully in front of the
yellow sofa.

"Can I get you anything, Henry? A cup of tea? Diet Coke? A
drink?"

"Thanks, but no. I never drink before five."

"You're probably still on East Coast time — and it's past five back
there."

"Smart girl, Alex. So very smart. But no, thank you anyway."

He sat on the sofa, crossed one leg over the other in what seemed to be a practiced rather than truly casual motion, and leaned back.

"So what did your Mr. Soyinka tell you, Alex? What did you think of him?"

How much did Henry know, I wondered? And why, suddenly, was I worried about it?

"Well, he told me about the publications he ran in Africa. About the fact that he and Everett had had some discussions about combining their interests, kind of a black version of Time-Warner. They were thinking about television—"

"Yes, and they're staffing up for this grand enterprise as if it's actually going to go forward."

"You think it won't?"

Henry looked smug. "It will. They just need the right person to run the Stateside end of the operation."

He stood and began walking about the living room, inspecting my pictures, picking up and replacing the little objets and mementos scattered throughout the room. He ran his hand thoughtfully over a bone mail opener with a handle carved like an alligator's body. I'd bought it in "my" Mr. Soyinka's Abidjan more than a decade ago.

"That person should be me, Alex. We both know it. *I've* been the person who has made *Diaspora* run. *I've* done all the heavy lifting. By rights, Everett's job should be *mine*."

"Oh, Henry. . . ." I didn't know where to begin. He was right, of course. He'd paid his dues to get into the game—but then the game had changed. Ben Soyinka was right too, in asserting that whoever ran the merged *Diaspora* would have to be an internationalist.

My face must have given me away, because Henry suddenly switched from thoughtful to furious.

"You think I couldn't do it? Is that why you didn't talk Soyinka into it?"

"Henry, I couldn't talk him into anything. He had his own thoughts about where he wanted this to go."

"Yes, of course he did. But you, who are so *very* persuasive on other occasions, couldn't sway him just a bit? I'm disappointed in you."

"Why on earth would you think I'd be any more persuasive than the next person?"

He smirked. "He's African. You're pale and moderately attractive. He's away from home . . . you know how they are."

I was genuinely insulted. "That's not fair to either of us. And, if it matters, Paul came along."

"Oh, well then. That probably wouldn't have worked very well." He paused, looked at me, and chuckled. "Oh don't get in a snit, Alex. I've been around rich African men enough to know how many of them think. It was an educated guess."

"If somebody white had said that to you, you'd call them all kinds of racist."

"No, I wouldn't," he said, unperturbed. "I'd call them accurate."

I rolled my eyes in disgust.

"So what's this I hear about a confrontation with Esmé Marshall? Is that how you got that scratch?" He gestured toward the bandage on my upper arm.

"I have a question for you first: How friendly were they?"

Henry smiled to himself and rubbed his nose, thinking. "Very. I mean, she wasn't going to be the next Mrs. Everett Carson, but they were quite close for a while."

"She says she's responsible for his new look—the weight loss and all. True?"

He laughed. "Oh, yes. You know, Everett was always a fried-chicken-and-short-ribs kind of guy. Esmé told him he was going to keel over eating that way. Did you know she actually engaged a meal delivery service to bring him breakfast, lunch, and dinner? They'd deliver food in little tin things to his home. Lunch came directly to the office."

"No kidding?" That must have cost a fortune; there were a couple of diet divas out here who'd made big money feeding finicky stars exactly the right combination of carbs and proteins—all incredibly palatable and packaged in travel tins that were delivered directly to the talents' trailers. Some actors and directors thought the diet divas were so good, they had them written into their contracts. But Ev?

"No kidding. And yes, it was a *lot* of money—but what else did Everett spend his money on? All his travel was business-related."

"Books?" I knew he loved books; we'd bonded over that years earlier.

"Comps. Or deductibles."

"Music?"

"Same."

"Women?"

"He took them to dinners and weekends on his expense account. I know—I did all the reimbursement approvals."

"That can't be right, Henry. Dinners in town, okay, but he went places like Aspen, Saint Thomas, San Francisco."

"Ever notice where editors and publishers choose to have their meetings? It's never Cleveland or Pittsburgh or Augusta, is it? It's always in fun places like—"

"Gotcha. Silly me."

"Yes. The married ones bring wives, if they have to. The unmarried ones bring the woman of the moment."

"Esmé."

"At that particular moment, yes. Believe me, I know. I had to make the reservations. First class all the way. Now, about Esmé . . ."

So I kept my end of the unspoken bargain and told him about Esmé, what she'd told us and how she'd ended up. He listened impassively.

"Frankly, I never saw what women saw in him. And I completely disagreed with his technique of juggling them. I figured, if anything, it was going to get him killed one day."

"Jealous woman?"

"Or jealous boyfriend. Or husband."

He was quiet for a moment, surveying the room. The midafternoon sun poured through the partially opened shutters, gilding the hardwood floors and splashing stray spots of light against the walls. The water in the pool gurgled. Down the street, the whine of an electric lawn mower sounded a little louder. Henry seemed lost in thought, so I made my own visual inventory of the living room. Mail from Thursday, still unopened, on the dining room table. A box of books from an online company that had been delivered sometime in the past few days, and left, perhaps by Josefina, in the corner. A tray table near the armoire that held assorted bottles of liquor and liqueurs. Half the tray was those little mini-bottles you're given on airplanes and in minibars. Georgie had taken to collecting them when she flew and passing them on to me. We'd sometimes open several and make drinks from them. "That way you don't waste a liter if you need to make something with Midori in it," Georgie once said. "Although why one would *want* to drink Midori in anything is beyond me."

I had to agree. The liqueur version of honeydew melon wasn't what I'd reach for if I was going to design my own drink, but it was, as the Girl Scouts like to point out, always better to Be Prepared. And it was definitely cheaper.

I sat bolt upright. Padgett Ross had said ordering the big bottle and splitting it could save up to 40 percent. And the bottle went to Everett's office, and was then shipped to Esmé!

"Henry?" I tried to sound casual.

"Hmm?" Henry looked up from a large book on glassmaking that he'd been browsing through.

"You said Esmé got Ev on this health kick. The vitamins, the diet. The echinacea."

Henry sat up a little straighter too. "Yes, I did, didn't I?"

"How did Ev and Esmé split the bottle? The owner of the Herb Garden told me he shipped it to your office first."

"He did. We'd put Ev's in his own bottle, pour the rest of the big bottle into the smaller bottle so the air couldn't spoil it, and ship it to Esmé. It still saved money."

"Who's *we*? Was Everett filling his own bottles?"

Henry smiled tightly. "Hardly. That kind of job was beneath him."

"Did he have an assistant do it?"

"For a while he did." Henry looked squarely at me. "Then I did it."

"Oh, Henry!"

"*Oh, Henry*, indeed. Do you know what it feels like to be *constantly* underestimated by those around you, to be told by your parents, in hundreds of little ways, what a disappointment you are to them? I do. My parents are Bajan, you see. They came to the States like everybody else—for their children. The class system is still very rigid in Barbados. Have you been there?"

"Yes, a long time ago. It was beautiful."

"And how did you find the people?"

"Proud. Welcoming, but proud."

"That's Eustace and Regina in a word: proud. And convinced we little Adamses had to be *better* than everyone else, always. So we were not allowed to hang around the playground after school—that was for the *Americans*." He leaned forward and winked, as if I were a fellow conspirator. "That's what they called you-all. '*They* can be directionless if they want,' Reggie would lecture me, 'but *you* cannot. You have to do better.' "

"So I did. Through elementary and high school, through Columbia College, and the first year of NYU Law. Then I did the unpardonable."

"Which was?"

"I dropped out. Law school was boring. I had the chance for a summer internship at *Newsday*, so I took it. You'd have thought I'd murdered someone." He smiled inwardly, because of course that's exactly what he'd done—just not then.

"Your parents weren't happy."

"That's putting it mildly. First the tantrums, then the tears, then the lectures, intended to produce guilty capitulation. They'd come to America for me, and struggled for me, and done without for me—and this was how I repaid their trust and sacrifice?"

"Henry, I don't get it: I mean, it's not like you're working in a porn store or something, you're the assistant managing editor of *Diaspora*! It's a good job, with a high profile and lots of respect—"

"Alex, Alex, Alex. *American* Alex. You don't get it: I didn't have an advanced degree; *that* was the cardinal sin. I was supposed to go to law school, get a job with a corporate firm somewhere, and allow my mother to brag about her three little professionals. Claiborne is a cardiologist in New Jersey, and Renée has an MBA from Chicago, while I have a job that requires no professional degree at all. Could have done it straight out of high school."

"And that's so awful?"

"To a West Indian, yes. *Better than*, remember?"

I guess.

"So for once I had a chance to redeem myself in their eyes: I was going to be the editor in chief of *Diaspora*! Everett had been saying for the past couple of years it was time for him to move on. He had his eye on other prizes. I didn't know whether he would leave to head the J-school at Howard or to run the first black version of *Meet the Press*, but he was very clear: This was going to be his last year at the magazine. I'd always thought I was going to replace him."

Henry was looking significantly more agitated now. It was probably better to move away from this particular subject, but I wanted to know more.

"Did you discuss doing that with him?"

"Of course. And that's when he told me I shouldn't set my heart on it. You know what he told me?"

"I'm afraid to ask, but tell me anyway."

"He said, 'You great, Henry, at what you do. You really make the trains run on time. That requires organization and prioritization. But the next person in this seat has to have vision, Henry, and that ain't you. Your organizational ability has killed your vision, if you ever had any.'"

Everett Carson, soul of diplomacy.

"I said that was unfair; I could be as visionary as the next person, under the right circumstances. He let me give him several story ideas and two dummy copies of the kind of magazine I'd run. That took virtually all my free time for two months. And I still had a magazine to get out."

"You must have wanted to do this badly."

"Obviously. But in the end, it didn't matter. While he said the dummies were perfectly serviceable, he thought they lacked something."

"Vision?"

Henry winced. "Vision. And that is when I began to drop infinitesimal amounts of nitroglycerine into his tincture of echinacea."

"Oh, *Henry!*"

"You're saying that a lot today, aren't you? Yes, 'Oh, Henry.' Good old dependable Henry. Want someone to explain skillfully why you aren't interested in talking to their community organization? Let Henry do it. Want to calm down the board of directors because you've spent more than you promised you would? Let good old Henry drag out the charts and graphs. Want to investigate the possibilities of expanding your outfit? Good old Henry will do the research, even if you don't pay him any more and you don't reinforce his authority with the rest of your tittering staff. Good old Henry."

I was sitting with a murderer—and something told me he wasn't going to let me call 911 to share the news. Now I was sorry that Sally was such a mind-her-own business kind of landlord. If she'd been more like the ones on TV, I might have some hope of a last-minute rescue. Didn't look like today was going to be my day.

Oh, well. The only thing worse than dying before you were supposed to is dying before you were supposed to with a whole lot of unanswered questions.

"How'd you do it?"

"My brother's a cardiologist, remember? Which means he's seated at the right hand of God, as far as my parents are concerned. So whenever we have one of our interminable family dinners, to which I must go because it's not worth Regina's tears and tantrums if I don't, most of the conversation at table is spent listening to Claiborne in adoration as he drones on about his Fascinating Case of the Moment. At Easter it was an inadvertent death from the combination of nitroglycerine and Viagra. I took mental notes."

"Ev took Viagra?"

"I told you." He smirked. "I knew practically everything there was to know about the man. Yes, he'd started taking it for—um, a temporary problem. He felt he had to maintain the legend. And the convention was coming up."

Yeah. A chaste Everett Carson, let alone one with erectile dysfunction, would have been the topic of the week. Ev and Viagra, who'd have thought it?

"Where did you get nitroglycerine?"

"One of the good things about community service, Alex, is when you've been at a place for a while, they trust you to do certain things. Like count out the meds that are going overseas as a contribution to clinics for the poor in the Caribbean and Africa—"

"You *stole* from donated materials?"

"Oh, get off your moral high horse!" he snapped. "It wasn't much—half a bottle here, half a bottle there. I just dissolved the little pills into the tincture when I filled the bottles. It tastes so bad he never knew."

The smirk was back, and Henry was fingering—caressing, maybe—something in his right pocket.

"I'll give it to you, Henry, you planned this meticulously."

"It actually took some—you'll pardon the expression—vision, didn't it."

"It did." All props, you little squirrel.

He smiled in satisfaction; then he frowned. I knew what was coming next.

"I am sorry, though, that you've dragged yourself into this. If you hadn't felt the need to be oh, so smart, Alex, I could have picked up and gone home and no one would have been the wiser."

"Henry, why do you think no one would have figured all this out?"

"It's been over a week, and you know what they say: If the police don't find the killer within forty-eight hours, they probably never will. I was feeling lucky."

I sighed. I wasn't.

"But even a lucky man brings insurance."

He removed whatever it was he was stroking in his pocket. It looked like a slim thermos.

"Coffee?" What was he going to do, caffeine me to death? Please.

He shook the bottle gently. "Acid."

I shrugged, uncomprehending.

"Very simple, Alex. I'm betting you'd rather die by drowning than by disfigurement. You're not beautiful, but I can understand why some men might find you physically appealing."

This from someone who looks like a frog in horn rims! I would have pointed it out, except I had other things I needed to contemplate. Like trying to figure out how to call someone for help.

"So I'm supposed to drown myself?"

"With a little help. Everett told me once you can't swim."

Shit. Everett was one of the few people who knew that. We'd been having a discussion about why he didn't either. Segregated swimming pools in Georgia were the culprit in his childhood; as an adult, he just hadn't cared to learn. I'd volunteered the info about my own inability to swim, thinking he wouldn't feel he was the only one. Instead, he'd been mystified that I could be in the same boat, so to speak, that he was. "Powell, you ain't got no excuse. You grew up in New England. Water all over the damn place—and no rednecks trying to keep you out, either."

I tried to explain about the accident, but he wasn't having any of it. Apparently, if you grew up in the integrated North and you couldn't do what all the white kids did—swim, ski, golf, play tennis—you'd let down the race.

"Henry, I hate to break this to you, but I'm not going to drown myself. You should have brought a gun."

He slapped his other pocket. "What makes you think I didn't?"

"You can't get through airport security with a gun."

"True, Alex, very true. Unless you're specially licensed to carry it and it's checked in your luggage, not carried aboard."

"And you're telling me you have such a license?"

He barked a short, nasty laugh. "Hell, no, this is L.A. It doesn't take vision to get a gun—just money and a few inquiries in neighborhoods I don't normally spend much time in." He patted the pocket again.

Great. Just great. So I was going to be shot, drowned, *and* disfigured?

"The gun is to persuade you to come out to the pool and slip quietly into the deep end. They say drowning is almost painless."

"Not if you've almost done it before."

"It's certainly less painless than the alternative." He gently shook the bottle of acid. I could hear it *sloosh* inside its insulated walls.

He walked over to me, and for every step he took forward, I backed up, careful not to place myself in a corner.

"C'mon, Alex," he coaxed. "Just think: If you let go, embrace the water, it's all over in a minute. So much better than the alternative." He uncapped the bottle, keeping an eye on me, and poured a little on one of my CD covers. The cover developed a nice little slump, like the center of a fallen soufflé.

"If it can do this to plastic," he whispered, "think of what it would do to eyes—and what good is a writer without eyes?"

There *are* blind writers, of course, but I hadn't anticipated joining their ranks.

"And think of your mother. Surely she'll want to come say good-bye to you. You don't want her last view of her little girl to be a melted face, do you?"

Another good point. I'd been trying to maneuver myself so I could get on the other side of the sofa; the door hadn't been latched and I thought I might have half a chance if I could throw myself across the room before Henry could fling his flacon.

But he'd had the same thought. He had made sure his back was to the door, and he stood firmly between the door and me.

I could see Sally's gardener in the near distance; he must have been the whine from down the street. Glimpses of him showed through the partially opened white lacquered shutters, but it probably wouldn't do me any good to yell for help. He was a little too far away—and like a lot of L.A. gardeners he was wearing earplugs to protect his hearing from the noisy drone of his equipment.

"Alex, you're going to think yourself to death—" Henry stopped and chuckled. "Matter of fact, you already have. Let's get this over with."

Octavio was walking toward the pool. I wondered if he was going to knock, as he sometimes did when I was home, and ask if I was writing. If I was writing, he always offered to do another part of the garden and come back to me last. I always thought it was lovely of him to ask, and I always told him not to worry about it. The newsroom floor isn't quiet as a tomb either.

"You're a smug little specimen, Henry. And frankly, I don't think you've planned this well enough. You're not going to get away with it."

"Frankly, I don't much give a damn *what* you think. Move it, right now, or—" He held up the uncorked bottle.

There was a small explosion outside my door, and Henry was so startled he dropped his weapon. It bounced on the floor and splashed a significant amount of the contents on his shoes and legs. I had been far enough away to escape unscathed.

After that, everything happened at once: Henry, howling, screaming, flailing frantically at his soaked trousers; Octavio, opening the door to apologize—"Sorry, Miss Alex, my blower, it backfired"—and stopping in amazement at the sight in front of him; and Paul, pushing through the door with Jim Marron and Georgie hard on his heels.

29

"**Are you hurt?**" **Paul asked, stepping past** Henry, who by now was rolling around on the floor trying to get his pants off. Not smart, since there was acid on the floor too. Now his legs *and* his butt were on fire.

"Jesus, what did you do to him?" Marron asked, stepping over to Henry. "Paul, better call 911."

Georgie just looked at me for an explanation. "I'm waiting," she intoned, gazing over her Very Expensive Shades at me. She was in an outfit that would have been astonishing anywhere but in Palm Beach—and maybe Nantucket; acid-green, pink, and lemon-yellow blooms rioted all over her skinny pants, which stopped several inches above her ankles, the better to show off her pink high-heeled thongs, trimmed in silk sweet peas.

"You look like Walt Disney just barfed all over you," I said in wonderment.

"I'm *still* waiting."

"Okay, here's the deal: Henry took a cheapie quick flight out here because he was pissed I hadn't returned his calls about Ben Soyinka, and one thing led to another and I figured out he'd been putting something in Ev's echinacea, so he decided he had to kill me and was going to melt me with acid if I didn't cooperate by drowning myself in the pool, and then Octavio's blower backfired

and scared him and he dropped the acid bottle—and y'all came in."
I looked at Henry. "Isn't that right?"

"*Yes! Now help me, I'm burning up!*"

"Octavio, is there a hose nearby?" Marron asked.

"*Sí*—I mean, yes. On the side of the house." Octavio pointed to
the wall that made up one side of the living room.

"Good. Would you mind helping me with this guy? We'll need
to step carefully."

So Marron and Octavio propped up a moaning Henry, dragged
him outside, and hosed him off. Henry was weeping like a baby.

Paul, shaking his head, called 911, as Marron had asked him to,
but before the paramedics came, more police were at the door, led
by Sally.

"Such an explosion! Is everyone all right?"

Mostly everyone, I assured her, and told her what the noise had
been.

"Thank heaven! You know the Malaysian ambassador lives just
down the street, and every now and then something happens there,
but not today apparently."

"Today, everything seems to have happened *here*." Paul smiled,
pulling out a chair for my landlady. As I went out to check on Marron, Henry, and Octavio, she and Georgie were trading gossip about
what was happening to the family that owned one of the most chic
stores on Rodeo Drive. Water seeks its own level, I guess.

In about ten minutes, an ambulance was in the
driveway and a phalanx of police was swarming through the courtyard. I guess living down the street from the Malaysian ambassador
does have its upside.

Two detectives, alerted by the uniforms' call-in, walked through
the door. Marron briefed them as to what had happened. That he
was there at all was happenstance: Paul had stopped at the West Hollywood station to thank him again and see if he'd be interested in
coming by for a drink. His shift was ending, so he'd taken Paul to the
rental place to return the car and then driven him home.

"Good thing, too," he'd added. "They'd of never been able to make sense of this mess in a timely manner if somebody with some institutional memory hadn't been here."

"Excuse me, but what am I, an Alzheimer's victim?"

"A *cogent* institutional memory, I mean."

"I *like* this man." Georgie grinned.

"See, Powell, a cogent institutional memory would have thought to ask Squirrel Nut over there when he'd gotten into town. *Before* the cooling waters were applied."

"Witholding medical treatment is illegal, Marron."

"In the theoretical world, for sure. In the real world it finds things out. Like who it was who tore the front off your car two nights ago."

"Smart." Georgie nodded approval.

"*Henry* did that?" Paul asked, looking over to the ambulance's open doors, where Henry's gurney was being loaded into the open bay. He looked like he wanted to hit him.

"Says so."

An EMT guy had cut off Henry's pants and squirted some sort of neutralizing liquid all over Henry's legs. They'd hooked him up to an IV, probably a painkiller, and a damp towel covered his privates.

"That towel was overkill. They probably could have used a wash-cloth," murmured Georgie, after a swift appraisal.

"Ooooh, I think I'm in love." Marron grinned. Georgie grinned back at him. Oh no, no, no, no, *no*! Life was complicated enough already without those two getting social with each other.

The ambulance left with Henry. The senior of the two detectives told Marron he'd call him in a couple of hours, "But I think we got it all. Have a nice day." They nodded to the rest of us and left to fol-low the ambulance to the hospital. The other cops—and Octavio—had followed Sally up to the big house, where Josefina had been told to put on the coffeepot, break out the iced Cokes, and "see what we can rustle up in the kitchen for these gentlemen. After all, they saved our Alex."

Well, the cops didn't, dammit. Octavio saved our Alex—or Octavio's old backfiring against-the-new-city-code gas-powered blower did. Which would not be forgotten come Christmastime.

Octavio could have my firstborn if he wanted it. If, at this ripe old age, I could squeeze one out.

The only people left behind were Paul, Georgie, Marron, and me. Georgie made quick work of getting Marron to open her Champagne bottles. Thanks to her mode of transporting them—some gel-filled sleeves wrapped around the bottles and stuck in a large black and beige tote with more insulation—they were still cold.

"Bottega?" Marron asked, admiring the bag.

"Bingo," Georgie murmured. "You must shop a lot for Mrs. Marron."

"I shop a lot, period. There isn't a Mrs. Marron."

"Really?" Georgie was batting her baby browns at him, big time.

"Have dinner with me tonight and I'll tell you all about it."

"Bet."

I was watching, slack-jawed.

"You'd better shut your mouth," Paul advised. "Little flies can come in."

A whole black cloud of flies could have flown in. This *couldn't* be happening.

"Should we ask them to join us?" Marron nodded in our direction.

Georgie smiled. "Something tells me they'll be able to entertain themselves quite nicely without us."

Paul put his arm around my neck and laughed. "Like I would have wasted my last night here having dinner with you guys!"

So after another half hour, Marron and Georgie made their excuses and left. He told Paul he'd be in D.C. in early fall for a DEA conference and promised to call. When they were walking out the door, I heard Georgie say, "Normally you can't get in without a two-month wait, but the maître d' is a good friend—"

Paul shut the door and shook his head. "Just think what she could do if she used her powers for good."

"The real world wouldn't stand a chance."

He kissed me on the top of my head. "By this time tomorrow, you'll be back in the real world."

I sighed, wrapped my arms around his waist, and pressed my forehead against his chest.

"There *are* advantages to being in the real world, you know," he said softly.

"Such as?" my muffled voice prodded. I could hear his heart beating through his pale blue shirt.

"You'll have a byline again. Front page. Maybe even above the fold. Tell me that doesn't make you fell better."

"Marginally." Actually, I lied. It made me feel a lot better.

"And maybe A.S. will be inspired to give you a raise. You can spend the extra money on cheap tickets to D.C."

I snorted. "You don't know my cheapskate boss. I don't think so."

"Well then, maybe *I'll* have to spring for a few cheap tickets to L.A."

"So you can do all the stuff you didn't get to do this time?"

"Sure. Rodeo Drive. The museums. A stupid Hollywood party. . . ."

"Disneyland. . . ."

"No need." He chucked me under the chin. "I've been sleeping with Goofy for a week."

"I been with a couple of the Dwarfs myself: Grumpy and Dopey."

"Not anymore, now I'm Happy."

I looked at him and smiled. "Me too." I sighed. "But I gotta write this thing and file it or I'll be Unemployed. And they don't have room for an unemployed dwarf."

I looked with regret at my pages-long handwritten account of the last several days and shook my head. If it wasn't Paul's last night, I'd be looking forward to finishing up.

"Quicker you finish, the quicker we'll have time for other things. I can go for a run, get out of your way, for a spell, if you're sure people have finished trying to knock you off for the day."

"I think I've run through my quota, thank you. I'm going to work outside for a while. It's cool enough."

So Paul shrugged into his shorts and sneakers and, shirtless, took off. I took my laptop out onto the patio (a corner was still damp from where Henry had been hosed off) and wrote, undisturbed, for about an hour and a half. When Paul came back, he slipped quietly into the pool and did laps while I talked with the desk about the cuts they needed to make. I wrote tight, so they didn't make many.

By the time the sun was turning the flagstones coral, I'd turned off my machine and snapped the lid shut. We walked up to Sally's and borrowed a few provisions for a quick dinner, polished off the unopened bottle of Champagne that Georgie had thoughtfully left behind, and tried not to think about how fast tomorrow was going to be here.

"My plane's early. Why don't you ride with me in the cab, and you can rent a car after you see me off?"

"What makes you think I'm planning to see you off?"

"Can't stand the thought of boo-hooing in front of strangers, huh, Einstein?" He kissed me lightly, then deeply. "Tough guy."

"Stop fishing; I told you I'd miss you. You're not getting anything else out of me."

"Bet I can," he whispered.

"Oh, sure, if you do *that* . . ."

An hour or so later, we were still awake, even though we were both tired. We were lying spoonlike, as moonlight made opalescent stripes on our naked flanks.

"What're you thinking about?" He nuzzled my neck where it meets the shoulder. I shivered with pleasure.

"Thanksgiving."

"Already defrosting that turkey TV dinner, huh?"

I turned to face him. "Not. I cook with some friends. We've been doing it for years. First on the East Coast, now here. About twenty of us get together every year. It's kind of a ritual. Georgie comes."

"Three kinds of dressing, game on in the den, little kids running around?"

"Yeah, now. We've been doing it long enough that some of the little kids are in high school; they were in grade school when we first started. Now they're old enough to help with the dishes. And we're old enough that the wine is extraordinary. Last year we had a Chateau Margeaux *and* a Pommerol."

"Sounds like fun." He smiled and brushed a stray strand of hair off my forehead. "And you're cooking real food—not stuffing tofu or anything, are you?"

"Want to come see for yourself?"

"Absolutely."

"Think you can live without me till Thanksgiving?"

"I don't intend to, Einstein."

"Oh, yeah? How're you going to get your fix?"

"Da plane, da plane!" His Tattoo imitation was pretty good. "That's why hardworking reporters—ones covered by the Guild, anyway—get comp days. I figure the crazy hours I work are finally going to pay off."

"You mean you're actually going to take vacation time for something that doesn't involve fly-fishing, skiing, windsurfing, or something equally inane?"

Signe had told me once that he liked to do Manly Things with a bunch of other (male) reporters on vacation, in places like rain forests, mountainsides, and remote campsites where they scratched themselves and didn't bathe for days. *So* attractive.

"Yep. I'm moving on to indoor sports." He rolled on top of me to demonstrate. "Not as dangerous as the luge, but thrilling nonetheless. The fan response can be amazing."

For an amateur, he was quite impressive. All in all, I gave him a ten.

30

I accompanied Paul to the airport at an un-godly hour the next morning. The young woman at the gate took one look at him and upgraded him to first class.

"See?" He smirked and swatted me lightly with the boarding pass. "*Some* women find a man with a black eye raffishly charming."

"Uh-huh. And others of us just think you look like Petey."

"Petey who?"

"Don't you remember the dog in *The Little Rascals*? He had a black eye too."

"Whatever made me think I was going to miss you, even a little bit?" He shook his head and took a last sip of latte.

"Can't show you here, would probably get arrested."

The last sip was now shooting through his nose, he was laughing so hard. A Japanese couple with matching monogrammed briefcases looked on with interest.

"Did I get any on my suit?" he asked, looking down at his tan gabardine.

"No, dammit." He was as pristine as ever.

"Maybe next time. Kiss me, Einstein. Gotta go." They were starting to board first class passengers.

We'd already had a conversation about how much I hated airport scenes and long-drawn-out good-byes. I'd figured out ages ago that the best way to leave was to do it quickly and cleanly. Kinder to everyone, all around.

So I kissed him firmly.

"These are for you. I got them while you were ordering coffee." He unfolded the papers. On top was the morning's copy of his own *New York Times*. He shifted that to the bottom and smiled broadly at the other paper, which was, of course, the *Standard*.

"All *riiiiight!*" he breathed.

There it was, front page, above the fold: "*Diaspora* Editor's Murder: A Real-Life Whodunit by Alex Powell, *Standard* columnist." I'd gotten up in the middle of the night to admire it in the online version. I could be cool about it now, but then I was jumping around, totally naked, and mouthing one word in the glow of the laptop's screen: "*Yes!*"

Attention all passengers: This is the final boarding call for United Flight Two from Los Angeles International to Dulles International Airport. All remaining passengers are requested to board now.

We looked at each other.

"It won't be too bad. I'll be back at the end of the month. And you can come to D.C. in October, when it's cooled off some."

"And you'll be back for Thanksgiving—"

"And the next month, if you want, you can come east for the Christmas party the White House gives for the Washington press corps."

"Really? Will the president be there?"

"Yup—if they don't put him in jail before then."

The current president had a bad habit of getting into litigious scrapes.

"Cool. You got a date."

He trailed his fingers across my cheek. "I do, don't I?" he said swiftly, and kissed me softly.

"See ya, Petey."

His black eye winked. Then he walked over to where a flight attendant, one of those all-purpose Creole-looking types, waited impatiently, hand on slim hip.

"If you promise to get help for that hitting problem," he called, from the mouth of the jetway, "I'll be back in three weeks."

The flight attendant immediately stopped looking pissed and blinked at him with sympathetic interest. "Let me help you to your seat," she said gently, taking Paul's briefcase and giving me one last furious glance before she slammed the jetway door.

The passengers waiting for the next flight looked at me with undisguised disgust.

"That's just *terrible!*" a doughy woman with a bad dye job hissed to her equally rotund husband, who looked at me balefully over his reading glasses.

I sighed. I'd told Signe and Georgie this boy was going to be a lot of work, and he was. But to paraphrase the model in the hair color commercials, he was worth it.

Epilogue

Just in case you don't live in a small colored world and don't have anyone to give you, as Aunt Edith would say, the 911, I thought it would be kind to catch you up:

Henry Adams went to jail after he got out of the hospital. Rupert Washington Jr. wasn't taking on new clients, and the lesser lawyer Henry retained couldn't get him off. He'll be there for about ten years, if he behaves. His mother got her wish: Henry *was* in the papers. But given the nature of the reason, I don't think she spent much time sending clips back to Barbados.

Esmé Marshall was lucky; she'd engaged Rupie before he was full up, and it went as Marron predicted: The judge bought diminished capacity, and all kinds of Very Important People came forward to plead clemency on her behalf. Thanks to those two things, Esmé is now making potholders and attending group therapy sessions in a woman's psychiatric facility somewhere in Westchester. It ain't Club Med, but she doesn't have a two-hundred-pound girl named Betty telling her she'd better go along with the program if she knows what's good for her, either.

Jim Marron and Georgie Marks continue to date, just to torture me. Marron has actually evolved into a pretty good friend. (And, let's face it, if you're a reporter it doesn't hurt to have a cop or two as a friend.) So when Paul comes to town, the four of us usually end up spending at least one evening together.

Chip Wiley is making millions with an Internet partner, in addition to running *Aspire*. He's scaled back on some of his time in the office in order to spend one day a week hanging out with Charles Mitchell Wiley IV, who, he informed me, is nicknamed Quatro. (Stupid move. Even in private school that poor kid's gonna catch hell.)

Jake Jackson actually broke down and had lunch with Jake Junior before the year was out and was astonished to discover that, gay or not, his boy knew something about publishing and had several fresh ideas that could revitalize *Onyx*. Junior is not bringing his partner to Thanksgiving dinner yet, but it looks as if things are moving in that direction.

Frankie Harper, as promised, told her editors at *Radiance* the truth about her background. She offered to resign and they promptly accepted the offer—but they also gave her a huge testimonial dinner for her favorite charity and continue to list her as Editor Emeritus. She writes for them from time to time. After the hubbub, she did a few media outlets: She spent an hour on *Oprah*, and talked only to guess which two print reporters.

Signe Tucker and I broke the story at the same time on the same day for our respective papers. We were *both* front-page above-the-fold, thank you (the *Times* headline: RADIANCE EDITOR CROSSES COLOR LINE UNWITTINGLY; ours—much better, in my humble opinion: BLACK, WHITE, AND SHOCKED ALL OVER: RADIANCE EDITOR REVEALS RACE TO STAFF).

Both A.S. and Signe's editor grumbled about not having exclusives, but we told them bluntly we'd both been in on it, we'd discussed it, and that was the way Frankie wanted it: Take it or leave it. They took it. Frankie and Neil are expecting their first child in the spring.

A.S. Fine still runs the Op Ed page and is more fair-haired and short-tempered than ever. Rumor has it he'll be given some Huge

Prestigious Responsibility in the next couple of months. Don't know yet whether that will make my life easier or harder.

Paul Butler continues to write his column at the *New York Times* Washington Bureau and to fly back and forth to see me when time and finances allow. Don't ask me how, but he always manages to fly first class. And he doesn't even have a black eye anymore!

Ben Soyinka did indeed merge *Diaspora* with *Black Africa Review* and *L' Afrique Noire*. He also got NPR to run a weekly hour-long segment of *Radio Publique d' Afrique* in English. Staffing is almost complete for Diaspora Network News, and Arthur French did, as predicted, leave the *Times* to run the whole shebang. He's doing a better job than Henry ever could have hoped to.

Eileen Stevens was awarded her doctorate in December and became Eileen Stevens-Soyinka in London on New Year's Day, with Ben's family and hers in attendance. The boys walked her down the aisle and received gold medallions with the Adrinka symbol for *I will love you always* from their new dad. Everett's aunt, Mrs. Weeks, having learned the truth about his death, is already looking forward to spending part of the year in Abidjan.

I know all this because I was one of the few non-family guests there. One of the others was my date, that guy to whom rumors persist in saying I gave a black eye. On my night table, there is a silver-framed picture of us taken in London that morning. I'm wearing a deep gray silk suit and (of all things) a matching broad-brimmed hat that Georgie and Signe twisted my arm to buy especially for the occasion. Very English-looking. Paul is handsomely attired in a dark suit and silvery tie. We are smiling and holding hands, and my free hand, the one not clasped in Paul's, is holding the huge bouquet of lilies and roses and stephanotis that Eileen, laughing, walked over and pressed into my hands as the newlyweds were making their getaway.

"Give in," she'd whispered. "It's going to happen anyway."

Maybe, maybe not. All a good reporter can do is try to find out.